## FOUR STARS FOR

### *THE BUTTER DID IT*

"Richman's prose is as smooth and easy to swallow as premium ice cream. . . . She brings a welcome angle and authenticity to the expanding menu of culinary mysteries."

—*Publishers Weekly*

"A rare find—a book you find truly hard to put down. Richman's culinary expertise and familiarity with the world of restaurant reviewing is evident throughout this delicious novel (which you won't want to read on an empty stomach or if you're on a diet). *The Butter Did It* grabs your attention from its opening pages. . . . A masterful whodunit."

—*Journal Inquirer* (Springfield, MA)

"A frothy little novel of murder, mayhem and meals. . . . A thoroughly fun read, with an unexpected ending."

—*Portland Oregonian*

# THE Butter Did It

## A CHARLES EATLY MYSTERY . . .

## Phyllis Richman

**HarperPaperbacks**
*A Division of HarperCollinsPublishers*

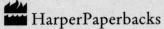 **HarperPaperbacks**

*A Division of* HarperCollins*Publishers*
10 East 53rd Street, New York, NY 10022-5299

ISBN 0-06-109625-3

Cover illustration © 1998 by Merritt Dekle

A hardcover edition of this book was published in 1997
by HarperCollins*Publishers*.

First HarperPaperbacks printing: June 1998

Printed in the United States of America

Visit HarperPaperbacks on the World Wide Web at
http://www.harpercollins.com

❖ 10 9 8 7 6 5 4 3 2 1

To Bob, the butter on my baked potato

# Acknowledgments

Writing a novel is said to be lonely work. Not so. My gratitude, in abundance, is due to many friends, relatives, technical experts, and combinations of the above: for sharing their expertise in law and criminal procedures, Judges Howard and Deborah Chasanow, and Charles E. Bailey (retired), commander of Forensic Science Services Section of D.C. Metropolitan Police; in toxicology, Drs. David Rabin, Kevin Cullen, David Rawl, Sanford Miller, Mike Medina, and Jack Segal; for culinary inspiration, Anne Willan, Mark Furstenberg, Patrick O'Connell, Jean-Louis Palladin, and Roland Mesnier; for guidance in police reporting, Elsa Walsh and Sari Horwitz; in theater, Lloyd Rose; and for all manner of support, my other wonderful inspiring colleagues at the *Washington Post*; for unstinting encouragement, Bob Burton and Joe, Matt, and Libby Richman; for kind and generous literary advice, Jody Jaffe, Wendy Law-Yone, Barbara Raskin, Aviva Goode, Russ Parsons, Anne Tyler, and Les Whitten; for shepherding me through the publishing process, my endlessly patient agent, Bob Barnett; for cheering me on to combine food and fiction, HarperCollins's distinguished cookbook editor, Susan Friedland; and for teaching me how to polish this first attempt at a novel, my generous editor at HarperCollins, vice president and associate publisher Gladys Justin Carr, and associate editor Elissa Altman. For the flaws in this work I have nobody to thank but myself.

# prologue

Laurence Levain's knees have been aching for the last hour. A chef's knees are the first thing to go; he knows that well. But, at forty-two, he refuses to worry about such things. Laurence still has his wiry, athletic good looks; his restaurant's stars keep shining brighter; and he's just finished turning a tub of flour and two dozen pounds of smoked salmon into ten thousand dollars' worth of pasta. He's not about to let aching knees spoil his satisfaction.

Outside Chez Laurence, November winds are slicing through Washington's darkness. Inside, the kitchen looks like spring. Laurence stands alone, massaging his legs amid hundreds of salmon-pink and herb-green stuffed pastas laid out like a patchwork quilt ready for stitching.

On the menu, these pasta squares are listed as *Les Nouilles en Quilt Multicolore*, and they're priced at twenty dollars per single four-inch piece. Familiarly they're called Laurence's quilts, and this world-famous pasta is one of the reasons people in

Washington say that the only dinner reservation more difficult to get is at the White House.

"Nobody would ever taste such pasta again if I died," Laurence boasts to himself as he stacks the quilts in the walk-in refrigerator. He's alone in the kitchen not only because it is late Sunday night, but also because tomorrow night's CityTastes gala requires that each chef prepare his signature dish without assistance. What's more, Laurence has never allowed anyone to learn the secrets of this paper-thin, translucent pasta. For years, other chefs have tried to duplicate its transparency, its ability to hold fillings in place as if they were stitched like cloth. Laurence's quilts look like patchworked fabric; his imitators' squares are merely ravioli.

Laurence is tired. Exhausted, in fact. He wipes the sweat from his chin and lurches from a sudden wave of nausea. "I should have eaten something earlier," he chastises himself. He tends to feel faint when he stands on his feet the whole evening without food.

"I'll grab something at home," he decides. "After a good, stiff, relaxing drink." Hurried by the thought, he stops briefly to comb his hair, then leaves the kitchen mess behind for the dishwasher and buttons his heavy coat for the walk home.

By the time Laurence arrives at his apartment, just a few blocks away on Massachusetts Avenue, he is no longer alone. He takes off his coat, trembling from the cold. "Calvados will warm us up," the chef promises his companion, pouring two small glasses of the apple brandy that, as orange juice is to

American kids, has been a part of him since his Normandy childhood.

He hands one glass to his guest, who's still wearing coat and gloves and examining Laurence's wall of awards. Laurence picks up his own glass as he always does, thumb and forefinger grasping it by the rim. He salutes his companion and tosses back the calvados in one gulp.

The companion, not feeling nearly as friendly, refuses to join the toast but instead responds with a few sharp words. Laurence is disconcerted, holds up a hand in a placating gesture. It doesn't work.

"You have no right to go public with this," the angry guest hisses. When that gets no more than a shrug from Laurence, the anger turns to begging. "Please don't do it. It will ruin me."

"You're overreacting," Laurence says placidly, without suggesting any compromise. "But let's not argue. Take off your coat and make yourself comfortable. Whew, I smell of fish. I've got to take a shower and find my heart medicine. I feel like shit." He pronounces it "sheet."

While Laurence has always been known to be obsessively neat, for the second time tonight he is sloppy. In the bathroom he strips off his clothes and drops them in a heap on the floor, then steps into the shower for a scrub that lasts hardly a minute. He wraps himself in a burgundy silk dressing gown and returns to the living room, ready for one more attempt at peacemaking and another drink.

Laurence fills two clean glasses with calvados and carries them to the nubby white sofa. He hands one to his companion. But the guest, still upset, spills half the calvados.

"Could you get me a towel?" The guest's tone is whiny, impatient.

"Sit still. I'll find one." Laurence sets his own drink down on the coffee table and goes to the kitchen. He returns with a towel, detouring for the calvados bottle. He refills the spilled glass and once again proposes a toast. This time the guest joins him, saying: "To your health."

The two drink down the calvados, both shivering from the impact of the eighty-proof brandy. Laurence's shivering doesn't stop as he returns the bottle to the bar. Instead, his tremors continue until he collapses to the floor and stops breathing.

The guest sits, riveted, on the sofa, staring at Laurence twitching and jerking for a moment as the body resists its fate. All motion stops.

Despite everything, the guest's first instinct is to aid Laurence, and to rush to the dying man's side. Stopping short, though, this silent witness never touches Laurence, merely stands immobile for several minutes watching death take over.

At last, the observer turns toward the door, then, with hand on the knob, stops. Something must be done. The guest turns back and pockets two of the four used glasses, rummages through Laurence's bedroom for a moment to find a few things, then arranges them in the living room to set the scene before leaving.

## one

Clams. They were what worried Georges.

I had ordered the clam fritters—*palourdes en beignets*—and today was Monday. It was lunchtime, and the fish delivery wouldn't be until the afternoon, so these were bound to be leftover from Friday. A cold snap like the past weekend's can cause last-minute cancellations and leave the kitchen full of expensive perishables. Marcel Rousseau, the chef and owner of the newly relocated La Raison d'Être, must have put the clams on the list of specials to get rid of them before the new shipment arrived. I would find out.

Georges, the eggplant-shaped maître d', busied himself straightening perfectly aligned silverware at the tables around me. I could see that he was anxious. In fact, the entire dining-room staff kept a wary eye on my table as I sipped my Sancerre.

Being a restaurant critic, especially for Washington's newest and fastest-growing newspaper, the *Examiner*, means that restaurateurs scrutinize every bite I take. And I was lunching alone, which apparently made everyone doubly nervous. The tension was so electric that I was afraid it would cause static on my tape recorder.

It's a strange life, being a forty-eight-year-old perfectly ordinary (and slightly overweight) medium-height, vaguely blond, green-eyed woman who creates a clamor just by eating lunch. I never make reservations under the name Chas (short for Charlotte Sue) Wheatley, and can often get by unrecognized, but not today.

I try to look unaware. I never order fewer than three courses, which I eat at a leisurely pace, sipping a glass of wine and observing the dining room openly rather than hiding behind a book. I don't take notes, but sometimes I use a tape recorder to whisper a few details.

When I come alone, restaurateurs know that can mean very good news or very bad news. It means their restaurant is being reviewed. Even more, it signals that I finished tasting my way through the menu on previous visits and now want to concentrate—on a particular dish or on the flow of the service around the dining room, on something I loved or something I hated before. In either case, my solitary meal is no fun for anyone.

Today's visit hadn't started well for Georges. I arrived at the same time as the secretary of defense, and Georges rushed to greet him as I stood a few steps behind. He was obviously about to usher the secretary to the best table in the house when he did a double take and registered that I was there. Reviewer panic set in.

Not one to lose his aplomb for long, Georges glanced at his seating chart again and led the secretary of defense to the second-best table. Such are the balancing acts of Washington. And such is the outlandish kowtowing to restaurant critics.

Nor was that the end of Georges's tests of diplomacy. La Raison d'Être's entrance was beginning to crowd up just as he was leading me to my table. When we were halfway through the dining room, Reginald Lonsdowne, the new Republican senator from Mississippi (who used to be the old Democratic senator from Mississippi), stopped me, thus delaying Georges as well.

"Chas, honey, you look perfectly beautiful today with your hair swept up like that," Lonsdowne oozed.

"Nice of you to say so," I replied, trying to sound sincere.

"You know, it's lucky I ran into you," he went on. "I was thinking of calling you, as it happens, to ask if you could recall the name of that Thai restaurant in Chicago you wrote about, the one where you described the entrées—I remember it exactly—as 'looking like a tropical garden just after the mist has evaporated.'"

I said I was flattered that he could quote me verbatim. Then I spelled the restaurant's name for him: Arun. While Georges discreetly shifted from foot to foot, worried about the crowd at the door, Senator

Lonsdowne held us, asking if he could use my name in getting a reservation.

"I'm sure your name is more than sufficient," I told him.

Georges seated me with barely disguised relief.

While Georges had showed a dignified unease over my visit, Brian, my waiter, looked as if he were about to fall apart. He was probably still quaking over the first time he had served me, three visits ago. He had decidedly not recognized me as a restaurant critic.

I was alone that afternoon, too, but then I was waiting for my friend Sherele, the *Examiner*'s theater critic, who is late for everything except the opening curtain. I had kept checking my watch and probably was fidgeting with my sunglasses. I usually try to pace myself better, but in my impatience I'd finished my glass of wine and two slices of olive bread.

This waiter, a lamb chop of a guy closer to my daughter's age than to mine, came up to my table and leaned one hand on it. Any waiter should know better. He affected what he must have considered a sexy smile, and came on to me.

"Hi, I'm Brian. Did I see you cleaning your sunglasses with chardonnay?"

I was already irritated with Sherele for being so late. And I'm the wrong woman for the casual leer. Having been a fat kid who slimmed down late in college, I am still inclined to take an attractive man's overtures as a gag rather than a compliment.

"If you'd been attentive, you'd know I was drinking sauvignon blanc, not chardonnay." I paused. "And you would have refilled my glass."

To his credit, Brian immediately served me an apology and a second glass of wine. He had gotten the message even without the added embarrassment of recognizing the messenger. The rest of the evening he was impeccably polite without pandering.

Unlucky guy. Here he was, now knowing I was a restaurant critic and having to serve me again. He must have been in a sweat. Each time he came from the kitchen he sniffed in the direction of his underarms as if worrying about whether he'd used enough deodorant.

So the maître d' was nervous, the waiter was panicky, and the busboy tiptoed around as if he were afraid he would drop the rolls or spill the water. An everyday lunch for a restaurant critic.

In contrast to the rest of the staff, the sous-chef was an oasis of calm. Stanley, the second-in-command, who actually does most of the work, came to my table when he heard I was there, to let me know that the chef, Marcel, wasn't around. Marcel, he explained, had slept late this morning after being up most of the night preparing his *soupe en chemise* for tonight's CityTastes benefit. Then Marcel had rushed off to Dulles airport to pick up his wife, Marie Claire, after her flight from Mexico had been delayed overnight.

CityTastes day definitely isn't a good day to lunch in Washington. Every chef in town would have been working late last night cooking for this hunger-relief gala that has become the fall fashion show of food.

Most chefs would've been feverish over a critic showing up on such a day. But I wasn't surprised at Stanley's insouciance. It would be Marcel's reputation on the line rather than Stanley's when I wrote my review. A sous-chef has nothing to lose and everything to gain. If a review is good, he'll attach it to his résumé and justly claim that he was the one who really did the cooking. If it's bad, the chef will take the heat.

Still, Stanley ought to have been embarrassed to serve last week's clams. After all, clam fritters demand so few ingredients. All he'd had to do to feed the entire dining room was open a couple of dozen clams and add their juices to two cups of flour, along with maybe a quarter of a cup of oil, a little salt, a dash of cayenne, and enough water to turn the flour mixture into a smooth paste. The hardest part would have been beating two or three egg whites until stiff and folding them into the batter, then deep-frying the mixture by spoonfuls. Some chefs use baking soda instead of egg whites; others add beer or wine instead of water, egg yolks or butter instead of oil. In this case, there was hardly anything to mask the taste of the clams, so their freshness was critical.

● ● ●

Stanley had hardly left the table when they arrived.

"Your clam fritters, Miss Wheatley," Brian offered with cool formality and not a trace of flirtation. Score one. He was learning.

I ate a fritter and smiled, not wanting to show that I had detected a bitter, overripe edge to the clam inside. Brian hovered, anxiously eyeing the clams.

"How are they?"

I changed the subject. "I hope you're going to CityTastes tonight. It's the one place you'll see every powerful person in the city at the same time. And get to taste all the best food of the year." I thought I'd show the guy that he was forgiven. He was probably still worrying that I would slap his hand in print.

Brian brightened. "I wouldn't miss it. I love these tax-deductible charity galas. Feed the hungry by overfeeding the affluent." With a suggestion of a bow, he went on to another table.

At the moment, Georges was answering the phone and simultaneously greeting a House committee chairman from Massachusetts. To my astonishment, I saw his smile freeze. His face turned the color of béchamel. He left the chairman standing with outstretched hand unshaken as he hung up the phone and rushed to the kitchen.

Now I was the one who tensed. I had thought it would take a nuclear attack to shake Georges's impeccable composure. I'd never seen him rude before, not even when he'd received a call telling him that President Reagan had just been shot only a few blocks away. I'd been in his dining room then and had watched Georges calmly announce the news to each group of White House staff and Congressional leaders, table by table, with never a crack in his veneer.

I caught Brian's eye and beckoned him over. "Something's happened that's got Georges upset," I said quietly so that nobody else would overhear. "I wonder if you'd snoop a little for me and tell me what's up." I gave him a new-old-friends smile.

Brian, probably, like most men who enjoy being with women, also loved gossip. He made a short detour to deliver a wine list and headed for the kitchen.

Georges burst out of the kitchen half a table ahead of Brian. He headed right for me, still pale, even trembling.

"Madame Chas," he nearly whispered. His face was twitching. "It's Laurence. His bad heart. He has died." At that, Georges's voice squeaked loudly, and the two men at the next table looked up.


Laurence the Only. The only chef to appear in *Time*, *The New Yorker*, and *People* magazine's "50 Most Beautiful"—all in the past year. The only chef to cook birthday dinners for both the President of the United States and Oprah. The only Michelin three-star chef who had established a chain of soup kitchens. Laurence Levain had been my mentor, my lover, and, above all, my friend. His heart had stopped. Mine was breaking. I couldn't believe it. I could not move.

Brian had seen my sudden paralysis. He showed up at my table with my coat just as I stood up, desperate to be alone. I grabbed a fifty from my wallet, sure it was more than enough to cover my lunch and unwilling to pause for change.

Brian took my arm and guided me to the door. We made our way through a sea of voices as I struggled to breathe.

I could hear some of the restaurant staff's reactions: "So young, only forty-two . . ." "What are we going to do about the senator's dinner next week? . . ." "I could name a few chefs who'll be celebrating at this funeral . . ."

On the street at last, I didn't know whether to scream or sob. By sheer will, I escaped without doing either.

## two

Most people would have hailed a taxi this stony-cold day even without being cramped with anguish. But I am a walker. Others feed their problems with alcohol and their illnesses with chicken soup. I deal with every kind of crisis by walking.

A walk from my Seventh Street loft to Georgetown is a treat to me. And I've been known to show up at a restaurant in Alexandria flushed and invigorated from a seven-mile stroll down the bike trail, carrying a leather pouch large enough to hold my dress shoes and, later, a menu. When my friends warn me that Washington is too dangerous for walking, I tell them that if I didn't walk off all the food I ate, obesity would kill me more surely than a mugger.

I had learned to truly value walking from Laurence—in Paris nearly twenty-four years ago. "It is the secret of our happy and healthy hearts," he'd told me, never anticipating the irony. "Parisians walk. Americans ride. That is why your countrymen grow tense and their hearts give out."

As he predicted, over the years my walks nourished a calmness. They introduced me to Washington more intimately and gave me time to let my thoughts run as free as an unleashed puppy's. It's while walking that words form prose patterns in my head and the problems of my day solve themselves. Not today, though. Not today.

I set off for my office, my shoulders hunched against the chill wind, my arms crossed and clutching my coat as if I were hanging on to a life jacket. I'd left my buttons undone, my gloves in my pocket. The wind stung my cheeks. Tears wet them and the cold turned them raw.

Hardly aware of where I was going, I crossed K Street against the light, then jumped back as a car swerved past me. I continued up Fifteenth Street until I found myself in front of *The Washington Post*. Startled, I realized I'd been heading in the wrong direction, and stopped short.

"I've got to write his obituary," I reminded myself. "I can't leave that to anybody else." After all, it was Laurence who had found the restaurant critic's job for me when I couldn't bear to cook in a restaurant any longer.

I turned back to L Street and headed toward New York Avenue to the *Examiner*.

More than two decades ago, when I left Paris for Washington, accompanying my husband, Ari, to his new job as chef of the French embassy, Laurence and I had been friends for two years and lovers for two months. He vowed that our separation was only temporary, assuring me that he would more than miss me. But he wasn't ready to let anything interrupt his Paris career.

I didn't tell him until after I was in Washington that I was pregnant. And as far as I knew, Laurence never even let it cross his mind that the baby might be his. I squelched that thought as well.

Someday I would leave my husband, Laurence had predicted. Then the time would be right and he would follow me. Eventually we would be together forever.

He was right about the first two parts, more or less. I didn't leave my husband, he left me. That was just around the time Laurence, after he'd won his third Michelin star, transplanted his career to Washington. He'd grown frustrated with the pressure of selling lavishness first and food second. He was tired of running a palace. He wanted to run a restaurant.

His older sister, Jeanine, the only family he had left, was in Normandy, widowed and with more time and money than she knew how to spend. She persuaded Laurence to join the American restaurant renaissance, the headquarters of which was generally identified as the nation's capital.

Thus, Laurence was the first to defect from France's small, smug circle of three-star chefs. He arrived with Jeanine, who had decided to run the dining room of his dream restaurant, which, of course, he named after himself.

As for our being together forever, that prediction underwent a good bit of revision. During our decade apart, Laurence had set aside what we had both thought was his consuming passion for me in favor of a string of momentary obsessions—models, starlets, dancers—always the same age and ever farther from his.

By the time he arrived in Washington, a cozy foursome was what he expected: Laurence, Jeanine, Ari, and me. Well, a fivesome, with my ten-year-old daughter, Lily, who, to my great relief, had Ari's high forehead and long pianist's hands. Laurence and I had over the years become, at least on the surface, comfortable old friends. And he mused that eventually we'd become a sixsome when he found another woman he could love as much as he had loved me.

But all his numbers went awry. He found Ari and me in the midst of our long-delayed divorce. To his surprise, this made him more miserable than our marriage had. He had to stand by and watch me fall apart.

Too much time had gone by. When Laurence took me to bed after my divorce, it turned out to be from pity. He wanted so much to make me whole again, but I was no longer the unquestioning, adoring, free-spirited young flirt I had been in Paris.

For my part, I went to bed with him out of desperation, hoping to recapture something from our long-gone carefree days together. But Laurence had not just lost his boyishness, his arrogance had swelled as maturity had filled out his face, neck, and belly. He wasn't much fun anymore. I found I could love him, at best, as an old friend. We settled for a close camaraderie, though I still yearned for the young man he had once been. Instead of filling in my love life, he helped me with my work life.

I had become a chef of sorts in the years after Paris, with Laurence's long-distance encouragement. At first, being the wife of a chef and the mother of a toddler was enough to keep me busy. But when Lily began kindergarten, I was bored. So I helped my friend Vivian start a small French restaurant that was open only for continental breakfast and lunch—perfect for our schedules because it allowed us to be home when our children returned from school. The job was more play than work. In fact, Viv, who did most of the cooking, said that making the croissants was like kindergarten—cutting and pasting and sculpting clay. I loved making simpler things: the soups, the bright-colored salads.

At first it seemed like a joke when the *Post*'s critic proclaimed that Viv's were the best croissants in town (aided by the headily perfumed jams Laurence found for us in Provence). But it was serious—so serious that other chefs began to stop by in the morning for their *pain au chocolat* and espresso.

My lunch dishes—attractive, wholesome, but no star-gatherers—went along for the ride. Nevertheless, within two years the restaurant had gone far beyond play. It was all-consuming work.

Ari lost his job at the French embassy when the new ambassador brought his own chef with him. But

Ari had amassed so many private clients through his embassy connections that being laid off was a relief. He was already virtually a full-time caterer.

As always, his was night work. But now my work was daytime, so we saw each other less and less. I felt I still had a closer relationship with Laurence, an ocean away, than to the husband with whom I shared a home. Ari gradually discovered that he, too, was lonely and that his life was a mess without me to keep him organized.

Like most divorces, ours was a long time coming. And as with many troubled couples, I had started out being the dissatisfied partner, but he made the move to break it up when he fell in love. He left me for another man.

I wasn't quite as surprised as Ari was to realize that he was gay. Looking back on our decades, I finally understood. Our marriage, my vague dissatisfactions, Ari's distance became illuminated.

Even so, while for Ari this new relationship meant a freedom he'd never before encountered, for me it meant humiliation. Embarrassment, self-pity, and the long habit of love churned inside me. Like a marble cake mixed too long, love and hate mingle into one mud-colored goo.

I became a dropout. Cooking had been so much a part of our marriage that I found the kitchen the most painful place I could be. I cut my fingers. The biscuit dough stuck to my hands. I cried in the soup. Everything was too salty.

Laurence heard through the grapevine that the new *Examiner* was looking for a restaurant critic, and he suggested I apply for the job. He remembered how much I had loved writing.

The *Examiner*'s editor was intrigued by the idea. Only San Francisco had a restaurateur as a food critic, and while that appointment had been considered a little dicey, her expertise gave her reviews particular authority. Besides, I would be an ex-restaurant chef rather than a rival of the restaurants I was reviewing.

So the *Examiner* gave me a trial, and I reduced my professional cooking to volunteering every other week at a women's shelter with Viv, who still ran her restaurant. Once I found another way to earn my living, cooking for free became a lark.

My editor's main worry was that since I had been a chef myself and was friends with many restaurateurs, I would be too easy on them. I laid that concern to rest when I reviewed my own Thanksgiving dinner. The editor thought it was an audacious idea, and he found the review hilarious. I was so hard on my own cooking that even I learned from it—and my Thanksgiving dinners improved from the exercise. The readers loved it when I declared that my mince pie would have been improved by using Mincemeat Helper. Then my reputation as a tough critic was nailed down when I wrote a one-sentence review of a new French restaurant: Le Duck is a turkey.

The other worry about my reviewing was that I couldn't be anonymous in restaurants. Like every critic, I made reservations in a fake name and showed up at restaurants unannounced, but I was often recognized once I arrived. That meant I had to work harder than most critics. I had to watch the entire dining room to see how the service was handled at other tables while I was being coddled. I had to observe how much larger my portions were and how more elaborately garnished than everyone else's. But after restaurateurs realized that I was going to tell my readers exactly how much caviar was on my plate and they were going to expect the same amount, the excesses were tamed.

But not entirely. Most diners don't have four waiters delivering their table's entrées in unison. Nor do they have to put up with being watched and overheard by every waiter and busboy on duty. Or with having to listen endlessly to the owner's complaints about the new tax laws and the weather. I couldn't hope to have a private conversation in a restaurant anymore.

What surprised me most was that even when restaurateurs recognized me, I often got bad food. Overcooked pasta at Giuseppi's Room, undercooked beans at The Cat's Pajamas, wild rockfish fillets with burned undersides at The Net, and damp, gray grilled steaks at Beefy Ben's—apparently many chefs just didn't know how inept their cooking was.

The hardest part was when I had to chastise Laurence's restaurant for losing the reservation I'd made under the name Smithson. To make matters worse, I had come when I'd known Laurence was out of town, and I'd made no bones about the food being not quite first-rate. I'd compounded the injury by revealing to the public that anyone could tell when Laurence wasn't in the kitchen because only he personally made *les nouilles en quilt multicolore*. This was the signature dish that had ignited his career, and he kept his method a closely guarded secret. Thus, *les quilts* were always on the menu when Laurence was cooking, but never when he was away.

Laurence had wished he'd never mentioned the critic's job to me. He said no other critic in town would have been as critical of him as I was. And the review had put an awkward distance in our relationship, which I mourned but also welcomed as befitting my new role.

If Laurence was stung by my candor, his sous-chef, Borden, was infuriated. Of course, Borden was habitually infuriated, and no restaurant where he'd worked had been able to keep him for very long. At thirty-five, he was skilled, but not quite as talented as he thought he was. And despite his public image as a charmer eager to make everyone happy, the only people who'd ever gotten along with him for more than a short time were Laurence, Jeanine, and my daughter, Lily, who had been in love with Borden for years. As soon as she was living away from home, Lily and Borden had actually had an affair. Fortunately, it had ended quickly—not, I admit, without my help. Lily's heart still burned for him, and Borden fanned the flames without being warmed by them himself. He kept up their friendship, and she kept up the hope that someday when she grew up and he settled down he would wind up marrying her.

# three

My morbid reflections ended abruptly at the *Examiner*. The doorway was clogged with schoolchildren jiggling impatiently and shoving each other as their teachers tried to round up potential escapees. The newspaper was being invaded by a field trip.

I dodged my way between careening children, flashed my photo ID to the distracted guard, and squeezed into an elevator. The diversion gave me time to collect myself and face the busy hush of the newsroom.

Newsrooms once were noisy places, with the clatter of scores of typewriters forcing voices to rise above them. Then computers edged typewriters off the desks, and the noise fell to an electronic hum, the clatter replaced by a visual cacophony of lighted screens set to color schemes ranging from riotous to sedate, from fashion editor indigo and taupe to investigative reporter khaki. Screen savers flash geometric dances in neon colors at empty desks, while at the occupied ones the monitors alternate pages of type with hands of solitaire or hearts.

Against this computer hush, voices drop to library level. A raised voice sounds naked, and draws every eye across the room. Yet everyone seems to be talking—mostly on the phone.

I love the newsroom even more than I had loved kitchens. It fills me with energy as I walk past the rows and rows of reporters playing out their complicated lives at their desks in full view of each other. I watch them working the phones—cajoling their sources, whining to their spouses, complaining to their mothers, promising to their children—and I feel inspired, even by their indolence. I've learned that often the most whiny and lethargic reporters are actually the most productive. I've watched some spend the first six hours of their workdays pacing the floor, cleaning off their desks repeatedly, talking to their boyfriends endlessly, yet by the end of the day turning out a thoroughly researched story. I marvel that most of the people in sight seem deeply engaged in doing nothing, yet they unfailingly produce a newspaper every single day of the year.

Today, though, I was grateful that newsrooms have unspoken but universally respected rules of privacy. If you are in a sociable mood, people sense it, and you'll be greeted by dozens of colleagues as you weave your way to your desk. But if you are rushing to meet a deadline or preoccupied with private worries, you can walk through the room as if you are invisible. I greeted nobody as I headed for the far corner, to the lifestyles section, where I would try to put Laurence's death into words.

The exception to the privacy rule—as to every rule—is the managing editor, Bull Stannard. "Hey, Wheatley!" he shouted from the door of his office halfway across the newsroom. "I hear Levain has checked out. Get on it and see me in an hour."

"Is that true, Chas, honey?" Sherele, not only the theater critic but my best friend on the paper, looked up from solitaire on her red and beige computer screen. Her dark eyes suddenly grew liquid and her face turned pale, as if milk had been poured into dark cocoa. "Oh, poor baby. What happened? You must be devastated."

Grant, the book reviewer on my other side, even forgot his habitual sneer as he scooted his chair over to me and left his Minesweeper game exploding its little mauve and yellow bombs. "Mr. Sensitive strikes again. If his own wife dropped dead, his first thought would be who'd write the story. You okay, kid?"

I raised my hands as if to fend them off, and nodded, not yet able to speak. After a moment I pleaded with them, "Look, guys, all I know so far is that it was a heart attack. I've got to hit the phones and find out what's going on."

"Heart attack, huh? Young, successful chef, the envy of every competitor and not shy about flaunting it. Sounds like a cracking-good murder mystery plot to me," Grant addressed to his computer screen and shrugged his shoulders elaborately.

"As David Mamet"—Sherele could never resist

quoting a playwright—"would say, 'Fuck you,' Grant." Turning to me, she added, "He didn't mean it, sweetie. Let us know if you need any help." She went back to solitaire.

To buy myself a little time to collect my thoughts, I switched on my computer and punched the phone button for my voice mail messages.

"Chas . . . Wheatley . . . you have . . . seventeen . . . new . . . voice mail . . . messages."

Groan. I hit two more buttons.

"Miss Wheatley, you don't know me, but I'm a fan of yours, and I wonder if you could tell me . . ." *Save.*

"Is this the restaurant department? My friend just opened a new restaurant . . ." *Save.*

"I'm just a reader, but last Saturday I went to one of the restaurants you reviewed, and you wouldn't believe . . ." *Save.*

"You bitch. You think you know everything, don't you? You don't know a sauce from pig swill, Miss High-and-Mighty Critic . . ." *Delete.*

The rest of my Monday-morning death threats would have to come later. My most immediate worry was about how I was going to get the information I would need to write an obituary, which was surely the reason Bull wanted to see me.

I wasn't sure who among Laurence's friends would know yet that he had died, and I definitely didn't want to be the one to break the news. His sister Jeanine's line was busy, his girlfriend Bebe's phone didn't answer, and Borden, his sous-chef, wasn't to be found. The police refused to tell me anything except that Bebe had discovered the body this morning, and that in light of the evidence and Laurence's medical history, the medical examiner was pretty much assured that it was a heart attack. The restaurant was closed.

So I steeled myself and started calling chefs I knew.

All their phones were busy.

Reaching my last resort, I dialed Ari.

The worst always brings out the best in my ex-husband. The more dire the situation, the more I can count on his civility.

In the dozen years since our divorce, our enmity had turned to truce as we were forced to deal with each other every time Lily had a crisis—which was often during her terrible teens. I came to realize that once I didn't depend on him as a lover, Ari could be a reasonably reliable friend. Eventually I was able to admit—and appreciate—that he was much happier and, despite his curly hair growing gray and his long body turning soft, he was even more attractive as a gay man than as the insufficient husband of a lusty young woman.

"Oh, Chas, I don't know what to do. I never realized he was so sick. Why did he keep on smoking?"

"Only to irritate Jeanine," I said automatically, then felt ashamed for being snide about Laurence's sister. Ari didn't bring out the best in me.

Still, he gave me the information I needed. He

hadn't heard much, but knew that CityTastes was going on after all, and that the evening would include a tribute to Laurence.

The city's most prominent chef dies and his public throws a party? I was stunned at the callousness under that frosting of doing good. "Maybe they're going to auction off his ashes."

I could feel Ari's disapproval crackle through the phone.

"The food is, after all, already made. And *les pauvres* will need the soup kitchens even if Laurence is dead." Ari's French accent always got stronger when I irritated him.

"I'm sorry, Ari. I'm just feeling so angry with life. With death."

"Go and write your story and I will see you there tonight. I will have a cognac ready to medicate you as soon as you arrive. I'll call you back if I manage to break through the keepers of gates and find out any more information for you."

Gatekeepers, I silently corrected as I turned to my blank screen.

"A musician leaves behind his recordings. A painter leaves behind his canvases. But a great chef leaves behind only the memory of flavors and textures never to be tasted again," I wrote.

# four

"Y ou don't like your salad?" It was a disembodied voice I heard two decades ago as I dozed over my plate of curly chicory with thick chunks of country bacon at the Bistro du Marche in Paris. The heat, the acrid cigarette smoke, the late hour, and the strain of trying to keep up with the rapid French of my husband and his clique of chefs had worn me down. One more night when I felt ignored and irrelevant. Maybe I should stay home next time.

"Oui," I answered. I'd only been in Paris a month, and my French was too clumsy to frame such an answer as, "I was just wondering how such a brilliantly simple salad ever got transformed into America's soggy spinach salad with its sweet dressing and cold, limp bacon bits."

As if he'd read my mind, this gingery young man with his chiseled features and awkward country haircut switched to English. "It is certainly better than your American spinach salads, isn't it?"

That woke me up. "I'm Chas Wheatley." I reached

across the table to shake his hand. "How do you happen to speak such good English?"

"Laurence Levain. I was a high school exchange student in a place called Bowie, Maryland." He enclosed my hand tightly in his, which already had the roughness and the scars of a chef's, though the rest of him looked freshly out of adolescence. Then he reached over and picked up a piece of my bacon and popped it in his mouth. "That was what all the girls ordered when we went out to eat—spinach salad."

"You couldn't have been a high school student very long ago." Too late I realized that this was an insulting thing to say to a man obviously several years younger than I. I'd already become so cranky in Paris.

But Laurence was sure of himself with women of any age. He lifted his glass of wine as if toasting me, and swallowed half in one gulp. Polite and practical young man that he was, he changed the subject. "Have you gotten to see much of Paris?"

"No, we've only recently arrived." I nodded toward Ari, deep in conversation with a fellow chef. Better let this young man with his seductive blueberry-syrup eyes know right away that I was unavailable.

"I am learning the city myself. I would be glad to teach you as I learn. And you will teach me your English."

Suddenly I felt very hungry. "That would be wonderful."

I had been lonelier than I'd admitted to myself

when I'd arrived in Paris with Ari. We'd been traveling around the world from kitchen to kitchen for three years after we fell in love—so quickly—in New York. Ari had been chef in a French restaurant where I worked as a waitress while trying to write a novel—and getting nowhere with it. He had shy, gray eyes and the soft, unkempt look of a professor. More than ten years my senior, he'd seemed mature and comforting to me. He spoke little, which I took as a sign of depth and strength. I was a chatterer in those days, and such a romantic that I even took our language barrier as interesting.

They say that opposites attract, and to this tall, quiet man who had been slaving in kitchens since he was fourteen, I apparently seemed spontaneous and full of life, all that he lacked. He was a baked potato and I was the butter, sour cream, and chives—ready to melt into him.

Within six months, Ari and I decided to marry and see the world together, starting off with the small inheritance from his grandmother and my college graduation money, supplementing our savings with Ari working in restaurants occasionally as we made our way from Asia to Paris.

Neither of us was as free a spirit as we'd thought we were before we set out on our adventure. Ari couldn't really turn his back on his career. He wound up working long hours in hotel kitchens and French restaurants wherever we went, then experimented with Thai spices, Malaysian herbs, and Chinese noodle doughs on his days off. He seemed to have professional connections everywhere. These were Gallic connections, though, and they had no space for me.

Thus, I rarely worked in a restaurant. Instead, I cadged a few freelance writing assignments here and there, and I kept Ari's accounts, since he was a disaster at organizing such things. I tried to convince myself I was happy. I enjoyed the research and interviews that gave shape to my days, and I looked forward to the late-night bar-hopping with chefs and their passively adoring girlfriends. Like these other young women, I mostly smiled and listened, though in my case it was because I felt uncomfortable speaking French. I loved hearing Ari declaim and argue with the other chefs—it was here that he came alive. And I appreciated his loyalty—faithfully bringing along his wife when the others rarely did. Yet, increasingly I brooded.

"Talk to me, Ari." I'd push the papers out of his reach on the rickety table we used for dining and working in our apartment in Bangkok.

"What would you like to talk about?" Ari never refused me anything—nor ever quite gave me anything either.

"About you. Tell me what you're thinking."

"What would you like to know about what I'm thinking?"

As usual, he deflected me with a question. He was always agreeable, certainly good-natured, never disapproving. But he hardly had anything to say. After I made the effort to talk to him, I'd wind up feeling foolish and tongue-tied.

Without girlfriends to talk to or family nearby to confide in, I took a long time to realize what a mistake I'd made. I knew that every new marriage had problems. And Ari was so nice that I blamed my growing unhappiness on myself. I was too demanding, a chronic complainer, I told myself. I'd try harder to be cheerful.

Our sex life was a fizzle. We were both pretty inexperienced, and our first awkwardness never became much smoother. A chef's long days and late hours didn't help. I was always the one to make overtures, and he was the one to plead a headache.

At first I attributed his passivity to his being so much older and working so hard. But by the time we arrived in Paris, I knew something was wrong. I told myself that settling in one place—where Ari felt at home—would cure it.

Through his old friend, Marcel Rousseau, Ari had landed a job as saucier at Laperouse, one of the two great restaurants overlooking the Seine. After cooking for a quarter of a century he ought to have been head chef, but his wanderlust had set him back. And in his passive way, he was content for the moment.

I wasn't, but hoped to be, once I got to know Paris.

To my surprise, Laurence called three days after our evening at the Bistro du Marche. "Have you seen the Rue Mouffetard?"

No, I hadn't even heard of it.

"It is Paris's most charming market. This would be a good morning for you to start to understand Paris. I have the day off from peeling asparagus at

Taillevent, so I will pick you up at ten-thirty. Do not eat first."

I hadn't really taken a good look at Laurence in the smoky bistro where I'd been so sleepy. On this fresh, sparkling May morning, he struck me like a roast beef sandwich after two weeks at Pritikin. I was jolted by his wiry energy and the unselfconscious handsomeness of him. While many Frenchmen wore jeans as if they were dress pants with knife pleats, Laurence somehow gave the impression that his were a hastily wrapped towel that might become undone at any minute.

If I felt guiltily attracted to Laurence that day, I fell openly and wholeheartedly in love with Paris markets. Laurence and I wandered down the narrow curving Rue Mouffetard like drunks staggering from bar to bar. A bite of runny Brillat-Savarin cheese here, a nibble of wild hare pâté there. Skirting baby carriages and squeezing past beggars reeking of three weeks' sweat, in the company of my talkative new friend, I felt I was coming back to life.

Laurence thrust a paper sack of crunchy fried chicken gizzards at me. I shook my head. I had always hated chicken gizzards.

"Try them. You must taste everything before rejecting it. Otherwise, you will miss many wonderful things in life."

I reached for one and took a small bite. It tasted delectable, gamy and soft, as if it had been massaged like a Japanese steer. Even more wonderful were the wild strawberries and tripe sausages, the long, crusty baguettes Laurence broke off and fed me as we walked, and the tiny green peas we ate raw as he scooped them from their pods.

"Ahh, from Normandy!" Laurence swooped a small bottle of cream from a counter set out on the sidewalk. "This is like mother's milk to me." He paid for it and took a swig as I watched in horror.

"Straight cream? You'll kill yourself." Those were my thinner years, but only because I dieted stringently between feasts.

"Show me your tongue." He drizzled thick droplets on my outstretched tongue as the wrinkled gray shopkeeper looked on in amused approval.

It was like no cream I had ever tasted. He was like no man I'd ever met.

He tucked his arm into mine as we left the dairy shop. "My mother used to churn this cream into butter. And now my sister eats margarine."

"In France?" I was shocked.

"Oh, yes. Even in Normandy."

"Does she still live at home?"

"My parents died two years ago, so she lives in our family home, with her husband. She has no children. And now that we have no parents, she likes to be my mother and make me her child. She is much older—twenty-six."

"Oops." I stopped short with an embarrassed laugh. My arm slid out of Laurence's, and I gave him a light punch. "Not so old. That's only two years older than me, you little cabbage."

"But she acts older." Laurence tucked my arm back in his. "And your mouth is just like a little girl's." He looked at it so long that I felt it had been kissed.

We had planned to have a picnic, but we were too full. Yet we certainly weren't ready to part. "I will show you the most important part of Paris." Laurence guided me from the street into a small, unmarked door. "This is the real café. It gets the city started each morning and keeps it going all day."

The few tables were unoccupied, but Laurence ushered me to the bar, finding us a place to stand among the silent men. Soon we, like everyone else, had a demitasse of thick black coffee and a glass of amber liquid.

"Calvados." Laurence picked up his glass, thumb and forefinger at the rim, and swallowed its contents in one gulp.

I wasn't used to drinking in broad daylight, but I did the same. The strong apple brandy burned a path from my throat to my stomach.

"Now we must walk it off," Laurence declared as we finished our coffee.

That was the first of many walks, across bridges and down narrow streets, along the Seine and through orderly tree-lined parks. I hardly felt the miles go by as we talked of our childhoods and our futures. He talked about his girlfriends. I avoided talking about my marriage.

Ari's days off never coincided with Laurence's, so I felt free to take day trips, often to Normandy, where I got to know Laurence's sister, Jeanine. She liked Laurence having an older married pal, and treated me like an accomplice engineering the future of our young charge. She hinted that I might introduce Laurence to a rich young American woman, and openly suggested that I might find him a job in America. Jeanine was a businesswoman, a dealer in antique fabrics—French laces and American quilts—and believed that the brightest opportunities for ambitious restaurateurs were across the ocean.

Some days Laurence borrowed a car and drove us into the countryside, where we visited cheese makers and wineries. We met other young men who were, like Laurence, as passionate about food as about women—they looked approvingly at me as I admired their lovingly cultivated pears and geese. These were the men who would revive France's culinary resources and would one day supply Laurence's restaurant, he told me. He intended to become a famous chef.

# five

I'd done what I could for the moment to sum up Laurence's death for *Examiner* readers, so it was time to see Bull in his china shop.

Surely Bull Stannard is the only managing editor of a major newspaper—or even a minor newspaper—to keep a complete Meissen tea service in his office. He's a big man, requiring an oversized chair and suits made to order. He has fierce blue eyes and a well-preserved 1950s crew cut. He would look far more at home on an NFL defensive line than in a newspaper office. And much as he dresses the part and uses his bulk to intimidate people, he likes to think of himself as a sensitive soul. So he cultivates dainties—the china cups, a marbleized green glass Tiffany desk set with inkwells that he actually uses, and a damask sofa in a muddy purple color he refers to as aubergine. Seated on it was Andy Mutton.

Where Bull is big and hard, Andy is big and soft. Flabby. Sloppy. As food editor, he might be expected to be a little overweight, but it isn't necessary to the job that every one of his neckties displays the menu of the restaurant where he last ate lunch.

And Andy is always hungry. Not just for food, but for adulation, for whatever crumbs of power he can forage in the corners of the food world. I had put up with him gracefully, even been amused by him in my early years on the job. And I had gladly done occasional stories for his food section.

At first I'd considered him harmless, and laughed it off when he corrected my pronunciation of *salade niçoise*—nick-OYS, he'd insisted. But I stopped considering him amusing when he edited my copy to make me look like a fool—changing "foie gras" to "fois gras" and inserting the definition of "aioli" as an Italian sauce rather than French garlic mayonnaise, presumably because it ended with an "i."

There he was, settled into Bull's office ahead of me, insisting that he, as food editor, was the appropriate person to write Laurence's obituary. I wasn't going to let him win this one. Laurence deserved better.

"Why you? Do you even know his middle name?" I tried to keep the sneer out of my voice. "Or his recipe for *les nouilles en quilt multicolore*?"

"Nobody knows that," Andy answered sullenly, and he was right about that. Which I would never concede in front of Bull.

"Both of you get out of here," Bull growled. "Andy, you cover the scene at CityTastes." Just what I'd hoped. That freed me to concentrate the evening on my usual whirlwind sampling of the chefs' newest creations. It was a particular advantage this year because the other two major critics in town were so new they were still trying to maintain their anonymity. They wouldn't risk being seen at public events for at least the next year.

Then Bull granted me my second wish. "Chas, I've already cleared it with your editor. Get that obit to me by four-thirty. It's going on page one."

What a way to get a byline on the front page.


By five-thirty, after Laurence's obituary had been edited and I was ready to go home and change before facing the food world at CityTastes, I felt split in two. I was totally immersed in Laurence's life, yet totally cut off from the events that surrounded his death. Nobody was answering phones. Anywhere. I'd have to piece the context together at CityTastes, after a hot bath, a stiff drink, and a long cry.

As I gathered up my notes, Helen Marden, the lifestyles editor and a good friend to everyone on her staff, hurried over to give me a hug and tell me I'd done a great job. I thanked Helen for running interference with Bull on my behalf, and wove my way through the newsroom's maze of desks. Those reporters not too frantic to look up from their screens tossed me a good-bye or a thumbs-up. Dave Zeeger, the *Examiner*'s star investigative reporter, was just coming into the newsroom, and grabbed my arm as I passed by.

"You okay?" He always looks at people as if he could read their secret thoughts.

"Yes, I'm fine. I guess. I've got to go to CityTastes tonight. An orgy and a wake in black tie. I suppose it's the right thing to do, but it seems so ghoulish. At least I don't have to write that story. Andy's covering it, though I'm sure he'll want my help." I sucked in a deep breath.

Someone called Dave's name and he gave an impatient wave without taking his eyes off me. "Hey, girl, buck up. And call me anytime if you need me. I'm having dinner at some fancy French restaurant with a couple of FBI guys after I finish here, but I'll be home recovering with a Domino's pizza afterward."

I left him with a mock grimace and a real smile.

As I headed for the elevator, I felt satisfied that I'd written the truth about Laurence's life. In a few days everyone would know that, all unawares, I'd written lies about his death.

# SILENCE IN THE KITCHEN

Three-Star Chef Laurence Levain
Fed Presidents and Panhandlers

By Chas Wheatley
*Examiner* Staff Writer

A musician leaves behind his recordings. A painter leaves behind his canvases. But a great chef leaves behind only the memory of flavors and textures never to be tasted again.

Laurence Levain, 42, chef among chefs in Washington and leading contender for the James Beard Chef of the Year Award next spring, died at his home Sunday night. He had a heart ailment. Mr. Levain had returned to his Massachusetts Avenue apartment after finishing the preparation of his world-renowned pasta squares, *les nouilles en quilt multicolore*, for last night's CityTastes, which he founded.

Mr. Levain, born in Normandy, France, trained at Taillevent in Paris from age 18 until he opened his own restaurant there seven years later. At age 28 he became the youngest chef ever to have achieved the maximum rating of three stars from the authoritative Michelin guide. When he immigrated to Washington ten years ago to open Chez Levain on N Street in partnership with his sister, Jeanine, Mr. Levain was the first three-star chef to bring that honor to this city. He was expected to repeat that achievement in Manhattan later this year in opening the restaurant Les Deux with his long-time friend, Marcel Rousseau, chef-owner here of La Raison d'Être.

Mr. Levain cooked not only for the well-heeled, but for the poor as well. He began feeding the homeless from his restaurant's back door, then gradually expanded his philanthropy until he had established a network of soup kitchens throughout the Washington area. He remained on the network's board and donated staff from his restaurant even when the pressure of planning a new restaurant recently forced him to discontinue cooking personally for the soup kitchens.

See LEVAIN, B5, Col. 3

# six

Tonight it took a long time to dress, because thoughts of Laurence kept distracting me. Twice I had to redo my hair, and still my upsweep threatened to collapse. My friends say they can judge my mood by my hairdo; this time they'd reckon me "on the edge."

I gave up on my hair and moved to the full-length mirror on my closet door, to see what my dress was doing to my unruly thighs. I've always loved soft, clingy clothes, but nowadays have to exercise more discretion in how clingy they are.

I used to diet. I suffered through vacation after vacation on carrot sticks and sixteen-ounce bottles of mineral water. I even got the *Examiner* to send me to a spa once.

It changed my life—but not the way most people say a spa changed their lives, not by making me a true believer in minimum portions and maximum exercise. No, the effect this spa had on me was to make me realize once and for all that strenuous dieting is a waste of one's life. Every woman at the spa was taking off the same pounds she'd taken off dozens of times before, and adding twice as many in the interim. Dieting is a losing battle, and I no longer wanted to consider life a battle anyway. I told myself that life was too short and my job was too good to waste my opportunities worrying about such things.

Thus I'd decided to stop feeling guilty about each bite I ate. I vowed to enjoy the abundance that accompanied my work, and to practice just a little abstemiousness at home—which is why my kitchen is stocked with bananas, cantaloupes, and fat-free popcorn, along with boxes and cartons of restaurant leftovers.

Not that I don't have my occasional doubts. Particularly when I look in the mirror.


I was dressed, but I wasn't ready to go. I picked an album that fit my mood and watched the last pink clouds of the sunset from my enormous windows while the McGarrigle Sisters strummed songs of loves found and lost.

My body and my mind ached. I settled for a moment into my favorite chair, a well-worn red velvet platform rocker. Surely there was time to hear a love-gone-astray ballad by Loudon Wainright III, to get the man's side of the story from the ex-husband of one of the McGarrigles—I could never remember which. There always is another side to a story.

The music made me think of Lily, who hates what she refers to as "Mom's guitar-plucking modern hippies." Lily is a musician with a passion for the classical, even though her Philadelphia piano-bar job requires her to play what she calls "supper-club pap." It pays the rent, she explains, while it gives her time to compose and practice her "real" music and go to afternoon concerts. I think of Lily as a poet having to make a living writing jingles.

I knew I had to call Lily, though I dreaded breaking the news about Laurence to her. I was relieved when Lily's phone wasn't answered, and for once was glad that Lily refused to own an answering machine.

The shadows stretched across the brick wall behind my chair, leaving me in the dark. I switched on a lamp, but knew I could no longer postpone the evening.

# seven

**T**his November evening the city was smudgy black and stinging cold, but it smelled warm outside the National Building Museum, as French tarragon, Thai basil, Mexican cilantro, and the garlic beloved of every cuisine rode on currents of steam from simmering sauces. As I ducked in a back door behind the delivery trucks to avoid the mob at the entrance, I realized I'd eaten nothing all day except a clam fritter. I was actually looking forward to sampling the showpieces of a hundred chefs.

You'd think that with so many food benefits every year, cooking for these events would become routine for chefs. And generally that is true. But CityTastes is different. For this, the largest cookathon of them all, the chefs prepare the dishes themselves rather than relegate them to their sous-chefs. That was a tradition started by Laurence, who never let anyone watch him construct *les quilts* anyway. Chefs being as competitive as they are, the others felt shamed into following suit, and eventually the competent chefs appreciated the fact that this ritual weeded out the fakes. After all, some celebrated chefs do no other hands-on cooking the rest of the year. In fact, in some unionized kitchens, the top people—the executive chefs—aren't even allowed to touch the food.

The format is that the senior chefs present their signature dishes (perhaps to show that they can still cook them), while the younger, less established chefs show off new dishes—the trends in the making. Thus, one year's Cajun spices fade in the perfume of the next year's kaffir lime leaves and epazote. And shimmering herbed custards in pools of pimiento *coulis* are replaced by towering constructions of fried vegetable chips and baby salad greens. Washington's CityTastes has matured into a stand-in for the legendary barrel-tasting dinners at New York's Four Seasons as the fall event to forecast next year's trends.

It always makes the network news, but this year the big guys were covering it live. The word was out about Laurence's death, though most of the party goers, having changed in their offices and rushed here without their daily fix of news, didn't know yet. They just looked curiously at the newsmen huddling together to milk each other for details, and figured that they were definitely at the right party.

As usual, the veal protestors were trying to get the cameras' attention by marching back and forth with their signs showing unhappy calves and bloody carcasses. They demonstrated against the mistreatment of calves at every food gathering, whether or not veal was to be served. I've always thought their time might be better used in helping to feed some of the city's hungry.

By seven P.M., the staging room was already a world-class headache as students from all the local cooking schools worked at breakneck speed to keep up with the steady need for plates, forks, and glasses, ten thousand of each. I maneuvered between the loaded carts to slip into the vast central hall with its eight, seventy-five-foot-tall Corinthian columns, a carpeted expanse that can seat two thousand comfortably.

Fortunately, I knew the layout well by then. The hundred buffet tables were positioned beneath the arches around the perimeter, arranged much like a cookbook—appetizers, soups, salads, pastas and other starches, fish, meat, vegetables, breads, and desserts. Wine tables huddled around the central columns, after-dinner drinks and coffee in the middle. That's where I headed, intending to start at the end, with the cognac Ari had promised me.

A stranger would most likely pick Aristotle Boucheron as a professor of some arcane language. He has that kind of vague, absentminded look, as if his thoughts are always escaping into the distant past. Despite or because of that, Ari is devastatingly attractive to middle-aged women and gay young men. More so since he's been living with Paul. At sixty his body has developed a lazy softness that suits his mismanaged curly gray hair—which Paul in vain tries to keep trimmed. Even in his pristine chef's whites, Ari looks unkempt. Maybe that is because his hands are always fiddling with something—plucking at his jacket buttons (which is why he's always losing them), ruffling through his hair. His hands are happiest with a mallard duck to pluck, a shallot to mince.

In the kitchen, his fidgeting is a wonder to watch. Those aimless putterings always end with something delectable and often astonishingly original. Such inventions seem to emerge reluctantly and absent-mindedly—the aspic jells, the mayonnaise fluffs, as if by accident. Ari's Chesapeake Bay chowder and his grape *bavarois* appear to be the simplest of dishes. But nobody has been able to duplicate them.

Unfortunately, his absentmindedness works productively in only the kitchen. He did just fine as a restaurant or embassy chef; such routines of management had been imprinted early in his teen years. But when he went into catering, he was prone to lose track of things. He would commit to a party with an unfamiliar address without even realizing it was in Baltimore. He would confuse names and dates, forget that white peaches wouldn't be in season by the time the dinner was to take place. He exasperated even those clients who went to every possible length to assure Ari's services.

Then, to the ultimate relief of those faithful clients, Ari found Paul. Or Paul found him. Just out of computer school in Asheville, North Carolina, Paul had been so desperate for a job in the big city that he answered every employment ad he could find his first week in Washington, even one as Ari's dishwasher.

Paul was everything Ari was not: young, quick, wiry, blond, with chiseled features and an alert look. He loved to organize things, whether a desktop or a laptop, a closet or a life. His Southern accent was a mystery to Ari's French ear, and vice versa. But their meeting was a lightning bolt that flung Ari out of a closet he didn't even know he was in. And from then on, Ari's clients could count on orderly dinner parties.

Paul's tenacity eventually won me, too. He worked hard and long at being a friend to Lily, and through her maddening teen years Paul made a point to take my side in every mother-daughter issue. Paul was often the lone voice of reason she would listen to. Eventually I couldn't resist accepting him as an ally and, ultimately, as a friend.

"Chas, darlin', you are a sight to gladden the eyes of this po' country boy. And that shimmery thing you're wearing makes my little gay heart go all pitty-pat." Paul laid it on thick as he stroked my midnight-blue silk sleeve. "Mmm. You look like blackberries and cream."

Paul didn't look half bad himself in his suede tuxedo, and I told him.

Ari beamed as if I'd cooed over his new baby, leaned over, and kissed me on both cheeks. "Are you feeling any better, *chérie*?"

"Now I am. There's nothing like a little gathering of a thousand friends to perk me up. And the prospect of the best hundred dishes on the East Coast." I was trying to keep up a brave facade. "Have you heard anything?"

"Nobody seems to know much. You'd be surprised by how many people here don't even know yet that Laurence is dead. But Borden, Jeanine, and Bebe are bringing *les quilts* that Laurence had prepared for tonight, and there will be a ceremonial sharing of the chef's last dish."

I shuddered. It sounded ghoulish. Even cannibalistic.

"I think you need a little strength," Ari suggested as he reached under the table and pulled out a tray with three snifters of cognac. "To Laurence. He changed all our lives."

I downed my cognac in one gulp, then gasped. "Ari, you old fool! That was Louis the Thirteenth." I'd just swallowed a hundred dollars' worth of alcohol.

The hall was filling rapidly. I began to get nervous about all I was going to have to accomplish tonight. What's more, two young chefs were heading our way, and I didn't want to get caught in an endless discussion of *beurre blancs*—or heart attacks. "I'd better go and get some real work done." I waded into the crowd.

Which way? The appetizer lines were, naturally, the longest, since the evening was at its beginning. Two couples, deep in conversation as they rushed toward the appetizer buffet, barreled into me as I stood, indecisive. "I gotta try Raisin Debt," said one of the men, who was wearing more gold around his neck than his wife wore on her fingers and wrists.

To the uninitiated it might have sounded like a

real-estate discussion, but I realized that he meant La Raison d'Être. Just as the woman looking for Lion Dior wasn't referring to designer men's wear but to the venerable French restaurant Le Lion d'Or.

Three chefs were huddled like white geese in a swirl of tuxedos and gowns. "Heart attack," I heard one say. All the chefs seemed to know, while a surprising number of guests didn't yet realize that this was a wake rather than a party. I pulled out my notebook and headed for the chefs.

Andy Mutton cornered me. "What a night. Already I've gotten some really good stuff about heart attacks from a few of the doctors here, and you ought to see people's reactions when I tell them Laurence has died. This is going to be quite a story."

I shuddered at his glee and didn't even bother to respond, while he changed the subject on his own.

"Chas, you are not going to believe how awful some of this food is. When are people going to wake up to these fakes? You can taste the canned broth in Jean-Louis's cream of chestnut soup."

Sure. Jean-Louis probably doesn't even know that broth comes in cans. But I held my tongue and decided to look on the practical side: That just meant more soup for me, and since Jean-Louis Palladin's restaurant at the Watergate had closed and he was now only an honorary Washington chef, I'd especially covet every spoonful I could get. I brushed Andy off with, "Excuse me, I've got to go say hello to Julia" (knowing he'd be jealous that we were on a first-name basis). And I marched purposefully toward Jean-Louis's cream of chestnut and foie gras soup with squab and chestnut *quenelles*. If Andy doesn't like it, it's got to be good.

It certainly was, though I had to spend ten minutes in line for just a cup of soup. I was torn between reporter and critic, but at CityTastes my job was to taste, and I was going to have to find a way to do that more efficiently. For one thing, if I let the time lag between tastes, I'd lose my appetite too early in the game.

I had long ago discovered that I could use diet spa techniques to my advantage, not just to lose weight but to enable me to eat enough for research purposes. I sometimes have to taste a dozen brands of butter or twenty different pizzas at one sitting, or even sample my way through CityTastes without flagging. Diet advisers teach you to eat slowly, to pause between bites and courses, so that your body has time to signal to your mouth that you're full. For me at food tastings, the trick is to eat fast, with as few pauses as possible. As long as I eat steadily, I can consume prodigious amounts without feeling stuffed. When I stop, my appetite disappears. Pacing is crucial in a job like mine.

For the second time today, Brian, that cheeky waiter from La Raison d'Être, came to my rescue.

"You want to know what they're saying?" He nodded toward two young chefs, Savio Vitale and Stephen Wang, sharing a booth and watching the crowd. They were paying so little attention to serving their creations—warm polenta salad and pan-fried three-meat dumplings—that the floor of the booth they shared was slick with spills. When Savio spotted me he waved his big wooden spoon in my direction, splattering polenta all over Stephen's white jacket. God, it's embarrassing being a food critic.

"I expect they are all thinking about what a great chef we've lost today," I said to Brian, not at all certain I was right.

"The older chefs are a pretty depressed lot, that's for sure. Watch how they kind of touch their chests when they think nobody's looking. They're all afraid they're going to be the next to have a heart attack."

"That's a chef's idea of empathy for a fallen comrade." I continually marvel at the egoism of the men behind the stoves.

"The young ones aren't even going that far. They're too excited about being here to think about anything but their own careers. That Chinese guy figures you're his ticket to fame and fortune. He thinks you're going to fall for his dumplings."

"It's hard to make a Chinese dumpling I wouldn't fall for."

"But the other guy, the Italian, he's warning him that you could be his ticket to the unemployment line. He says he worked under a chef who suffered from your double-edged pen. An ex-chef."

I just shrugged.

"See those two over there?" He pointed to two other chefs hovering over pumpkin-tofu flans and black bean pâtés with fronds of dill garnishing them. "He's calling her flans health food, and she's telling him his plates of pâté look like weeping willows in mud piles."

"She's right." I couldn't help giggling.

"He's bragging that he's got an inside track with *Food & Wine* magazine. She says those New York guys never write about unknowns, so she's waiting for you to discover her and make her famous enough for them to bother with."

I was beginning to enjoy this. "And what's he about?" I pointed to Victor Hernandez at the next table, arms folded and watching the two bickering chefs with a scowl.

"He was complaining to his assistant that his poblano soufflé with jicama salsa wasn't going to make him famous anyway. That just doesn't happen to ethnic chefs. It's only when gringos like Rick Bayless and Mark Miller cook with Mexican ingredients that chiles and cilantro become chic. He's never going to be in the Beard-award league."

"I'll have to see if I can prove him wrong. If I ever get past this bottleneck. I'm dying to taste more of the food, but it wouldn't look good for me to butt in line."

"I can take care of that." Brian left me standing and headed for the front of my line.

In the meantime, Stephen Wang, the dumpling chef, had counted the number of people ahead of me and had swung into action. He rearranged the rows of plates in front of him and reached back to a pan he'd reserved at the side of his stove. These must have been perfect dumplings he'd been saving in the hope of their making him a star. He lined them up where I would be sure to get one.

Brian stepped behind the table and, nodding a greeting, picked up a plate of dumplings—ordinary ones—and another of polenta. He carried them off to the side, waggling his head for me to follow. While Stephen watched in dismay as I was handed an imperfect plateful, I broke off from listening to three blue-haired women in crepe gowns and sensible shoes who were talking about Laurence.

"They say he was—you know." One rolled her eyes and sealed her lips.

"Fucking," filled in the second. That got a frown from her friends.

"Shh, Eleanor. People will hear you."

"Beautiful dumplings," I said between bites, passing half back to Brian in exchange for half the polenta salad. It's wonderful how food can blot out all other thoughts. "I love the combination of ham and venison. If I didn't know it was illegal to import, I'd think this was Yunnan ham." I dug into the polenta salad. "Interesting idea, combining stalk celery with celery root in this *mirepoix*."

Brian nodded in agreement. "You're the expert. I couldn't taste the difference between Yunnan ham and honey-baked, not that I know what Yunnan ham is. But I'm good at hunting." Brian took off for the next course.

Stephen Wang was so disappointed that his dumpling plan hadn't worked that he didn't notice me until I tapped him on the shoulder.

"You're Chas Wheatley," he stammered.

"I know it," I said and grinned. "And you're Stephen Wang, aren't you? I wanted to ask you about those dumplings. You must have studied in Kwangchow."

Stephen's mouth dropped open. "How did you know? After Harvard, my parents got me an apprenticeship at Pan Hsi." That's China's most famous dim sum restaurant. "I spent two years learning to make a hundred different dumplings."

I was impressed. "I didn't think anyone outside China made that particular shape. And was that Yunnan ham?"

Stephen shook his head. "It's not really Yunnan ham. I could never sneak enough past customs to use for my restaurant. But I finally worked out a formula for simmering Smithfield ham in soy sauce and rock sugar and drying it so it tastes pretty close to Yunnan."

"Great job." I finished my notes and shook Stephen's hand. Then I turned to Savio, who was glowering jealously. "That's a lovely trick with the two-celery *mirepoix*," I said, reaching to shake his hand, too. Savio lifted my hand and turned it over, kissing it with a little bow.

"You are a very smart lady. You have an admirer for life."


Thus Brian and I ate our way around the hall while I eavesdropped on the rumors. Hot dishes and cold dishes. Heart attack and suicide. Gentle dishes and chile-hot explosions. Drug overdose and seafood allergy. Delicious inventions and abominations. Died jogging and died at the stove.

Those who knew Laurence looked stricken. Those who merely knew of him were seasoning their dinner with morbid curiosity. I wanted to shut ignorant mouths, slap smirking faces. But I had to keep reminding myself that my job here was to eat.

I worked my way from the new young chefs to the old masters, for good reason. Just as it would be a waste to start a meal with the best wines, the raw young chefs' dishes would be likely to suffer in comparison with their more seasoned elders'.

For one thing, they were usually so complicated. The newer the chef, the more likely he or she was to throw in too many seasonings, to make the dish too rich, to sauce and garnish it to death.

Thus it was a treat to come to Roberto Donna's game risotto—only Roberto would dare (and succeed) to make a risotto for five hundred. Anyone else would turn it to mush. And nobody but Yannick Cam would have the confidence to serve a simple codfish and potato puree—albeit with enough caviar to seriously deplete the Caspian Sea's sturgeon population.

It was with great relief that I encountered Patrick O'Connell's specialty from the Inn at Little Washington, the tiny Virginia inn that's considered the best in the country. A chef with considerable wit and instinct, he knew tonight's diners would be buttered and olive-oiled to the groaning point, so he served a tiny sundae of savory sorbets: rosemary, asparagus, and winter tomato (where did he find such summery tomatoes in November?), drizzled with a remarkable lime-jalapeño syrup that was more perfumed than sweetened. As a classic palate cleanser was meant to do, it refreshed my taste buds and made them ready for the next course.

Brian was orchestrating our feast even more finely than I'd realized. At the prime moment, we were right next to La Raison d'Être's booth, ready for Marcel's *soupe en chemise*.

French onion soup had become a joke before Marcel Rousseau reinvented it as an hors d'oeuvre rather than a soup. Once the staple of Parisian bistros, this hearty beef broth with its slowly browned onions and cheese-glazed baguette slices had been bastardized in chain restaurants, coffee shops, and cafeterias. It was seldom made with anything resembling meat stock anymore, and rarely with onions sautéed slowly enough to fulfill their sweetness. It was usually canned or reconstituted from dried mixes, topped with gluey factory bread and waxy cheese. It was the kind of mass-produced dish that made Americans say, "I don't know what all the fuss is about French food."

Marcel made real onion soup in his restaurant. But most of his customers wouldn't order it. They mistrusted any onion soup, or even if they trusted Marcel's cooking, they'd be embarrassed to be seen eating it, just as they'd never be caught tucking into beef Wellington.

So Marcel had transformed it into fritters. He started with the classic soup—sautéing thinly sliced onions slowly with butter in a covered pan for about fifteen minutes, then removing the cover, adding a touch of sugar, and stirring over moderate heat for at least half an hour, until the onions were deeply brown. Then he added rich brown beef stock and a splash of wine, and reduced this broth over high heat until it was mostly onions. He poured it into a shallow pan, refrigerated it until it jelled, and cut it into small cubes. These he coated with a batter thicker than the one he used for his clam fritters, making sure the cubes were thoroughly coated. He rolled them in a mixture of grated parmesan and Swiss cheeses, and refrigerated them again. Frying them was a tricky process, the textures and temperatures needing to be exactly right so the batter wouldn't burst and the soup run out. Eating them was a trick, too. You had to pop them whole into your mouth so the broth didn't spill down your chin. I loved them.

Marcel was not in good shape. A fidgety man with a beaky nose and darting eyes, he had always looked like a sparrow. And now he looked like one who had been prematurely pushed out of the nest. His eyes were rheumy, and he hadn't shaved very well.

No wonder. He and Laurence had been friends and competitors for decades; what's more, Marcel had once been Laurence's mentor in France, when Laurence had been a young apprentice and Marcel a full-blown chef. Recently they had been planning to work together again, to open a restaurant in New York, each one of them spending one week a month there, and eventually expanding to other cities. The project had been getting a lot of attention in the press, since it was the first time Washington chefs with a national reputation were planning a triumphal march into New York. This was the scheme that would support their old age, and the two had been gathering investors for the project.

When I first caught sight of Marcel, he had just eaten a single spoonful from one of Patrick O'Connell's savory sundaes and had handed the rest to his wife, Marie Claire, to dispose of.

"These stupid Americans," he said to her. "They make everything a dessert."

The French aren't willing to give Americans credit for anything.

Marie Claire saw me first. She dumped the sundae in a trash can, glass dish and all, then rushed over to embrace me and drag me over to Marcel's booth. I wished that time could pause right there and let me cry on her shoulder before I faced the rest of the evening. Here was a woman who would know how to rise above grief. I told her how sorry I was to hear about her brother's death last month and welcomed her back from Mexico.

"It is very hard to lose one and then another in such a short time," she said, and thanked me for the flowers I'd sent to the family. Marie Claire and I had been almost-intimate friends since my years in Paris, when I'd watched her closely for clues to being a selfless, adoring chef's wife. She is one of those women who are solid, warm, dependable, and ready to help you through any trouble. Yet with all their generosity, they reveal little of themselves.

"I cannot go on. Laurence was my son," Marcel

sobbed as I took both his hands. I reached out to hug him, but he recoiled. "*Les chemises!* They are burning!" Marcel fished out a dozen blackened cubes from the fryer. It hadn't seemed possible that he could look more dismal, but he did.

Marie Claire seemed embarrassed. Even more than usual, she looked like a warm biscuit in her draped white blouse and golden-brown long velvet skirt. She caressed Marcel's shoulder and brushed back a stray hair as if she were patting him into shape.

I didn't know how to comfort him. So many people were watching that I felt we were on stage. "It's too crowded here, Marcel. I want to see you later." I picked up a plate of his little fried soups, which won a wan smile from both of them, and I made my escape.

I was glad I'd waited until I left to eat my *soupe en chemise*. It tasted as tired as Marcel looked. Poor guy. I dumped the rest and went to face the desserts.

While all around the hall chefs were bickering, whining, and trying to upstage each other like children vying to become the teacher's pet, the pastry chefs acted like grown-ups. Teammates. Colleagues. Maybe it was all that sugar that sweetened their dispositions. Or the appreciation—everybody loves desserts, even third-rate desserts.

Probably it had to do with the fact that pastry chefs' names are seldom known to the public. So few become celebrities that it's pointless to cut each other's throats for attention.

Whatever the reason, there they were, scooping ice cream for each other, drizzling chocolate in decorative swirls, passing out each other's tartlets and *vacherins* and telling everyone how delicious each other's creations were. The dessert tables were a happy place, like the nursery in a hospital.

If Cinderella had lived in Washington, she never would have met her prince. By midnight, when she lost her slipper, the prince and all the other important people would have been long gone from the ball.

The movers and shakers of the capital city have an unwritten curfew. On the stroke of ten P.M., at dinner parties, meetings, tête-à-têtes, and galas all over town, they get up to leave. They say it's because they must get up early, but at least for the politically inclined (which includes nearly everyone in Washington), it's really because they want to get home in time to watch the late news and *Nightline*. New Yorkers go to clubs until the wee hours; Washingtonians stay up late to see if they are mentioned on the news. Thus, it doesn't matter whether the coffee's been served or the poetry reading is finished. Any hostess worth her salt knows that her table is going to empty at ten.

This November night at the National Building Museum, a thousand people were beginning to stir. It was nine forty-five.

Borden, Laurence's sous-chef, arrived just in time, arm in arm with Laurence's sister, Jeanine, and Bebe, the bereaved girlfriend who had discovered the body. They were surrounded by a flock of chefs carrying trays piled with *les quilts*. The procession looked like geese, swans, maybe even angels— Borden in his white chef's coat and the two women in long white gowns. Against all the white, the salmon pinks and herb greens of *les quilts* were breathtaking.

"Ladies and gentlemen," Borden shouted over the public address system. His voice was lost in the noisy burble of the half-drunk crowd. "May I have your attention, please." People started shushing each other. "Ladies and gentlemen, let's have a moment of silence.

"Laurence Levain, our dear friend, died late last night of a heart attack. He had exhausted himself preparing for this CityTastes. He finished preparing his beautiful salmon quilts and went home where, sometime after midnight, he collapsed. He went quickly, I've been told."

The silence was broken by sobs. Everyone knew now.

"We are here to honor and to mourn the passing of a great chef and a beloved friend. We will do it in the way he would have wanted it. Let us bow our heads and say a silent farewell. And let everyone partake of his final gift, *les nouilles en quilt multicolore*, that he prepared last night for this event."

The room was silent for a moment, then someone began to sing the French national anthem. The crowd joined in, the Francophiles singing and the others humming along. Tears glistened, coursed down a thousand cheeks. As the last notes died, the clatter of serving trays filled the silence. Dozens of students waded into the audience, handing out small plastic plates of *les quilts*.

At first, nobody quite knew what to do with this steamy little reminder of death. A few isolated people started to take a bite, but paused as they saw they were alone. Finally, nearly everyone carried a plate to the coat check, then out the door. Some eyed the trash bins wistfully, realizing that it would look rude to discard this precious morsel. The homeless dozing in nearby doorways would eat well tonight.

I made my way to the podium to pay my respects to the family. Poor Borden, losing his mentor and his friend, though probably gaining a lucrative new position in the process. Surely Jeanine would crown him with Laurence's toque, a great honor for such a young chef. Jeanine's shattered dreams—she had devoted her life to Laurence's career. And Bebe, poor child, she had so obviously idolized him.

Although I never exactly understood why most people found Borden greatly talented and charming, I'd always figured he had qualities that were beyond my perception, since Laurence had chosen him as sous-chef. I recognized that he was a good technician in the kitchen, mildly good-looking in a Yale kind of way, and had an instinct I lacked for always saying the right thing (if not the interesting thing). We had become, over time, friendly acquaintances.

Yet Borden and I had felt a little edgy about each other in recent years. Lily had come between us. No sooner had she reached the age of consent than the two of them had had a secret fling that still lingered for Lily, but had turned into mere friendship for Borden. I felt he was keeping her dangling. Besides, at thirty-five he was too old for a twenty-two-year-old. He, of course, resented my interference, though I suspected he'd also concede that I was right. Borden reminded me of an artichoke—did you ever notice how, delicious as it is on its own, it destroys the taste of any wine you drink with it?

Tonight was not a night for resentments, though. When Borden saw me squeezing through the crowd around him, he reached out to me and pulled me into the inner circle of chefs. "I called Lily," he whispered as he enfolded me in a hug. "She's hoping to hear from you." I felt a flash of jealousy that he'd reached my daughter first. Here was one more chance for Lily to measure these two rivals for her affection and find me coming up short. Borden dropped his arm from my shoulder as he continued his conversation with the group in attendance.

I couldn't reach Jeanine and Bebe. They were moving toward the exit, wrapped in a crowd of weeping women. Borden remained in front of the podium, surrounded by dozens of chefs, answering their questions.

"Yes, Bebe found him late this morning. She called

an ambulance, but of course it was too late. The medical examiner said he probably went very quickly. The funeral will most likely be on Thursday."

The questions accelerated.

"Look, I'm exhausted. I've been fielding calls all day and getting all this stuff ready for tonight. I've got to get out of here." He started shaking hands and clapping shoulders and kissing cheeks, telling this chef and that one that he'd see them tomorrow. As the crowd thinned to two or three close friends, Borden answered one more question.

"Is it true that it happened when he was fucking some broad?" The question came from a chef I couldn't see.

Borden didn't notice me behind him as he looked around to make sure the women were gone, his mouth twitching halfway between a grimace and a smirk. "Yeah, you know the old stallion. Never too busy for a flying fuck. Apparently he picked up one of his Fourteenth Street floozies on his way home. She was gone by the time Bebe showed up in the morning, of course, but the police told me Bebe knew he'd been with a prostitute."

My heart was racing.

"I can think of worse ways to go," another chef said and shrugged.

They all guffawed. This dignified group of chefs broke into horseplay, nudging one another and adding coarser and coarser obscenities. The dam of emotion had broken, and they were releasing their tension with a little gutter humor. I escaped.

It wasn't true.

Yes, it was common knowledge that Laurence sometimes picked up prostitutes on his way home from work, having become a pig about women once he'd passed thirty-five and feared he was losing his youth. But not last night. I was sure he wouldn't have brought a woman home last night, just as I was certain nobody else but I would know it was impossible.

## eight

D ave, I have a problem. Got time for company?"
An investigative reporter would know how to
help me sort this out, especially such an experienced one as Dave, who'd covered everything from
inspection frauds to organized crime. I cradled the
phone on my shoulder as I rooted through my purse to
check that I had mugger money—just enough but not
too much. "I've got to talk to you about Laurence's
death. Something's wrong. What I've been hearing
doesn't fit together. Someone's lying about what happened before he died, and I'm beginning to wonder
whether his death really was from a heart attack."
Only a few stragglers were left in the hall. I caught
sight of a white jacket behind me and lowered my
voice. "I need your help."

"You think there was some foul play? Goddamn,
Chas, get right over here. I'll even save you some pizza."

Distracted by the chef hurrying around the corner, I didn't bother to chide Dave about his infernal
pizza.

"Chas, are you there?" He sounded worried.

"I'll be there in an hour," I told him. That would worry him more.

"Don't walk, you idiot. Take a taxi."

But I was already hanging up. Thank goodness I'd brought my sneakers. I needed the walk.

The nighttime sky not only felt cold, it looked cold. Neither stars nor streetlights contributed much illumination, though every tree and each darkened building threw sinister shadows across the cracked and buckling sidewalks. I strode up Fifth Street past the Gospel Mission, where I saw a huddle of men scraping the last of *les quilts* from plastic plates.

From this perspective, Washington is a city of misery and hopelessness. A few blocks south lies the great American corridor of power, Pennsylvania Avenue, where mostly white men push the buttons and issue the orders. The residential districts to the north and west are wealthy and white. To the east and south, the black majority lives, some in splendor and most in poverty. Squeezed in between blacks and whites are the Hispanics.

I turned onto Massachusetts Avenue, eerily uninhabited, and headed northwest and up the economic ladder. A man came out of the NPR building and crossed the street. I was relieved to have someone share the sidewalk with me, though he hurried as if propelled by a fast-breaking story or a hold-up man.

I didn't want to think about death. I wanted to remember Laurence. I returned to Paris, to the year we became lovers.

● ● ●

As Laurence and I became frequent companions during my two years in Paris, at first I persuaded myself that Ari was looking on us not with jealousy, but with relief. I no longer needed him as much. And I was happy, which made him happy.

Yet I wondered, when Ari insisted I bring Laurence to Laperouse so he could show our young friend his new sauces and his latest pasta experiments. Such are a chef's weapons. Sexual fantasies and guilt began rumbling through my dreams, nightmares of gladiators trying to obliterate each other.

I still joined Ari at the late-night chefs' gatherings, and often Laurence was part of the crowd, sometimes with a woman—a very skinny and giggly model or a darkly quiet student, but never the same woman twice. I added jealousy to my guilt. And I retaliated by pointedly ignoring Laurence on those evenings. My reward was getting to know some of the other chefs' wives, particularly Marie Claire, whose husband, Marcel, was Ari's closest friend. She was a mother hen of a woman, but not just because she was ten years my senior. She even mothered Marcel.

I've always considered it a waste that Marie Claire never had children. On the other hand, over the years I—and later Lily—enjoyed the generous fussing she might have expended on her offspring. Marie Claire was as soothing as rice pudding, and as sweet. She helped me to find a new apartment when we needed one, and to decorate it on our meager budget when we moved in. And she inspired me to try harder to be a chef's dutiful wife. Marie Claire devoted herself to caring for Marcel—watching what he drank, gently steering him away from overeating. Like most of the wives I knew, she worked in her husband's restaurant. It was the only way she could have a chance to see him, she said.

I wished I could be as understanding of Ari as she was of Marcel. Apparently Ari, too, had such wishes. One night we were with the usual group of chefs and their women, sipping cognacs and talking about restaurant critics. Marie Claire was reminded of the time an American critic had claimed that Marcel's pistachio ice cream had food coloring in it. Even though the rest of the review was good, Marie Claire was infuriated that the woman would print such a lie.

I'd never seen Marie Claire wound up like that. Her soft cheeks grew rigid and her pink-and-white complexion turned splotchy red. She couldn't drop the subject. She was still seething, and this was years later.

"Enough already!" Marcel pounded the table. It was the first time I'd heard him raise his voice to her. All of us were embarrassed for her and for him.

The next day, I brought up Marie Claire's obsession to Ari. "Why did she go on about it? It happened so long ago, and it was such a small part of the review."

"You American women cannot understand the French chefs' wives," Ari said in his usual quiet way, but with an edge to his voice. "They give up so

much. They live on nothing in the early years when
the restaurant is making very little money. And they
spend the same long hours working in the dining
room and doing the accounts that their husbands
spend in the kitchen. Cooking is the husband's
whole life, and she takes care of everything else—
the books, the reservations, the taxes, the children.
But it is all for him. The restaurant is his, the glory is
his. His talent is her life. He is her only future. And
so she feels protective, even more than a bear with
her cubs."

Did Ari sound resentful? I didn't want to know it.

I had my own life. I now had a best friend and a
language in common with my surroundings, occasional writing assignments, and a beloved new city
to explore. I kept frantically busy. Sleep was something to indulge in as little as necessary. And sex—
well, where was the time for it? I no longer had to
blame Ari, I could blame my busy life.

After nearly two years of pretending to treat me
like a beloved sister and confidante, Laurence began
openly to treat me as a woman. When he took my
arm, I felt him pressing it against his side. When he
greeted me with a kiss on both cheeks, the second
kiss lingered. I assumed he was short on girlfriends
at the moment. I didn't want to spoil our friendship
with dangerous expectations.

Then one dreary gray day we were sitting in a
café, hunched over an insufficient little round table.
The pale wintry sun struggled to warm us through
the glass. We drank calvados after calvados to burn
away the chill. Laurence began fidgeting with his

glass. "All married Frenchmen have mistresses. And American women like to think of themselves as equal to men. So married American women should have mistresses. Or masters."

I didn't get the logic, but I got the drift. I never was much good at responding to men flirting with me, so I babbled. "But American women refuse to have masters."

I wasn't sure he would understand that play on words. I glanced up at his face just as I was taking a sip of my calvados, and it splashed on the table.

He quickly reached over with his napkin to stop the spill before it dripped into my lap. "Then certainly an American woman would not turn down the opportunity to have a servant."

His English is better than I gave him credit for, I thought. I looked off at the bare chestnut trees and skim-milk sky to avoid his eyes as I put down my glass. My hand brushed his. And stayed. He linked his little finger with mine, just as that first day he had linked our arms.

When I looked back at him, a grin was twitching wickedly at the corners of his mouth. "I would like to be your servant. I would be devoted to you forever. I would polish you carefully every day and make you shine."

My hand felt on fire. The heat jolted through me like the calvados. It went straight to my groin, and made me feel weak. "Not my servant and not my master. My lover. I know. But I can't." I can't? What was my stupid mouth saying? After two years of waiting for his towel to drop? Some prim, terrified

Chas inside me was answering. "I could not hurt Ari that way."

"Ari." The name sounded bitter from Laurence's mouth. His face looked stripped down to the barely twenty-year-old that he actually was. "You know what they say about Ari . . ."

"No, I don't. And I don't want to know." I couldn't bear to hear him say more. I'd spent five years avoiding saying more to myself.

I grabbed my coat and stalked out, leaving Laurence stunned, his face collapsed into crushed adolescence.

For two days I heard nothing from Laurence. He might have called, but I wouldn't have known. I was never home. He had taught me to walk, and I used that lesson well. I didn't know what—or whom—I wanted to walk away from, so I just kept walking.

The third day, Ari was going to be out very late, going over the last-minute details for the next day's competition for *le meilleur commis cuisinier de France*, for which young chefs prepare one dish ahead and another on-site with a mystery basket of ingredients. Ari was a judge. Laurence would be a contestant. In my turmoil, I had forgotten it was coming.

The least I could do was wish Laurence well.

By midnight he would certainly be home. I would just apologize for having walked out on him, and see how he was doing before his contest. But if that was all, why had I taken a perfumed bath and put on silk underwear?

A freezing rain had turned the street slick and the traffic slow. As I dashed from the taxi to Laurence's front door, hoping he was there, I realized, as I should have before, that I had a bigger worry. What if Laurence had a woman with him?

He didn't. That was apparent when he opened the door and saw me dripping before him. He crushed me in a hug that nearly turned my sodden coat to steam.

"I'm sorry I ran away." My voice was muffled in his shirt.

"I'm sorry I gave you reason to run away. I love you, Chas, but I am willing to love you any way that you will have me."

I pulled away and searched Laurence's face. He looked terrible. Lines of tension creased his forehead. His Mediterranean-blue eyes looked as if a storm had churned them cloudy. I was dumbstruck.

Laurence filled the silence. "I don't want to hurt your life." He stroked my hair and wiped the corners of my eyes, where tears had begun to collect.

"You have made my life very happy these past couple of years." I led him inside and sat on the threadbare velvet love seat that was his only living-room furniture. I pulled him down beside me and stroked his cheek. "I don't know what I want right now. My life is cut in two. And I don't know which half is the right one. But I think it is time for me to start figuring that out. I don't want to hurt you either."

"We have never talked about your marriage. I didn't want to intrude. But I have seen that you are not quite happy."

"I just don't think about it. I love Ari." Was that still true? I wasn't sure. Maybe I was just used to saying it. "He is good to me. He does what he can. He tries." Why was I talking about Ari?

"I'm not asking you to decide anything. I just want to have a little more of you for now. Ari's leftovers. I would like to have what he is not using. For now."

I liked the way that sounded. Thrifty. "That's why I'm here." I reached up to kiss Laurence. I was ready to melt.

He didn't melt back. His lips were as tense as refrigerated dough. I pulled back and gave him a surprised look.

"Oh . . . I . . . this is not the right night for this. Excuse me." He dashed for the bathroom.

I was stunned. I looked around his apartment while I waited for him to return, which wasn't soon. Clothes were strewn on the floor, along with scraps of paper and sketches. A half-empty bottle of calvados stood on the windowsill next to a small, empty glass. The apartment looked as tense as his face had. I took off my damp coat and picked up one of the sketches. It was a plate of food.

Laurence returned, looking sheepish. "It is the competition tomorrow. I have never been good with tests. I cannot sleep, I cannot eat. My stomach is bad. I have always had this difficulty, since I was a small child."

I was relieved that the problem wasn't me. I

stroked his forehead and gave him a motherly hug. "There's nobody better than me to cure such a problem. Do you have chamomile?"

I brewed him chamomile tea and massaged the back of his neck in between his trips to the bathroom. I talked about his sketches and his plans for the competition. I poured calvados into his second cup of tea and took a slug myself. Then, when Laurence seemed less agitated, I turned down the lights and set about the ultimate relaxation therapy.

"I'm going to make it all right." I piled pillows at one end of the love seat and eased his head back on them. I took off his shoes.

"I wish I could . . . I have always been afraid it would bring me bad luck."

"Shhh. You'll be fine." I unbuttoned my blouse and let it slip to the floor.

"Ohh, you're so beautiful. If only—"

"Don't say anything." I unzipped my skirt and let it drop.

"Oh, *mon dieu*. So beautiful."

I unbuckled his belt and unzipped his jeans. I reached into his shorts.

"Oh, I. I must . . ." He bumped me onto the floor as he bolted to the bathroom. I sat fuming in my silk underwear as I heard him retching.

After that embarrassing fiasco, I wasn't sure Laurence would want to face me again. And my own confidence had taken a bruising as well.

As it turned out, Laurence was sturdy beyond his years. Or, as he later put it, he was used to such pre-test panic and by now knew enough to avoid such situations. He'd never gone to bed with a woman before a big cooking event, and he never would. Not only was his stomach a mess and his manhood limp at such times, he stubbornly believed that sex would rob him of the concentration—or the luck—he would need. I was the first woman to ever face his jitters, and obviously would be the last.

The day after the competition, as soon as the sun warmed the glass-enclosed roof deck he'd borrowed from a friend, he showed me that his impotence was temporary. We made love on the chaise, then spread cushions on the sun-warmed stones. We writhed among tubs of geraniums and pansies. Laurence sprinkled me with petals. I decorated him with leaves. We giggled and moaned and panted until the sun went down.

Now it was my turn to panic. For days my body vibrated with memories of Laurence, but my heart pounded with guilt. I was afraid to see Laurence again. I clung to Ari. My remorse drove me to seduce him while I yearned for Laurence. I begged Laurence for a respite, for time to think.

Two months went by in turmoil, as Laurence and I alternated abstinence and passion. At first I'd talk to him endlessly, but always in harsh sunlight and public places. I couldn't face abandoning Ari. Then I'd cave in to guilty abandon. Finally, to my secret horror, I discovered that I was pregnant.

Fate made my decision for me. Laurence might be

ready for love, but I didn't believe he was ready for responsibility. When Ari was offered a job as chef at the French embassy in Washington, I took the coward's way out. I went with him. Any regrets I had were swept under the carpet of a loving family: Ari the doting father, Lily the spunky baby, and me immersed in mothering her.

As I walked along the deserted Washington streets, icy suspicions turned my Paris memories stone cold. From our first fruitless groping in Paris and occasional commiserations in years after, I knew Laurence would never have attempted to make love to a woman, or even have one around to witness his misery the night before such an important show as CityTastes. If Laurence hadn't had a woman with him, someone must have made it look as if there had been one.

Why?

To mask the fact that somebody else had been there, to conceal the real encounter in an anonymous sexual assignation.

To hide what?

Murder—what else?

The lights of the Henley Park Hotel appeared as welcoming as a front porch. I nodded at the doorman, then averted my eyes as I passed Laurence's apartment. At Fourteenth Street, I felt the hostile stares of the street women in their small skirts—or no skirts—and big hair. They wore little but makeup to keep them warm. I wondered how Laurence could have found their company appealing.

By the time I reached Columbia Road, an hour had passed since I had called Dave. But the walk had done its job. I was calmer, and looking forward to Dave's probing questions to help me answer mine. And more. A back rub, for a start. I tucked stray hairs back into my upsweep and stopped under a streetlight to put on fresh lipstick.

Columbia Road always cheers me after the sterility of the tourist-hotel neighborhood. Its mingling of Hispanics, blacks, and whites, of single graduate students and middle-class families makes Washington feel more like a big city than does any other part of town. Even near midnight it was pulsating with Latin music.

I turned off at the Barney Senior Center and walked that last dark block to the Ontario, where Dave lives. Since no structure in Washington is higher than the Washington Monument, this massive apartment building on a hill has a clear view of the city's magnificence, and it outclasses everything else in the neighborhood. It's Washington's answer to New York's legendary Dakota. But instead of *Rosemary's Baby*, its literary claim to fame is that Nora Ephron commuted here from New York when she was married to Carl Bernstein, and thus presumably tested her recipes for *Heartburn* in an Ontario kitchen.

As I approached the iron grillwork protecting the glass doors, I saw that Dave was waiting inside. He burst out and grabbed my arm. "God, I'm glad you're here. I've been standing here for half an hour wondering which emergency room to call first. Your nighttime walks are going to do me in, Chas."

"You investigative reporters worry too much." I reached up and ruffled his lank beige hair, then pulled his face to mine and kissed him as thirstily as if he were a Perrier in the desert.

Dave is tall and commanding, and probably too handsome for his own good. He makes me think of Thrasher's french fries with apple cider vinegar—irresistible and dangerous, substantial and consoling, with a tantalizing, sharp edge. One look at Dave leads people to three conclusions, all of which hold true so far: He'll never gain weight no matter what he eats, he'll never lose his craggy good looks, and he'll never stick to one woman. Because he is so open about his wanderlust, women somehow find him trustworthy. They confide in him. And they vow not to fall in love with him. Usually they break that vow. I did.

When I entered the warm entry hall I discovered I was not quite as calmed from my walk as I'd figured. My teeth started chattering, and it wasn't from the cold.

My silky midnight-blue dress couldn't have looked glamorous twisting around me as I huddled in the corner of Dave's sofa, having run a stocking on the cracked leather. My hair was dangling from dislodged hairpins. I had a mug of coffee with a shot of bourbon in it warming my hands.

Dave was eating the piece of cold pepperoni pizza he'd magnanimously saved for me.

"How can you be so sure he wasn't with a hooker?" he asked me as he picked at the bits of cheese sticking to the box. "The guy was a letch, and everyone knew it."

"But there were times he didn't want a woman anywhere near him." I wriggled out of my stockings. "He would never, ever have a woman around the night before a big show-off cooking event. His nervous stomach was too much of an embarrassment. Not to mention his impotence. And the older he grew, the worse it got. Laurence was too vain to let any female see him in such a state." I sipped my coffee and examined a small stain on my skirt.

I felt disloyal telling Dave this, but I needed his help, so I went on. "Even his sister didn't know. He was too embarrassed. Everyone had to think he was a stud all the time. So he'd find ways to get around the issue. He'd fall asleep in his kitchen or he'd pretend he was drunk. Or pick a fight with his girlfriend. Anything so he wasn't put in the position of having to perform before a big day."

"Okay, I can understand that. But if nobody else knew, how did you know?"

"He first told me in Paris. We were so close, even then, that there were no secrets between us. And we were too young to be wary of trusting our best friends." I didn't want to admit to Dave exactly what the circumstances had been, since even he didn't know Laurence and I had been lovers long before my divorce. "Early on, we made a game of telling each other things that we would never dare tell another person."

"So what did you tell him?" Dave sounded more jealous than curious.

I ducked my head and sipped my coffee. "I only tell my secrets in Paris, in case you want to really get to know me sometime." My answer was a surprise even to myself, and I felt my face flush as I heard my words. "Oh, forget that. Let's stick to the problem."

Dave moved over to the sofa, having finished the last scrapings of pizza. He massaged my left foot, which, at that moment, he seemed to feel more comfortable addressing than my face. "Yeah. Now, we've got this guy. With a heart problem that everybody knows about. And a steady girlfriend but an irresistible impulse for hanky-panky. He shows up dead one morning. The medical examiner seems pretty sure it was a heart attack. And there are signs of hanky-panky."

I was nodding. Dave felt encouraged to progress—with the massage as well as the monologue.

"But you say the hanky-panky was a fake. Does that mean the heart attack was a fake? Nobody would bother to establish a fake scenario if the guy just happened to drop dead of a heart attack. You'd just walk away. The only reason for pointing the finger at a prostitute is if you want the finger pointed away from you. Have I got it right?"

My breathing quickened. Dave's hand had worked its way up my leg and was massaging my most delicate parts. I wouldn't have believed that grief could so quickly cross the line into passion, or that strong emotions could be so readily interchangeable. The diversion from my pain was irresistible. "You've got it right."

Dave took my coffee mug and placed it on the floor, then leaned over to lick the caffeine-flavored bourbon off my lips, ending with a long, deep kiss. He nudged aside my stockings and dropped them off the sofa into the coffee mug.

"You want to pursue this?" he continued.

"Yes, I want to pursue this." My body flooded with relief.

Our clothes didn't melt away as they always seem to do in books. My dress bunched under my back when Dave stretched out on top of me. I shifted to straighten it, shoving Dave half off the couch. He reached out to brace himself, his hand splashing into the mug with my stockings.

I was somewhere between laughing and crying, but Dave wasn't the least bit daunted. His arms wrapped around me, his body clung to mine, right down to our toes.

I moaned. Then the world intruded again and my breath caught.

"You're thinking bad thoughts."

"I'm thinking he was murdered."

"I know." Dave pulled away and kissed my eyes closed. He gently massaged my temples. So sweet, so safe, so chaste.

My body began to melt into him again. I took one of his hands and placed it strategically, then for the next hour he showed that he knew all about me.


Dave and I have a ritual after our lovemaking that is almost as good as the sex itself. After dozing on the couch—which is where we usually make love, since we're too impatient to get beyond the living room— we take a bath together in Dave's big claw-footed tub. We talk about starting out in the bathtub some- day, but so far we haven't gotten around to it, and we've been trying for two years.

The bath is a kind of delayed and extended fore- play. Dave's bathroom is as large as some bedrooms, and it not only has this enormous and picturesque tub, it has a dimmer switch for the lights, strategi- cally placed candles, and a picture window that frames a perfect view of the Washington Monument.

Dave and I have our best talks in this tub. And our worst.

First we got the night's sad business out of the way. Dave agreed that Laurence's death was begin- ning to sound fishy. He would call one of his friends on the police force in the morning and set up a meet- ing for me with the detective in charge. Then he encouraged me to just talk about Laurence's life, to begin to lay him to rest.

Dave was trying hard to cheer me up. He even started to tell me what it was about me that turned him on. It's not something he talks about easily so, like most serious subjects, he treated it as a joke.

"You describe yourself rather well, you know," he began.

"Me? How do I describe myself?"

"You don't really know you're describing yourself. You think you're describing a wine. Every time I read what you write about cabernets, I think about you," Dave said as he traced my lips with his finger.

"Am I going to like this?" I wondered if he was setting me up for a punchline. Dave knows I'm uncomfortable hearing people recite what I've written.

"Don't get your back up. Those are lovely things you say about cabernets. And just what I'd say about you: You've got backbone. And structure." His hands were showing what he meant. "I love your bouquet. You're mellow. You have depth. And just enough acid for balance. Not to be forgotten, you have great legs." He stroked them to prove it.

Wow. I was speechless. But just for a moment. "It's a pleasure to be appreciated by such a connoisseur. I'd be glad to write more, in case you run out of text."

"The point is, Chas, I'm in love with you. And it's time that more than the two of us know it."

So far, we'd been utterly secret about our relationship, and I'd grown to like it that way. I tell him it's just that keeping it to ourselves has, over the past two years, become a habit that's hard for me to break. But he knows there's more to it.

The odd thing is that the secrecy started with him. Dave exposes so little about himself that I suspect few of his friends outside the business know about his two Pulitzers—one for uncovering drug use in city government, another for revealing construction kickbacks. Few even inside the business know about the wife who died and the baby who lived, severely retarded and institutionalized from birth until a quiet death four years ago. It took years for Dave to stop blaming himself for the car accident that killed his pregnant wife, even though she had been driving and he was asleep in the backseat.

Once he started dating again, he kept women physically close and emotionally at a distance. And he kept his affairs private. Everybody loved Dave, but nobody knew him. That's the way he liked it.

I figured that's really why Dave refused to go to restaurants I was reviewing. He says he hates tablecloths and valet parking. He particularly can't stand waiters fawning over me. And food that doesn't have enough grease seems to upset his stomach—or so he claims. Besides, he only likes to eat food that's familiar, in places where he's been before. Even when we find a common ground—pizza—he always orders pepperoni and sausage, and I prefer pancetta and prosciutto. Or anchovies.

So we stayed home. I never expected our little fling to lead anywhere, given Dave's reputation, so I found the secrecy convenient. I'd been through humiliating endings before; this time I'd avoid being embarrassed when he dropped me. I just assumed we could go on like this forever (which meant until Dave traded me in for someone else). But to my surprise, lately the secrecy had been making Dave uncomfortable.

Tonight he tried a lighthearted approach. "Let's just test the waters. It'll be easier if we rehearse. Here's the scenario." He pulled himself up straight and shook his shoulders, slicking back his hair and pursing his lips. "I'll be Sherele."

I wiggled to an upright position, too. "I'll be me. Or I'll try, anyway."

Dave put on a falsetto. "How long have you two been going out, did you say?"

"Oh, not long. Just a couple of years." I rolled up my eyes in mock innocence. We broke into whooping, splashing laughter at the thought of Sherele missing two years of such juicy goings-on, right under her nose.

Then I sobered us up, saying, "You know she'll feel betrayed. And so will everyone else."

I realized it was a pretty lame excuse for avoiding any public commitment. I was too much of a coward to admit that I didn't trust him, that I'd had enough embarrassments from men to last me a lifetime.

Dave wasn't ready to let the subject drop. "Maybe we could dream up a brand-new first date. I could sort of saunter over to your desk and . . ."

Better that I should play along than drag us into a real argument and force the issue. "Yeah, and what would you do then?"

"I could say, 'We never have actually been introduced, have we?'"

I was beginning to enjoy this. "Yeah, and then I could ask you if you had any plans for dinner."

"And of course you'd invite me to go along with you to L'Auberge Chez Francois."

"No, that wouldn't work. Nobody would believe you'd drag out to Virginia with me for dinner in a fancy French restaurant."

"Maybe I could ask you about a recipe and invite you over to teach me how to make a grilled cheese sandwich," he suggested.

That set off my giggles. I was laughing so hard I

could hardly talk, but I managed to blurt out, "But how will you explain to everybody, Mr. Zeeger, that you are already six months pregnant?"

That got him. Dave slid down into the water and stuck out his belly like a beached whale, covering his eyes in mock embarrassment. Now we were both choking on our guffaws.

When we got our breath back, Dave tried one more tack toward reassuring me. "Look, Chas, I've never kept anything going with one woman for this long before. In case you're afraid of my wandering eye . . ."

"That's not the problem," I lied. But only in part. I took a deep breath and decided it was time to reveal at least some of my fears. "Right now our relationship is just between us. If we're known to be a couple, it affects my job, too. People will expect you to accompany me to dinners and parties, and they'll be insulted if you cop out. I know you'd hate going to those things." What could I expect of a guy who's never even owned a suit?

"I'm going to buy me some of that caviar and practice. You'll see," Dave said, standing up and nearly dunking me in the process. He ruffled my wet hair and got out of the tub.


I couldn't sleep. Laurence and Dave were both haunting me. From experience I knew that the only thing to do was to get out of bed and try again later. I pulled on one of Dave's soft gray sweatshirts, which came to my knees, and padded barefoot into the kitchen, tucking my hair behind my ears only to have it fall forward again.

A glass of warm milk usually worked, but not tonight. I couldn't calm down. I couldn't even concentrate on the crossword puzzle Dave had left unfinished on his scarred lavender Formica kitchen table. I looked at it. He hadn't found a four-letter word for "House of worship, in Munich"; nor could I at the moment. I purred at the silly cat clock with its broken pendulum tail. It was already two A.M. Lily would be home from work and wide awake—as I well knew after all the times Lily had awakened me with the moment's crisis. Like last night. So it was time to turn the tables.


"Mama! Where are you? I've been trying to call you for hours. I even tried the shelter, but they said you and Viv didn't cook today." Lily somehow begins most of our conversations with an accusation, particularly when I am the one who calls. I uncurled myself from the corner of Dave's sofa and planted my bare feet on the uncarpeted floor, ready to stand up and fight.

"No, we weren't scheduled to work at the shelter today, with Viv being out of town and tonight being CityTastes. I'm at a friend's. I tried to call you earlier, but it's hard to leave a message when you don't have an answering machine." There I go, wading right into the battle, I reminded myself. I pulled Dave's sweatshirt over my cold knees and resolved to put a little forbearance into the exchange. Nobody needed an argument at two A.M.

"What friend?" Lily said, deftly deflecting the accusation. As she waited for an answer, I could hear from her breathing that she was practicing her yoga stretches.

"It's a friend I'd like to talk to you about some-time. But I'm too tired at the moment. I just wanted to hear your voice and see how you are doing about Laurence. You two always had such a special thing going on between you, from the time you were a little girl. I knew you'd be upset about him, and I guess I could use a little mothering myself, too."

"Oh, Mama, I can't stand his being gone. I don't even want to believe it."

"I don't either, Lily." My voice began to crack.

"I know it must be so awful for you. You two were so close. Are you okay? Have you talked to Dad? I got an E-mail from Paul telling me Dad wanted to talk to me tomorrow. I guess this is what it was about." I could hear tears in Lily's voice, too. "I love you, Mama. Tell me what I can do. Would you like me to come home?"

Philadelphia isn't all that far, and yes, I would love for Lily to come home. We fall into our old inti-macy so easily when we are face to face. I imagined her wiry dark hair falling over her face as she arched into a cat stretch, this thinner and far more limber version of me at twenty-two. "I'd love to see you, but I know you don't have any vacation time, and it's not worth risking your job. Just hearing your voice is a big help. I'll let you know when I find out about the funeral."

"Look, Mama, I know it's hard to reach me. I'll try to keep in better touch. And I know you don't like to do it, but in an emergency you can always call me when I'm playing at the club. That's where Borden found me."

I tensed again, stood up, and started pacing the floor with the phone in one hand, the receiver in the other. Lily was always putting me in competition with Borden, but this time I wasn't going to rise to the bait. Our talks are so volatile, always ready to boil into anger, then settling again into a soft, warm simmer. For a change I averted a fight. "I'm always afraid to call you at work. But I'll do it next time."

"After our talk last night . . . I didn't make it easier for you. I'm sorry. I was in a foul mood because Borden wasn't home after he said he would be, and I was worried that he was with some new woman." Lily was trying hard, too. She rarely admits to me any imperfection in Borden. "But that's just me, Mama. I always take it out on you, I guess because I trust you to love me anyway. And because even when I'm angry I'm always sure that I love you."

I laughed. "In that case, I might prefer just a little more indifference." Lily laughed, too. The tension was gone. I eased into the sofa again, rubbing the corners of my eyes. Lily trusted me. Maybe I should trust Lily.

I started, hesitated, started again, my voice husky. "Lily, hon. I don't know if I should say anything . . ."

Lily, when she stops to listen, has that daughter's

instinct. "Whoa, Mama, you really aren't okay, are you? You don't sound okay at all."

I started choking. "Lily, I'm scared. I think Laurence was . . ."

Lily finished the thought for me: "Murdered."

# nine

The sunlight was in my eyes. I pulled the pillow over my head and nudged the comforter aside with one leg. It didn't help. Reluctantly I admitted it was morning. I vaguely recalled Dave kissing my neck and saying good-bye. I sat up and leaned over to see the clock radio. 9:12. I'd have to get by on six hours' sleep and a hangover. I picked up Dave's sweatshirt where I'd dropped it beside the bed, and padded into the kitchen, my head pounding.

Dave had anchored a note with a jar of instant coffee. Once again I vowed to buy him an espresso pot and a bag of Starbucks. At least he had aspirin.

"Good morning, love," he'd written. "Called Det. Homer Jones. Set up lunch for you. He insisted on I Ricchi. 1:00. He'll make reservation. See you back at the salt mines, C. W. Great bath." I rubbed the note against my cheek. Poor substitute for Dave. No bones, no whiskers, no lusty smell.

I called my boss, Helen—remembering to dial through the switchboard so she wouldn't see Dave's number on the caller ID—and said I wouldn't be in until after lunch, but in case anyone needed me I'd be checking my voice mail.

I thought I was ready to get moving, but my body told me otherwise. It sat stubbornly in a kitchen chair, refusing to budge—not until I paid some attention to the questions I was avoiding.

Who would want to kill Laurence, and why? The reasons that immediately came to mind sounded like bad movie plots: Jealous lover (Bebe). Jealous colleague (Borden). Jealous partner (Jeanine).

That covered love as a motive, as far as I knew. What about hate? He hadn't stolen any guy's girlfriend lately. He hadn't fired anybody recently. He could be exasperating, but he wasn't the kind of person to make real enemies.

Money—that's the motive I'd bet on. Surely some competitor would benefit by removing the top chef from the restaurant lineup. But the flaw in that theory was that no one chef could be sure of getting the business Chez Laurence would leave behind, and it was just too farfetched to imagine a consortium of French chefs agreeing to bump him off so they could all share his leftovers.

I tried another avenue. The restaurant business is fueled by corruption. In a restaurant like Chez Laurence, millions of dollars a year pass through the coffers. Much of it is cash, not readily accounted for, thus easily siphoned off. Great quantites of costly ingredients are always on hand, which means that restaurants are rich sources of stolen goods—steaks, wines, caviar. Silver and artwork are heisted from restaurants, too. Everyone steals; even patrons have been caught trying to sneak out giant potted plants. I should look into whether anyone's been skimming profits from Chez Laurence, someone who could have been threatened by Laurence discovering the losses.

The trouble was, each of these possibilities sounded ridiculous if I gave it more than a moment's thought. I'd just have to act as if I knew what I was doing, and maybe I'd figure it out along the way. I called Jeanine.

Jeanine's voice was hoarse, but she sounded composed. She was on her way over to Laurence's apartment, and I suggested we meet there in an hour.

It would be a rush. I swallowed half a cup of instant coffee, showered, and pulled on the jeans and sweater I kept in Dave's bottom drawer. His comb would have to do. I gathered my hair into a ponytail, found a shopping bag for my wrinkled evening dress, and left, buying the *Examiner* from a vending machine to read in the taxi. No time to walk today. I'd have to stop by my loft to change into proper I Ricchi clothes.

After all that rushing, I had to wait for Jeanine in front of Laurence's apartment. I sat on the front steps and unfolded the *Examiner* to reread Laurence's obituary, wishing I could write it over again and do better this time. The sun felt shrill to my tired eyes and I kept closing them, craving being back in Dave's warm bed with the clock turned back to, say, two days ago.

Jeanine stepped out of a taxi looking as if she'd

had her steel-gray suit fitted to her after she'd put it on. Her hair suggested that a hairdresser had been hiding in the taxi to smooth any bangs that had dared to stray. Her hips were narrow and her neck was firm. Nobody who saw Jeanine could doubt that she worked out at least once a day. Except for a leatheriness to the backs of her hands, Jeanine could have passed for Laurence's younger sister rather than as eight years his senior. I feel like yesterday's chopped liver next to her foie gras in aspic.

On closer look, though, today Jeanine didn't look so good.

We exchanged kisses on both cheeks. Jeanine's felt clammy. Her hand shook as she unlocked the door to Laurence's building. Her voice, under the bright chatter, still sounded scratchy.

"Chas, my dear, I am so grateful for you to come here with me. I could not have faced this apartment alone. I have had no sleep. No sleep. I keep hearing his voice and seeing his face." Jeanine always sounds as if she's reading lines someone else wrote.

At the apartment door, we both hesitated before stepping over the threshold. I took Jeanine's hand and gently led her into Laurence's living room, which looks a little like a cloud. All white, with a silver lining.

You'd think that a chef, after wearing a white uniform in a stainless-steel kitchen all day, would like to come home to a little color. Not Laurence. He'd decorated his apartment with white carpet and modern furniture of white wool, glass, and chrome. His tables were glass. And like the white plates against which he arranged the vivid food in his restaurant, the white walls displayed the only color in the room, gilt-framed still lifes and landscapes he had inherited from his parents. Those and his tableware and glassware were what he'd kept from his childhood home, while Jeanine had taken the old-fashioned furniture.

I settled us both on the long, low white sofa, feeling Laurence everywhere. Not knowing how to comfort either of us, I waited for Jeanine to pick a subject.

The funeral.

"I thought to take him back to France, but there is nobody left there. And so we will bury him here. That way all of his friends will be here to say good-bye. I think it will be Thursday. Friday is too hard for the chefs to leave their restaurants."

Talk of practical matters was a relief. I volunteered to check over the funeral notice in the paper. "I suppose you will use that same church, out past the CIA, where that chef—what's his name?—had his funeral?"

Jeanine rooted through her purse. A handkerchief? No, a business card. "Yes. And the cemetery in Fairfax. We will have it early, so that those who need to get back to their kitchens can do so. I must see to so many things. So many things." The small white card fluttered as Jeanine's hands shook.

For a moment Jeanine's eyes filled with tears. "I am so alone. I have nobody now. We were always such friends. When we came here, we did everything together." She dabbed her eyes. Carefully, so she wouldn't smudge her makeup. "Do you remember that night we went to eat sausages and dance the polka at that strange place in Maryland? And there was a funny little man watching Laurence and me having such a good time? He asked Laurence, 'Is she your sister or your girlfriend?' And Laurence answered him, 'A little of both.'"

Jeanine's monologue ran down. She straightened her shoulders and took a deep breath. "How could he leave me? I never thought he would leave me here alone."

I was dumbstruck. I knew it was natural for people to feel anger at the loss of a loved one, but I was embarrassed to hear Jeanine openly blame Laurence. What could I say? Agree that he was a shit to be so inconsiderate as to die?

I didn't have to say anything. Jeanine carried the conversation on her own, ranting at the dead Laurence. She hardly noticed me until I reached to stroke her clenched fists. Suddenly she paused, flustered. She had gone too far. But she didn't exactly back off, just tacked in a new direction. She switched her monologue from what he'd done to her to what he'd done to himself.

"I told him to stop smoking. You'd think, after the doctor gave him that scare, he'd stop. His own father, after all. And his only uncle. Both died of heart attacks. He had to prove to himself that he had no such weakness. He jumped from parachutes with those foolish, crazy friends. They drove all night to hunt for game. He thought that sleeping for minutes would be enough. He never stopped. He insisted on killing himself. And now he has done it."

With that Jeanine really ran out of steam. She crumpled back against the pillows and covered her eyes with both hands like a small child hiding. Her vehemence had shaken me. I stood up and began to straighten up the room, unwilling to look at her. What had driven that excruciating soliloquy? Grief or guilt?

There was nothing plain about Homer Jones. You might even call him a fancy-clothes detective. He was the kind who'd wear a Hecht's sale suit, Filene's Basement shirt, and street-vendor tie, and carry it off as if it all came from Neiman-Marcus. Smooth-skinned, loose-limbed, closely cropped and mani-cured, he looked as scrumptious as the tiramisu being served at the next table. He was the only African-American in the dining room at I Ricchi, but he would have stood out anyway as he unfolded from his chair to greet me.

"I want to tell you, I'm a big fan of yours, Miss Wheatley."

"Chas."

"Chas. I'm Homer. You know, I scan your reviews into my computer. That way I can search for oyster stew or chocolate mousse or whatever I feel like eat-ing. I keep them on my laptop, so when I'm cruising I don't have to get stuck with a McDonald's."

"Well, I'm flattered, Homer. I hope I've covered enough neighborhoods to do you some good." I felt like a panelist who's just been introduced to the studio audience.

"Yeah, you do okay. Though I sure could use some more tips for Prince George's County."

"So could I."

Homer caught the waiter's eye and signaled him for menus. "I'm afraid I might not have a lot of time today, but when Dave called, I wanted to fit you in. So we'd better order, in case I get beeped. I'm real excited about watching you at work." He reached for the focaccia—which the waiter had just replenished even though neither of us had eaten any. "How do you do this reviewing?"

"We just have to choose different things and taste each other's. Or at least I have to taste yours." I hoped the interview stage of the lunch was over. I pointedly opened my menu and examined the list of specials. I already knew the regular menu by heart.

Homer didn't order like a man in a hurry. "I think I'm going to start with the tagliolini with rabbit sauce. I've got to see whether their pasta is as good as mine. I roll it out by hand—I don't believe in pasta machines. Then I'll try the fritto misto. I remember you thought it was—how did you put it?—'gossamer.'"

I groaned inwardly. I hate hearing my words quoted back to me. Why is it always my most trite descriptions that people remember? "I'll have the ribollita," I told the waiter. The bread-thickened vegetable soup would be balm for such a cold, hard day. "Then a grilled fish. Do you have wild rockfish today?"

Homer ordered his tagliolini without fuss, but got

into heavy technicalities with the fritto misto. "I want it without shrimp, just with scallops and squid. And any fish the chef might want to include. Go heavy on the zucchini, too. Then—after the fritto misto, not before—I'll have an arugula salad with just a little fresh lemon and coarse salt and some Parmesan—shaved, not grated. I'll put the olive oil on myself."

After he had the waiter repeat his instructions, Homer sat back with a grin that anticipated great satisfaction. I figured that now we could get to talk about murder.

"How do the police know . . ."

Homer hadn't noticed I'd said anything. "I never order shrimp unless I'm absolutely sure they're fresh. I've had waiter after waiter insist they were fresh, and then they come all mushy and with no taste at all. Frozen shrimp are just a waste of time."

I couldn't agree more, but I didn't really want to talk about shrimp at the moment. I persisted.

"I heard the police thought there was a woman in Laurence's apartment the night he died."

"It sure looked like it. Silk dressing gown with nothing on underneath, porno flick on the VCR, napkin smeared with lipstick, and stocking snagged beneath the sofa as if somebody left in a hurry and didn't have time to look for it. Two used glasses. Didn't matter anyway, though. Looked like a natural."

"A natural?"

"Heart attack. We normally wouldn't even bother with an autopsy in a case like this. It's an expensive proposition, you know, and when we found out the guy had preexisting heart disease, we almost went with a no-post. There were no signs of a struggle, no trauma, no stangulation. Not even any seminal fluid. There didn't seem to be any theft, no forced entry, not much to investigate in a case like this. But we had enough conditions here that we decided to play it safe and go with an autopsy after all. We're still waiting for the results, but the medical examiner said the signs were classic. Just a natural."

Homer had done his job, told me what he thought I wanted to know. He turned his attention to the pasta with rabbit sauce. My soup didn't look so good to me at the moment.

I preferred arguing to eating. "That's too easy. I think he was murdered, and that's just what the murderer wanted you to think. I know he didn't have a woman with him, but somebody obviously wanted you to think he did."

"How could you know he didn't have a woman around?"

I explained his CityTastes jitters and his queasy stomach.

"Men do strange things, honey. You think you know all about them, and then they go and surprise you." He gave me a superior look.

"Homer, I've known Laurence for more than twenty years. In all that time this is one thing he's never changed."

"Amateur detectives. Everybody watches too much television. O. J. Simpson, Columbo. Everything's a conspiracy. And every homicide detective's got nothing to do but chase down a hundred blind alleys. Do you know this city had more than four hundred homicides last year? Not deaths—we had thousands of those to investigate—but actual sure-thing homicides. And we haven't solved more than about half of those. I'm working fifteen cases right now. We've got to have something to go on."

Homer had that bored, patronizing tone that waiters use when someone who wasn't listening the first or second time asks them to repeat the specials a third time. But he was twirling the last strands of his tagliolini with all the passion that his voice was missing.

"Look, Homer, this wasn't some drug dealer who was gonna get his sooner or later and deserved it. This was Laurence Levain. One of the most talented chefs you or I will ever see. You, of all people, ought to appreciate that. If there is any chance at all that his death was not a natural, as you call it, this city owes him a little more respect than to shrug it off."

The pasta had taken its effect. I had no illusions it was my speech that had softened Homer. "Hey, sweetheart, don't get me wrong. I may sound hard, but that's just how we detectives get when everyone expects one hundred percent of our attention at the same time. I'll bet you do pretty much the same when somebody interrupts your little romantic evening out by stopping at your table to ask you how come you haven't reviewed his brother-in-law's restaurant."

He was right. I was expecting too much. "I know what you mean. I don't really expect a full-scale investigation, just a little poking around. I'm sure you're curious, too, as to who this mysterious woman was who might have seen him die."

The waiter had taken my full bowl of soup with a worried look and an "Anything wrong with it, Miss Wheatley?" I figured I should make a better show of eating my rockfish, so I let Homer off the hook for a few moments while he and I both paid loving attention to our entrées.

"Italians truly understand fish." I changed the subject to placate Homer as I eased the flesh from the backbone of my rockfish. "All but one of the kitchen staff here are Latin American, but even though they aren't Italian, they're cooking Italian." I knew he'd like that insider's tidbit.

His mouth full, he nodded for me to go on.

"They've kept it simple: just a glistening of olive oil, a sprinkling of oregano leaves, coarse salt, and a squeeze of lemon. And they've grilled the fish whole, to catch all the nuances of flavor from the head and bones. Would you like a bite?"

"Sure would," Homer answered, holding out his bread plate. "Great wood smell."

"It was grilled on charcoal embers scooped from that wood oven after the fire had burned down," I explained, pointing out the bread oven in the rear. "That's how they got such a crisp skin and those lightly blackened spots." My little lecture was reawakening my own appetite. "Notice how it's stayed moist, how the flesh has barely turned milky and just opaque." I had Homer's complete, smiling attention now. I'd made peace.

"What were you doing Sunday night?" Homer's question from nowhere made me choke. So much for the power of my culinary prose. "You know, nobody likes to talk up a crime more than the one who did it."

"But I'm a restaurant critic." I just blurted it out, as if that were enough of an alibi. Realizing how defensive I sounded, we both laughed.

Homer also beeped. At least something under his tweed jacket did.

"Damn, I was afraid I wouldn't make it to the salad. But at least I got through the fritto misto." He took one last bite as he stood up. "Miss Wheatley . . . Chas . . . I've got to go. I can't promise you much. I've already worked all night once this week, and I'm working the three to eleven shift today. Then tomorrow I've got to spend all day testifying in court.

"But this was the best lunch I've had since I went to Venice in ninety-two, and I really enjoyed meeting you. So I'll do what I can. I'll check out the girls on the street and see what they can tell me. Give me a few days, and I'll talk to the medical examiner again and the technicians from the mobile crime unit. I'll get someone to doorknob the neighbors. If something wasn't right, we'll find out."

I was skeptical, but grateful that my whining had nudged him into some action. "I'd really appreciate that, Homer. And I figure I'll owe you a good dinner at the end of all this."

"Why don't you give me a call in a week, and I'll tell you how it's going." He handed me his card. "Thanks for the lunch, Ms. Restaurant Critic."

A week, huh? Nice brush-off. I signaled for the check. I'd been a self-taught restaurateur and a self-taught restaurant critic. I guessed I could be a self-taught detective, too.

# ten

No schoolchildren today, thank goodness. Instead, the entrance to the *Examiner* was blocked by three furtive-looking men with plastic lima beans in their ears, whispering into their lapels and eyeing me as if I were a criminal rather than a budding detective. I'd forgotten that the mayor was lunching with the top brass today. Dave had been hoping he'd be invited.

And so he was. Otherwise, his desk would have been littered with Cheetos bags and Heath Bar wrappers and he'd be buried in a pile of computer printouts from the city auditors.

The newsroom was nearly empty. Any minute the editors would start pouring in from lunch, rushing to the two-thirty news conference. It would be at least an hour before I'd have a chance to tell Helen about my plan to investigate Laurence's death. Or to ask Dave how I could go about it.

I made a list of people I'd need to talk to, again giving thought to the scenarios I'd sketched mentally this morning. I ought to have picked up more tips from detective novels. I'd read enough of them that I should know the formulas by now. Bebe: The girlfriend's always a suspect, though I couldn't imagine why this one would want her sugar daddy dead. Borden: History tells us the climb to power makes a habit of leaving a few bodies in its wake. Jeanine again: Sibling rivalry gone wrong—maybe Mama had loved him best. Then there was every jealous chef in town. The list grew, and I realized I still didn't know what the hell I was doing.

When in doubt, listen to your voice mail. It makes you feel you are getting something done.

Three pandering publicists, five readers wanting suggestions for their office Christmas parties, an old friend from Boston, and a cookbook author coming to town and wanting to meet for dinner.

Then: "Hey, lady. I was told to deliver this message to you. I guess if you're not there I'll do it anyway. It says, 'Keep your nose out of things that aren't your business or you'll get a heartache, too.' Some kind of joke, I guess. Okay, I delivered it." It sounded like a teenager, the kind of flat voice a kid gets when the teacher makes him read *Romeo and Juliet* aloud to the class. I could practically see his face flush. I felt sorry for the kid.

Heartache? Why had it taken me so long? The kid might have thought it was a joke, but what I'd just heard was a halting, monotone, death threat. My skin felt hot and my mouth went dry. I was scared.

Homer Jones hadn't believed Laurence had been murdered, but somebody did. So there were two of us, but only one of us knew who the other was.

I realized I was more than scared. I was also elated. And mad—not just at the murderer, but also at that I've-seen-it-all detective, Homer Jones.

I played the tape again, transcribing it on my computer and saving it in my voice mail box. Then I called Homer to mobilize him—and to gloat.


"Glad you called, Miss Wheatley."

Before I could get a word in, he rattled on. "I never got a chance to ask you one important thing. I had a reservation for Laurence's restaurant because I wanted to propose to my girlfriend at the best restaurant in town. Obviously, that's not going to work now, but maybe you've got another suggestion."

"Detective, I've just had a pretty scary call."

This guy doesn't listen. "I want a restaurant that will be around for a long time, so we'll be able to go back for our anniversaries."

"Hey, you didn't seem to hear me. I just got a threatening call."

"What'd you do? Dump on some chef's duck à l'orange?"

"No, I got a message from Laurence's murderer."

That got his attention. "What did he say? What did he sound like?"

"He sounded like a kid. It was on my voice mail, some kid just delivering a message somebody'd written out for him. It said, 'Keep your nose out of things that aren't your business or you'll get a heartache, too.'"

"Wait, give it to me slower so I can get it down. Who else have you been talking to about this? Save the message." At least I'd done that right. "Did this call come in on a published number?"

This guy liked to ask his questions in pairs. Didn't wait to hear the answers. Probably wouldn't even hear his girlfriend turn him down. Anyhow, I'd gotten his attention, and he was beginning to take me seriously.

I repeated the message slowly. Hearing it again myself, it was really beginning to sink in, right into the pit of my stomach. I was starting to wish I'd left Laurence's death for somebody else to worry about.

"Anybody can get my number just by asking the switchboard. And I haven't talked to anybody about this. Except Dave, as you know. But that's irrelevant. And my daughter."

"Your daughter?" I didn't like his suspicious tone.

"My daughter is in Philadelphia. She works nights." As if that was proof positive that she was incapable of murder. Then I recalled the phone call I'd made to Dave from CityTastes. Something had distracted me. What was it? White. Someone wearing white. A chef. Or one of the hundred or so women wearing white gowns.

Homer said he'd get someone to listen to the tape to see if anything could be learned from it. And he said he was going to move this case to the top of his list.

"In the meantime, Miss Wheatley—"

"Chas." Afraid as I was, I'd feel better if Homer considered me a friend.

"Chas. I think you ought to be a little more careful than usual. I don't think anything is really going to happen. These threats don't usually mean much. But, if it's after dark, you might get the *Examiner*'s security guard to accompany you to your car when you leave."

"I walk."

"No you don't. Not this week. I'll alert the patrolmen in your neighborhood to keep an eye on your building. And keep tight-lipped about all this."

So I immediately poured it all out to Sherele, who'd just come back from the hairdresser and was hurling questioning looks at me as she booted up her computer.

I edited out the parts about Dave.

"Let's take this step by step. First, file that wormy little message. You don't need it staring you in the face," Sherele said.

I hit a couple of keys and made it go away. Sherele was right. It's hard to think with a death threat on your screen.

"Okay, now. Let's look at this calmly," she continued. "You're not going to die. That message is only first-act stage business, and you're the heroine of this play."

I had to laugh. My obsession with food is only casual interest next to Sherele's eating, drinking, waking, sleeping fixation on the theater.

"Maybe it's a tragedy," I worried.

"Nope. Only a mealy-mouthed second-rate minor slob gets a kid to deliver the message of doom. A coward. Even if we accept the probability that this lame play on words was referring to Laurence's death, it sounded more like 'I'm gonna tell on you' than 'I'm gonna spill your blood.' Anyway, if you're scared, you can come and sleep at my place tonight."

"Thanks. But I think I'll tough it out." I couldn't tell her I had a better offer—or expected to, from Dave.

"In any case, you've got to tell Helen what's going on. Then let her tell Bull about it. You don't want to have to waste the rest of the afternoon hearing about all the death threats he's received."

"Yep, I know what you mean. When I asked him last year about doing a story on a diet spa—figuring it's only fair that the *Examiner* pay for me to take off some of the flab I accumulated on its account— he sucked in his stomach and bragged that he still weighed exactly the same as he did in college."

"That's only because his brain's been shrinking. Look, Chas, just stick to bright lights and crowded places. And let the receptionist know where you are so the paper can keep tabs on you. These folks know how to handle this."

That did it. If Sherele the Cool was nervous, I could really be in trouble. I put my face down on my keyboard and took a few deep breaths. Sweat beaded on my forehead.

Sherele lifted me by the shoulders. "You're gonna short out your keyboard, honey. Let's take a break. I haven't had lunch yet, and I'm taking you with me. My treat."

"That's a break?" Sherele knew that the last thing I needed in my life was another restaurant meal, much less a second lunch.

"Yep, we're going to the *Examiner* cafeteria."

She was right. No temptation to stuff myself there.

The *Examiner* cafeteria has a crowd that never quits. It's open all night and all day, for computer staff and printers, ad reps and reporters, hardly finding time to change from the breakfast-bread buffet to the salad bar and from grits and pancakes on the steam table to lasagna and fried chicken. Despite the enormous variety, it is food with a theme: heaviness. The salads emphasize pasta, cheese, and thick, creamy dressings. The hot pastas feature cream sauces or tomatoes with an oily surface and a blanket of cheese. The entrées are mostly fried—the vegetables, too.

No wonder the staff is logy in the afternoon. Even what passes for a light lunch here would put me to sleep.

That's not the only reason I avoid eating at the cafeteria when I have a free lunch hour. Here's the other:

"Hi, Chas, are you going to write a review of this place?"

"Hey, Chas, are you really going to eat that stuff? I'll never trust your reviews again."

For a restaurant critic, it's no break to eat in public, even on home ground.

I took a cup of coffee while Sherele stood at the salad bar pulling the crust off her fried chicken and slicing the bare meat, then cutting thick slices of seven-grain bread to make a sandwich. She topped it with red onion, red peppers, and olives from the salad fixings and dabbed on a little blue-cheese dressing. She already had a big, gooey, apple brown betty. With ice cream. Sherele is a dessert freak. The thinnest women often are, for some unexplainable reason.

We carried our trays in search of a table. In an unspoken agreement, the dining room is segregated. Not by race or sex, of course. But the National staff huddles in one corner, Metro reporters nearby and overlapping but not really invading the center. Hard news and features mingle only intermittently. And advertising keeps plenty of distance from the reporting staff. As for editors, they eat elsewhere unless it's raining.

"Who's that?" I asked Sherele.

A tall, bony woman I'd never seen before was taking a tray at the cafeteria entrance. She caught my eye because she was wearing what looked like a French baker's shirt, big and blousy, with its balloon sleeves buttoned tightly at the wrist. On second look, though, it seemed like a baker's shirt adapted by Ralph Lauren or somebody else expensive. She reminded me of some kind of food, but I couldn't put my finger on it.

"That's the new Golden Girl in Investigative," Sherele said with just a bit of a sneer. "Dawn something. From the *Orange County Register*."

"A Californian, no less," I said. "Replacing Ed Welcher, isn't she? He was a Golden Boy who didn't last long."

"They don't."

"But you lasted," I reminded Sherele.

"Yes, but I was a twofer. A black and a woman. It's harder to get rid of a double minority. Particularly if she's the only female black theater critic in the United States." Sherele bit into her sandwich as if it were Bull Stannard's hide.

I hadn't really thought about it before, but Sherele was right. In the newspaper's drive for diversity, it had hired blacks, Hispanics, Asians, Arabs, all kinds of minorities. But most of them were women. That saved the rest of the slots for white males.

Sherele wasn't finished with her lecture. "Besides, just because I'm still here doesn't mean I'm still a Golden Girl. Bull hasn't said a good word about anything I've written this year. He only growls that I cover too many depressing plays."

"At least he notices you."

"So far. I'm only at the Bad Girl stage. The next step is I'm wallpaper," Sherele said through bites of sandwich.

At that moment, Dawn left the cafeteria line, her nearly bare tray holding only a container of plain no-fat yogurt and a bunch of grapes. I wondered if she was going to peel them.

"This one will last awhile," Sherele predicted. "What I didn't tell you was where I met her: at the theater, with Hamilton Asterling."

Suddenly I understood the designer shirt. Hamilton Asterling was the ancien régime at the *Examiner*, the paper's first editor and the one who put us immediately on the map. He is old money and a tough newspaperman. Blue blood and steel balls. He'd come out of retirement to start up this paper, and promised to stay with it for five years, no more and no less. He drove us hard, backed us to the hilt, pushed us with his gutsy stands and his foul mouth. Then he had left us—mourning his departure—in the hands of the bean counters. Ham—never did a name fit better—was gone from the newsroom but was still on the paper's board, and remained as influential as he cared to be.

"She was with him?" I stammered.

"With them," Sherele answered. "His wife was along, too."

Dawn had been searching the dining room systematically, but apparently hadn't found whomever she was looking for. So she settled for second best. Us.

"Mind if I join you?" she asked, seating herself without waiting for an answer. "I'm Dawn." She held out her hand to me.

"Nice to see you again, Dawn," Sherele lied. "This is Charlotte Sue Wheatley, our restaurant critic, generally known as Chas."

"What a day." Dawn nodded a greeting and started right in, one of those people who immediately turn the subject to themselves. And she actually began peeling her grapes. "I've got this incredible scoop. From a California congressman, no less. And Bull won't let me go with it. He says it needs another confirmation."

"Oh, that's—" Sherele started to murmur sympathetically, but she was cut off.

"There's this cute guy in Investigative. You probably know him. Dave's his name. He's been putting the make on me, so I asked him to help me out. It's the least he could do after all his free stares at my boobs. He was supposed to meet me here, but I guess he got stuck in that lunch with the mayor."

I was aghast. It was one thing to have been expecting Dave to eventually throw me over for some other newsroom chick. But to come face to face with the possibility hurt more than I'd anticipated. Particularly someone young, beautiful, and bosom buddies— quite a bosom, I'd noticed through her mostly unbuttoned shirt—with Hamilton Asterling.

"Honey, if it's Dave Zeeger you're waiting for, you're risking starvation," Sherele said as she started in on her apple brown betty, never one to be diverted from eating.

"So, Charlotte Sue, how do I get to go to a restaurant with you?" Dawn turned her attention to me.

I hate being called Charlotte Sue, but I decided to give the woman a chance. "It's not that difficult. You just have to be willing to work your way up from the E list—the bottom of the barrel. All my friends serve duty going to the unknown Filipino or Indian holes-in-the-wall in the far suburbs before they have a chance at Kinkead's or Galileo."

"Count me in for one of those Korean restaurants with a grill in the center of the table. I love to cook," Dawn said as she peeled another grape. I'd never seen anyone consume calories so slowly. Each grape was washed down with maybe a third of a teaspoon of yogurt. At this rate she'd be here to greet the dinner crowd.

Sherele, in the meantime, had scarfed down her dessert and scraped up every stray driblet of ice cream. She looked ready to go, so I swallowed the last of my coffee in order to escape with her. Sherele, ever maternal, piled my dishes and hers on her tray, stacked the two trays, and stood up. "Sorry I've got to run, but I can hear my computer calling. Welcome again to the *Examiner*, Dawn, and let me know when you've got time for a real lunch."

We all exchanged the friendliest of good-byes. I tried not to hope that Dawn would choke on a grape. I finally realized what food she reminded me of: an under-baked bread stick.

By the time I got back to my desk, I had myself under control. I'd looked at the situation logically. One: I knew Dave was a wanderer, so I'd never expected him to be exclusive or even last with me half as long as he had. Two: I had only Dawn's word for Dave's interest in her. And while she was savvy enough to be a big-deal investigative reporter, she might have misinterpreted friendly looks as leers. I wasn't rushing to judgment.

Heavy into the argument with myself, I jumped when my phone rang. It was Dave, calling from six desks away, wanting to know how my talk with Homer went. I said I'd get back to him in ten minutes, which meant I'd meet him in the stairwell to the composing room, a corridor nobody had used since the computer began beaming page layouts to our desks.

● ● ●

"I filled in for you with your lunch date," I started before Dave could get a word in.

"Lunch date? I went to the lunch with the mayor. I didn't have a lunch date," Dave said as he ran his thumb softly across my lips.

"That's not what Dawn said." I licked his thumb, finding it hard to stay angry with him.

"Dawn?"

"Don't pretend you don't know the new Golden Girl in your very own section, Dave Zeeger." I was also finding it hard to stay un-angry with him.

"Of course I know her. Or I've met her, at least. But I hardly made a lunch date with her. I only encountered the woman once, in a group of about half a dozen people. Even I don't work that fast," said Dave in a totally convincing tone, punctuated with a hand creeping into my blouse.

Dawn must have mixed him up with someone else. Dave wasn't the only good-looking guy in the Investigative section.

"Back to Homer," I said, changing the subject. And I told him about lunch at I Ricchi and its aftermath.

At first Dave tried to persuade me to leave the investigation in police hands, but he knew that in my place he couldn't resist doing a little digging on his own either.

"First, let's talk about your safety," he said. Dave's reported on countless scumbags, right up to the Mafia. He's investigated jails and judges. And he's sent some of the latter to the former. So he's no stranger to death threats.

I promised him I'd follow Homer's and Sherele's advice.

He added some of his own: "Don't just tell the receptionist when you go anywhere, even to the bathroom, tell me, too. Call a taxi whenever you have to go anyplace. Have dinner with me."

That sounded like the safest bet to me. What's more, if anyone saw us, we could always say Dave was helping me with my case.

Once I agreed to be sensible about protecting myself, I pressed Dave for more advice. I was itching to move from the defensive to the offensive. He agreed to help me launch my own personal investigation of Laurence's murder.

The police will look at the closest relationships first, he explained. Laurence's girlfriend, Bebe, and his sister, Jeanine, were both bound to come under police scrutiny, though neither of us could see a motive for either of them. Both would have been better off with Laurence still alive. The sous-chef, Borden, would be considered: Was he jealous of Laurence? Did he feel his career was being squelched? Marcel, because he was going into partnership with Laurence in New York, would undoubtedly be questioned, though Laurence's death was surely going to kill the project and leave Marcel in the lurch. Still, except for the women in Laurence's life, Marcel was the person closest to him. And partnerships are second only to marriages as relationships with enraging possibilities.

"What can I do that the police can't do better?"

"You're the expert on restaurants, and on Laurence. You've got to work the phones. You'll be surprised by how much you can get with a few phone calls, even on a murder," Dave lectured.

Though I'd been thinking along the same lines, I was uncertain as to where to begin. "In the restaurant world? Call whom?"

"It's easiest to start with the money. Call the restaurant's accountants. Its investors. Its suppliers. Chat them up a bit, share the grief. Then zero in and ask them whether they've noticed any problems, anything funny going on. At that point, stop talking. Create an awkward silence. You'll be amazed by what people will say just to fill a gap in the conversation," Dave said, then stopped, leaving an awkward gap in our conversation.

Sure enough, I was driven to fill it. After several silent moments I found myself asking, "Dave, you wouldn't sleep with someone else in the newsroom, would you?"

It wasn't the conversation filler he'd had in mind. He looked as if I'd slapped him, his face flushing and his eyes darkening in anger. "Sounds like you want it both ways: both secret and exclusive. If you're going to make all the rules in this relationship, you could at least make them consistent."

I started to get angry, too, and to argue back. But for once I thought better of it. I was probably being overbearing. Instead of mouthing off, I gave a test run to Dave's own technique. I created an awkward silence.

He filled it. Sort of. He kissed me. "Goddammit, you should know by now that I'm not going to hurt you," he murmured into my hair.

"Hey, your technique works," I said with a grin.

Dave shook his head and laughed. "You're a fast learner."

I sneaked a peek at my watch and looked up to find him doing the same. We both smiled sheepishly, each relieved not to bear the burden of practicality alone.

"Time to go." We said it simultaneously.

Then Dave added, "One more thing. Never end a conversation without asking whether your informant knows anybody else you should call."

"Okay, good advice," I said.

"And I have to go to New York tomorrow afternoon. That's where Laurence was opening a restaurant, right? Give me the information and I'll discreetly nose around among the money guys I know there." With that, Dave disappeared into the newsroom. I waited a couple of minutes so we wouldn't be seen together. And I tried out feeling that I could trust Dave not to hurt me.

I hit the phones running. I called accountants and suppliers and rival chefs. I called investors and friends of investors. I didn't find out who the murderer was, but I unearthed a lot of snakes under the stones that my calls dislodged.

The people who spend a day's salary on dinner in a fancy restaurant would certainly be surprised to learn that almost all restaurants are creepy-crawly underneath their glamorous facades. The garbage that is inevitably stinking and attracting rats outside the back door of a restaurant is just a metaphor for the workings inside.

Bribes and kickbacks are as common as Caesar salads. Restaurateurs pay some suppliers' employees under the table to get the best fish or raspberries, better than their competitors' restaurants are getting. Other suppliers with less competitive goods ante up a regular retainer to whomever is contracting for their services in order to keep their business. Employees pay middlemen to get jobs. Customers bribe the maître d' with Christmas booze and vacation houses in order to get a good table. In other words, everyone pays extra for what should be ordinary services. And hardly anyone pays taxes.

That afternoon I drew up a list of restaurateurs who were in trouble with the IRS—or should be. I had a sub-list of which restaurants were so behind in their bills to suppliers that they were on a cash-only basis. It would have been shorter to make a list of those that weren't in financial trouble.

I knew which investors had made money (very few) and which had lost it all (most of them). Yet these doctors and dentists and lawyers continued to invest, probably as much interested in the cachet as the return on the dollar.

I began to compile a list of the Caribbean getaways that had been loaned to Laurence's sister, Jeanine, as hostess, the cases of champagne offered to Borden as Laurence's sous-chef. I learned of whole chateaubriands being resold after being smuggled out of the kitchen, tins of caviar being carefully lightened, their skimmings going for big bucks.

I found out enough to make me lose my appetite. But I didn't know if I really had discovered any clues to the crime—or even if there really had been a crime.

I'd been on the phone constantly, not bothering to pick up incoming calls, but leaving them to voice mail. Late in the afternoon I got a message from Homer, delivered by hand from the receptionist. He hadn't been able to get through to me and wanted me to call him.

Homer wasn't in his office, but had left instructions for me to call him on his beeper.

"Chas, I've got this thing rolling. The medical examiner took a harder look, and he says the guy had an overdose of digoxin, his heart medicine. It's hard to detect a digoxin death because it just looks like a normal heart attack, so there didn't seem to be any reason to do the toxicology until I talked to you. The M.E. is grateful. Plus embarrassed, of course."

"What kind of death would it have been? Was he in pain?" I could hardly get the words past the lump in my throat.

"No, not any more painful than a heart attack, Chas. It could have taken a couple of hours to work; it's hard to tell with a guy who's already got a weak heart. But once it happened, he would have gone fast."

"Thanks, Homer. I'm glad to know."

"Anyway, this digoxin business could be an accident. Not likely, though. Could be a suicide. Could be murder. In my opinion, murder is the best possibility. The dose was highly concentrated and the scene just didn't look like a suicide."

"What's the next step?" I asked, hoping the answer would direct me to my next move as well.

"All this news made me want to talk to his girlfriend right away, and that's where I am now, at her place."

"What does she say?" I felt a wave of nausea as the news began to sink in. The reality of murder was hard to face close up.

"She didn't say much. In fact, nothing at all. She's gone. She didn't show up at work today. Nobody's heard from her. And her apartment looks as if she went on a quick trip. Neighbors say she and her boyfriend fought a lot, and the word is that she'd recently found out he was cheating on her. I've issued an attempt to locate. You got any idea where she might have gone?"

As I thought about how upset I'd be in Bebe's situation, the message to me from that kid on the telephone made my skin crawl again. "No, I know hardly anything about her. But if my boyfriend had been whoring around on me like Laurence did, I might want to kill him."

"You'd never pick a guy dumb enough to play around on you," Homer said.

I hoped not as I craned my neck to see Dave, who, as usual, had some nubile young ballerina-turned-copy-aide leaning over his desk.

Homer continued, "It just goes to show, it always pays to shine the spotlight on the bereaved innocent who discovers the body. I'll let you know as soon as we track her down. Keep your nose clean, Chas, and keep looking over your shoulder." I started to hang up, but Homer had more to say: "Hey . . . thanks for your help in this."

So the supposedly unconcerned D.C. police

seemed to have solved this crime almost before anyone knew it was a crime. Bebe would be easy enough
to find, so by the time I left the office I probably
wouldn't have to watch my back after all. My shoulders unhunched, my knotted stomach relaxed, my
whole clenched body began to ease. Helen was waving to me from her office. I went to tell her the news.

The *Examiner* ground into action to proclaim
Laurence's death a possible murder. Den Ranger, the
police reporter, started working the phones, as Bull,
Helen, the city editor, and I huddled in Bull's office.
Bull was just about to assign me a sidebar on the
CityTastes scene, when Andy Mutton, probably in
the midst of stirring up some amazing new canned
soup back in the food section, got wind of what was
happening and oozed in on us. He wanted to do the
sidebar. This time Bull declared a pox on both our
houses, and told us both to feed our information to
Den so he could work it into his story.

I wished Andy would impale himself on a
corkscrew, but he probably only drank screw-top
wines anyway. I decided to expend my fury on my
computer, and spent the rest of the afternoon writing up the worst restaurants I could think of for my
upcoming dining guide. (It's called "Pats and
Pans"—get it? Not my idea.)

> The busboys are so quick to snatch your
> plate as soon as you rest your fork, you won-
> der whether they are selling your leftovers
> out the back door.

This General Tso's Chicken should be demoted to Private, or even court-martialed. The meat tastes as if the chef began with frozen breasts, those pale, mushy slabs of ex-chicken that had little flavor even when they were fresh. They're lodged in nuggets of batter as gummy as peanut butter. And the sauce—two asterisks promising to enflame your palate—tastes like nothing more than sugar dissolved in vinegar.

Dinner with Dave was a compromise, but the good kind. We ate at Coppi's, where Dave could get pizza for both dinner and dessert, while I could have a jicama-pancetta salad and gladly help him finish his chocolate-hazelnut-stuffed pizza dough.

Coppi's dessert of chocolate-hazelnut calzone is one of those brilliantly obvious ideas that makes you wonder why nobody thought of it years ago. A round of regular pizza dough is filled with Nutella, that smooth, thick, chocolate-hazelnut paste that comes in jars, the same stuff the French street vendors slather on crepes. The dough is folded into a half-moon, crimped tightly, and baked. It's served hot, so the filling oozes all over the crust and your mouth as you eat it. The slight saltiness of the dough seems to intensify the sweetness and the richness of the melted chocolate. Never have two ordinary components done more for each other.

As usual, we started out talking about work—as well as the murder that had become part of it. Dave seemed proud of my baby steps as an investigative reporter, but since Bebe's skipping town made her look pretty suspicious, there didn't seem to be much more to say on the subject. So Dave talked a little about the organized crime story he was working on. Dave doesn't reveal much about his work unless I patiently draw him out. His decades of investigative reporting have encouraged his natural secrecy.

Work talk ran down, so Dave switched to books. Usually I enjoy hearing about whatever historical period is his current obsession, but this time I was having a hard time paying attention. My thoughts kept returning to Bebe.

I'd never known a murderer before. I felt I had a pinball machine inside me, flipping my heart from fury to pity to morbid curiosity. Everyone knew that Laurence was always on the prowl, and Bebe must have, too, before she went out with him. But maybe she fooled herself into thinking she'd changed him, that she was enough woman to reform him. It could be that if I found out my guy was alternating between me and other women, I'd want to kill him, too.

That was the pity part. But even in a court of law, infidelity is not a capital offense. Who has the right to take a life? I raged at the idea of someone wielding the power to wipe Laurence off the face of the earth.

As for the curiosity, Bebe seemed such an innocent. Just another cute, young, bleached-blond bimbo with an inclination for gold-digging and star-fucking. Nobody knew why she'd managed to stand out in Laurence's crowd of adorers. Pretty and talentless and just smart enough to know how to hitch a ride on a wagon that was going somewhere exciting. Looks like she was smart enough to know how to administer concentrated digoxin, too, and almost get away with making murder look like a sex-induced heart attack. I'd always seen Bebe as a little crass, but still couldn't quite think of her as dangerous.

No matter. She was the concern of the police now. Her face flashed on the evening news behind the restaurant bar. Pert blondes must find it hard to hide.

Above all, I felt relieved. And exhausted. It was time to go home and drink a private toast to Laurence and try to put my life back in order. And to steel myself for the funeral the day after tomorrow.

Dave reluctantly dropped me off at my apartment and promised he'd try to get back from New York by tomorrow night. I enjoyed his reluctance. Maybe I should work at being less available to him. It might do our relationship some good. I smiled to myself all the way up in the elevator. Home safe and sound.

# eleven

I still get a rush of excitement every time I step out of the elevator and anticipate the high ceilings and immense windows that make my apartment feel like a stage set. This time, though, I didn't even have time to get my key out before I saw her coming.

As Bebe raced silently down the hallway toward me, my first thought was how stupid I'd been not to let Dave come home with me. Then even that thought fled, and I just panicked. I'd never faced an attacker before in my whole life, and here was a murderer on the run, barreling my way.

I struggled to free my key ring from its zipper pocket, without success. My voice caught in my throat, but even if I could have screamed, there would have been no point. The doors are thick in my building, and the only other apartment is at the far end of the hall. Too late for the elevator—it would never arrive in time. The stairs were behind Bebe. Nothing to do but fight her off. She had height and youth on her side, I had weight. Not much of an advantage.

Then I saw the glint of silver.

Omigod. A knife. How do I handle this one? My only weapon was my purse.

For once I was proud of all the stuff I lug in my shoulder bag. It must have packed the power of a baseball bat as I swung it right for Bebe's head. She went down with a yelp.

But she was quick. Even while she was catching her breath and swearing "fucks" and "goddammits" at me, she was back on her feet faster than I can get up from the couch on a good day.

I swung again. But this time she was ready for me. She grabbed my swinging arm with her left hand and my throat with her right.

I was so scared I could do little more than croak. "Bitch. Murderer. Anorexic star-fucker."

Bebe's peaches-and-cream face turned a furious blotchy purple. Where was the knife? I prayed that I'd knocked it out of her hand when I'd caught her with my purse.

"You call me a murderer?" she hissed. She backed me against the door, using both hands on my throat now that she was in too close for me to wind up for a swing. I tried to kick, but she easily sidestepped me. Her hair was wild. Her eyes were fierce. My arms flapped in silly little punches as I tried to beat her off, no more effective than a sofa pillow attacking the rump that sits on it. My teeth were snapping in a vain attempt to bite arms that were nowhere near them. I struggled for breath. My head was exploding. I couldn't last.

The door caved in behind me and I tumbled backward, pulling Bebe along with me. My arms flailed, trying to cushion the blow. I waited for my head to crack on the bare wood floor, but instead it bounced against something soft. Another body. There were three of us on the floor, arms and legs flying, three voices shouting.

The third one was Lily's. My daughter had come home, and I'd brought a murderer along as a coming-home present. Where was the knife?

"Lily! Call 911!" I shouted as my agile daughter untangled herself first from the melee. My breath was still coming in gasps, and I felt a red-hot pounding in my head.

"Quick, call the police!" Bebe echoed me. "Aargh!"

I'd just stepped on her right arm. I kept my foot there and pinned her other arm with my elbow, but as I regained my breath, the fight seemed to have gone out of Bebe.

"What are you madwomen doing? You could hurt yourselves, you know," lectured Lily. Young people never take their mothers seriously.

"Your mother tried to beat me to death," Bebe whined.

"Beat you to death? What else would you expect when you come at me with a knife?" I was frantically sweeping the floor with my feet, trying to find that knife or at least kick it out of the way before Bebe got hold of it again.

Bebe started to cry. "A knife? I don't have a knife. I waited all this time just to talk to you, and then you called me a murderer and practically knocked me out with your purse. You broke two of my nails." She held up her left hand, with three shiny silver talons still intact, glinting in the light.

"I thought you were trying to kill me," I said.

"I thought you were my friend," Bebe answered.

"Forget the police, Lily," I said, regaining both my breath and my sanity, feeling my anger dissolve into a flush of embarrassment creeping right up from my toes. "I think we can straighten this out ourselves."

I paused and surveyed the wreckage of Bebe and the rugs, the former sobbing and the latter bunched up around her legs. I took in Lily's mix of confusion and disapproval. I retrieved my purse and felt my face and neck for injuries. No serious harm. "Red wine, everyone?"

I went to the cabinet for the bottle even before I took off my coat. As I opened the wine, I was reminded of a scene Sherele had quoted to me from a Neil Simon play.

"Did you hear the one about the guy in New York's Central Park?" I started the tale as I took off my coat and helped a badly confused Bebe with her jacket. "One day, this guy—let's call him Joe—was out jogging, and a man running the other way brushed past him and bumped him in the shoulder.

"A couple minutes later Joe realized his wallet was gone. He turned around and raced back in the direction he'd come. He overtook the guy who'd bumped him in the shoulder and knocked him to the ground.

"'Give me the wallet,' Joe demanded. The guy handed over the wallet, then ran off. Joe limped away, congratulating himself all the way home. Where he found his wallet on the dresser."

Nobody laughed.


Such is my lot in life that I always seem to be settling people on sofas and salving their psychic wounds. Bebe at one end, Lily at the other. Pouring wine for them both, two bewildered children.

"You're the only one of Laurence's friends who's been nice to me. Outside of Laurence, I didn't really know anybody else all that well," Bebe blubbered into her glass, wiping her runny nose on her sleeve. Her makeup had melted into smears of mascara and lipstick, as if she'd never learned to color within the lines. "I was so scared, and I kind of thought you were like a mother. I didn't know where else to go."

Mother? She must have really been low on friends if I was her first resort.

"I thought you'd killed Laurence." There was my tact again.

"I didn't even know he was killed. I thought he just died. And the next thing I knew, the police were saying he was murdered, and they were looking for me."

I rubbed my bruised neck. Bleary and miserable as Bebe looked, I wasn't ready to buy her innocence that easily. "You looked like the best suspect. Neighbors reported that you two had been fighting lately, and the police seemed to think you'd found him cheating on you. I'd probably want revenge for that myself."

"Revenge, yes." Lily swallowed the rest of her wine in one gulp, and began choking and crying at the same time. "But killing him wouldn't be revenge. That would be too fast. I'd want him to suffer like I did, not to die quickly."

Lily pulled further into her side of the sofa and looked as if she were going to throw up. "Would somebody please explain what's going on here? I take time off from work and come home to comfort my mother and wind up in the middle of a knock-down, drag-out fight with everyone yelling for the police. Mama, you never tell me anything."

As usual in any crisis, Lily had found a way to see herself as the victim and find me at fault. On the other hand, she had gone to great lengths to be here for me. And she had saved me from being strangled. I knelt on the floor beside the sofa, wincing as my elbows and knees reverberated from my ridiculous battle.

"I'm very glad you came, my love," I said belatedly. Lily hugged me. It was Bebe's turn to look as if she wanted to throw up. Instead, we all grew teary. I told Lily the real story of Laurence's death. It quieted us all.

Bebe was the next to explain. At first, she didn't believe it when a "friend" told her Laurence had been cheating on her. But one night she made a surprise visit and found him in bed with a prostitute.

"Our bed," she wailed.

She and Laurence had fought. Then made up. And fought again. She'd left him and come back. But he started acting secretive again. So on Saturday night

she walked out again. Monday morning, figuring he
would be busy at the restaurant preparing for
CityTastes, she had gone back to his apartment to
pick up some of her things. She'd found him dead
and called the police.

As she waited for the police, she was angrier than
ever, because it looked as if he'd had a woman with
him. Yet, increasingly, she was grief-stricken, not to
mention guilt-ridden for having abandoned him. By
the time the police arrived, she felt she owed it to
Laurence and his friends to keep the sordid details to
herself. That's why she went to CityTastes with
Jeanine and Borden, pretending nothing had changed
between Laurence and her.

But the anger had returned. She loved him and
hated him. She was furious that he'd escaped her
revenge, and brokenhearted to have lost him. She
was so confused that she didn't think she could face
his funeral, so she had decided to leave town and try
to get a grip on herself. But she'd had no place to go.
She'd turned around and was back in Washington
when she heard on the radio that Laurence had been
murdered and that the police were looking for her.

"I didn't kill him, but I was the only one who had a
right to. It's not fair," Bebe fumed. Her logic escaped me.

"You must be hungry." Lily made her own leap of
logic from Bebe's impassioned monologue. "Mama,
you got any good doggie bags in the refrigerator?"
Lily has always loved to fiddle around with leftovers
and make never-to-be-replicated combinations of
Italian, Chinese, and Salvadoran bits of food. Since

she'd left Washington I seldom brought doggie bags home anymore, so she was going to have slim pickings. That wouldn't inhibit her much.

Lily found a package of Arborio rice in a drawer, a piece of dried-out cheese in the refrigerator, and a tiny packet of saffron in the spice cabinet. Sure enough, after a search through the freezer, she came up with a container of turkey stock from last Thanksgiving. She launched into a risotto, with Bebe chopping onions at her side.

Lily heated the stock, tinged golden with the saffron, to a simmer on the back of the stove. Then she sautéed the onions in olive oil until they were translucent, and stirred in the rice until it began to turn opaque. She ladled a half cup of stock into the rice, stirring as it was absorbed.

While I hovered over the kitchen activity, I nervously broached what was worrying me. "We have to call the police and tell them Bebe's here."

Bebe sort of whimpered, and Lily shot me an angry look. Before either could contradict me, I took a firmer stand. "We have to. No arguments. If we don't, Bebe could be in worse trouble, and we'd be in trouble with her."

I picked up the phone and called Homer Jones's office.

The man who answered the phone put me on hold even before I could ask for Homer. Then I was disconnected. I dialed again with the same results. The third time, I was prepared.

"Hold it," I shouted into the phone. That stopped him. "I've got to talk to Detective Jones."

"Ain't here," the voice told me.

"Ask him to call Chas Wheatley," I began.

"Yup," he said, and cut me off before I could even add "please."

"Don't sweat it, Mama," Lily said, interrupting her risotto making to squeeze Bebe's shoulder. "You can say you tried. It's in their court now, and they couldn't do anything this late at night anyway—except maybe lock Bebe up until they could deal with her in the morning. Bebe will sleep more comfortably here, and, in the meantime, we can work out how we are going to solve this murder."

That's my daughter, my beautiful blue-eyed, black-haired, long and lean daughter. Whips up a risotto with one hand and solves a murder with the other. There's nothing like the confidence of youth.

Ladling in the stock by the half cupful, Lily continued to encourage the rice to gradually swell and soften. At the same time, she eased Bebe into talking more about Laurence. I stood by silently, pouring the rest of the bottle of wine a half cup at a time into my glass.

"All the chefs were jealous of him," Bebe said. "He was not only successful, he was so nice, even to his rivals. Personally, I think it just made them all feel meaner. Everything came so easily to Laurence: money, fame, admiration, women." With that, she faltered and grew pensive.

I was surprised to hear such insights from this frowsy-looking over-painted blonde. The more she talked, the more I began to understand what Laurence saw in her. I felt satisfaction that she had qualities even the young Laurence might have appreciated.

Lily, still stirring and pouring, nudged her on. "Were there any specific chefs who seemed to have it in for him?"

"Actually, they all liked him, even though they were jealous of him." One step forward, two steps backward. Befuddled little Bebe was getting us nowhere fast. "But things began to change after Laurence and Marcel started planning Les Deux."

That perked me up. Les Deux was the new restaurant Laurence and Marcel, each putting in half-time, were opening in New York as a prototype for a chain of restaurants. It was the first restaurant a major Washington chef was opening in the Big Apple—a reversal of the usual trend. And the partners expected it to eventually finance a comfortable retirement.

"So you think that other chefs were jealous because Laurence and Marcel were jumping the gun on what they wanted to do?" I asked Bebe.

"No, it was more that they were feeling abandoned. Laurence was their leader, the captain of their home team. And he was going on to play in another league." Bebe was clearing up the onion debris and wiping off the counter. I didn't know she had it in her.

"Hardly motive enough for murder," Lily interjected.

"I agree," Bebe said, collecting dishes and silverware to set the table. "But we've got to start somewhere." Surprisingly efficient for a fluff of a girl with silver talons.

Then Bebe added, "The most jealous of all, of course, was Borden."

Lily bridled. "Borden is the last person to want Laurence dead. He was Laurence's protégé. He loved him like a father."

"That's what everyone thought. Me, too, at first. But Borden's more complicated than that," Bebe said.

"I would say so." Lily had acid in her voice as she turned off the stove and began to fiercely grate Parmesan into the pot.

Bebe ignored Lily's warning signals and barreled on. "I've heard Borden tell other chefs that he was afraid Laurence was going to fire him because he was too good and Laurence felt threatened."

"Well, Laurence should have felt threatened. Borden probably is as good as Laurence. Or will be before long." Lily had grated the cheese right down to her knuckles. She grimaced as she dropped the grater and abruptly removed the pot of risotto from the stove, forgetting the pot holder and burning her hand in the process. "Damn. Where'd you put the pot holder?" she accused Bebe.

"I'm sorry. I don't think I moved it—it's right next to the stove." Bebe scooped ice from the freezer and applied it to Lily's hand.

Lily looked wounded as Bebe heedlessly continued. "Borden was always complaining that Laurence took credit for dishes that he developed. He even claimed that he could makes *les quilts*—better than Laurence's."

"Oh, c'mon, Bebe. You know what complainers chefs are. Underneath it all, Borden and Laurence were inseparable," Lily protested while she folded the cheese into the risotto as vigorously as if she were beating a rug. Poor rice.

"No, it was Borden and Jeanine who were inseparable. They've been lovers since last summer."

"Shit!" Lily had dropped the pot of risotto on the floor. She ran from the kitchen toward the bathroom.

"What happened? Is she all right?" Bebe looked bewildered.

"She must have burned herself again. I'll go check on her." I left Bebe cleaning up the sticky mess and followed Lily to the bathroom.

She was, as I expected, in tears. "I knew something was going on. He never had time to talk to me anymore, and he was never home when I called."

"Shhh. It's all right." I didn't know what else to say, so I just hugged her and let her sob.

"Maybe I was too young for him. I guess I knew that. But Jeanine? She's too old for him."

"I know, dear." Not much motherly wisdom coming from me tonight.

"I didn't even know if I really wanted anything to happen with him anymore. I just wasn't quite ready to give up the idea altogether. And it's too mortifying to imagine him with that uptight old toothpick."

Old? Well, yes, I admitted to myself. Jeanine and I are old, if you look at it from Lily's point of view. Or Borden's, one would think. Even Laurence's. He must have hated the idea of Borden and Jeanine.

Lily washed her face and composed herself. "I can't imagine what I saw in a guy with such weird taste."

Her recovery couldn't be that easy. I expected I'd hear more about this later.

Bebe had cleaned up the floor and salvaged enough of the risotto for a respectable supper, particularly since I'd already eaten dinner. She cooed over Lily's hurt hand and ushered us all to the table, which she'd set rather charmingly.

Lily looked morose but alert, and after wolfing down half her risotto she even began to look relaxed. I probably should have eaten some risotto, too, to sop up the wine that was beginning to make my head swim. Or was it the conversation?

Bebe and Lily had dropped the subject of Borden and found common ground in speculating on Jeanine as the culprit.

"She hated the idea that Laurence and I were going to get married," Bebe said.

That sobered me up immediately. Was Laurence, the eternally uncommitted, actually planning to marry at last? Marry this near child whom all his friends saw as just a bottle-blond waif? Now I was the one to feel a stab of jealousy.

"She sabotaged us every chance she got," Bebe continued. "She made up stories about me. She intercepted messages and then told Laurence I was meeting him earlier than I said, so he'd wind up waiting and angry with me. She was always trying to put me in embarrassing situations."

"I could see her doing that," Lily said, joining right in. "She was always subtly putting Mama down, too."

Was that true? I began to search my memory for times I'd felt demeaned when Jeanine was around.

This was getting out of hand. I felt that as the mother figure, I was responsible for reality checks. "Look, Bebe, even if Jeanine was possessive, she wouldn't have killed her beloved brother in order not to lose him."

"But she'd already lost him." Bebe was full of surprises. "She went into a rage when Laurence told her he was sending her to New York to manage Les Deux and replacing her as hostess here. With me."

I was shocked. Of course Jeanine would feel discarded. She'd put up the money for Laurence's restaurant when they'd come to Washington. And now she was being kicked upstairs—or up to New York.

Lily wasn't buying it. "I'd think she'd be flattered to be put in charge of the New York restaurant," she said. "It's a much bigger deal. Not to mention a much more important city."

"That's what Laurence tried to tell her," Bebe said. "But she didn't care about New York. She cared about being with Laurence. And with keeping me out of the picture. But maybe most of all, she cared about staying here with Borden. Though I really don't expect that to last very long."

A small smile of satisfaction crossed Lily's face. "No, I can hardly imagine it would."

My mind was reeling with the wine and with Bebe's revelations. They still didn't add up to a sister murdering her baby brother, in my book. Then again, no motive was sufficient for murder in my book.

"It's past midnight. And this is beginning to sound

like campfire ghost stories." I stood up, yawning, and started to clear the table. By now I'd assumed Homer wasn't going to return my call tonight. "Let's get to bed. We'll think more clearly in the morning."

Lily and Bebe made quick work of cleaning up, while I distributed nightgowns and pillows. How opposite they seemed—Lily, dark, wearing little makeup, naive and idealistic; Bebe, pale under all that mascara and eye shadow, hard-boiled and worldly wise. Yet both were ready to give their all to anyone who showed interest in them.

I said good night to my two young coconspirators. Then I tossed and turned for hours while I listened to their innocent snoring.

I woke to the sound of denim sliding and creaking over Bebe's bony legs. As I resisted consciousness it occurred to me that quiet little Bebe always wore noisy clothes: clanking jewelry, swishing silks, clickety-clack sorts of shoes.

Two young women, nearly the same age, height, and weight, Bebe and Lily, even with names the same shape. But they dressed so differently. Bebe's clothes clung, while Lily's hovered. You could only guess at Lily's shape under the flowing layers of shirts, blouses, and long skirts—a cloud of blues and greens this morning.

"You know, I was your age when I first met Laurence," I said as I poured coffee for the three of us.

"He told me about it." Bebe stirred three spoons

of sugar into her coffee while Lily went in search of the honey. "At first I was jealous, but then I figured we had a lot in common, and I thought of you as a friend. I knew that you were the woman he had loved most. Until he met me."

"Weren't you married then?" Lily asked me, settling in on Bebe's side of the table. We'd never actually talked about those days. I'd hoped Lily would never ask.

"Yes, although Ari and I were already having problems." I started to get up from my chair, under cover of getting the coffeepot from the kitchen.

"I'll get it," Lily interrupted. She brought the coffeepot back to the table and this time sat down next to me. "It must have been hard, being married to Dad. I love him dearly, but even I get frustrated with his distance."

I was touched by Lily's sympathy for me: She had always defended Ari fiercely from my slightest criticism. Her gesture freed me to tell her, "I loved him, too. And still do, in a way. But I always knew there was something missing in our marriage. God knows we both tried hard for a long time to make it work."

"Why didn't you run off with Laurence?" Lily must have been harboring this question for years.

"He was my best friend," I tried to explain. "It worked better that way. And he was too young to settle down. Besides, I loved being a family—with you in it."

"Was Dad angry when I was born with blue eyes?"

Everything stopped—Bebe's spooning sugar into her coffee, my hand reaching for my cup, my heart.

"Is that what you've been thinking? That you're Laurence's daughter?" I reached toward those eyes that must have caused her private pain. "Oh, no, my dear. Your beautiful eyes came from Ari's father. Ari always said that his father's eyes could make a gray sky look blue."

Lily leaned back in her chair and turned her thoughts inward, leaving us all in silence.

"I'm sorry," I whispered. "I wish I'd known."

Lily's always been mercurial. "I'm glad I was wrong. I didn't totally believe it anyway, just kind of toyed with the idea." She wrapped me in an ardent hug. "Hey, we've got a murder to solve."

Lily, of course, wanted to go and confront Jeanine immediately, accuse her of murder, and have her arrested. I, as usual, put a damper on her impulsiveness. I was having serious misgivings about our playing detective.

I said as much, which got both girls grumbling. Nevertheless, I became more specific.

"Bebe is going to the police, first of all," I said, throwing Bebe into rigid alarm. "Don't worry. I'll call them and explain it all. And then I'm going to work, where I am supposedly earning a living. And you, Lily, ought to go and see your father so that he doesn't have to hear thirdhand that you're in town."

"Yes, sir, sir." Lily saluted me and went off to find a few more layers to throw over her morning accumulation. I figured I'd just waylaid her slightly. She'd be back giving me an argument before long. Either that or she had plans of her own.

I dreaded the next step. And wouldn't you know it,

just when I hoped Homer would once more be impossible to reach, he was answering his own phone.

"I've got Bebe for you," I said in the most matter-of-fact voice I could muster. I didn't feel like getting into how long she'd been here or what had happened to the message I'd left for him.

"Say, Miss Chas, maybe you are a detective after all. Where is she?" Homer sounded as if he'd just been served a full plate of fettucine *al pescatore.*

"First you've got to tell me what's going to happen to her. She didn't do it. But she's afraid she'll be arrested."

"Sounds like you're treading on dangerous ground, making demands on the police. What makes you think she's innocent?" Homer's voice had curdled, as if he'd hit a spoiled clam. Bebe was crowding me, trying to hear what he was saying.

I started pacing the floor to get a little distance from Bebe. I knew this was going to sound lame: "She told me."

"Good thing you weren't interviewing Jeffrey Dahmer," Homer spat out.

"No, really, Homer—"

"Have you checked her alibi?" His voice was patronizing.

I had a lot to learn as a detective. I'd never even thought to ask. So I held my hand over the mouthpiece and made up for lost time. "Where were you Sunday night?" I whispered to Bebe.

"You mean she's right there with you?" Homer was shouting.

Bebe cowered in the corner when she heard his

voice. "I was hostessing," she whimpered, as if she were telling me she'd been snorting coke. "Borden asked me to do this friend of his a favor. He knew Laurence would be busy cooking for CityTastes. And his friend's regular hostess had to go visit her mother."

"What time?" I pursued, bringing the phone close enough that Homer could probably hear for himself.

"I got there about five, and got to talking with the owner afterward, so I didn't get home until about one A.M. It was in Maryland, outside Columbia, nearly an hour's drive."

"I heard. I'll check it out," conceded Homer. He and I both knew by now that the digoxin was likely to have taken a couple of hours to kill Laurence, and he had died long before three in the morning. "Just get her down here to talk to me, and I'll try to make this as easy as possible for her."

I was going to get a recess from this mess after all, I thought. But not for long. Homer had one more question: "Did you ask her about the kid's threatening call?"

I'd forgotten all about it. Or, more precisely, I'd assumed the message had come from Bebe. Then once I decided that Bebe was not a threat, I altogether forgot about any danger to me.

"What call? What kid? I don't even know any kids," was Bebe's bewildered response when I belatedly asked her.

My recess was over.

• • •

Walking to work turned out to be just what I'd been needing. Washington looks cleaner in winter than in warmer seasons when its inhabitants are constantly blowing their noses and spitting in the gutters, symptoms of the city being the allergy capital of the universe. Today noses were pink only from the chill, the air was clear and cold, and I wanted to breathe it in by the bucketful. I couldn't get enough of being outdoors after the past two miserable days. I wished my apartment was in Silver Spring so I could look forward to a real walk to my New York Avenue office.

After two blocks, questions began once again to bounce around in my head. Who was behind that call? Was there any real danger? What did I know that somebody didn't want me to tell?

And what about that Sunday-night job of Bebe's? Did Borden have some reason for wanting her so far away from Laurence?

# twelve

This time the crowd around the front of the *Examiner* was ogling an ambulance that was just racing away as I reached the front steps. Who was in it? Nobody seemed to know.

The newsroom looked empty, which didn't surprise me since few of the staff come in before ten-thirty. I looked at my watch: 10:30 on the nose. It should have been busier.

It was, actually. I just hadn't noticed that everyone was gathered in Bull's office. Was he the casualty? No, I could hear his voice, growling for everyone to get back to work.

"What happened?" I called out to Sherele as she fled Bull's impatient snorts.

I couldn't hear her over the stampede.

"Who's sick?" I was shedding my coat as she reached our adjoining desks.

"It's Andy. He had a heart attack."

Andy? Oh, poor Andy. I immediately forgot all my disgust with him and welled up with pity. "Just like that? No warning? Is he going to be okay?"

"I don't know. It looked pretty bad. They were giving him CPR the last I saw." Sherele looked shaken. She'd seen it, seen him fall.

"I'll go check whether there's anything I can do," I said, heading toward the food section.

"I'll come, too," Sherele volunteered, putting her arm around my shoulder and clickety-clacking alongside me in her high heels.

I didn't know exactly why I was rushing off to visit the scene. Maybe it was voyeurism, maybe I needed to make it real by seeing that Andy actually wasn't at his desk. He was one of the few people who regularly came into the office early, which I took to mean that he didn't have much of a life outside the *Examiner*.

As always, Andy's desk was a mess of grease-stained papers, coffee-stained envelopes, and books opened to pages stained with tomato and egg. He ate most of his meals at this desk. I started to pick up errant mail that had scattered on the floor.

Some of the envelopes were addressed to me: "Ms. Chas Wheatley, Food Editor, *The Washington Examiner*." It was an ongoing battle between Andy and me, this mail. Readers often assumed that my title was food editor, or they just didn't know the difference between a restaurant critic and a food editor. And the mailroom was so sloppy that half the time I got Andy's mail and he got mine. The difference was that I returned his to him. He kept mine.

My hands felt sticky. The envelopes were smeared with red and brown goo. On closer look—and smell— it was something very familiar. Chocolate-covered cherries, my favorite. Sure enough, buried under a pile of newspapers was a small box with four empty pleated paper cups. A box of four chocolate-covered cherries—at least it had been once. Beneath the box was its wrapper, brown paper with a card taped to it. The card had my name on it. The candy had been sent to me.

In my years as a restaurant critic I'd often made a public joke of my addiction to chocolate cherries. I even kept a life list of the best I tasted. These were from a new chocolate shop I hadn't tried yet.

Yesterday's threat, my chocolates, and Andy's attack clicked into place.

"Sherele, it was supposed to be me!" I held up the wrapper.

"Chas, honey, you know Andy ate half the goodies that were sent here for you," Sherele said, unperturbed.

"No, the heart attack was supposed to be me!" I shook the paper under her nose, making her back off and look at me as if I were crazy.

I was crazy. With fear. I grabbed her shoulder, feeling a bubble of hysteria in my throat. "Andy ate this candy addressed to me. Then he had a heart attack. We've got to call the hospital and tell them to look for digoxin. Somebody's tried to kill me the same way that Laurence was murdered."

Sherele got the point.

So did Homer. He eventually arrived to find me sitting numbly in Andy's chair, staring at his mess. The nervous crowd chattering around me included Dave, who was trying to act like just a colleague but occasionally couldn't remember to keep his hands from stroking my hair. I wished everyone would go away so I could just snuggle myself in Dave's arms and cry for, say, a day or two.

"I'm sorry, I've messed up the clues," I said stupidly. Now I knew what scared silly meant. I also felt sick with guilt that Andy might have died because of me.

"Naw, there wouldn't have been any clues," Homer reassured me. "Anybody who went to all that trouble wouldn't have left fingerprints on the wrapper. The only evidence is in Mutton's stomach."

In a city known for the sluggishness of its public services, the police rapidly swarmed the *Examiner* to secure the crime scene and ogle the newsroom. Bull was nervous having cops on the premises, but there was nothing he could do about it. Nothing but grouse at us all to stop wasting the publisher's money and get back to work.

My colleagues, who had gathered in horror around me in the food section when the news spread, sneaked embarrassed glances at me as they retreated. Even Dave muttered something about being late for an interview. There I stood, one of those bewildered characters you see in TV ads, everybody whispering around her but nobody daring to tell her she has dandruff. Sherele put her hand on my arm and steered me back to my desk.

"It's not your fault," she argued with the thoughts I hadn't spoken. "Just remember, you didn't do it to

Andy. He was the victim of his own greed. And you would have been too smart to eat candy from an anonymous source. I hope."

"I think I've just gone on a diet," I answered her miserably.

Nothing made me feel better until a message popped up on my computer screen. The entire newsroom was informed that Andy was doing fine. Most of the digoxin had oozed out when Andy ate the chocolates. So Andy owed his life to his sloppiness. The digoxin dose he'd ingested had been small, and he'd merely fainted. A cheer went up. Probably the first and last cheer Andy was ever going to inspire, and the poor guy wasn't around to hear it.

Even though I was relieved, I still felt angry and afraid. I also felt exhausted and nervous. What I didn't feel was hungry. But my job is to eat, and I didn't know what else to do at this point but get on with my job.

How was I going to do that and stay alive? I called Dave.

"Look, hon, you can always just pretend to eat."

"Then how am I going to write about it if I haven't tasted it?" We were in our private stairwell. My voice was muffled by his shirt, in which I'd buried my face.

"The hell with writing about it. Your job isn't worth your life. If the police don't catch this guy soon, Bull will just have to give you a week off from your column."

"Is this the same investigative reporter who's shown me his scars from being beaten, run down by a motorcycle, and grazed by a switchblade in pursuit of his stories?" Dave was acting more protective than I wanted him to be. Well, it wasn't that I didn't like being protected, but I needed him to treat me like a professional, too. He should be giving me advice on how to safely conduct an investigation, not how to run and hide.

Dave cocked my chin so he could look in my eyes. My gaze slid past his, to settle on the thin exclamation point etched down his left cheek, the scar from that knife attack. His mouth widened into a one-sided grin, and he conceded the point. "Gotcha. Let's think this through. Point one: Before every bite, consider where the food came from. Who could have known you were going to eat it? Or that you might eat it? Who bought it, who cooked it, who had access to it on the way to your plate? Who else might be eating it? The more people it's being served to, the safer. Point two: When in doubt, spit it out. Hey, I like that—when in doubt, spit it out." Dave tapped the rhythm on my forehead.

"That'll sure do a lot for a chef's confidence: 'The restaurant critic couldn't even swallow the food.'"

"Aw, c'mon. You can be discreet. Spit it into your hankie or something."

Faint bells rang. The church around the corner.

"Shit," Dave responded to them. "I forgot about my plane. I'm gonna miss it. Look, Chas, just don't take any chances, okay? I'll be back tonight, or tomorrow, latest. Leave me a voice mail message if you need help, and I'll be checking in."

I waited for Lily in front of La Raison d'Être. This time I didn't feel like going in alone. She swooped in like an early spring bird, layers of blue and green sweaters and blouses flapping around her as she rushed up to me, cheeks flushed and eyes sparkling.

"Mama, have I got the goods on Borden." She planted an excited kiss on my cheek. It seemed as if Lily was going to enjoy hating Borden even more than she had enjoyed loving him. "Dad and Paul had been hearing rumors that he was taking kickbacks from suppliers and reselling the caviar."

"Slow down, Lily." Under my hug she felt as if she were about to take off. "Every kitchen is a hotbed of such rumors. That doesn't make them all true."

She threw me an "Oh, Mom" glance.

"Even if they are true, it's a long way from petty embezzling to murder," I cautioned her, ever the mother.

"I'm not accusing him of murder. But we've got to start somewhere," Lily conceded, slightly contrite. Then, as she always does when the conversation doesn't go her way, she changed the subject. "I'm starving."

Georges wasn't at the door. Wednesday was his day off. Instead, his boss's wife, Marie Claire, was greeting the customers, pivoting from one to the other in a filmy wool dress the color of plums. On her, roundness looks appropriate, from her cheeks puffed like biscuits to her pillowy bosom. Marie Claire has a sweet pink face like the grandmothers of our dreams, and a voice like softened butter.

When she saw me, her face turned to margarine. Restaurateurs never manage to hide that moment of shock when I walk in unannounced. But the good ones, like Marie Claire, instantly recover from their panic and welcome me as if all my reviews were raves.

"My dear Chas," she trilled. "And Lily, such a blossom you have become." A cloud of kisses sprinkled the air around us. Marie Claire was a woman so secure in her life that after the first involuntary alarm she could greet me with the effusiveness of a friend rather than the wariness of a restaurateur about to be critiqued.

"How are you doing, Marie Claire? And how is Marcel?" I felt sorry for this couple, for so long friends with Laurence and with such hopes for their future together.

"We are carrying on, my dear." Her face clouded, but she controlled it from any further display of emotion. This was, after all, a public place, and she was responsible for the comfort of her customers. "I will come and talk to you when the lunch is over."

Restaurants are indeed restorative. The sponged yellow walls and the masses of flowers turned La Raison d'Être into a springtime afternoon. Lily and I settled into the soft banquette and opened our menus as if the curtain were rising on a brilliant new play. For the moment, the ugly and dangerous world outside was too far away to care about.

But just for a moment. What was I going to do about eating?

Nobody had known I was coming here, I reminded myself, so it was impossible for anyone to have doctored the food in anticipation. Furthermore, even I didn't know what I was going to order. And the chance of someone having digoxin on hand just in case I showed up would be ridiculously slim. Nothing—no shelf, no coat, no pants pocket, not even a purse—is safe from prying eyes in the chaotic, crowded back of a restaurant.

I grew hungry.

On the other hand, anyone who knew my pattern could guess I'd be back at La Raison d'Être sometime soon, since I was obviously reviewing it.

I lost my appetite. I ordered a whole bottle of wine and a large bottle of mineral water so I could watch them being opened and poured.


Lily was hungry, I noticed. Not so much for food as for Brian, who was having a conversation with our waiter, a few feet away.

"What a hunk," Lily said, confirming my observtion.

I chafed with a prickle of jealousy. Suddenly I felt very fifty.

Brian must have bribed our waiter with the promise of filling in for him on a Saturday night, because suddenly he was at our table, pad in hand, ready to take our drinks order.

"How nice to see you again, Ms. Wheatley. Are you back to finish Monday's lunch?" Brian looked genuinely happy, from his lanky gold hair to his chiseled chin. But while his greeting was directed to me, his eyes were on Lily.

I gave in to the inevitable. "Brian, this is my daughter, Lily. She's visiting from Philadelphia."

"I went to Penn. I love Philadelphia," Brian cooed to Lily as if he were talking about blue eyes rather than cities. His hands, with pen and pad, had dropped to his sides, abandoning the pretense that he was a waiter. I wanted our other waiter back.

"What year?" Lily was addressing Brian as she might a guy she'd just met at a bar, and she was getting to know him. Next she'd be asking his major. This was going to be a long lunch.

Lily and I negotiated over what to order, a familiar dance for both of us. Perversity is her middle name: In restaurants she always wants something simple, often vegetarian—a green salad, a plate of vegetables—or maybe something as daring as plain grilled fish without the sauce. I was working, which meant I needed to test the chef. The complicated dishes were the most relevant.

Today Lily was unusually cooperative, perhaps because she wanted to look agreeable in front of Brian, or more likely to please Marie Claire, who had always taken a particular interest in Lily. From babyhood until I became a restaurant critic and called a halt to Marie Claire's generosity, Lily's prettiest dresses had been gifts from her. Thus, in order not to offend Marie Claire, Lily merely mentioned the salad and grilled fish to me before she accepted our ordering the mousse of monkfish with garlic, which Marcel makes with olive oil and no cream at all, followed by his updated version of bouillabaisse and his rosy, tarragon-scented, garlic-crusted rack of lamb with the bones crisped and arranged alongside for nibbling. Of course, I again ordered the clam fritters.

My reason was telling me I could safely eat, but my stomach balked a little. As I contemplated the fritters, I reminded myself that it wouldn't make sense for someone to poison a guest in a restaurant where he or she worked. Too easy to trace the poison. And if the poisoner was not an employee, the odds against our crossing paths at a moment opportune for a poisoning would be astronomical.

When Lily picked up her fork to taste the mousse, though, my heart began to pound as if I were having a heart attack in anticipation of a chemically induced one. I had belatedly realized that Lily could be poisoned, too, on my account.

"I can't let you do this," I said, grabbing the plate from her and putting it beside my own. Lily looked aghast.

I beckoned Brian from the next table, where he'd been unable to keep his eyes off us even while he plated the Caesar salad he'd been mixing. He plunked down the other table's salad plates unceremoniously and was at our side in an instant.

"Brian, I know that what Lily really wants to try is

one of those Caesar salads. Would you mind? Why don't you just wheel that trolley over here and bring the romaine when you have a chance."

"I have the chance right now," Brian said as he reached for the trolley and rolled it to Lily's side—where I could unobtrusively keep an eye on it.

Brian took the large empty salad bowl and the small dish from the coddled egg back to the kitchen while I explained to Lily that it had been such an upsetting week that I didn't have the heart to make her eat more than she wanted on my account. I could sample the dishes we ordered without her needing to.

Brian returned instantly with a fresh bowl of romaine and another coddled egg. He whisked together the mustard, pepper, anchovy, vinegar, Worcestershire, and olive oil from the cart and poured that dressing over the romaine. He squeezed in a freshly cut lemon, cracked the egg over the bowl, and grated the Parmesan on top. He tossed it again, added croutons, also from the cart, and gave the salad a final toss. Somehow he made the process look like a dance of seduction, and he presented the plate to Lily as if he were offering himself.

In the meantime, I mushed around the mousse and cut the clam fritters into small pieces, hoping to look as if I were eating. I figured that with two appetizers and two entrées being served just for me, nobody could expect me to finish them, and it is remarkable how shrunken a pricey restaurant dish looks after you've attacked it with a knife and fork. I was a little worried that Lily might ask to taste my food, as she often finds an appetite for rich dishes, even meat, once they are on the table. But after I'd been so unexpectedly considerate of her abstemiousness, she didn't dare admit she'd love a lamb chop.

I waved away the dessert menus. Far too full, I claimed. When Brian asked if we wanted coffee, before Lily could answer I said that we wouldn't have time, because I had to get back to the office. Having gotten away without actually eating anything but two rolls—rather, the insides of two rolls—I was a little tipsy from the wine and drenched in relief from having maneuvered through this meal safely.

Marcel, coming from the kitchen to greet us at the end of the meal, had had no such respite from tension. His face looked beakier than ever as he shifted from foot to foot, inquiring as to how we'd liked our lunch. I never answer this question directly when I am reviewing a restaurant, so I muttered something about being glad to be here. The dining room had nearly emptied, so Marcel asked if we minded his joining us.

He nearly fell into the chair. Marcel looked as if he hadn't slept since Monday. And he probably hadn't. His hand shook as he lifted the espresso cup Brian had delivered to him. When Brian gestured an offer to bring us coffee after all, I lifted my glass to signal we'd just continue sipping our wine.

"They don't really think Laurence was murdered?" Marcel asked intently. He was having a hard time accepting the truth. "Nobody would want to do such a thing, not to Laurence."

"It's not a matter of thinking he was murdered, Marcel. We know for sure it was murder," Lily chimed in. I couldn't have been quite that direct.

"But the police don't have any evidence, do they?" Marcel tried again, fastening his eyes on me as if I would deny what Lily had declared as a certainty.

"Now they do. The same person tried to poison me," I blurted out, actually putting it in words for the first time. Marcel lowered his cup, incredulous. Lily gave a yelp. I hadn't meant to tell her about the chocolate cherries, and now I'd let it slip.

And so I had to explain, though I didn't mention my hesitation over eating Marcel's food. Lily grew silent and her jaw hardened.

"Oh, Chas, I cannot believe such a thing," Marcel said with tears in his eyes. He reached over to take my hand. "I couldn't bear it if you died. These are terrible times."

By now we were the only guests left in the dining room. Marie Claire pulled up a chair and joined us.

"Have the police caught that awful woman yet?" she asked me without preamble. "After you, Laurence always chose bad women."

That didn't exactly seem like a compliment to me, but coming from Marie Claire it was undoubtedly meant kindly. In the backbiting world of food, she was one of the few who was never the source nor the subject of gossip.

"Bebe turned herself in," I explained. Marie Claire looked relieved, but not when I added, "She hadn't killed him after all, and she had a clear alibi."

"What are the police thinking now? Who do they think did it?" Questions tumbled out as Marie Claire leaned closer. More and more questions piled up before I could answer the first.

"Mama's been working with the police," Lily chimed in to brag about me. She does that on occasion. I call it her my-mommy-can-beat-up-your-mommy mode. "She's got some clues she's working on." As usual, she got carried away.

I no longer relished talking about murder, since it seemed to be further upsetting my friends. I answered with something innocuous about there being various leads to follow, and I tried to change the subject. I began to hash over the food at CityTastes.

"Isn't it great that so many more chefs are participating these days?" I sounded like I was prattling, even to myself.

"Tell me about what they served." Lily leaned into the table, looking fascinated. I knew she was just helping me out. She usually tires pretty quickly of talk about restaurant food.

"Roberto Donna somehow managed to make a perfect game risotto for five hundred, and Yannick Cam's codfish puree had enough caviar to pay the national debt," I told her.

Marie Claire chimed in, "I hope you tasted Jean-Louis's cream of chestnut soup."

I could still taste it in my mind. "It did make some of the young American chefs' concoctions seem a little outlandish."

Marie Claire laughed, her face brighter as she conjured up the more bizarre presentations. "Oh, yes, that little black bean mud pie with those green things waving over it. Marcel, remember that pumpkin and tofu thing?"

Marcel, too, was getting into the spirit. "I will never understand why Americans put all those hot peppers in everything. And the idea of dessert in the middle of the meal. Next Mr. O'Connell will try to clean our palates with chocolate mousse."

I disagreed with him there. Just because Patrick O'Connell's creation looked like a sundae it need not be classed with desserts. I thought the dish was rather witty. But Marcel has never had much of a sense of humor.

Marie Claire must have agreed with me. Although she didn't contradict her husband, she abruptly diverted the discussion. "Wouldn't either of you like coffee?"

I looked at my watch, realizing that Lily and I were eating into Marcel and Marie Claire's much needed afternoon break. "No, thank you, we've really got to go. We'll just take the check." I felt a stab of guilt about how much this uneaten lunch was going to cost the *Examiner*.

Marie Claire signaled to Brian, who had returned to the dining room and discreetly stood far enough away not to be suspected of eavesdropping yet close enough to be beckoned if we needed anything.

"I'll let you be on your way," she said as she stood up, tucking her arm affectionately in Marcel's when he stood to join her. "The saddest thing is that Laurence did not get to see his dream. We have decided to name the New York restaurant after him, and we will run it as he would have done."

Marcel's face looked as if it were about to crumple. He opened his mouth to speak but couldn't quite manage it. Marie Claire patted his hand and took over for him.

"Chas, we have all known Laurence for so long, I would like very much to help you in any way to find out what happened. Will you call me and tell me how the investigation is progressing? And to let me know that you are safe and sound?"

At last, here was someone who wanted to take care of me for a change. I liked the idea of sharing the burden. "I'd be glad to. Thank you," I said as I kissed Marie Claire directly on the cheek, not two inches away as we usually do.

"If you are not feeling safe, my dear, you are welcome to stay at our house," she added, kissing me warmly in return.

Lily, in the meantime, was exchanging business cards with Brian. These young professionals.

I was hungry. Much as I grumble about having to devote my stomach and my thighs to an endless stream of professional eating, that's the part I love about my job. For one thing, while I'm eating I don't have to be writing. And the writing is always hard— at least the getting started is.

Lily decided to head home for a nap, being two days behind in her sleep by now. She promised to meet me later for dinner. I was even further behind on my column, and was determined to get some writing done. But not before I found a Burger King. A Whopper was the safest thing I could think of eating at the moment.

• • •

I know writers who precede their writing sessions by sharpening their pencils—even when they use a computer. Others line up all their notes in some ritualistic way. Or grind and brew a perfect cup of coffee before getting started. Every writer has a secret ceremony, a magic charm to get the words flowing.

I walk. The first block or two I am aware of the curbs and ramps under my feet, the varying textures of cement, brick, and metal grates. Gradually my thoughts shake off gravity. The squooshes of tires and clip-cloppings of high-heeled shoes fade, the smells of soggy wool dissipate. I no longer see blanket-wrapped panhandlers and shop windows. My eyes wander to the upper floors, to stone carvings that hide from passersby who keep their eyes nailed at human level. I begin to notice the chirps of birds. And my meal begins to digest into words.

Usually, but not always. Not today. Trying to release myself to words was like trying to fall asleep with a car alarm outside the window. I couldn't let go. My unconscious wasn't doing the work I wanted it to do. Instead, it meandered in a direction all its own. It brought me to Ari's door.

# thirteen

It amazes me that after all those years of being first a lonely wife and then an angry ex-wife, I sometimes feel more at home with Ari than with anyone else. I suppose it has to do with his being the father of my child. Or perhaps more important, when I was Lily's age, he was a father to the child-wife that I was then.

The smell of his kitchen took me right back to Hong Kong. Ari was pressing the carrot and leek residue from his fish stock through a conical sieve. I don't know what the Chinese call it, but the French named it, in honor of the vaguely cone-shaped coolie hat, a *chinois*.

Ari was making his famous Chesapeake Bay chowder to warm the mourners after tomorrow's funeral. His cooking always adapts to its locale. When we lived in Hong Kong, his fish soup was flavored with ginger, and a few mashed smoky, fermented black beans gave it a salty mystery. Here he had replaced the black beans with Smithfield ham.

"Remember when Laurence tried to use black beans in his soup—but got Spanish ones instead of the fermented Chinese kind?" I leaned over the butcher-block island, where Ari was chopping a fresh batch of carrots, and snatched one. Paul reached for one, too, and Ari playfully slapped his hand.

A thing he would never have done with me, I realized with a pang. Before Paul, Ari'd never had a playful bone in his body. I could probably learn a lot from Paul.

"Laurence was like a baby who's trying to run before he can walk," Ari said, testing the edge of his knife with his thumb. "He wanted to learn all the cooking, all at once. Nobody could slow him down." Chop chop chop chop chop. Ari's hands barely moved as he reduced whole carrots to tidy little cubes.

"I know. He never stopped asking questions," I said. "He had to meet absolutely everybody who had anything to do with food, to pick their brains. He followed Marcel around like a hungry puppy." I'd begun wandering around the kitchen, opening cabinets and peeking into drawers. I love seeing what people keep behind their doors. Paul gave me a mischievous grin and strolled ahead of me, opening the doors before I reached them. As I reached the end, Paul stood in my path and turned his pockets inside out, which made me choke on a giggle.

Ari, of course, noticed none of this. He just continued chopping. And reminiscing. "Do you remember when the chefs started making up dishes to talk about in front of Laurence? Those *fantastique* things? And he thought they were real and tried to make them work?"

I'd forgotten. But it was beginning to come back. "You did one with carrot tops. I didn't think you did it on purpose. I thought Laurence had misunderstood some Chinese ingredient you'd used. Did you really mean carrot tops?"

"Actually, yes. I did tell him I used carrot tops." Ari abruptly scooped the carrots into a bowl and turned toward the stove. Only half the carrots made it into the bowl—he clearly just wanted an excuse not to meet my eyes. With his back turned to me, he continued. "Sometimes I could not accept any longer that he copied me so much."

"Oh, Ari, he didn't really mean anything by it. He was young. He admired you and wanted to emulate you," I blathered defensively.

For the first time, Paul stepped into the conversation. "At some point it's called stealing." He took the bowl of carrots from Ari and put an arm protectively around his shoulder. "You loved him, Chas, so you wouldn't have given it such an honest label."

I was shocked. To cover my chagrin, I started searching through my purse for hairpins. Repinning my hair kept my hands busy and gave me a moment to collect my thoughts. "It's such a fuzzy line. All chefs are influenced by other chefs. One season everyone is cooking with balsamic vinegar; the next, it's beets with goat cheese. Who knows where an idea starts?"

"You're right, my dear," Ari conciliated. But Paul wasn't such a pushover.

"There's a difference between ideas and inventions," he said, wading right in. "Sure, everyone latches on to the vegetable of the month. That's an exchange of ideas. Paul Prudhomme's blackened redfish, it got copied all over the place but everyone knows that Prudhomme originated it. He gets the credit."

I started to argue back, but Paul cut me off.

"The theft is when a chef claims it as his own. And then, even worse, accuses the original chef of stealing it."

"You don't mean Laurence," I protested. My face grew hot. How could Paul make such accusations with Laurence not even buried yet? Paul was an outsider, not a chef. He'd never even worked in a restaurant. "Laurence watched, he played around with ideas, he learned from other chefs. He never really stole anything."

"Well, he tried, didn't he?" Paul gave me such a piercing look that it was obvious he was no longer talking about recipes. I felt a sick dread spreading through me with the possibility that Ari had resented Laurence, even after all these years.

Paul and I both jumped when Ari slammed his knife into the cutting board.

"Paul." Ari's voice was quiet. He retrieved the bowl of carrots from Paul and asked, "Would you mind getting the fish broth from the other refrigerator?"

"Sure, Ari." Paul left the room.

Without a word, Ari finished scooping the carrots into the bowl. Then he reduced a pile of leeks to a fine dice. I sat on a stool at the counter, watching fearfully, sadly. Ari and I had never talked about Laurence, not seriously. We'd just always pretended that nothing had happened.

Ari, in his usual silent way, skirted the issue yet acted the peacemaker. He started chopping a mound of parsley, then paused to extract a sprig. Without a word he walked around the counter and tucked it into one of my hairpins. He stepped back to look at his handiwork.

"Beautiful," he said.

"Thank you," I said.

This kindhearted man, this passive man, I could not credit him with anything worse than avoidance.

Ari gathered all the chopped vegetables and poured them into a large stockpot. My attention was jerked back to the chowder making: I'd assumed Ari would be sautéing the vegetables, but he hadn't heated the pot first, or added any butter. Instead, he opened one of the cupboards I'd seen filled with bottles, and took out one containing a pale green liquid. He poured the contents into the pot and adjusted the heat. A wonderful smell of herbs began to fill the room.

"What's that?" I asked, revived and intrigued by what seemed to be a new method of sweating aromatic vegetables.

"My secret." Ari was smiling right up to his eyebrows. "No fat," he added proudly.

I walked over to the cabinet to look at the bottles more closely. Three rows of wine bottles filled the cabinet, and each row was filled with a different liquid—one the color of tomatoes, one green like the one Ari had just poured, and the third a sunny yellowish orange. I uncorked an orange one and sniffed.

"Citrus," I said.

"Right," Ari confirmed. "Orange, lemon, lime, grapefruit, and a dash of that new ugli fruit."

The contents of the bottle had separated into several layers, so I covered the mouth of the bottle with my thumb and shook it. The liquid turned an even orange, then quickly began to sort itself out into layers again. I licked my thumb.

"Yum. No oil at all?" It tasted like essence of fruit in an oil base.

"None at all," said Ari. "It is my new discovery. I am going to market it as soon as I finish working on the tomato flavor. A very good company in France has expressed interest in it. And a very big company in Minnesota. I am deciding which would be the best direction for me to go."

"That's really exciting. You deserve it." This was the Ari I admired. I walked over and kissed him on the cheek, then dipped a spoon in the stockpot and tasted a bit of the simmering vegetables. "Amazing."

Ari has never been much of a moneymaker. He works hard, but only at what he wants to do, which seldom includes record-keeping or billing, much less the kind of production cooking that is profitable. His financial stability improved when Paul took over the mechanics of the business. Yet as busy as Ari is, he still doesn't make much of a profit. And at nearly sixty he can't plan to be in the kitchen too many more years. I've always worried about his future. But with this new elixir of his, it looked as if I wouldn't have to worry any longer.

Paul returned, lugging a plastic bucket of fish broth.

"Ari's shown you his pot of gold, I see," Paul said, giving me a friendly wink as he dipped a spoon into the pot and blew to cool it before he tasted.

"It's fabulous," I said, feeling kindlier myself as I went back to the cupboard to taste the tomato-red version. It, too, filled the room with its smell as I opened the bottle, then stoppered it with my thumb and shook it. But when I licked my thumb this time, it was a letdown. The tomato flavor was too faint.

"You can see that the tomato doesn't have the right intensity yet," Ari said before I had a chance to comment.

"That's what I was researching last weekend," Paul chimed in. He started wiping down the counter where Ari had been chopping vegetables. "Some Pennsylvania Dutch farmers have crossbred a new tomato that maintains its flavor better when it's processed, but I found it a pain in the neck to deal with their religious restrictions. The guy said I could come anytime, so I decided that this weekend, before CityTastes, would be perfect. What a mistake. He wouldn't talk business at all on a Sunday. God, it was frustrating. And I forgot that you couldn't get a drink around there either."

I remembered how silent Pennsylvania Dutch country was on a Sunday afternoon. "So what did you do?" I asked Paul.

"Oh, I managed. I just ambled on to Philadelphia

and stayed over with some friends who happen to
have one of the great wine cellars of the English-
speaking world."

I was glad the afternoon was ending on such a
friendly note, and left them fussing together over fish
stock and bottled herb essence.

# fourteen

One lone placard carrier marched, under an impatient sky, back and forth in front of the *Examiner*'s entrance. From the rear this protester looked stalwart, back straight and shoulders lifted. When he turned and faced me I could see that his eyes and the message on his flapping cardboard sign were pathetically confused. Something about taxicabs and judgment day. I felt sorry for the guy, and gave him a smiling thumbs-up as I passed. He broke his stride and rushed to open the door for me, in the process whacking himself on the head with his own sign. He didn't seem quite sure who the enemy was.

Dave hadn't come back from New York today after all, which was disappointing. I'd hoped I could persuade him to come to dinner with Lily and me. I was even willing to pick a place where he wouldn't need a tie. Instead, I asked Sherele.

"I'd love to see Lily," Sherele said immediately. "But I've got to show up at some little experimental theater thing that starts around nine-thirty. So I might have to leave before dessert."

"No problem," I assured her.

"No problem for you," Sherele grumbled. "I don't suppose you'd be willing to start with dessert."

"No, but I'd be glad to find a place that doesn't serve dessert, or at least one where the desserts aren't very good," I said.

Sherele leaned over and pinched my cheek. "You're just a Christian martyr," she crooned.

"Where's that from?" I hate it when Sherele expects me to just know.

"*The Glass Menagerie.* Tennessee Williams never did write enough about food," she mused.

"Sherele, do you suppose there's a twelve-step program for dessert addicts?"

With reluctance I turned to tackle my pileup of work. Fortunately I'm one of those people who can switch into overdrive when necessary, doing two or three things at a time. I think it comes from being a working mother. You learn quickly when, all at one time, a child, her school, your spouse, and your boss are clamoring for your attention. You cook dinner, braid your daughter's hair, and conduct a telephone interview, jotting notes in between brush strokes. You help your daughter with her homework by phone as you check messages on the computer, organize notes for your column, and sample three new mustards on a rice cracker you found by rooting around in your desk drawers.

So, in quick succession, I called Stephen Wang's restaurant to make a reservation in Sherele's name

(Chinese restaurants never have much in the way of desserts). Then I left a message on my home answering machine and another with Ari for Lily to meet us there. I sped through my E-mail, voice mail, and U.S. mail, setting aside most of it to deal with next week. I exchanged computer greetings with my boss, Helen, wherein she assured me that if I didn't get my column done by my usual Friday deadline, early Monday would be fine this time. She also, to my great relief, told me that Andy Mutton was out of danger, and that she had assigned him a story on hospital food. I wrote up my notes on La Raison d'Être (which were frustratingly short), gathered my file on Wang's to see what dishes I shouldn't miss, left a message for Dave explaining about Lily and Sherele and dinner, for when he got back from New York tonight, and saved the best part until last: returning a call from Homer Jones, whose message said the police department was making some progress and he wanted me to call him.

"What's cooking, Homer?" I knew "cooking" was the wrong word almost as soon as I said it.

"Hi there, Ms. Wheatley. Glad you called. And glad you reminded me of what I wanted to tell you. I found this little Nepalese restaurant that I think you ought to take a look at. The owner says he's going to have to close down soon if he doesn't get more business, so I told him I'd pass the word on to you."

Spare me. There's no way I can save every one of the innumerable undercapitalized and nearly identical

Asian restaurants that open in little storefronts, usually in neighborhoods where nobody likes spicy food unless it's Tex-Mex. But I needed Homer on my side. I dutifully took down the name and address.

My dues paid, it was time for Homer to pay his. "What's going on with the murder investigation?"

"Now that's an interesting thing, Chas." Homer had called me by my first name. That must mean he'd switched from restaurant-critic groupie mode to in-charge detective mode. "After talking to the victim's girlfriend—and I thank you for calming her down and getting her to come in voluntarily—we've been looking harder at the victim's other nearest and dearest. The sister seems to have had a more complicated relationship with him than in most happy families."

"That's what I was trying to tell you yesterday," I cut in excitedly.

Homer didn't pause. "But after talking to the neighbors again, we're headed in a new direction. One of them had an overnight guest, and today we tracked him down, which turned out to be interesting. It seems that he couldn't sleep, and opened a window because the apartment was stuffy. Lo and behold, he heard angry voices coming from Levain's apartment."

"Did he hear what they were saying?" My heart was pounding. What the argument was about could tell us who the arguer was.

"No, he couldn't hear the words. But he could definitely hear that it was two men." Homer had a note of satisfaction in his voice.

"Not Jeanine, huh?" I felt oddly disappointed. And appalled at myself. Why did I want Jeanine to be the prime suspect? I hoped it was just because I wanted the murder solved.

"Not Jeanine. At least not directly. Anyway, after hearing what the girlfriend had to say about the sous-chef, we're taking a look at him. Any ideas?"

"Borden? What did Bebe tell you about him?" I asked even though I sort of knew the answer. I wanted to hear Homer's version.

"Well, she trotted out all the usual motives: jealousy, frustration, money. And we have been finding bribes and kickbacks like worms after a rainstorm. Seems that Levain had recently found out about two of those bribes and didn't like them one bit. That, believe it or not, came from the bribers. Levain hadn't yet uncovered the others, but it wouldn't have taken him long once he'd set his mind to it. In light of that, we were mighty curious as to why Borden sent Bebe into Maryland for a Sunday-night job. Right now we're trying to track down who initiated that contact."

"Borden certainly had easy access to Laurence," I agreed. But somehow it all seemed too obvious. Kind of a letdown, which surprised me since I'd never much liked Borden, who treated women with far less respect than he showed asparagus. "How can I help you get the evidence?"

"That's my job, Chas," Homer retorted. "Unless you'd like to trade for a week and let me write your review."

I saw his point.

He went on. "What you can do to help is to keep yourself out of Borden's way. Remember, whoever killed Levain also tried to kill you."

The funny thing was, while I could entertain the possibility that Borden had killed his boss, his mentor, his closest friend, I couldn't imagine anybody I knew killing me. "I'll watch what I eat," I promised Homer. "But then I always do." Lame joke.

"We'll keep an eye on Borden. But you stay in brightly lit places and in the company of other people anyway," Homer cautioned.

"I suppose I'll see you at the funeral tomorrow morning," I said.

"Yes, unless I have the good luck to be busy booking a murderer. You know where to reach me if anything makes you the least bit uneasy," Homer said. "And don't forget that Nepalese restaurant." Homer signed off.

Stephen Wang's hands were so sweaty that they left damp streaks when he wiped them on his white chef's jacket every few seconds. He was hovering over my table, telling me the history and ingredients of every noodle and dumpling on his menu, his words chasing each other as if they were racing toward a finish line. I felt out of breath just listening to him.

Sherele was late, of course, and so was Lily. Thus, I was not displeased to have the company and the rapid-fire noodle education. Stephen's restaurant held a dozen tables in a room decorated with far more taste than money. Whole walls were tinted persimmon and lit softly so that they glowed like a sunset, while others, a dark and glossy eggplant hue, had spotlights positioned over them to suggest a starry night sky. The tablecloths, too, were dark, which played up the small clusters of white flowers in Tabasco bottles, giving them the impact of expensive bouquets. And against the dark cloths, the white plates of food at nearby tables were like paintings in an intimate gallery.

Stephen insisted I try a bottle of the new white wine China was producing and, while I was waiting, he suggested that I might sample the new dumplings he was working on. They were from an ancient recipe, he explained, which used wheat flour to make them supple and rice flour for translucence. Thus, when he eventually gets the proportions right, he should be able to roll the dough thin enough to show patterns in the colors of the filling. Stephen ran back to the kitchen to show me what he meant.

What he brought were slightly bulging half-moons of dough in which a faint marbling of green and beige showed through.

"These are pork and spinach," Stephen explained as he cut into one triangle with the chopsticks that he wielded as nimbly as if they were fingers. "I don't have the dough fine enough yet, so you can't quite see the pattern of the filling."

I snagged a bit with my chopsticks and tasted it, figuring a nibble couldn't hurt. Nobody but Sherele, Lily, and Dave knew I'd be dining here, and Laurence Levain had lived in a different world from Wang's all-Chinese staff. This food couldn't be dangerous.

It was scrumptious. Juicy pork and velvety spinach with a hint of anise and plenty of garlic. The dough had a slippery quality to it, reminiscent of something I'd tasted a long time ago. I could almost smell the teahouses of Hong Kong as I tried to figure out what made it so familiar. I hate it when my almost fifty memory plays hide-and-seek with me.

"I guess I can't blame you for starting without me." Sherele jolted me back to the present when she came up behind me and squeezed me with a hug. "As long as you haven't gotten to the desserts."

She turned to Stephen Wang and held out her hand, introducing herself. He took her hand with a small bow, just short of kissing it. "I'm very flattered to have two distinguished critics in my insignificant restaurant," he gushed as he frankly examined Sherele from her curtain of braids to her pearl-gray high-button suede boots.

"I see your cover's blown," Sherele said when Stephen left. "I'm glad. That means we get to eat the good stuff." She shook her chopsticks out of their paper sleeve and reached for the dumplings. "Wow! I like the way that slips down my throat."

"You don't think there's any danger here, do you?" I asked Sherele, on whom I'd always depended for reality checks.

"Danger? Of what?" She looked puzzled. Then she remembered, and began to gag. I quickly handed her a glass of water.

"I ate some, too," I reassured her. "It's got to be okay here. This is a Chinese restaurant. Nobody here could have wanted Laurence killed. It's just too far-fetched."

"You're right," Sherele said, eyeing another dumpling hungrily. "But just to be safe, let's insist Stephen Wang sit down and eat with us. The restaurant is nearly empty, so that shouldn't be a problem for him."

Brilliant. I waved him over and suggested that he dine at our table so that he might explain the dishes and show us how to eat them. He said he was flattered, and would sit with us as soon as he'd finished supervising the preparation.

I was reluctant to wait for Lily, since Sherele was on a tight schedule. And people who wait for Lily spend many hungry hours. So we ordered, with plenty for Lily to share when she arrived.

"To my friend the sleuth, who is learning too soon that only in fiction do the good end happily and the bad unhappily." Sherele held up her glass of white wine to toast me.

"Okay, what play's that?" Once again I felt illiterate around Sherele.

"*The Importance of Being Earnest.* Sort of." She took a sip, then wrinkled her face as if she'd just bitten into an unripe persimmon. "Bleechh! What's that?" She peered and sniffed at her wine as if it were roadkill.

"You've never had a Chinese chardonnay before?" I grinned, but kept my voice down out of concern for Stephen's feelings.

"I'll stick to tea," she said. "Or orange soda. Isn't that what the Chinese really drink at banquets?" Sherele waved the waiter over and inquired about what brands of orange soda might be available.

She caved in after one horrified glance from the waiter, and ordered a beer. Tsingtao. Then she turned her attention to the day's special, murder.

"Do the police have any evidence on Jeanine or Borden?" Sherele was already planning the prosecution of one or both.

"Nothing on either, at least that I know. Fingerprints wouldn't count, since both of them were at Laurence's place practically every day. Since the voice the neighbor's houseguest heard with Laurence was male, they are working to pin down Borden's whereabouts and to find somebody who can identify him as the man who was with Laurence that night. Also, the cops are trying to link someone to the purchase of digoxin. It's hard to get in such a concentrated form, probably liquid. The trouble is, I'm having a hard time imagining someone I know murdering someone else I know," I said, feeling more tolerant of the wine with each depressing sentence.

"Why, Chas, honey, I've known you to want to murder both of these men yourself from time to time," Sherele said, dropping her voice an octave. She put on her James Earl Jones accent. "Where did you say you were Sunday night?"

Sherele could always turn my gloom to laughter. She has such an amazing range of voices to call on. If only her readers could hear her recite her reviews. Yet she always refuses to do television. She likes her privacy, she says. She doesn't want to be recognized in the supermarket in her sweatpants and high-tops. I couldn't agree more, which is the selfish part of why

I've always tried to protect my anonymity in restaurants.

When our dishes and Stephen arrived, he recited a little introduction to each of his creations, and I insisted he eat along with us. We silently concentrated on those first bites and all the fresh nuances they had to offer. Sherele understands how important it is to me to fix the tastes—and the words to describe them—in my mind before I am diverted by conversation, and Stephen was clearly caught up in his own critical examination.

He didn't stay long, though. A waiter came to whisper that he was needed in the kitchen, so he left with bows and apologies.

"You know, I'd bet my money on Borden. I've never liked that oily twerp." Sherele launched right back into our discussion as if it hadn't been interrupted. "He's always thrown Lily just enough crumbs to keep her hope alive, when he was really just toying with her."

She knew, of course, that she was voicing my thoughts. "At least Lily wasn't so encouraged that she decided to settle in Washington," I reminded Sherele. Where was Lily, anyway? Anxiety, as it invariably did, carved big empty spaces in my stomach. My chopsticks were nervously roaming from dish to dish for a third and fourth round of sampling, while Sherele had finished with hers and set them on her plate. The more we talked of Borden, the more unsettled I felt about Lily. "Where is that girl? It would serve her right if there was nothing left by the time she arrived."

"But it wouldn't serve you right." Sherele gently eased the chopsticks from my right hand. "Go call and see if she's left you a message."

No message on my voice mail. And I never could remember the code for retrieving messages from my home answering machine. Lily knew that, and if she weren't leaving a message on my voice mail, she knew she could call the restaurant and ask for Sherele without blowing my cover.

Lily was two hours late. And even for her that was alarmingly tardy. I decided to leave with Sherele, and go home to see if she'd left me a note or something.

I made awkward excuses to Stephen Wang, who looked crestfallen that we were leaving without dessert. After a hurried good-bye to Sherele, I raced home.


"Lily?"

As I unlocked my apartment door, I half expected her to be sprawled contentedly in front of the television or puttering around the kitchen.

No answer.

Maybe she'd fallen asleep.

Her bed was empty, as was mine, the sofa, and the bathroom.

No note, either.

I felt that surging, rolling fear pound in my stomach, my head, down to my toes, and out to my fingers. That thundering anxiety a parent feels when a small child disappears in a crowd or breaks free to run into the street.

I was overreacting. I was jumpy from the tension of this terrible week. Lily was a grown-up and sensible, if slightly irresponsible, young woman who forgot to leave her mother a message.

What's more, I was a silly menopausal hysteric who forgot to check the answering machine.

"Hi, Mama. That was a really nice lunch. Haven't eaten so well since the last time I was home. Haven't had such warm and fuzzy mealtime conversation either. Thanks for both." There she was, just as I might have expected, leaving me a message on my answering machine. She must have forgotten I can't call in for messages.

She went on: "I'm going to beg out of dinner tonight. I hope you don't mind, but I'm not used to such big meals anymore, and I just can't face another one so soon. Besides, this whole dreadful murder is beginning to sink in, and I don't feel very public at the moment. I've steeled myself to go pay my respects to Jeanine. You've convinced me that it's important to keep up appearances, so I'll get that over with. Then I'll probably come home and veg out for the evening. I may see you before you go out, or certainly when you get home after dinner. I hope you don't mind, Mama. I love you."

The next message was mine, telling Lily to meet us at Stephen Wang's. She'd never gotten the message. She'd never come home.

I took a couple of slow, deep breaths and called Jeanine. The phone woke her up.

"Lily? Oh, yes, she came by this afternoon. It was so sweet of her. I told her Laurence loved her as if she were his own child. You know, I always wished I'd had a child." Jeanine's voice was slurred, and her thoughts were wandering. My edge of suspicion caved in to a momentary gush of sympathy. I'd probably get drunk, too, alone at home the night before the funeral of my last family member.

Why was she alone? I tried to find out without blatantly asking her.

"Did you and she have a good talk?" I blathered, not wanting her to know I was alarmed.

"Talk? Oh, yes. We talked of what women always talk of: men," Jeanine said, her voice sliding around the scale. "She remembered so much about Laurence, from the time she was a very little girl. She said he was the only one who could persuade her to taste those things that frighten children. Frogs' legs. And brains. Crayfish."

"Did she stay long?" I worried that Jeanine would be alerted by my abruptness if I came right out and let her know I'd called just to track down Lily.

"Why, yes, we had such a sympathetic talk that we both lost track of the time. I had quite forgotten my appointment with the funeral director until Borden interrupted us. I was so embarrassed that I had not yet gotten Laurence's jacket from his apartment, and Borden had to do it." Jeanine was maddeningly slow, her voice winding down as if she were falling back to sleep.

I lost my patience. "Jeanine, did Lily go with Borden? What time did they leave?"

"Such a sweet girl. Do you remember when Laurence bought her a tiny chef's jacket when she was just a little girl?" She was wandering hope-lessly.

I tried again. "Jeanine, did you notice the time when Lily left? Do you know where she went?"

"Borden was so glad to see her. He said he had been trying to find her everywhere."

"Do you mean he came to your house because he knew Lily was there?" I felt like wrapping that tele-phone cord around somebody's neck.

"Yes, that's exactly right. I had called him about Escoffier." Jeanine seemed to be talking nonsense. Why would she be calling Borden about a 150-year-old chef?

"I think that's what happened. Or maybe he had called me about Escoffier. It doesn't really matter, I suppose. And then he asked me who was with me. I told him Lily, of course. And he said he would come right over to see her. They always were fond of each other, weren't they? Such a lovely girl, so young," Jeanine drifted, mumbling.

"Jeanine, what time did they leave? Where did they go?" I persisted, trying to shake her awake with my voice.

"Borden turned the lights on for me when he left. It had grown so dark, and I was so tired," said Jeanine.

At least that was something. They must have left in the early evening. It was clearly going to be up to me to find out where they'd gone.

"Jeanine, I think you should get some sleep now. I'll see you in the morning." She was continuing to mumble, so I reminded her, "Don't forget to hang up the phone. Good-bye, Jeanine."

Mumble.

"Jeanine, don't forget to hang up the phone."

Click. She didn't forget.

I immediately rang Borden's number. No answer. Not even an answering machine. They could have gone anywhere. I couldn't possibly track them down. What could they have been doing for all these hours? Surely Lily would have called and left another message if she were going to be this late.

I couldn't think. I didn't know what to do next. I didn't know where to call next.

Of course I did. Somebody would know exactly where Borden was: Homer Jones. He'd said the department would keep an eye on Borden.

Fortunately, Homer answered on the first ring. I was so strung out by now that I was pacing the floor in ever-widening circles and had just about pulled my phone line out of the wall.

"Homer, where's Borden?" I didn't bother with hello. I even forgot to tell him who I was.

He knew anyway. "Hey there, Ms. Food Critic. How was dinner?"

"Homer, I don't know where my daughter is, but I know she's with Borden. And she should have been home hours ago." I wasn't quite lying. In my opinion, she not only should have been home hours ago, she should never have been with Borden at all.

"Nothing to worry about, Chas. Stay cool. Borden's right at home. Our boys saw him go in, and his car is still out front. They did tell me he had a woman with him, but the guy isn't dumb enough to hurt anybody in his own apartment," Homer said in the most irritatingly self-confident tone.

"If he's home, why doesn't he answer his phone?" I asked, sitting down to keep myself from yanking this conversation out of the wall.

"Lots of reasons people don't answer the phone. Particularly when there's a member of the opposite sex visiting," Homer said.

"Goddammit, that's my daughter," I exploded. "And you may think he's smart enough not to harm her, but I don't think you're smart enough to trust with my daughter's safety!" I was yelling by now. "I'm going over there right now."

"Hold on a minute, Chas. I'm sorry." That was a new one from Homer. "I was talking out of turn. Look, we've got men right in the neighborhood. I'll send them to the apartment and make sure everything is all right. You just sit tight where you are. Our men can get in there a lot faster than you can."

He had a point. Besides, there were more of them.

For the next five minutes I literally sat tight. I sat on a chair with my hands clenched, my neck muscles taut. I dared not use the phone, but I didn't want to move out of arm's reach of it. Lily had been alone for hours with that lying, cheating—and probably murderous—son of a bitch. Somebody had to get her out of there.

*Bbrrinngg.* I jumped as if I'd never heard a phone ring before.

"Chas, don't get excited, but they're not there. They left the lights on, so the guys who went by didn't realize at first that they'd gone." Homer sounded almost as bad as I was beginning to feel.

"What kind of fucking observation is that?" I screamed into the phone. "How long have they been gone? You've got to find my daughter!"

"Now calm down. That's exactly what we're going to do." The louder I got, the quieter Homer got. "You've got to listen to me. We'll need your help, so you have to simmer down and listen. Yelling won't get her back. You've got to calm down for your daughter's sake."

That got my attention. "What can I do?" My voice was shaking.

"They can't have been gone too long," Homer reassured me. "There was evidence that they'd eaten dinner at Borden's place."

"Poison? Could he have poisoned her?" I cut in, my voice rising again. By now I was huddled in my chair, wishing I had a blanket to wrap around me. I felt so cold.

"No, I'm sure he didn't poison her. Nobody poisons someone and leaves the dirty dishes in the sink. There are no signs that it was anything but a friendly get-together. Hold on a minute. That's my other phone."

Homer left me hanging, and to keep from exploding I began to make a list. I had to feel I was doing something. I began to write down places they might have gone, people who might know where they were.

Homer returned. "We've determined that they're not at Laurence's restaurant. That's been locked since the murder, and nothing's been tampered with there. We've got men checking the neighborhood bars. They wouldn't be at another restaurant, since they've already eaten. And they're probably on foot, because Borden's car is still there. We'll give the neighborhood a thorough going-over. I promise I'll keep in close touch, so you just stay there in case she calls home or shows up. And don't worry."

Those were two orders I was going to ignore. What kind of guy expects a mother not to worry? And did Homer really think I could just sit quietly in my apartment, waiting for the Keystone Kops to fumble around until they found my daughter?

"Just as you say, Homer," I lied.

This time when I left my house I had the code for retrieving my answering machine messages. Lily might just call in. Or Homer might actually come up with something.

I was out the door and tapping my feet nervously in the elevator, as if my impatience could make it go faster, when I realized that I had no idea where to go. I'd have to trust to instinct.

Outside, I started walking toward Borden's apartment. Then I turned back in indecision. I didn't want to encounter one of Homer's cops. For lack of any better idea, I headed for Laurence's restaurant. Maybe those incompetents had missed something there.

Impatient as I was, I didn't want to run. That might attract attention, and I'd be out of steam too fast. I didn't want to take a taxi because I needed to feel I was combing the neighborhood on the way. So I walked at about double my normal pace, my feet practically flying off the ground. I was panting by the time I reached the restaurant.

One look made my heart fall with a thud somewhere in the vicinity of my stomach. Homer was right. Nobody had been there for days. Mail and debris had piled up at the front entrance, so soggy by now that the door couldn't have been opened without disturbing the muck. I walked around the block to the alley and the rear entrance. Spilled garbage had crusted across the doorway. No footprints, no sign of anything having budged there for days.

It took all the will I could muster not to sit down amid the grime and cry. I had to go on.

"I'll find her," I told myself.

"Yeah, but in time?" I answered back.

"Yes, in time. I'm her mother. Besides, Lily's a smart girl. She knows all about Borden, and she wouldn't have walked into the situation blindly."

"Oh, shut up and do something."

I'd been walking without noticing where I was going. Some kind of sleuth. I figured I'd better give up and go home, but first I wanted to call Homer to see what he'd come up with.

I looked up at the dark sky and wished on the first star I saw—it was too late to play the game right, so I decided that in a pinch, any old star would do. Then I looked around me. I was on Massachusetts Avenue, just half a block from Laurence's apartment. I'd taken the same route he'd taken every night going home from work. For a moment my worry over Lily was drowned out in a flood of sadness. I had a lot more tears waiting to be shed over Laurence.

I knew there was a pay phone on his corner. Maybe Homer would have some news.

No late-night businesses light up this part of town. The people who live here do so behind closed curtains. And tonight there was no traffic at all on the avenue. Washington at night can be so silent that you'd never guess it was a world capital.

Murder capital, yes.

Out of habit I watched the side streets and bushes for signs of potential muggers. I even stepped onto the scrubby grass alongside Laurence's building and peered into the yard that runs between the two adjacent apartment buildings. I don't know why. Maybe to feel safe enough to stop and use the outdoor phone. Or more likely because I was busying myself, reluctant to give up and go home.

In retrospect, I'd call it intuition.

From the narrow passageway between the buildings I could see that Laurence's kitchen window was lit. Somebody was up there. The lights hadn't been on when I'd been there with Jeanine, I was sure. It had been daytime. And she obviously hadn't been by this evening to accidentally leave them burning. Something was wrong.

Okay, maybe I was exaggerating. The lights could have been left on yesterday, I reminded myself. Or the police could be looking around again—though why Homer wouldn't have told me, I couldn't imagine.

"God, I wish I knew," I almost said out loud.

I didn't need to.

Lily appeared in the window, hands above her head as if to ward off blows, her forehead pressed against the glass. She looked utterly slumped. But she was still alive.

"Lily!" I shouted, though of course she couldn't hear me.

I should have called for help, I know. But I couldn't stop. I had to get up there before anything worse happened to Lily.

Not that I knew how to get in.

I stood at the door, frantically trying to come up with some idea. I certainly didn't want to ring the bell and warn Borden.

I used to have a key to this door. That was a decade ago, but facts didn't stop me from rooting around in my purse in some hopeless attempt to conjure up that old key. I felt around the bottom, unzipped pockets, tried every one of the keys on my ring.

"God, I wish I could find it."

This time I did say it out loud.

A shadowy, half-lit face loomed above me, attached to a tall body in a black leather jacket slashed all over by silver zippers. I automatically jumped half a step backward, slamming my purse shut and clutching it to my chest. His hand reached out and grabbed my arm.

"Be careful, you'll fall," he said. "Do you need help?"

"I . . . I . . . I . . ." Too many scares tonight. I could no longer even spit out a simple sentence.

"You've lost your keys?" He spoke for me. Now that he was fully in the light, I could see that he was a dark, skinny young man, his face pocked with acne and more unsure than mine. The only sinister thing about him was his jacket. And that was plastic.

Even so, I still could do nothing but nod.

"Hey," he continued sympathetically, probably having been a stammerer himself on occasion, "I live next door. My uncle's the super here. I know he's a pain in the ass when people forget their keys. But you can't just stand out here."

I shook my head. At this point I figured it was better to continue as a mute.

"Happens a lot, huh?"

I nodded.

"Okay, I got ya. I'll do it for you." He reached past me and pressed the superintendent's button.

"Yeah?" a voice growled through the speaker.

"Hey, Uncle Stan, it's me. Benny. We got some letters in my building that belong to your building. I just figured I'd bring them by." This quick-thinking young man shrugged his shoulders and gave me a sheepish grin as he glibly told his lie.

"Fuck, Benny, it's practically the middle of the night," grumbled the disembodied voice.

"Sorry, Unc. Didn't get home till late. Just buzz me in and I'll take care of it. Good night, Unc," Benny said, placating the voice.

"Yeah. Good night." The voice sounded more irritated than grateful, but it was accompanied by a buzz.

Benny pushed open the door with his shoulder and held it for me, sweeping his arm toward it and ushering me in with a little bow. "Have a nice evening," he said and disappeared as soon as I was safely inside.

I pounded on Laurence's door. Lily opened it.

"Mama! What are you doing here?" She looked a mess. Nothing bloody, nothing that I could see broken, but her face looked ravaged.

"Lily, you didn't call," I blurted in that age-old guilt-provoking motherly fashion. Get right to the heart of things—not "Are you hurt?" or "What did Borden do to you?" or even "Did you get any evidence?" but right to the complaint that my daughter hadn't called me.

"I'm really sorry, Mama. Once we started talking, I totally forgot about the time." As Lily said this, she took my arm and urged me inside. There at the table was Borden, motionless, his head cradled in his arms. At first I thought he might be dead, but he gave a little hiccup. And another. The kind that children get when they've cried themselves dry.

I turned back to Lily. Now I realized that what I saw on her face was not pain or fear but a mirror of Borden's despair.

Borden looked up at me, but didn't focus. His eyes roved until they settled on Lily's face. "I can't bear to let him go," he said, his voice so hoarse that it came out as a half whisper.

Lily sat down beside him and stroked his hair, suddenly looking older than Borden. She was the mother, he the child. She didn't say anything, but I could see from her look that she considered Borden a mourner, not a murderer.

I didn't yet know what had changed her mind, but looking at Borden I could imagine why she was feeling sympathetic. I sat down next to Lily and pored over Borden's face as he gradually came back to life.

"We came back here to get Laurence's Escoffier." Lily slowly, with obvious fatigue dragging at her mouth and the corners of her eyes, began to tell me about the evening—at least the last leg of it.

"Jeanine wanted the book to be buried with him." Borden had roused himself enough to enter the conversation.

"So that's what Jeanine was babbling about— Escoffier the book, not Escoffier the man," I blurted out, sounding as dotty as Jeanine had.

Lily watched me quizzically, but went on anyway. "We'd gone back to Borden's apartment because we wanted to talk and because Borden couldn't handle being in public." With that, Lily shot me a guilty glance and shrugged her shoulders, which I took to mean that she knew she shouldn't have trusted him at that point and had knowingly put herself in danger.

But it had worked out all right, and Lily looked as if the evening had been punishment enough. I reached over and stroked her cheek, which only served to start fresh tears coursing down it.

Borden didn't seem to catch our undercurrents. He obviously didn't know that Lily and I suspected him of murder—or at least that I did and Lily had. Even so, he went on to explain himself to me. "I hadn't been able to talk to anyone, Chas. At first I felt so angry at Laurence for dying and leaving me in the lurch. And I also felt so guilty."

The hand stroking Lily's cheek stopped cold. "Guilty?" I shot Lily a questioning glance.

Borden continued, "Well, not as if I'd murdered him. But I felt I had hurt him."

"We talked about Borden taking kickbacks," Lily interceded, trying to build a quick bridge between his confession and what I already knew.

"I guess I didn't really think of it as kickbacks, at least until Laurence died. I just considered it—I don't know—little favors. Or friendly gifts. Or sharing the wealth. Everyone does it, you know."

I reminded myself not to confuse candor with innocence, and even if I might eventually accept the fact that Borden was innocent of murder, I wouldn't declare him innocent of everything. Still, I restrained myself from voicing my judgment. Borden wasn't asking for my opinion anyway.

"Chas, ours was a complicated relationship," Borden said, continuing his case. "I owed Laurence everything, yet I was jealous of him. He knew it, and sometimes that spurred him on to make me more jealous."

So far, it was the Laurence I knew.

Borden paused for a long, thoughtful breath and stared at his hands as if he had his notes written on them. "What made it worse was Jeanine." He stopped short, confused. "No, I don't mean that Jeanine made it worse. I mean that the attraction between Jeanine and me made it worse. For a time I thought I loved her. But eventually I realized that that was just some weird way of being closer to Laurence. Like wanting to be part of his family, as crazy as that sounds."

Borden put his head in his hands again, until he pulled himself together. He looked up and went on, "Instead, I became his rival."

He hiccuped. "I couldn't stand what my affair with Jeanine was doing to the three of us. By the end I was only using Jeanine, and she was doing the same with me." For a moment a sheepish smirk crept across his face. "Jeanine's the one who put an end to it. She convinced me that we would do better as friends."

Only Jeanine could pull that off. If I had three lifetimes I'd never learn how to handle men the way she could. How had she managed to turn rejection into a choice of friendship over passion?

By now I needed a drink, even if they didn't. Two nights in a row I'd been cleaning up the debris of Laurence's relationships. I was being worn down by everyone else's troubles and didn't even have time for my own.

I surely creaked as I dragged myself out of the chair. I couldn't face calvados. Laurence had kept his Campari in the kitchen. That was what I needed to settle my stomach as well as my nerves.

I no longer remembered which cabinet held the aperitifs. I started searching. The third cabinet stopped me short. Cinzano, Lillet, and Punt e Mes were lined up, not quite blocking the view of a familiar bottle of pale green liquid.

"Mama, I'm exhausted," Lily said from the other room. "Maybe we should all go home."

"Mmmm," I answered. I slid the other bottles aside and took a good look at the green one, almost afraid to touch it.

"You didn't drive, did you?" Lily continued.

"No," I answered absently. I turned the bottle, searching for a label that wasn't there, then lifted it out. The liquid had separated into layers, which smoothed into an even green when I shook it. Here was Ari's secret essence in Laurence's kitchen; clearly, it was stolen.

"I'll walk you both home," said Borden.

Moments of my dinner at Stephen Wang's flashed through my head. I was searching for a memory. What was I looking for? Dumplings. Slippery dumplings, made from those glossy rice-and-wheat noodles that Stephen had said were from an ancient recipe. Now I know where I had tasted them before: Hong Kong.

When Ari and I had lived there soon after we were married, he'd begun experimenting with Chinese noodle doughs late into the night and again each morning. He was trying to recapture the old formula for nearly transparent noodles. He'd loved the idea of creating pictures between the thinnest sheets of dough.

Pictures. Patterns. Omigod!

Quilts.

Ari had continued his dough experiments in Paris, but I wasn't paying much attention by then. Obviously Laurence was. The wonder was that in all those years since Ari and I had been in Paris I had never once made the connection between Ari's Chinese dough and Laurence's quilts. And now it seemed so blatant. That slick, glossy texture from the rice flour, the suppleness from the wheat, the very idea of using dough as a clear wrapper for the picture within.

Ari must have been enraged when Laurence stole his idea and used it to nourish his career. Yet Ari never let it show—not to anyone. At least not to me. He'd somehow managed anyway to maintain a lifelong friendship with Laurence. So I'd believed. Maybe I wasn't as accurate an observer as I'd thought.

I uncapped the bottle of green liquid and, thumb over the mouth, shook it again. I licked my thumb. It was Ari's retirement.

"Mama, what are you doing there? Didn't you hear me?" Lily's voice had a quarrelsome edge.

I felt afraid for her, even more afraid than when I'd thought she was in danger from Borden. She'd take almost any physical pain more easily than the pain of losing her father.

I'd been wrong about Bebe. Maybe even about Borden. I wouldn't make the same mistake with Ari. I was going to keep my suspicions to myself this time.

"Mama!"

I jumped as Lily put her hand on my shoulder.

"I'm sorry, sweetie. I was thinking about Laurence," I said as I quickly put the bottle back on the shelf.

"We're ready to go," she repeated. "Borden wants to walk us home."

That brought me to my senses. Borden would walk right into a police alert if I didn't do something right away. "Just let me stop in the bathroom first," I told Lily, and strode into Laurence's bedroom.

I washed my face and flushed the toilet in the bathroom at the far end, then used the bedside phone to call Homer. I didn't tell him much, just that I'd found Lily safe and sound, and that Borden hadn't revealed anything of obvious importance to the case. He told me, in an exasperated voice, to get a good night's sleep.

# fifteen

The sky was metallic Thursday morning as the
stream of cars passed CIA headquarters on
the Virginia side of the Potomac, and turned
off Georgetown Pike to Saint Luke Catholic Church.
Its slim triangular tower, cut at an angle like a
baguette, showed six bells to the passersby, and on
each side a plain, spare iron cross.

Mourners filled the parking lot beneath the leaf-
less sycamores. The only sounds were the soft hums
of motors and the closing of car doors as Laurence's
friends and enemies, backers and suppliers, colleagues and groupies mutely crossed to the entrance. Even the television cameras kept a discreet
and quiet distance in a rare show of respect.

At first glance the lawn might have looked
snowy, though the day was dry. The greenery was
peeking through a sea of white. An ever-growing
group of chefs had spontaneously gathered there to
whisper and smoke after paying their respects to
Jeanine, Bebe, and Borden in the church. The chefs

had left their coats—along with their wives and girl-friends—inside, and had flocked outdoors in just their white jackets, spotlessly clean, stiffly starched and buttoned up the side, right to the neck.

Every chef wore a hat. The French chefs wore tall toques. The Italians' white hats were soft and floppy, like brioches left to rise too long. The Americans wore baseball caps, brims turned to the back.

I wouldn't have joined this group, being neither a man nor a chef, but as Lily and I reached the sidewalk Marcel hurried over to greet us and tucked my arm in his, so I couldn't gracefully escape. Lily was quicker than I, and stayed out of Marcel's reach.

"You go on with Marcel, Mama. I'd rather meet you inside," she whispered to me, then turned to give Marcel a fleeting kiss and a good-bye.

I was surprised that she didn't stop to greet her father—it was as if she were acting out my secret reluctance. Then I realized what she was hurrying after: I saw Brian in the open doorway. Lily probably hadn't even noticed Ari in the crowd of chefs.

As for me, while I dreaded having to face Ari, I was also perversely curious to see if he looked different to me today. I felt sheltered from any danger by this familiar group, as well as relieved to postpone offering Jeanine condolences with all the voyeurs standing by to gather details for future gossip.

Marcel, looking as if he'd aged a dozen more years since yesterday, kept me clamped firmly in his grasp. He seemed to need a crutch, and, at the moment, I was the best substitute he could find.

The chefs' buzz was not about Laurence. This was a funeral, but the subject was the same as it is with chefs anywhere: money. The outside world assumes chefs constantly talk of food, of techniques, of ingredients. That's only true for the very young and naive. Seasoned chefs talk unceasingly of financial things—of profit, of price increases. Oh, they talk football, too, but even much of that discussion is about who bet how much in the pools and how many bucks the last winner got.

I, of course, am an unreliable reporter. I hear that when I'm not around they talk about sex. In French.


For a few minutes I was able to pretend I hadn't seen Ari, since he was in heated conversation with an enormous chef whose girth blocked Ari's view of me. I'd pay my respects to Paul Prudhomme later. I nodded to Michel Richard and Jean Joho behind them, then to Wolfgang Puck, who had just joined Jacques Pepin. But I couldn't leave Marcel yet, so I stood with him on the fringes of a group that was figuring how much Borden and Jeanine were losing by keeping the restaurant closed for the week.

"They can't afford a Saturday night," one said.

"It's not just the loss of revenue," another suggested; "they can't afford to let the public wonder for too long whether Borden can carry the kitchen."

One of the younger chefs started a side conversation with, "What's going to happen to the New York—"

He was cut off by a poke in the ribs and a side-long glance at Marcel, who looked as if he were trying to listen to the two conversations at once.

I had no patience for this; the grief that awaited indoors would be less crass. "I've got to go see Jeanine," I whispered to Marcel.

"Mmm? Oh, yes, *chérie*. Marie Claire is with her." Marcel's mind was elsewhere, so I easily made my escape.

Almost.

"I've been looking for you, Chas," Ari said, startling me as he came from behind. Somehow he had circled from the far end of the crowd without my noticing. And his voice was not only unexpected, it was menacing.

"There you are. I wondered where you were," I tried to respond normally, sounding like a fake to my own ears. I couldn't face a friendly kiss from Ari at the moment, so I ducked my head and started rooting through my purse as if I were in desperate need of a handkerchief.

"Chas, I have something to ask you," Ari said. I hoped he hadn't sensed my frostiness.

"Sure," I squeaked.

"I need your help. I need you to keep a secret." His voice had dropped.

I finally met his eyes, and was shocked. They looked exactly the same as always, a shadowy far-away gray and crinkly at the corners, as if he were squinting at distant thoughts. I'd expected them to look like the eyes of a killer. Hard and mean. Scary.

And now here he was, the Ari about whom the worst I'd ever been able to say was that he was frustrating or exasperating. In his presence I couldn't bear to think of him as a murderer.

"A secret?" I squeaked.

Not much of one. It was only that Ari wanted me to keep quiet about his new essences.

I headed into the sanctuary, looking neither right nor left. I didn't want anyone to divert me now that I was steeled to pay my respects to Jeanine.

If I was steeled, she was armored. Jeanine was wearing designer battle wear—stiff shoulder pads, tight waist, fabric that look as if a bullet wouldn't pierce it, all in black right down to the faint smudge of eyeliner across one cheek. She sat under the watchful eyes of Marie Claire, who stood behind with her hands on Jeanine's shoulders, patting them every once in a while like one might absently pet a cat. Marie Claire turned a sad, sympathetic glance my way and threw me a silent kiss. At Jeanine's side was Maguy Le Coze, whose brother—and partner in her New York and Miami restaurants—had died just a couple of years ago of a heart attack. She was someone who could truly offer Jeanine comfort, I thought as I caught Maguy's eye and mouthed a greeting.

Jeanine, a crowd jockeying in position to extend her their condolences, looked composed, but was answering questions one beat behind, as if she had to have them transmitted a long distance. I couldn't think of anything worthwhile to say, but it didn't matter because Jeanine wasn't absorbing much.

Borden was worse. He didn't even make a pretense of responding. He had disappeared into someplace far inside. Bebe clearly wished she could do the same thing, but instead was greeting people and commiserating with them over their loss of her fiancé. She grabbed my hands with both of hers and lifted her face to kiss my cheek.

"Oh, Chas, I'll never be able to thank you enough," she whispered as she did. "I would be in such trouble without you."

"You'll be just fine," I reassured her. "You have a lot of life ahead of you." I felt inane. Sometimes I wish I could write out my conversations and edit the clichés before they pop out for public consumption. I think my fingers are smarter than my mouth.

Bebe didn't seem to notice. She just smiled at me, bittersweet and beautiful. "I'll never forget what you did for me. And Lily, too. I won't often find women like you two."

That was the cue I'd been waiting for. "Have you seen Lily?"

"Yes, she was with some handsome guy. I think they went to find a seat," Bebe said, nodding her head in the direction of the main chapel.

Sure enough, Lily was already seated and saving a place for me. But by now she wasn't with just a handsome guy, she had two. Brian was guarding Lily on the left, and Paul was on her right.

Paul the romantic. He'd quickly sized up the situation and was playing cupid by weaving connections between Lily and Brian. "I remember when Lily was reading Molière and Batman comics at the same time," Paul said, testing the waters as he addressed Brian. "Do you read French?"

"Yes, but I'm a Spiderman guy, myself," Brian responded to Paul, but kept searching Lily's face to see how she was taking his answers. From the content look in Lily's eyes I concluded that they'd already found common ground in music, movies, and wine vintages.

"Chas!" Paul leaped up to usher me into the pew. "Do you know that these two young people have both backpacked in the Alps and prefer Mozart to Haydn!"

Who wouldn't, I thought. Let's see how identical they feel about universal health care. Paul the Matchmaker knew just what to avoid. As I slid in next to Lily, I scoured Paul's face for guilt, hypocrisy, fear, or any other emotion that might seem compatible with being an accomplice to murder.

None. Paul looked relaxed and innocent.

Even after Ari joined us, meeting Lily's enthusiastic hug with a passivity I knew well, Paul seemed his usual comfortable self. For the first time, it occurred to me that maybe he didn't know. Of course. He'd been away in Pennsylvania when Laurence was murdered. He couldn't have kept track of Ari's activities. Maybe Paul didn't just look innocent, but actually was innocent

The first notes of the organ broke my reverie. The

Mass was beginning. My eyes leapt to the casket, and the dreadful reality began to sink in. Laurence was gone. Really gone. Forever gone.

I don't remember a thing about the ride to the cemetery. I have the sense that it began my true mourning for Laurence. And since I stood by the grave with Lily on one side and Ari on the other, I must conclude that we all went together.

Fortunately the ceremony was brief. Jeanine's stony silence couldn't have lasted much longer, and I didn't want to be around when it broke. Borden was at her side, standing within an inch of her but not touching her. Bebe, recently so central to Laurence's life, had been shunted to the edge of the crowd, and looked lost. Marcel seemed about to topple, held upright by Marie Claire.

I'd forgotten about Homer. Surely I'd seen enough *Columbo* shows to know that he would be at the cemetery, watching for the murderer to drop some clue. But I'd never had to connect TV mysteries to real life before. There he was, standing apart from the mourners, positioned so they would all have to pass him on the way to their cars. Of course Homer wasn't wearing a rumpled trench coat like a fictional detective. He had a golden-brown leather one that looked soft enough to melt under a strong sun.

At the moment his eyes were fixed on Borden. With a start, I realized that, as far as Homer knew, Borden was still the prime suspect. Did I want to suggest otherwise to him?

Not yet. Maybe not ever. I needed time to think it through. So for once, instead of seeking out Homer, I avoided him. As I walked back to the car I kept to the far side, with plenty of people between me and the detective. He didn't look happy about it.

# sixteen

The restaurant business demands enormous fealty. It imposes schedules on its servants that set them apart from the civilian population. Restaurant workers are night people. Chefs in particular eat long past the hour when normal people have gone to bed. They wake up when nearly everyone else has been at work for hours. Their moments for relaxing are not anywhere near those prime-time hours the entertainment industry fills with sitcoms and football. Their break is in mid-afternoon, between late lunch and early dinner.

Restaurants are like newborn infants. They require constant attention. Weekends, holidays—when everyone else is playing, that's exactly when cooks and waiters are working their hardest.

Even more important, a restaurant cannot tolerate excuses. Illness? An emergency? Sorry, but the reservations are already booked, the food will not stay fresh, the revenue will be lost forever. Like the show that must go on, like the mailman who must deliver through snow and sleet, the restaurant must feed its customers and its creditors.

So Laurence's memorial gathering did not immediately follow the funeral, but would come only after a pause in which the workers who feed Washington would go back to their kitchens and dining rooms for the lunch and dinner services. Late Thursday night the mourners would come together once again, bringing platters and chafing dishes of food, bottles of wine and beer, to celebrate Laurence's life at the restaurant of his no longer future partner Marcel.

Since the cemetery was in Virginia and the funeral was over before noon, I decided to be efficient and test out a suburban restaurant at lunch. It would take my mind off the murder, and surely in an out-of-the-way place where I wasn't known, I could eat safely.

The hostess at Mamma Maria's didn't glance our way once during the five minutes Lily and I stood in the entry hall listening to her telephone argument with somebody she kept calling "sweetheart." Finally she hung up and turned to us without apology. "Two?"

At least she could count.

She seated us in a narrow red leatherette booth and handed us menus without another word. Lily looked irritated and puzzled. "A dozen readers called and wrote to tell me about this place," I said defensively. I always feel responsible and apologetic when I take people to a disappointing restaurant (which is most of the time). I tell myself that I shouldn't feel guilty. After all, being the restaurant critic means that I don't have a critic's advice to go on, so how am I to know? But I worry that my friends think I intentionally save the good restaurants for someone else.

"The people who recommended this must have been the owner's relatives," Lily said. "Or creditors." Then she saw how flustered she was making me. "Oh, don't worry about it, Mama. I'm not really hungry anyway."

I was. And I was thirsty. Since nobody showed any sign of voluntarily approaching our table, I waved over a waiter.

"Yes?" He looked at me as if I'd interrupted an important train of thought.

"We'd like to order some wine," I said.

"White or red?" the waiter asked without looking up.

"Don't you have a list?" I asked.

"No, we've just got white or red." He was still looking down, with pencil poised.

I started to ask him what kind of red, but thought better of it. "Red," I said.

"Ditto," Lily said.

The waiter said nothing, just walked off.

I opened the menu and saw that it was identical, even to the typeface, to three other Italian restaurants I knew. I could have listed its dishes without looking: fried calamari, mozzarella and tomato salad with fresh basil (tomatoes in midwinter? hah!), clams casino, minestrone. A half-dozen pastas with probably identical tomato sauces, fettuccine Alfredo for sure.

The special of the day was a big platter of all the seafood in the house—calamari, clams, lobster, and shrimp—with tomato sauce, served over pasta, at a bargain price. Business must have been slow this week, and the chef wanted to get rid of all the tired shellfish before the weekend delivery. The tomato sauce would drown out any suspiciously muddy flavors.

"I'll just have a salad," Lily said. I started to argue with her, since a salad wouldn't help my review much, but I didn't have the heart. Not when the restaurant seemed so unpromising.

"I'm going to get the special." I must have said it with an air of resignation.

"Oh, Mama, you know it's going to be awful."

"Yes, it probably will be," I agreed. "But I don't want to waste a visit by not making sure."

The wine didn't raise any hopes. Red was an exaggeration. Our glasses of wine looked more brown. A little oil, and they'd be salad dressing. The slices of lemon floating in our water glasses had brown edges to match the wine. And so did Lily's iceberg lettuce salad.

"A theme restaurant," Lily said as she unearthed bits of brown-edged carrots and cucumbers in her salad.

The waiter plunked down my platter of seafood and pasta, a mountain of food that looked as if it were meant for one of the large round tables for six. Given my forced restraint after the poisoned chocolates, I thought the portion was just about right. "Will there be anything else?" he asked, then turned and left before we could answer.

Lily and I rooted through the pasta's thick red sauce to find curled up halves of lobster tail no big-

ger than jumbo shrimp, far more shell than meat.
The clams, on the other hand, were large enough to
need a knife and fork—if one had a knife sharp
enough to pierce these tough bivalves. We each tried
one, and kept chewing it, like gum, as we turned our
conversation to more interesting subjects.

"Mama, with all that's been going on this week,
I've never gotten around to asking you something."

Uh-oh. My mind began quickly searching through
possibilities. In the meantime, I gave a noncommit-
tal, "Hmmm?"

"Who's the friend you were with when you called
me Monday night?" Lily stretched out along her side
of the booth, having given up on lunch, with a faint
mischievous twitch to her mouth.

"Monday?"

"You know, when you called to tell me about
Laurence. You weren't home, and you said you had a
friend you wanted to tell me about. What's going on?
You got a new guy?" Lily didn't look challenging, she
looked eager.

"You don't mind the idea of my having a new guy?"
I stopped digging and nibbling the red lava flow on
my plate and gave her my full attention. After the sexual confusion of my divorce and Ari's moving in with
Paul, Lily had been so upset by my dating that I was
extremely cautious about mentioning men I was seeing. I figured she'd let me know when she was ready
to hear more. Only lately had she begun to ask about
my social life. I took it as a good sign, that she was
feeling more comfortable altogether about men.

"Mind? Why would I mind? You think I still have

fantasies of you and Dad getting back together? No, it would be a relief to know that you weren't lonely. And not to worry about your needing me when I'm too far away to be much company for you."

In some vague way I knew Lily worried about me, just as we worry about anybody we love. But it hadn't occurred to me that she worried that I was lonely. "You know I have plenty of friends," I started to protest.

She interrupted. "I don't mean just friends. Lovers. A guy. That's what I worry about."

"You're worried for me? Not for yourself?" I was probing a sensitive area.

"Sure I wish I had a guy. But wishing and worrying are different matters. Besides, I've got plenty of time," Lily said, taking another sip of her wine, then looking as if she wished she hadn't.

Vinegar or not, I needed mine. I swallowed half of what remained in my glass and mentally blocked my nasal passages, concentrating on swallowing it without tasting it. "Hey, thanks for the compliment," I said sarcastically.

That made Lily realize how insulting she'd sounded. "I didn't mean it so negatively. You're not over the hill. I'm sorry I put it that way. But you've got to admit that there are more men around the corner at my age than at yours."

She was right, of course. And we were wandering off the point. It was enough to know that Lily would welcome rather than be jealous of my having a man in my life. "As it turns out, I do have a guy. Sort of."

Lily leaned forward with both elbows on the table

and smiled like a kid with a present to open. "I knew it! Tell me!"

"Well, it's a little complicated."

"The best ones always are," Lily said in a conspiratorial girl-to-girl voice.

So I told her about Dave, about how sweet he was to me, and how reassuring. I told her about how he hated restaurants with awnings and doormen, or even with wine lists.

"He'd be happy here," Lily said, then chuckled.

She was right. I also told her how sexy he was, and how he seemed to be a magnet for every female in, or out, of the newsroom. Lily uttered an occasional knowing "Umm-hmm."

Then I talked about the secrecy. Nobody knew we were seeing each other, not even Sherele.

"That doesn't sound good, Mama. This is a guy seriously afraid of commitment."

"No, not he. Me." The words had a hard time coming out of my mouth. "I'm the one keeping it a secret. I just can't stand the idea of everyone in the newsroom smirking behind my back and gossiping about me being another of Dave's short-lived conquests."

"Short-lived?" Lily contracted her eyebrows in a puzzled expression. "Sounds as if it's been going on for a while. How many weeks have you two been seeing each other?"

Now I felt really embarrassed to admit how long I'd been keeping this secret from her. But I didn't want to openly lie. "Something over a year," I fudged.

"A year!"

Good thing I'd softened the blow.

"Mama, you listen to me. This is not about a little newsroom tittering. This is something more. This is about not yet having lived down the humiliation of being married to a homosexual."

Lily's arrows always shot straight. This one appeared to be two-headed. She drank her entire glass of wine.

She wasn't done with me, though. "It's been ten years, Mama. And look what's happened. You have a wonderful career. The city is full of people who won't take a bite of food until you approve of it. And even your enemies grudgingly admire you."

She was getting a little carried away, but I wasn't about to stop her.

"As for the old divorce gossip, that ran dry probably nine and a half years ago. And you and Daddy are good friends now."

That brought a lump to my throat and a wrenching to my gut. For an hour now I had suppressed the thought that Ari might be a murderer.

Lily didn't notice any change in me, so she went on. "If this guy has had a million, even two million women before, so what? Right now he's with you. And he's been with you long enough to show you that's pretty important to him, right?"

I nodded.

"And he's been faithful to you so far, right?"

I nodded again, but with less vigor. Until lunchtime two days ago, I'd thought he'd been faithful.

Lily went on. "Nobody can predict the future. Sure, he might leave you. Or you might leave him. One of you might die."

Ahh, my romantic daughter.

"Love is for right now. And if the time comes that it doesn't go on, you just pick yourself up and work the next room." End of lecture.

I was tongue-tied for a minute. We both sat silently, lost in thought.

"Are you going to be able to do that?" I said as I reached for Lily's hand. I knew she was thinking of Borden, who had been her lopsided love for all her adult life.

The melancholy Lily gave way to the tough, resilient Lily. She squeezed my hand and lifted her chin. "Why not? I'm your daughter."

"Then I'd better behave like a proper role model. Want to come out to dinner with Dave and me before the memorial tonight?" I asked. And while she nodded vigorously, I added, "If I can get him to put on a tie."

Mother and daughter, best friends as well, we left the restaurant arm in arm, happy to be in each other's company.

In the parking lot, Lily looked alarmed. "You forgot to steal the menu," she said.

"No I didn't. I just figured that I'd leave the restaurant in peace. No point taking up twenty-five inches of space to tell umpteen thousand people not to go to a restaurant they've never heard of anyway."

"If the chef only knew," Lily said, climbing into the car.

As I was pulling out of the driveway, Lily slammed her fist on the dashboard and said, "Oh, shit, I forgot."

I slammed on the brakes. "Do we need to go back?"

"No," she said. "That's not it. I'm so tired I don't know what day it is. I made a date to meet Brian at Cashion's Eat Place for dinner tonight. And it's probably too late to call him at the restaurant to postpone it. I guess I won't be able to meet Dave yet. Will you hang on to him long enough for me to get a rain check?"

Lily planned to spend the afternoon sleeping ("I don't know how you do it, Mama," she'd praised my going on to work) and reading. "Have you got any good books in the apartment?" she asked as she dropped me off at the *Examiner*.

"I've finished the new Sue Grafton—*N*, I think, or maybe *P*," I suggested. The only advantage in a failing memory is that I can sometimes get two reads out of a novel before I realize I've been through it already. Twice the value, I figure.

"A mystery, I suppose," sneered Lily. "I don't know how you can bear to waste your time with that junk."

An old argument. We both took comfort in settling into well-worn roles.

## seventeen

The protesters in front of the *Examiner* today looked so clean-cut and agreeable, I could have believed they were here to compliment the paper rather than complain about an editorial last Sunday. I ignored their signs as I picked my way through the gathering, preferring to imagine that they'd painted such messages as "*Examiner*: E for Excellent" and "Citizens for Giving Wheatley a Raise."

The newsroom had settled into its quiet post-lunch drone, most of the reporters on the phone, tracking down sources and pinning down details before they launched into frantic deadline writing. A few nodded or twiddled a pencil in my direction but, at the moment, nobody seemed available for chatting. Even more disappointing, Sherele's desk looked as if it had been straightened up for the end of the day. She must have gone off to do an interview for her Sunday feature.

I took one look at the stack of mail, the packages, the faxes, the notices, the messages, and the newspapers on my desk and wished I had an interview to escape to. And that was only the visible log-jam; I hadn't yet checked the volume of traffic on my E-mail or voice mail.

I slumped into my chair and tried to figure out where to start. My mind wandered back to the funeral and, like letting go of a stretched rubber band, it returned me right to what I'd been pushing to the back of my mind with exhausting persistence. Ari the murderer. The possibility was too sad, too overwhelming.

And it wasn't my business, I reminded myself, putting my head on my desk for just a moment. I wasn't a police detective. Nobody deemed it my job to solve Laurence's murder. If I had my own twisted suspicions, probably overreactions to flimsy evidence, I'd just better keep them to myself. I shouldn't be trying to wear Homer Jones's shoes.

"Chas?" A woman's voice startled me. "Are you all right?"

"Huh?" I had dozed off. I lifted my head from my desk and shook it to clear the cobwebs.

"The restaurant critic syndrome. Too much wine at lunch, right?" It was Dawn. Her voice sounded sympathetic.

"Oh, hi, Dawn," I said, not projecting the image of the hotshot professional I wanted to convey.

But my napping hadn't led Dawn to write me off as a doddering, dozing old-timer unworthy of her concern. She pulled out Sherele's chair and settled in, swiveling to face me.

She, too, looked exhausted. She leaned back and stretched her legs out, resting them on the edge of Sherele's wastebasket.

"They sure do keep you on the go here," she said. "I thought I was working hard in Orange County. How're you doing?" She took a long survey of my face. "I heard that the chef who died was a friend of yours, and I wanted to tell you I'm sorry. I had a good friend die last year, and nobody knows what that's like until it hits you firsthand."

"Thanks," I said, belatedly warming to her. Reporters get to be a crusty bunch, usually leaving the soft-hearted things unsaid in their competition to be the most hardened observer of the world scene. Newcomers like Dawn take time to learn how cool they're expected to be, so it's sometimes nice to be around them before the scar tissue develops.

This unexpected invitation to unburden myself caught me at a vulnerable moment. With Dawn's gentle encouragement, I told her about my relationship with Laurence, those beautiful days so long ago. It felt good to talk about them.

"I once had a guy like that," she said, taking off her shoes and rubbing her stockinged feet. "Part mentor and part lover."

"Most of the lover part was fantasy for us," I corrected. "But it was the kind of relationship you don't forget."

"Don't I know it. For me, every guy since that first one has been nothing more than a roll in the hay. Sometimes I think my life is never going to be more than one-night stands, and I know it's my doing, not theirs."

It took me aback that Dawn and I had quickly slipped into such intimacy. She must be lonely, having recently moved here. Yet her revelations made me a little uncomfortable, because I wasn't ready to make her my confidante in return. So I changed the subject. "What are you working on?"

"It's that thing I was talking about in the cafeteria when I met you, the leak I got from the congressman," Dawn said, sitting up straight and swinging her feet to the floor. Talking about work brought life and color back into her face. "I found another source. In New York. Bull sent me up there yesterday to persuade him to go on the record."

"Good going," I congratulated her. "No wonder you're exhausted. What did it take you—half the night?—to get him to talk?" Her enthusiasm was infectious. I know how great it feels to pin down an elusive story.

"That wasn't quite what wore me out," Dawn said, a little grin playing at the corners of her mouth. "The really exhausting part was how I celebrated. You know that guy I was telling you about?"

My spirits began to sink, and a lump started to grow way inside my stomach, expanding to squeeze the breath out of my lungs. "You mean Dave Zeeger?"

"Well, sugar, it turns out he was in New York yesterday, too," Dawn continued, apparently unable to see that gigantic, ominous growth that was choking off my air. "And he became my Flavor of the Week."

"Flavor of the Week?" My voice must have sounded like a faint squeal.

"You know," Dawn said by way of explaining. She even, by god, winked.

"Must be a California thing," I suggested. "You don't mean . . ."

By this time Dawn was leaning closer, in a conspiratorial way, lowering her voice. About to get to the good stuff. "Ordinarily I don't like to mix business and pleasure like this," she said. "But it was just too convenient to pass up."

Convenient! My Dave!

Dawn hardly paused for breath as she told me how she ran into Dave in the hotel lobby. "Sure enough, we were both staying in the same hotel."

Which made sense, since the *Examiner*'s travel agent had undoubtedly booked the rooms for both of them, and she always chooses the hotel that gives her the biggest kickback.

"So we had a few drinks—or rather, I had a few drinks and he nursed a beer . . ."

That sounded like Dave.

"And the heating in the hotel wasn't very good," Dawn continued relentlessly, "so he volunteered to keep me warm."

"You do mean Dave Zeeger?" I asked hopefully.

"Sure enough, honey, that cute one over there." She pointed to Dave's desk, where he had materialized since I'd last looked, and was now earnestly talking on the phone. Probably to his next lay.

"You went to bed with him?" I wanted to get the

first of my two required sources clear and on the record.

"You ought to try it yourself sometime," she said generously. "He's good. I like that quietly passionate type. And he's got this thing he does in the bathtub afterward."

That did it. Enough. I had a murder to think about. Dave's.

"Doesn't sound like my type," I said from some well of strength I didn't know I had. And I elaborated, "You know, Dawn, I hope you didn't get too attached to him. He's got the busiest pecker in the newsroom. Certainly not somebody to pin any hopes on. In fact, you'd be safer scaling back your expectations and considering him nothing more than Flavor of the Day."

"Don't worry, I'm in no danger. I already told him I'm never more than a one-night girl when it comes to somebody I work with. He didn't like it, because we both had a great time. But I've already kissed him good-bye. Anyway, much as I enjoyed the guy, I only seduced him as an antidote to Ham."

"Hamilton Asterling?" I couldn't believe she was telling me she had slept with our patrician, gutter-mouthed, and very married retired editor, even though Sherele had said that he and Dawn were at least acquaintances.

"Now, that's some guy. Biggest schlong in the Western Hemisphere," Dawn told me to my dumb-founded amazement. "Must be a foot long. That's a man who could make me break my rules."

At that moment my phone rang, and I could see

on the caller ID screen that it was coming from Dave's extension. How indiscreet of the two-timing schmuck. I reached for the phone and turned it away from Dawn so she couldn't see the number.

"Hi, gorgeous," Dave crooned. "You must have come in while I was in the john. Sorry I couldn't get back last night. How did the funeral go? Are you okay?"

"Just fine. Having an interesting little heart-to-heart talk with my new friend Dawn," I said, seething.

"Oh yeah?" Across the newsroom I saw Dave turn my way and lean forward, as if that would let him see, or maybe hear, us better. At the same time, Dawn unfolded herself from Sherele's chair and stood up, stretching.

"I thought that was Sherele you were talking to. I could only see the top of her head," Dave said. Did he sound nervous? I couldn't tell. "Does she know who you're talking to?"

"Not so far. A surprise, huh?" I was digging my nails into the desktop in my silent fury. Dawn finished stretching and looked around the newsroom, undoubtedly for another relationship she could break up. She signaled to me that she was leaving, and blew me a little kiss that got stuck in the back of my throat like a fish bone.

Now I was ready to really talk to Dave. When she was out of listening range, I switched into attack mode. "Dawn says you got together in New York," I said, readying my ammunition.

"Yeah, it was quite a coincidence, especially after

what you said about her," Dave said in an innocent voice.

"Did the two of you have a good time?" I had him in my sights.

"I don't know about her, but I found the whole thing exhausting," Dave said in a maddeningly matter-of-fact tone.

I was just about to fire back, when Dave's other line rang. He interrupted my first word, saying in a rush, "Look, Chas, this is the call I've been waiting for. I've got to get this guy on the record for deadline. But I want to see you tonight. I found out some interesting gossip on Laurence's business dealings in New York, but I can't talk now."

Click.

The one thought that kept me from stomping across the newsroom and wrapping the phone cord around Dave's neck was that at least I'd been smart enough to keep our relationship a secret.

My boss, Helen, is such a sweetie that we all wonder how she ever worked her way up to one of the top positions on the newspaper. Most editors only get there by way of a trail of blood. And any sign that they think of their reporters as human beings is considered evidence of managerial incompetence.

Helen alone knows her reporters' families and their problems. She respects our frailties and plays to our strengths. She believes that compliments are an important part of an employee's diet, whereas most editors think they only make their reporters grow fat.

When Bull calls me into his office, I cringe. When Helen calls me in, I look forward to the encounter. And I suspect it is about something confidential, since otherwise she would come to me rather than summon me to her.

This time she wanted to know how the funeral was, what was happening with Lily, and how I was weathering Laurence's death. She also wanted to tell me that Andy was doing fine and had gotten a good story on hospital food (not so subtly trying to clear away any lingering guilt I had over his poisoning).

I thought our talk was over, when Helen asked whether I'd checked in with Den Ranger. I was too embarrassed to tell her that I'd totally forgotten that our police reporter was assigned to follow up on Laurence's murder. Nor did I want to rat on him and mention that I hadn't seen him at the funeral or heard his name mentioned by the detective on the case. Den had long ago lost his energy for his reporting job, and spent most of his time writing rather than solving murder mysteries—writing fictional ones. When it comes to dealing with real crimes, he tends to wait for the police to call him and tell him what they want reported by the press.

"Den's having a hard time getting any information out of the police department," Helen said.

"I can understand that," I answered noncommittally.

"He's got the idea that nothing much is happening there," Helen elaborated, looking at me quizzically, as if she expected me to confirm or deny.

"Hmm," I said cooperatively.

"Den thinks that the police are more seriously considering the possibility of suicide."

I couldn't help it. I snorted with laughter. "Suicide! He killed himself and then he planted the lipstick and the stockings? And what about the voices the neighbors heard? Next the police will suggest that Laurence accidentally overdosed on digoxin, and nobody was to blame at all."

I guess I was yelling, because Helen looked as if she were under attack. She moved her chair back from the desk, ready to stand up, and the fine lines around her hazel eyes deepened. I regretted my tone. After all, Helen was only reporting what she'd heard.

"I'm sorry, Helen." I dropped my voice to a conversational decibel. "I'm just wound too tightly at the moment." I didn't want to further attack Den, so I blamed my reaction on my mood.

I promised to check in with him this afternoon and share any information I might have. And I thanked Helen for giving me leeway on my deadlines this week. I know that pushing the deadlines adds to her stress, so she was really doing me a favor.

Whenever you want to get me going on a task I've been avoiding, just give me a worse task. I returned to my desk, dreading talking to Den. So I tackled my mail and messages.

I got a good rhythm going, punching keys on my phone for voice mail and my computer keyboard for

E-mail, opening envelopes every time there was an electronic pause, then sorting my letters into piles, the biggest one destined for the recycling basket.

Within a half hour my tally was up to seven reporters from other newspapers and networks wanting to interview me about Laurence, twelve compliments on Laurence's obituary ("It made my eyes tear and my mouth water"), eight restaurateurs hoping I'd stop by to try their food, fourteen readers with restaurant suggestions (including three more for Mamma Maria's, all suspiciously similar), three parents claiming their children had such discerning palates and literary talents that it would be amusing and instructive for me to have them write guest reviews, one teen-ager with enough talent to write her own letter, more hate messages than I cared to count, and two wrong numbers. That didn't include the friends and family, who would just have to understand my keeping them for later. I piled up the books, still in their wrappers, and in light of the week's events, I dumped the packages of food directly in the trash. Oh, yes, there was one item that fit no other category: Dave had called. I deleted the message.

Having tried the phone, Dave switched to the computer. "I'll meet you in three min. Usual place." I saw him from the corner of my eye, heading toward the door.

I toyed with leaving him to enjoy the musty aroma of the abandoned stairwell alone, but I lost my nerve. Besides, I hadn't really had a chance to fire a barrage at him. So I waited four extra minutes, then sauntered to the stairs.

● ● ●

Dave is so much better at this than I am, I thought when I caught sight of him leaning against the wall, as relaxed as if he were staring at Sunday afternoon football rather than a blank mold-green wall. He's had decades of loner life, honed by the secretiveness of investigative reporting. His face never shows emotion unless he intends it.

"Hiya, shortcake. Sorry I had to cut you off before. I wrote up these notes for you," he said as he heaved himself off the wall and handed me a yellow sheet from a legal pad, folded into quarters. His hands free, he reached for my shoulders.

I shrugged him off as I stuffed the paper into my skirt pocket. "Look, Dave, I haven't attached any strings to our relationship, but I never thought you'd embarrass me by sleeping with someone from the same newsroom." I'd meant to release more firepower, but it got toned down on the way out of my mouth.

"Same newsroom? I haven't even been tempted to sleep with anyone from the same universe. What gave you the idea I'd do that?" Dave's limbs had lost their relaxed ease and had come to attention. His jaw was clenched, his stomach was taut, and his hands were on their way to fists.

"You did. Just because you and Dawn were in New York—'exhausting yourselves' out of town rather than on home territory—doesn't make it any less humiliating for me," I spat out, trying not to raise my voice lest someone walking by the door hear us.

"How can you jump to such conclusions? It's just plain paranoid for you to assume that because both of us were in New York at the same time we were fucking each other." Dave was really working up steam, and while I was, too, more than ever I didn't want us to be discovered by the outside world.

"Shhh," I warned him. And I tried to calm myself in the hope that he would follow. "All right, Dave, maybe I have no right to ask you to be faithful. But I do expect you to be honest. Dawn's already told me about it."

"Dawn what? She told you about what?" His voice boomed through the stairwell and caught itself bouncing back.

I clapped my hand over his mouth. He tore it away. But it did quiet him. "She's lying, Chas. Or maybe you misunderstood her. We did have a drink together."

"How can she be lying? She described you to a tee. Even your little tête-à-tête in the tub afterward," I said, my voice thickening and tears ramming my barricades.

"Tub? What tub? I don't know what she said, but it's simply not true. She's just made up details and guessed right. I'm not even attracted to the woman," Dave finished lamely. He knew it was the wrong defense, and cringed slightly as he waited for me to renew my attack.

I didn't. I was close to tears, and I didn't want to cry in front of him. I simply turned around and walked out. My eyes stayed dry all the way to the women's room. Which wasn't very far.

A few splashes of water later, I returned to my desk, the tears replaced by a headache. While I was gone, Dave had filled my message screen with his successive thoughts:

"Do you really think I'd do anything to risk our relationship?"

"How can you know me so well and call me a liar? Why would you believe someone you hardly know instead of me?"

"Why don't you come over and hear what she has to say with me standing right there?"

"Who's the one of us who wanted to keep all this a secret, anyway?"

"Hell, I shouldn't have to defend myself. If you were any kind of friend, you'd defend me instead of her."

"Delete all of the above. Delete everything. I thought I'd at last found a woman who'd bothered to really get to know me. Wrong."

My headache had traveled down to my stomach, and I broke into a hot sweat as if my tears had overflowed to my entire body. I turned to see Dave, but all I could see was his back as he stomped out of the newsroom, not even waiting for the elevator but swinging open the door to the front stairway.

Let him go, I told myself. I didn't know whether that advice was based on anger, shame, or inertia.


I'd have to think about that later. At the moment, Den Ranger was heading my way, shambling the way he does, kind of like Ray Bolger as the scarecrow in *The Wizard of Oz*. Den always looks as if his limbs are only temporarily connected and might shake loose at any moment. He flopped down in Sherele's chair, which I was beginning to think of as the Witness Stand.

"Say, Chas," he said.

"Hi, Den. How's it going?" He doesn't inspire much in the way of repartee.

"Not bad. Not bad." He paused, as if to consider whether a third repetition was necessary. It was. "Not bad."

"Good." I hammered another nail into the conversation to make sure it was truly dead.

"So what about this Levain thing?" Den bravely forged a new direction. "The dead chef?" he added, in case my memory couldn't reach back beyond three days.

"The dead chef." I said it with such an assured tone that Den could be confident I remembered.

The subject established between us, Den got to the heart of it. "I talked to the detective. Jones? Jones. He said there's nothing definite yet. He promised he'd call me as soon as anything heated up. But I thought I'd check with you, seeing as how you've been involved. Just to make sure I haven't left any loose ends."

"No, Den, I think you've probably got all the loose ends tied up for now," I comforted him. "I'm going to the memorial tonight. I'll let you know if I find any new strings to follow."

"That'd be mighty helpful," Den said, shaking his various limbs in preparation for mobilizing them.

"Most of these cases never do get solved, you know. And as often as not, it's the guy who did himself in. Accidentally, more likely than not."

I breathed a sigh of relief when Den left, partly because his slo-mo brain made me want to shake him until his arms and legs fell off in a heap, and maybe a little bit because, deep inside, I wanted to believe Den's theory that no living person was to blame for Laurence's death. Believing in Den is hard to do when you're face to face with him.

Mostly, I needed to get out of the newsroom. I was desperate to be alone or to collapse with someone around who would comfort me. I tried to put everything aside for a moment to concentrate on my options.

If I went home and was alone, I'd wind up—as I tend to do when I'm depressed—falling asleep. And I'd never be able to rouse myself to face Laurence's memorial. I could go somewhere else to be alone, but in my miserable state I couldn't face a restaurant and I couldn't think of any other place to go. I needed a friend.

Sherele wasn't home. I left her a long, rambling message, saying something about just wanting to talk . . . nothing urgent . . . was going home . . . but don't feel obliged to call . . . only if you feel like it . . . I'll be just fine . . . don't worry about me.

## eighteen

All that reassurance must have scared the hell out of Sherele. She didn't even stop to call, she just showed up at my door. And as Sherele always does, she brought the antidote to whatever might be ailing me. She calls it her heart and soul food. The smell was unmistakable: her own carefully perfected skinless, greaseless oven-fried chicken (can't hold a candle to the real thing, but beats anybody else's low-fat attempts). And I knew what would be accompanying it: Sherele's fantastic tangy new-fashioned potato salad made with no mayonnaise; corn bread that crumbles on your tongue and then melts right down your throat; and beet greens—my favorite—slowly simmered with bits of smoked turkey to give them a doctor-approved old-timey smokiness. Probably ambrosia for dessert. A full-course Southern recovery package—home-cooked food I could safely eat.

"Hi there, baby," Sherele said, kissing me on the cheek and pushing past me with her basket of food.

"Brrr. It's gotten colder out there. You sounded like a person who shouldn't be alone this miserable winter night."

And so I wasn't.

As Sherele, continuing her best-friend chatter, walked into my living room and set her basket on the truncated printer's cabinet that serves as my coffee table, she closed her mouth mid-sentence. She took a long, slow look at Homer Jones, top to bottom and back again. By the time she fixed on his eyes, they were returning the compliment. He leapt to his feet and held out his hand, as if he were impatient for me to introduce him instantly so he could have the excuse to touch her.

"Sherele, this is Homer Jones, the detective who's handling Laurence's case." I couldn't seem to call it murder.

Like a shot, Homer's hand grabbed hers and held on.

"Homer, this is Sherele Travis."

"You're the theater critic," Homer said. "I can't tell you what a fan I am of yours."

Hadn't I heard that before?

Needless to say, after Homer investigated what was in Sherele's basket, he invited himself for dinner.

Except for the chance to eat my fill of food that nobody could have tampered with, my evening didn't improve. With Homer around, I didn't have a chance to pour out my heart (or as much of it as I dared reveal at this point) to Sherele. He had called to ask if he could come by for "just a few minutes" to go over some things he'd overheard at the funeral. But with Sherele here, he didn't seem inclined to leave, or even to talk about the case.

He just wanted to chat about the theater with Sherele. It turned out that except for food, theater was his first love. (How many first loves did this man have?) And soon he and Sherele were trading opening lines like cooking students exchanging recipes.

They got around to recipes, too.

"Is that potato salad? My, it's been a long time since I've eaten potato salad," Homer said as he began to unpack Sherele's basket. "I'm trying to hold down my fat intake." He patted his flat-as-a-board stomach in case Sherele hadn't noticed it already.

"No fat in my potato salad," Sherele said in the same tone I might use to declare my kitchen free of cockroaches. Strike one.

Homer wasn't daunted. He cracked a lopsided half grin as if she'd been boasting about the absence of fat on her trim bottom. "I've tried that, but my potato salad always winds up tasting like pure vinegar. Or with no taste at all."

"You've just got to know how to do it," Sherele said as she took the bowl from him, turned her back, and marched it to the dining table. Sure enough, trim bottom. "A real cook knows you have to season your potatoes while they're still hot. The trick is to stir together your vinegar with a big spoonful of mustard, then dilute it with water, tasting as you go along, until the vinegar isn't too sharp. Toss it with those hot potatoes and lots of scallions, and you'll never miss the oil at all. Lucky for you I didn't bring my pecan pie."

Sherele, who's always watching my weight for me, wouldn't have brought a pecan pie to my house unless I was at death's door.

"I do love a good pecan pie." Homer said, salivating. I wondered whether the cause was pecan pie or Sherele.

"Oh, mine's good, all right. I make it with fresh pecans my cousin sends me from Georgia."

"What part of Georgia?" Homer asked, walking right into the kitchen as if he owned it, and pulling out silverware, napkins, place mats, and dinner plates.

"Cordele." Sherele found the glasses and set them on the table.

"I know Cordele," Homer said, warming to the subject. "It's got those two great catfish restaurants next door to each other." He folded the napkins into triangles and lined up the silverware at each place.

"Yeah, Daphne Lodge and the Olde Inn. How'd you know that?" Sherele was looking at Homer skeptically. She removed the hot beet greens from the microwave and added them to the table display.

"I've got a cousin in Cordele, too. Do you know the Terrys? They favor the Olde Inn." Homer noticed the candles on top of the bookcase and arranged them on the table.

"Sorry. Haven't met them. My family always goes to the Daphne Lodge." Strike two.

"But I'll bet they both like the same barbecue—Ken's." Homer had swung again.

"Sure do."

That got Homer to first base.

"In fact, I've got some of his chopped pork in my

freezer. I was going to defrost it for dinner Sunday night. Perhaps you'd like to join me." Amend that: second base.

"As it happens, I already have plans for Sunday night." Homer paused. "But in light of this new development, I think I might have to do something about those plans. Can I let you know tomorrow?" There went Homer's engagement.

Once I accepted the fact that I was irrelevant to the conversation, I found certain advantages to Homer's company. He's a guy who knows his way around a kitchen. After having set the table, he took it upon himself to do the dishes. And in my wounded state, I was actually comforted by being served and talked around without being expected to help in any way. I let my thoughts run free.

Besides, I had a lot I didn't want to talk about.

I didn't want to talk about Dave to Sherele if I could get through the breakup on my own. That way, I'd never have to reveal my sneakiness or face the stupidity of my having gotten involved with such a stud.

I didn't want to talk about Ari with Homer. I still believed some other miraculous solution to this crime would absolve my ex-husband, and in case it didn't, I couldn't bear to be the one to point the finger at him.

We'd finished dinner, and were listening to Homer wax poetic about Sherele's succulent chicken and extraordinary potato salad, when the phone rang.

Homer answered it. I figured he was the kind of guy who automatically assumed it was for him.

"For you," he said, waving the receiver in my

direction. Then he turned to Sherele and recited, "Never send to ask for whom the bell tolls."

Sherele groaned.

"Hemingway, right?" Homer asked with a boyish grin he had probably practiced before a mirror.

"Only partial credit. John Donne first." Sherele isn't conquered easily.

I left them to their foreplay and took the receiver from Homer.

"Hi, Mama." Lily's voice sounded reinvigorated. "Was that Dave?"

"No, sweetie, it was Homer Jones, the detective. Sherele's here, too. I'll explain it all later," I answered, wishing my guests would disappear so I could talk openly to Lily. She was the one person, I realized, to whom I could tell all.

But not tonight.

"I'm having a wonderful time," Lily volunteered, a statement I rarely hear her make. "Brian is going to help serve for the party tonight, so I'm going to just go on over there with him. I'll meet you there. Okay?"

What could I say? "Okay. Enjoy yourself. See you there."

Homer and Sherele were exchanging phone numbers when I hung up. Suddenly, it seemed, every woman but me had a guy. Lily had Brian, and Sherele seemed to have diverted Homer from that woman he was supposedly going to propose to.

It occurred to me that maybe Homer had so much time on his hands to dog my steps because his girl had already turned him down. Either that, or he was another two-timing, double-dealing stud like Dave.

Sherele reached for her picnic basket, but Homer beat her to it, asking if he might walk her to her car. This is a woman who routinely attends street-theater performances in the most dangerous sections of town without hesitation. To my astonishment, she only started to protest, then changed her mind. "Why not?"

Even Sherele.

Maybe I was better off without a guy. Depending on nobody. Taking care of myself.

Freedom. Time to recapture it.


While Homer escorted Sherele to her car, I changed my clothes. I wanted something fresher, more independent to wear to tonight's gathering. As I took off my skirt, I heard a rustle, and felt in the pocket. I'd forgotten Dave's paper, the notes he'd taken for me in New York.

I straightened out the crumpled sheet and turned on the bedside lamp. One needed every possible advantage to decipher Dave's gnarled script. It was addressed to Homer and me. After mentally filling in the missing articles and sounding out Dave's phonetic spelling, I concluded that Dave had tracked down an investor in Laurence and Marcel's New York restaurant project. This unnamed moneyman had told him that the Thursday before the murder Laurence had called a meeting of the investors for this week. Very secretive. Warning them to tell absolutely nobody else about it. Laurence wanted them to be prepared to postpone the project but not to put their wallets away. If after the meeting they decided not to go ahead with the project as planned, he would offer them an alternative.

The note detonated a series of questions in my head. Why would Laurence call off the project? Did Jeanine know about it? Marcel? Borden? Who stood to gain from this, and who to lose? I assumed the alternative investment Laurence had referred to was Ari's essences—or the essences he seemed to have stolen from Ari.

I'd have to talk to Dave. Maybe he had a sense of whether the emphasis was on the decision not to go ahead with the project or on the alternative investment. Did it sound as if something was wrong on the project, or that Laurence was looking for an excuse to divert their investment to a more lucrative possibility?

My thoughts were interrupted by the doorbell. Homer was back. The weather had turned so cold that he assumed I'd want a ride with him to La Raison d'Être. While it didn't seem quite appropriate to me that Homer was going to show up at this memorial gathering for Laurence, I wasn't about to tell the police how to conduct their business. Besides, I reminded myself, what's the worst that could happen at a funeral party—that he'd put a damper on it?

Whatever my misgivings, I was grateful for the ride tonight. The air had grown so damp that even though I was wearing my red-and-black wool coat designed for winter fêtes in Finland, the dark and cold insinuated themselves through every protective layer of clothing. I was glad I'd remembered hat and gloves for the walk home, and that I'd opted for boots tonight. Under the circumstances I was even relieved that Homer'd brought an official car that he could park right in front of the restaurant. The valet parking was sure to be slow with everyone arriving at once.

On the short ride, I gave Homer Dave's note and explained what it said. While he responded that this was important stuff and he'd get somebody right on it, he seemed to be only half paying attention. I guessed that the other half of his mind was replaying Sherele's best lines—or even more likely, his best lines to Sherele.

# nineteen

Noise rushed out to the street every time the door to La Raison d'Être opened, exploding party sounds like firecrackers on the quiet block. Outside, television cameras and reporters attacked each new arrival. Inside, the dining room was so crowded that tables had been pushed against the wall in clumps, like seaweed at the shoreline. There was a note of hysteria, of people desperately pretending to have fun. Though the night was young, everyone already seemed a little drunk.

I abandoned Homer, kept my head down to avoid catching anyone's eye, and headed right for the bar. I needed a calvados.

I watched the bartender uncork a sealed bottle and pour me a hefty dose. I held the snifter up to the light and silently toasted Laurence. I swallowed it in one gulp and, coughing, ordered another.

Now I was ready to be sociable.

I turned from the bar to find a wicker basket staring me in the face. Its smell took me right to the coast of Maine, to hot oil and crunchy batter and ocean salt. It was a basket of *palourdes en beignets*, the clam fritters I'd been served for lunch here last Monday just before I'd found out that Laurence had died.

"You must try these tonight, Miss Chas," said Georges, the maître d' who was holding the basket to my nose. "The clams were flown in from Maine today."

Georges's eagerness to have me taste the fritters rang an alarm in my head. On the way over, Homer had renewed his plea: I should keep in mind Andy Mutton's digoxin poisoning and continue to be cautious about what I ate at the party. He didn't have to remind me.

I didn't think I needed to abstain altogether, though. As I'd been doing right along, I'd be careful to eat only things that couldn't have been tampered with. I reached across the basket and took a clam fritter from the far corner. Nobody would poison the whole batch.

Sure enough, the clams were spitting fresh, unlike those three-day-old ones I'd been served on Monday.

"I made them myself, with you in mind," said Stanley, La Raison d'Être's sous-chef, who had come up behind Georges. Stanley's never been shy about taking credit for anything, especially with a restaurant critic. "I was really embarrassed about the fritters you had on Monday."

"Do you mean Monday lunch or Monday evening?" I asked, remembering that the onion-soup fritters from La Raison d'Être at CityTastes were even worse than the clam fritters at lunch.

"Monday lunch," Stanley said. "I had nothing to do with the cooking for CityTastes. That was all Marcel. Weren't his *soupes en chemises* good?" Stanley's voice had an annoyingly hopeful note.

I didn't want to criticize Marcel in front of his sous-chef, so I skirted the question and asked him instead if he'd seen Brian. Then I set off in the direction he pointed.

This was a potluck party. All the attending chefs had contributed. So I was ducking outstretched trays at every turn, each held by a beseeching chef wanting me to taste. I smiled wanly and held up my hand as I wove through the crowd. "Later." "Thank you, but not at the moment." "Lovely. But not right now." I fended off calories by the million, feeling both guilty about seeming rude to these chefs and nervous about eating such eagerly offered food.

The next hand didn't give, it took. It took my arm and pulled me into a relatively quiet and food-free corner of the room. It belonged to Ari.

"They're trying to force-feed you, my little goose," he said, laughing as he leaned over to kiss my cheek.

For a moment I felt as if I'd just reached home base. Then I remembered my suspicions. Did my cheek turn to ice?

Apparently not so that Ari would notice. He didn't flinch, but went on as usual. "Where is Lily? Surely she didn't leave already, without saying good-bye?" Ari's gray eyes darkened as he looked for her, and his long face looked more sad than it naturally does.

"No, she's here, but she didn't come with me," I explained. "She's suddenly became glued to that waiter who sat with us at the church. Brian. He works here. They're probably in the kitchen."

Paul arrived from nowhere, psychic that he is, carrying two doubles of calvados for Ari and himself. He was just in time; not only did I crave another drink, but I was falling short on safe subjects to address with Ari. I held up my empty glass, and he poured half of his into it.

"Hey, darlin'," Paul said, and kissed me on the forehead. Tonight he was dressed in somber gray, though his jacket felt like rose petals as I brushed against it, and when he moved I noticed it was lined in silk the color of a nectarine.

I sipped my drink, set it on a ledge, and snagged a smoked salmon tart from the far side of a passing tray while I launched into the only safe topic that came to mind. "How's Jeanine doing? I haven't seen her yet."

Paul grabbed a tart, too, grimacing as he took a bite. "Whoooo. Salt city." He dropped it on a teetering tray of dishes being carried past his shoulder. "I'd say she's doing amazingly well, at least since she's simply decided Laurence's death was an accident rather than murder or suicide." Paul, ever the gossip, wound up for a juicy exchange.

Ari wasn't eating. He took a long swallow of his drink. "Everyone else is saying it was accidental, too. But what do the police say?"

I was surprised to hear that question from Ari, who treats gossip like a language he can't manage to pronounce. His eyes bored into me as if I were a side of beef and he its potential buyer.

"I haven't heard anyone suggest an accident. Or even suicide." I was telling the truth, but not much of it. I took a bite of my tart in order to keep my mouth more safely occupied.

Not so safely after all. Paul was right, for the wrong reason: The salmon was inedible, but not because it was salty. It had that slightly fermented taste of old lemon juice.

"The newspapers haven't said much. Do the police have any clues telling them for certain it was murder?" Ari asked. I felt increasingly uncomfortable with his pursuing this topic.

"I don't know. Ask the police yourself. That's the guy who would know," I said, pointing out Homer Jones scarfing down Thai squid salad across the room.

"Well, let's go find the man." Paul gleamed with the possibility of a new adventure and launched himself in Homer's direction.

Ari didn't move. "I don't want to interrupt his eating," he told Paul. Lame excuse, particularly after Paul shrugged and continued his beeline toward Homer. Homer was going to be interrupted whether or not Ari participated. But Ari held his ground.

I held his ground with him. My deep-seated drive to be a busybody was getting the better of me. I took another sip of my drink, for courage.

"Ari, tell me more about your essences." I approached the subject in a low voice.

Even though I was nearly whispering, Ari looked around as if he were afraid of being overheard. He waved away a tray of skewered shrimp. "You must not say anything about them to anybody, Chas," he warned. His voice had an icy edge that made me shiver.

"Doesn't anybody else know about them?" I continued.

"No, I have been very careful this time. Nobody else has tasted them. I do not yet have the money together to start the company to make them, and I have still to perfect the recipe," Ari said, his accent growing more French, as it always did when his emotions were aroused.

"Didn't even Laurence taste them?" I ventured.

"Certainly not." Ari had actually lapsed into French: *Non. Certainement.* "Not this time."

I had never quite known what the word "glowering" meant until I watched his face responding to my question.

Despite Ari's certainty, somehow Laurence had gotten hold of a bottle of Ari's essences. It was hard to imagine how he could have done so without Ari knowing. Still, Ari's response seemed genuine.

Could Ari lie with such sincerity? Could he kill with such apparent innocence? Could I stand calmly discussing the murder of one of my dearest friends with the man who was possibly his murderer and who had nearly poisoned me as well?

Not for long.

"I have to go pay my respects to Jeanine," I said, excusing myself from Ari and giving myself permission to be a coward.

• • •

Jeanine was easy to spot. I just headed to where the crowd was thickest, and apologetically elbowed my way into the center. I fortified myself along the way with a blini and caviar, reaching my arm into a tangle of eager nibblers who had swarmed the tray. Nobody would poison a whole tin of caviar in the hope that I'd come by and pig out on it.

Jeanine was dressed in something a French couturier might design for a deathbed wedding. It was black, ankle-length. It looked like a sleeve that Jeanine had wriggled into and it suggested a figure too grief-stricken to have eaten for the last four days. Jeanine's eyes, on the other hand, swam in a sea of alcohol.

"Of course it was not murder," Jeanine was saying in a stiff voice that sounded as if the phrase were automatic. Murder was the last subject I expected people to be badgering Jeanine about at her brother's memorial, but restaurateurs are a hard-headed bunch.

"What about the overdose of digoxin?" The questioner was hidden in the throng. I stretched to see over the heads to find out who she was. No luck. This was a tall crowd.

"Oh, poof," Jeanine countered. "You know how absentminded Laurence was. Especially before a big event. He probably forgot that he took his medicine, and took some more."

"Then you don't think it was suicide?" That, too, was a disembodied voice, but to my surprise it sounded like Homer.

"Never." Jeanine's voice had dropped to a dark, suddenly sober utterance, her eyes clear and hard.

Then she looked around like a cornered animal seeking escape.

I was the way out. "Chas," Jeanine cried out, smiling as if I was the best thing that had happened to her this week. "I'm so glad to see you. Come and sit with me."

People shifted to let me through, and I gave Jeanine a reluctant hug, in the process spilling a few drops of my drink on her. Jeanine didn't notice; in fact, she hugged back as if she hadn't seen me in a year. Come to think of it, she hadn't given me such a warm hug even after she hadn't seen me in ten years.

Not that she had much to say to me. After that emotional greeting, Jeanine seemed to disappear behind her eyes and respond to my conversation as if she were only pretending to understand English.

I'd served my function of fending off unwelcome subjects, so Jeanine began to survey the crowd again. I'd had enough, too. I excused myself, saying I had to go look for Lily. Which was true.

I stopped for another drink on the way, switching to cognac just in case my calvados preference had been noted by someone who wished me ill. I also snagged from the middle of a passing tray a very small slice of rare filet of beef on the tiniest—and crunchiest—potato pancake.

I found Lily at Brian's side, handing out napkins to go with the hors d'oeuvres he was passing. It was the first time I'd seen Lily openly and voluntarily playing a supporting role. Usually she'd press the guy into passing napkins or—more typically—turning pages at the piano. She looked a little embarrassed when I hugged her and took a napkin but waved away the hors d'oeuvres. I'd already tried the clam fritters.

"How was your dinner?" I asked, putting down my drink and my napkin, neither of which I needed at the moment.

"I hardly remember what I ate," Lily whispered with a dreamy grin. "He's really nice, Mama."

I seemed to be the only woman in my circle without a romance, but seeing Lily happy—for good reason this time—compensated for a lot.

"Seems so to me, too," I assured her, watching Brian offer some appropriate greeting to each person as he passed the tray. Thoughtful man. That'll be new for Lily.

"What happened to Dave?" Little frown marks between her eyes changed Lily's expression. I looked around, wary about who might be listening, but she had kept her voice low, and Brian was absorbed in his hors d'oeuvres mission.

"I've dumped him. He'd been off in New York with another woman in the newsroom," I said, stopping short because my voice was shaking. I picked up my drink, realizing that I did need it after all.

"Oh, poor Mama. How did you find out?" Lily looked as stricken as I felt.

"The other woman. Dave denies it, of course."

"Are you sure? Women can lie, too, you know. Maybe she was out to get you."

"She didn't know I had anything going with him. And she had intimate details to relate."

"Look, Mama, don't jump to conclusions. We'll talk about this later," Lily said, this time the practical one.

Brian and his tray of hors d'oeuvres had moved beyond her reach, and she scurried to catch up with him. Or maybe to avoid Borden, who was approaching from the other direction, with his arm around Bebe, of all people.

Borden and Bebe? A new motive? No, I couldn't bear to think of it. Or of any new complications to Laurence's murder. I began to wish I had Jeanine's ability to block out all the possibilities except an accidental overdose. I shouldn't have been drinking so much. It was making me feel sorry for myself. I swore off for the moment and set my drink down again.

Borden's hysterical unburdening of last night might never have occurred; he seemed fully restored to his old oily self. After the usual moist greetings, he got right down to business.

"We're reopening tomorrow," he said. "We just can't afford to stay closed, and the wait staff needs the income, too. We also think it's important to show as quickly as possible that the restaurant can go on as well as before."

As well as before? It would take a lifetime to show me that, I thought, reaching for my glass like a security blanket. But what I said was, "I'll mention it as soon as possible. It's too late for tomorrow's paper. I'll see that it's in on Saturday." I didn't need that drink after all; I just held it.

"Thanks, Chas. I appreciate that," Borden said with the patronizing tone of a chef who's just been told by a customer that his *boudin blanc* tasted every bit as good as the Frugal Gourmet's quick, low-cal version.

"Are you going to be working for Borden?" I asked Bebe, not caring if the question sounded rude.

She looked startled. Then she noticed Borden's hand on her shoulder and she looked more startled. She changed her expression to an apology, and shrugged out from under his hand. "At the restaurant? Oh, no. In fact, I was just wishing Borden good luck. I've had enough of the restaurant business. I've decided to try to get back in the theater."

"I'm really sorry about Bebe leaving, but I guess it makes sense, with the New York project up in the air," Borden said, as usual opaque about anything but economic considerations.

By then, Marcel and Marie Claire had joined us. I put my glass down and kissed cheeks with them. "Are you all right, Chas? You are taking good care of yourself?" Marcel clutched both my hands as if they were ice cubes and his were burned. I reassured him with another kiss.

A waiter with a tray of the salmon tarts was ready for us as soon as we finished our little greeting ceremony. I shook my head no, having already tried these dreadful little overripe hors d'oeuvres, but I didn't warn the others in time. Each took a tart.

Marie Claire turned to Bebe. "My dear, I'm sure we could work something out until the New York restaurant opens, but I understand your wanting to get away from all this," she said in her soothing way that made all problems seem tractable.

"Is New York opening?" I was surprised, since Borden had just said the project was up in the air. But he wasn't one of the owners, so surely Marcel and Marie Claire would know more. Borden looked as surprised as I was.

"I have been in touch with the investors," said Marcel, taking a bite of his tart. "They seem reassured that we will be able to work it out." He took another bite.

I couldn't imagine the restaurant project continuing without Laurence's name. But maybe I was underestimating Marcel. I'd personally never believed his talent was in Laurence's league, and he didn't have nearly the charisma. But he was undoubtedly a fine chef, and there were critics who thought him the equal of any in the country.

Besides, it seemed that although Laurence was dead, his name was still being kicked around.

"Jeanine certainly isn't giving up," Marcel announced. "We are going ahead with using his name."

"She's been very sweet about that," Marie Claire chimed in. She bit into her salmon tart and puckered her mouth. I wished I'd warned her. As always, she was the soul of politeness. Instead of criticizing some other chef's food, she discreetly turned to Marcel and slipped his tart out of his hand to save him the experience, then deposited both tarts in a napkin on the window ledge.

Marcel gave her a rueful look and wiped his hands on his white jacket. "Jeanine thought it would be a tribute to Laurence to open a restaurant in New York that carried on his name."

I didn't say it out loud, but I wanted to add, "And if you promote it carefully, half the diners will never know that Laurence isn't alive and cooking dinner for them."

I was offended on Laurence's behalf. But then, who was I to judge? I still had a job. These people'd had their financial security murdered last Sunday night. Why should I prefer that the murderer claim them as victims, too?

While Borden and Marcel launched into business details, I excused myself. I was here to mourn Laurence, not package him.

Bebe slipped away from the group, too, and came up beside me, handing me the glass of cognac I'd left behind. She apparently wished to set me straight.

"I just wanted to leave in peace," she explained. "I wanted to say a polite good-bye to Jeanine and to Borden and then try to get all of this out of my mind." She looked no more than a child, one hand tugging at a blond curl, the corners of her mouth turned down as if a teacher were about to consign her to detention.

"You're on the right track, Bebe." I didn't want to send her to detention, I wanted to give her an A for effort. "I know it will take time to get over Laurence even if he treated you like shit. In any case, it is a good time to make a change. If there is any way I can help, you know where to find me."

"Yeah. Just let me know if you hear of a job anywhere in a theater. I'll start out selling tickets if that's what it takes."

"I'll keep my eyes open."

"And, Chas," Bebe started, hesitantly.

"Yes?"

"I hated him at the end, but I also loved him. He could paint such pictures in my head. He could make me taste the world and smell it in a way I never did before."

That was what I had come here for. I wanted to start mourning Laurence properly, by unpacking my memories and savoring them and then folding them away for permanent storage. Bebe alone in this crowd seemed wise enough to understand that.

While we talked we were occasionally interrupted—by Homer telling me he'd call me tomorrow, by restaurateurs pressing their cards on me and hoping I'd get a chance to try their holiday menu. Yet nothing stopped our flow of reminiscences. The crowd was beginning to thin. I was taken aback to realize it was after midnight.

Bebe had provided just what I'd craved. The catharsis had calmed me more than I'd even known I needed to be. We lifted our glasses in a silent toast and drained them, then embraced for a long time. We'd done each other good.

I went to get my coat. It had been a long, wrenching day.

# twenty

Istepped outside to a transformation. The metallic sky I'd noted on my way in had been a snow machine. It had dumped a good four inches and created havoc on the streets. The scene was white and sparkling. But interrupting the quiet were frantic sounds of spinning wheels and racing engines.

Washington, the arsenal of the free world and architect of global defense systems, cowers before the slightest snowfall. Offices and schools close in the face of a mere half-inch accumulation, and the very threat creates a run on the dog food and toilet paper supplies of every 7-Eleven. Immigrant taxi drivers who have never seen snow race their cabs and slam on their brakes like kids on sleds. Timid civilians creep along at five miles an hour. Traffic becomes a hopeless snarl. Even after midnight it was going to be a mess.

I gave thanks to my warm red-and-black coat and boots, and started walking.

I'd hit a lull in the crowd. The block was empty

except for one man huddled against a lamppost at the corner. As I approached him, I wondered if he was sick—not surprising, considering the amount of booze that was being poured at the party. His shoulders were heaving. Surely he was retching.

"Do you need help?" I asked, feeling anxious but unable to simply ignore a sick man.

"No. No. *Es nada.*"

"Mateo?" As he turned to me, I saw that he wasn't sick, he was crying. Mateo was a dishwasher at Laurence's restaurant, but more than that. He'd been there for years, in a job that generally lasts weeks or months. Most dishwashers are not only poorly paid, they are the kitchen's whipping dogs, the underlings on whom chefs vent their tension. Mateo had instead been considered part of the team; he was probably the highest-paid dishwasher in Washington, and most likely the only one entrusted with keys to the restaurant. Mateo and Laurence had become friends; Laurence had found temporary jobs for Mateo's relatives whenever any arrived from El Salvador, and in return Mateo's mother had always invited Laurence for holiday dinners, taught him to make *pupusas* and fried yuca. In Laurence's restaurant, Mateo had evolved from an undereducated street kid to a serious part-time college student with dreams of becoming a cartoonist.

"You'll freeze here, Mateo," I said, putting my arm around him.

"He was my *padre*," Mateo sobbed into my shoulder.

"You had a wonderful relationship," I said lamely.

I couldn't begin to find enough to say for such a loss.

"I couldn't believe it when I heard he was dead."

"How did you find out?" My talk with Bebe had taught me that at least it was a help to talk about the loss.

"It was terrible. Laurence's lawyer or something called to the kitchen, but I was the only one there. He told me that Laurence was dead and that I should tell the other staff when they came. But I was alone. All alone. I went crazy."

"I can imagine."

"No. Nobody could imagine. I could not have imagined. I howled like a dog. I tore my shirt. I could not stay in that place and wait for anybody."

"So you left?"

"I didn't even know what I was doing. I had been washing up the dishes from the night before. When I got home I realized that I never finished the washing. I just shoved all the dishes into a rack and put them someplace. In the storeroom, I think. I could not go back to that place. But now I must, because we will open tomorrow. I must clean up." Sure enough, talking had calmed Mateo. His eyes had dried and his jaw was set firmly. He'd gone from stricken to stoic.

"Are you going tonight?"

"I think that would be best. I would not like any of the staff to see how I left it."

"I'll walk with you," I volunteered. It was on my way, and I was glad to have the company this sad and eerie night.

We didn't say much along the way. Nothing more than asking each other if we were cold and assuring each other that we were not. Mateo was clearly dreading the encounter with the kitchen, and my mind had switched into an investigative gear, wondering what I might find in this place that had been frozen in the time of Laurence's murder.

Suddenly the brilliant snow became dim. The electricity had gone off along Massachusetts Avenue—the streetlights, the illuminated doorways, the glow from apartment windows. Moonlight was enough to guide our way, but I worried that Laurence's kitchen would be too dark for us to see anything. Mateo shared my worry, adding to it his concern that there wouldn't be enough hot water for the dishes.

"If I can't finish tonight, I'll have to come in the morning very early to clean up for the opening," he said as he picked up his pace.

Although Mateo was no taller than I, his legs were muscular from his obsession with soccer. I had to scramble to keep up with him.

The lights were working on Laurence's street. Mateo put his soccer legs to good use at the restaurant's entrance, shuffling and stamping to sweep away the snow and debris with his feet. He unlocked the door and turned to say good-bye to me.

"I'd like to come in," I said.

Mateo hesitated. He knew he really shouldn't bring an unauthorized person in with him.

"Please, Mateo. I need to see his kitchen again. You know it will be all right," I wheedled.

Mateo shrugged his shoulders and flicked on the lights, then led the way to the kitchen.

It looked dead.

I'd never seen this kitchen without Laurence in it. Yards of stainless-steel cabinets emitted a cold shine. Crowded stalactites of hanging copper pots gleamed like pink ice. The marble pastry counter radiated a chill. No food. No steam. No exciting spicy smells.

My stomach churned and I felt sick. I shouldn't have come. Not when Laurence's home base was so dark and empty.

Mateo, too, looked spooked. He stripped off his jacket and gloves, leaving his hat on, and started scrubbing the countertops.

"It doesn't look so bad, Mateo," I said, trying to sound energetic. "This shouldn't take us long. Let me help you." I stuffed my gloves in my pocket and unbuttoned my coat.

"Now I remember," Mateo said, interrupting my offer. He dashed into the walk-in refrigerator. "They're here," he yelled. He returned, struggling to carry a large metal rack piled with dishes. He eased it onto a counter and stood back to assess the task ahead of him.

"There's not too much," I said encouragingly. As I looked over the jumble of plates, bowls, and silverware, my heart thumped. "Don't touch it!" I shouted as Mateo began removing dishes.

He stopped abruptly, startled.

I moved to block him from the rack, knocking him against the counter in my hurry.

"What the—"

"That's Laurence's mug," I said, pointing to a large glass beer stein.

It wasn't quite a mug or a stein, more an oversized crystal tumbler with a handle and with Laurence's initials etched on it. A Viennese crystal company had designed these years ago for its anniversary promotion, and had given a dozen to each honored chef in a solemn ceremony inaugurating its culinary hall of fame. Laurence took great pride in his mugs and always kept one at his side as he cooked, for sipping one of those garish green sports drinks that he said kept him going. He would have been better off with a real beer mug, because these fragile crystal vessels cracked easily. But when one broke he just went on to the next. He must have been down to his last one by now.

"You want it?" Mateo reached around me, but I caught his hand.

"Yes, I want it. But not for a souvenir. That could be the drink that poisoned him. We should turn it over to the police."

I don't know why it hadn't occurred to anybody before, but if the digoxin took two hours to work, Laurence might have ingested it at the restaurant rather than at his apartment. And since nothing had been found in the glasses at his apartment, this could be a promising lead. Neither the killer nor the police would have anticipated that Laurence's drinking glass could still be in the kitchen, unwashed.

Mateo whistled. "You mean it's evidence?"

"Could be. Where are the plastic bags?" I was opening drawers, but only out of nervousness. I had no idea where anything was in this kitchen.

Mateo handed me a plastic bag and examined the

glass, pointedly clasping his hands behind him so I wouldn't worry.

"There's nothing in it," he said, frowning in disappointment.

"I don't think that matters," I reassured him. "It will have some traces the police can test. And it might even have fingerprints." If it did, the murderer could prove to be anybody who might have had the opportunity to visit Laurence in the restaurant Sunday night, not just somebody Laurence would invite home for a drink.

"Those fingerprints could be mine," Mateo said in alarm. "I picked it up to put it there."

"Don't worry. They'll understand that. The question is, who else's are on it?" I handed the bag to Mateo, indicating that he should hold it wide open. Then I picked up a spoon and snagged the mug's handle with it, lifted the mug from the jumble, and lowered it into the bag without touching it.

"Just like *NYPD Blue*," said Mateo, smiling for the first time this evening.

"Yeah. I tape it every Tuesday," I said, feeling kind of smiley myself.

My sense of satisfaction didn't last. After my flush of discovery I had to face the fact that I might have saved the glass that would hang Ari. Could I be the one to direct suspicion to him? The question kept renewing its attack.

But now I had no choice. Mateo was a witness to this evidence. It was a relief to not bear the responsibility alone.

"I think it's okay for you to clean up the rest," I told

Mateo, not wanting to keep him here any later than necessary. With the restaurant reopening tomorrow, he was going to have a long day ahead of him. I went to call Homer Jones.

The electricity was working, but the phones weren't. I picked up every phone I could find in the restaurant. All dead. I was so frustrated I felt like throwing up. I jiggled buttons and banged receivers and dialed anyway. No juice. As I walked back into the kitchen, the lights began to flicker. Mateo was cleaning like a whirlwind.

"The phones are out of order, and I don't know how long the lights are going to last. I think I'd better just take this to the police," I told him, picking up the plastic bag with the mug.

I didn't know how the police authenticated evidence, but I figured I should do something to prove the mug's source. So I tore a sheet from the notepad in my purse and wrote where and how this mug had been found. I initialed and dated it, then asked Mateo to do the same. I rummaged through Laurence's desk until I found a stapler, then, in full sight of Mateo, I used it to attach the note and seal the bag. I stuffed the package into one of the big black patch pockets of my coat and left Mateo to his washing.

The dark sky had a faint yellowish cast, and exhaustion rolled over me. My stomach clenched and churned as I thought about carrying in my pocket the weapon to imprison someone, probably someone I cared about. My legs were sluggish, and I felt increasingly dizzy, so weary that I passed two phone booths before I remembered that I was supposed to be calling the police. Was I really on my way to the police station? I wasn't sure. I was suddenly too tired and sickened to know where I wanted to go.

Even if Ari had poisoned Laurence, I could imagine why he'd feel justified—Laurence had been, after all, stealing Ari's lifeline. Now that I had lost Laurence, could I bear to lose Ari, too? I trudged on, so worn down by death and guilt that I felt like dying.

I stumbled over a chunk of broken sidewalk hidden by the snow, and I went down hard, not quick enough to stop myself with my hands. I'd only scraped my knees, but sprawled in the cold slush, I felt my energy seep out as the dampness seeped in. I didn't have the strength to get up. Ripples of dizziness and nausea radiated through me as the whole world turned a sour yellow. I closed my eyes against the acrid color. Just a little nap, and I'd be ready to get on with my walk.

# twenty-one

I nearly did die.

It was probably my coat that saved me.

I might not have been noticed in the snowdrift I'd chosen for my collapse if I hadn't been wearing such a bright coat. Even once I'd been spotted, perhaps nobody would have considered me an emergency case if I'd been wearing plain gray, or some other neutral color. I might have been treated more casually, as the usual homeless drunk just sleeping it off. As it happened, the passerby who called for help on his cellular phone had realized that the night was too cold for even a street person used to sleeping in the open. Miraculously, he got me to the hospital probably minutes after I'd fallen—though, as I was to learn later, not before somebody had stolen my purse.

I woke in a hospital bed with three anxious faces welcoming me back to consciousness. Lily, sprawled on a molded plastic chair she pretended was a sofa, looked groggy and tear-stained. Homer stood in front of the window, arguing quietly but fiercely with someone on the phone. The third, and least expected, was Dave. He was slumped in a chair next to Lily, staring at a wall as if it were showing *Nightline*. The surprise of seeing him here was nothing compared to my amazement at noticing that Dave and Lily were holding hands.

Only then did I realize how sick I must have been.

Lily was the first to notice that I was awake. She greeted me in utterly Lily-like fashion: She burst into tears.

That brought the others around. And I must say, it was nice to see how happy I could make them by doing nothing more than opening my eyes.

I can put two and two together as well as the next guy, so I didn't need anyone to tell me that I'd been attacked by the killer digoxin. But Dave filled me in without my asking.

"Someone must have doctored your drink at the party," he said. "It was a bigger dose than Andy got, probably too big to hide in an hors d'oeuvre. This killer is learning as he goes along. Fortunately he didn't take into account what a strong heart you have—all your walking, I suppose. Apparently, enough digoxin to kill Laurence wouldn't even keep you off your feet for long. What were you drinking, anyway?"

"Just calvados. And a cognac."

"Maybe now you'll give up that overpriced battery acid in favor of good beer," he suggested, obviously needing something to growl about so he wouldn't come off like Alan Alda.

Homer stepped in, not wanting to be left behind

as the last softy. "Gotta get going. Just wanted to ask you a couple of questions," he said, so no eavesdropper would assume that he'd stayed around out of concern. "Anybody you can think of who might have had a chance to mess with your drink?"

"Sure, a couple hundred of them. Anyone who was at the party." I felt dangerously stupid.

"Did anybody bring you a drink?" Homer had decided he'd need to be more specific with a mush brain like me.

"Yes, Paul. But he poured me part of his, which had to be safe. I got the others myself at the bar, and made sure the calvados was from a freshly opened bottle. The cognac came from a bottle everyone was drinking from, and a tray that wasn't intended for me, but was being passed around the room."

Homer wrote that down. "Did you put your drink down at any time?"

"Lots of times. I always park my drinks, then pick them up later."

At that, Homer hitched up one side of his mouth and gave me an exasperated look. "You ever been poisoned before? No, scratch that. I'm outta line. Sorry. It's been a long night."

"Look, Homer," I said, realizing that he'd gotten a lot less sleep than I had. "It could have been anybody. I'm sorry, but that's just what the situation was. I moved around a lot, talked to a lot of people, had several drinks, and I thought I was being careful, but I guess I really didn't keep track of them."

The edges softened around his mouth and eyes. He rubbed his face with both hands, massaging it back in order. "I know. It was just that I'd hoped—"

I interrupted him with a whoop. At least it started out as a whoop. It came out as a sad little croak. Not all parts of me were back in working order yet. "Gurgle," I said. "I do have some evidence for you. I was bringing it to you last night because the phones were out." I tried to get up but discovered that that was well beyond my capacity at the moment.

"Don't get up," Dave said, reaching out a hand to stop me, and winding up by stroking my hair. It was a comforting feeling, but didn't last long when I heard what else he had to say.

"The glass. I know. We found it, in your pocket," he continued. "But it must have broken when you fell on it." He had the tone of a parent telling his toddler her pet goldfish had died.

"You could still get fingerprints off it," I protested.

Homer came to the side of my bed. "We can still examine it for traces of digoxin, and ultimately that could help the prosecution. But I'm afraid we aren't likely to get any fingerprints."

"It's nothing but a bag of glass crumbs," Dave said.

"I don't know why you didn't leave it to the police," Homer couldn't resist adding.

Not only were these two making me feel guilty and defensive, they were ganging up unfairly in what sounded to me like a bad cop–bad cop routine.

"I was afraid the glass would be cleaned up with everything else before the police got there," I said. Besides feeling attacked, I was disappointed that all the sweet protectiveness was disappearing almost before I got to enjoy it.

Dave made another U-turn to defend me. "At least she found the glass. What happened to your crack investigative team?"

The heat was off me. Dave and Homer were glaring at each other. "We went over the entire kitchen, or so I thought," Homer muttered through clenched teeth.

Visions of firing squads ran through my head. I couldn't let Homer mete out undeserved punishments.

"They couldn't have known that was Laurence's glass," I said. "It was in a pile of dishes. In the refrigerator."

"In the refrigerator?" All three of my guests formed a chorus.

"The dishwasher was so upset when he heard about Laurence's death that he just dumped everything and fled."

"He didn't say anything about that when we interviewed him," Homer said, not much cheered by my explanation.

"Obviously you didn't ask the right questions," Dave said, landing another punch.

"I think I'll take a little nap," I interceded. I must have looked awfully dismayed, because the two of them practically stumbled over each other trying to make me feel better.

"You did good, Ms. Wheatley," Homer capitulated with a half bow.

"Damn good," Dave echoed. "It was a brilliant find. Maybe you'd like to move over to the investigative reporters' side of the newsroom."

He was laying it on a bit thick. Which made me realize that Dave was seeing Homer as competition. And trying to get back in my good graces after his get-together with Dawn.

"As I said, I've got to get going," Homer repeated. "I hear the press is clamoring for your attention, but the hospital is holding everyone off for the time being. I'll check back later." Homer left with the plastic bag of clear, sparkling shards.

Lily wasn't saying anything, but she scooted her chair right up to the bed and laid her head beside mine, to give and get some cuddling.

"How'd you two get here?" I presumed Lily had still been with Brian, and I had no idea who'd called Dave to my bedside.

"Dave found me," Lily said. "Pretty good sleuthing, I'd say."

"But who found Dave?" I wondered.

"It was a fluke," he said. "I was out in a squad car last night. An old police buddy of mine invited me along, seeing that I had nothing to do." With that his mouth curled into a pout and his shoulders dropped to mock the slouch of a victim. Too obvious to have much effect on my heartstrings.

"It was a miracle," Lily said. "If Dave hadn't been there, the hospital might not have figured out that you'd been poisoned with digoxin. You might have died."

The idea that my survival was due to such a far-fetched set of circumstances made me feel dizzy all over again. "So you heard my name over the radio?"

"No, it wasn't quite that simple. They couldn't find

any identification on you, so they just broadcast your description. But how many red-and-black coats do you think there are on the streets of downtown Washington after midnight?"

I hardly heard the last part of that. I was distracted by the question of identification. "No identification? Where was my purse?"

"Don't worry," Lily said, running a cool hand across my brow. "They found it in a trash can a block away. Somebody had stolen it."

"Yeah, I got one of the guys to go back and search the neighborhood. Usually it's ditched in the nearest rubbish heap. And you were lucky this time because all the thief took was the money."

"The credit cards are there?"

"Amazingly enough, they are. I figure whoever took it was afraid that you might be dead and he might get nabbed for murder if he tried to use your credit cards. So he settled for the opportunity to make off with just the quick cash." Dave looked proud of himself, as if he'd personally nabbed the culprit.

I was proud of him, too. Sometimes it's nice to have someone with all those investigative reporter skills to take care of you.

Sucker, patsy, a voice inside me interrupted. Dave might have saved my life, but he still hadn't saved my confidence in him.

"I really don't want to leave you, Chas, but I've got to file my story today and I have a dozen calls to make first. I'll check on you later. I know I'm leaving you in good hands. I'll see you tomorrow."

Tomorrow? What was Dave going to be doing without me on a Friday night? How come he wasn't coming back here?

Dave gave me a lingering kiss that held promises of pizzas by candlelight and fluffy bath towels. I wondered with whom.

He and Lily embraced like foxhole buddies after an artillery-rocked night.

When he was gone, Lily fixed me with a knowing smirk. "You didn't tell me what a hunk he was, Mama."

I was too tired to blush, but I enjoyed the sound of admiration in her voice. "You liked him?" I asked the obvious, but even moms crave an excess of reassurance from time to time.

"I think he's a wonderful man. Sexy, too, of course, but a really solid person. Someone you can rely on." That was high praise from Lily, from whom men, starting with her father, had tended to slip away until she had to go out and drag them back.

But I wasn't so sure about the relying on. I told her so.

The boasts of Dawn didn't faze Lily. Her generation takes everything sexual more easily than mine does. But that wasn't the only reason she was unconcerned.

"Women lie," she insisted.

"So do men," I countered.

"True, but we expect that. Women who lie are protected by the fact that we don't expect them to.

We give them far more benefit of the doubt than we give men."

"Maybe you're right. I don't know. I just can't think about it all right now."

"What you need at the moment is a nap," Lily said. "And so do I."

"You go on home and sleep, sweetie," I said, growing a little foggy and beginning to drift off.

"No such thing. You know I can sleep anywhere. This chair is fine. I'm going to take a nap right here. We both are."

And we did.


My nap was longer than Lily's. Half awake, I could hear simmering voices, Lily's and Ari's. I was so sleepy, though, that I couldn't rouse myself to join them, but kept slipping back into dreams and mere shards of thoughts.

Laurence was dancing. His white jacket, flapping as he dipped and swirled, became wings. He began to fly, tossing squares of quilted pasta in iridescent colors over the heads of people far below. His jacket turned into a parachute, floating him slowly back to the ground. As he drifted and twisted, I saw that his bare chest was bloody. Yet Laurence didn't seem to be in pain. He caught the blood in his hands as it dripped, and transformed it into more shimmering pasta squares.

When he touched the ground, he was surrounded by outstretched hands begging for food. Laurence began picking from among the supplicants, handing each of the chosen a square of pasta. One by one, people took a bite and beamed with happiness. Laurence continued to dole out pleasure.

At the front of the crowd someone looked familiar, but I couldn't identify who it was or even whether it was a man or a woman. All I could see was a cape as white as the snow that I'd slept in last night. When Laurence's eye fell on this familiar figure, his face darkened. The pasta quilt in his hand lost its color, and its edges turned brown. The person in the white cape, seeming not to notice or care, just reached out to take the ugly bleached pasta and, like everyone else, ate it eagerly, desperately. But for this unlucky creature the pasta meant not joy, but pain. Every limb jerked twice, and the figure collapsed at Laurence's feet.

Laurence went limp, his arms hanging useless at his sides and his face expressionless. People filed by, each holding a lipstick. Every person made a mark on the fallen figure, until a hundred of their streaks joined in blood-red knots binding the body to the ground.

I woke up trying to figure out what was so familiar about the person in the cape.

I'd never, in a quarter of a century, seen Ari cry before.

"I still can't understand why anybody would try to kill your mother," he was saying to Lily, wiping his eyes with a big, rumpled handkerchief that was edged in blue stripes so bright it had to have been borrowed from Paul. And Paul wasn't there. That meant Ari was probably crying even before he left home.

"Dad, she's going to be all right. I promise," Lily was pleading with him. "You heard the nurse. She said that Mama is not in any danger at all. Stop worrying. She's going to be fine."

"I never understood how a man could do murder," Ari said. "But when I heard that somebody had attacked her I thought that maybe, after all, I could kill somebody. Anybody who harms her deserves to be hurt."

This was not the talk of a real murderer. At least not of somebody who could have murdered Laurence. And certainly not anyone who could have poisoned me. I didn't need evidence. Ari's tone was enough. He couldn't be that good an actor.

For days I'd been stuck in a terrible place, not really believing that Ari could have murdered Laurence, but not honestly being able to dismiss the notion. My conflict had made me want to stop thinking about the murder altogether. But listening to Ari immediately freed me. Now that I'd heard enough to satisfy myself about Ari's innocence, I could get working on figuring out what had really happened.

"Hello, Ari. I'm awfully glad you're here," I said, opening my eyes, watching a smile spread across his face and easily returning it.

Ari came over to kiss my forehead and stroke my cheek.

"I'm all right. I really am," I said.

"I tried to tell him that," Lily chimed in.

"Now that you are awake, I am prepared to believe the doctors," Ari said ever so gently.

"I'm hungry. Did you bring anything good to eat?" I asked Ari.

"Now will you believe she's back to normal?" Lily shook her finger at Ari in mock severity.

Ari looked much relieved. He walked over to the windowsill and lifted the lid from a ceramic tureen, which released wonderful smells into the room.

"Chicken soup!" I guessed, happily. "With dill. And parsnips."

Nobody ever made better chicken soup than Ari.

"Just what the doctor ordered," Ari said, carefully spooning chunks of chicken and carrots, tiny dumplings and fronds of dill into three bowls. He handed one to me and one to Lily. Then he sat down, crossed his legs, folded his hands on his knee, and waited expectantly for me to take the first spoonful.

"Aren't you going to eat?" I asked him.

"No, my dear. I have no appetite yet."

"Then who's the third bowl for?"

Lily answered, choking on a laugh that got tangled up with a mouthful of soup. "It's for the doctor. Daddy really meant it when he said it was just what the doctor ordered. When I asked your doctor whether it would be all right for people to bring you food, he said that he hoped they would. And he asked that if Ari brought you any of his famous soups, could we please save him a bowl."

● ● ●

Chicken soup is indeed a magical restorative. Yet its powers come not only from the broth itself—which is probably curative simply because it is warm and wet—but from its circumstances. How well it works depends not just on its nutrients but on who makes the soup and with whom it is shared. Ari's chicken soup might be one of the great chicken soups of the world, but what made me feel stronger was that he'd made it for me, and that I was eating it in the company of my daughter and my dear ex-husband.

Plus the knowledge that any doctor who was offered some of this soup was going to be so grateful that his efforts on my behalf were going to be unflagging. Ari had made sure that I was in good hands.

Lily set her bowl back on the windowsill and became all business. She had a stack of notes she was ready to discuss.

"I called Grandma and told her to tell all the family that you're fine, they needn't worry, and you'll call them later. The same with your best friends," she began. "Probably everybody who works for the *Examiner* has called. Helen, of course, and Bull—at least his secretary called on his behalf. Even Andy Mutton—I thought you two didn't like each other. Some guy named Den who wants to ask you some questions. And Sherele sounded distraught. She says she's going to visit even if she has to steal a nurse costume."

"The hospital must have erected quite a barricade if it could keep Sherele out," I said. "I'd love to see her in a nurse's uniform. Chanel, of course."

Lily didn't have time for my weak humor. "I think every chef in town must have called. Marcel and Marie Claire have left several messages. Everyone wants to bring food."

"Did you tell the cafeteria kitchen it could close down for the duration? Of course, we'd have to run a digoxin check on everything." I was tickled by visions of chefs lined up with their dishes, waiting for a lab assistant to draw off a sample.

Lily looked impatient. "Mama, you don't know how frustrated the nursing staff is. We've got to get back to some of these people. Take the pressure off the nurses' phones. So far the doctors have restricted visits to the immediate family."

Ari gave a proud smile to Lily for including him.

"I think I'm ready to see people," I said, though I felt a stab of panic about how I must look. "Is there some way we can get permission to allow visitors but limit the list to just a few? The idea of being a captive audience to chefs who want to tell me about their new holiday menus doesn't appeal to me."

"I'll talk to the receptionist. I think that's possible. We can make up a list," Lily said, shuffling through her notes.

Ari began to bustle around, packing up the dishes. "I must go back to my kitchen, *chérie*. I will take this soup to the doctor's office. And I will try to be back later with something for your supper. Paul wants to come, too, as soon as he can be allowed." As only an old restaurateur could do, he balanced the tray and bent to give me a good-bye kiss without a drop spilled.

"Ari, there's something I need to ask you about. Do you have one more minute?" I was bolder today than I had been yesterday. I was more sure of my direction and no longer afraid to head toward it.

"Of course."

"Did you know that Laurence had a bottle of your essences?"

Ari's grin was one part sheepishness, two parts bitterness, not holding together well. "Laurence thought he had a bottle of my essences. I knew him too well by now. And I was prepared this time. What he had was—how shall I say it?—a temporary essence."

"You mean you gave it to him?"

"No, but I predicted that he would acquire it. So I made sure he could get nothing but an old batch, one whose flavors will not hold up for very long. You see, capturing the essences was the easy part. Fixing them so that they would keep their flavor has been much harder. But I have worked that out now."

"Laurence didn't know that?"

"He did not. He would have found, once he had opened the bottle, that ten minutes after the air entered it, the aroma would be gone and it would be merely bitter colored water."

"You're amazing." I felt lighter than I had in days.

When Ari walked out the door, he left me in much better shape than I'd been in even before I'd drunk the poisoned cognac.

Lily had finished with her sheaf of notes and was going through the newspaper, making marks with a pen. For the first time it dawned on me that this was Friday, and she was supposed to be in Philadelphia.

"You'd better leave, too, hadn't you?" I asked.

"No, I'm staying."

"Is that all right with your boss? You don't have to stay, you know. You've been wonderful, and I've been grateful to have you around. But you really should get back. I have enough people around if I need help."

"I know you do, Mama. But that's not the only reason I'm staying. My job has been shaky for a while, but my boss didn't want to leave me in the lurch so he's kept me on even when he couldn't really afford it. I'm more or less doing him a favor by leaving."

"You mean you're really staying? For good?" This was a thunderbolt, that my fiercely independent Lily was willing to live within a hundred miles of her parents.

"Would you mind?" My surprise must have frightened Lily. She stood up and turned to straighten her papers, so I couldn't see her expression.

"Mind? It's the nicest thing that could happen to me." Surely she could hear that in my voice.

Now I'd gone too far. Lily looked embarrassed, backed away in an unconsciously wary reaction. I decided I'd better smooth things over. Let her know I wouldn't hover. "As long as you recognize that I'm used to having my place to myself and we agree on a few boundaries."

Lily's expression flip-flopped once again: horror-stricken. "You wouldn't expect me to live with you, would you?"

"I thought that was what you meant. No, of course I wouldn't expect you to live with me, though you're welcome to stay as long as it takes to find an apartment. You won't mind going out to dinner once in a while, will you?"

"Mind? I'll love it. Half the reason for moving here is that if I don't find another job before my money runs out, I can be sure I won't starve."

"And the other half?"

"Oh, lots of things, Mama." Lily was back in the plastic chair, shredding the newspaper into confetti. "I know you think I'm throwing myself at a man again," she began defensively.

"Well, I . . ."

"Brian isn't the reason for my moving back here, he's just sort of a catalyst. Meeting him got me thinking about why I've had to stay away. And how I've wanted Borden, but only at a distance because I knew it wasn't real.

"But I've missed you and Dad, and I love this city. In an odd way, it's a good place for a young musician. Since there is so little chamber music available here, musicians feel much more intense and serious about what they do. And everything is more unstructured, more open to young people than in a city like Philadelphia, which is so officially music-oriented."

"I'm sorry. I didn't realize. I thought you liked Philadelphia." I was dismayed that I knew so little about Lily's life. I hoped that would change.

"I did. And it's been good for me, musically. But I feel I've sort of used up what's available to me there. And more interesting things are happening here now than a few years ago. I'm tired of having to play nightclub schlock in order to support myself.

"And it's not just the music. I've also been away long enough that I feel I can come home as an adult."

"You've certainly proved that to me."

Lily looked down and realized that she had a lapful of shredded paper. She burst out laughing. "Now that I've shredded the classifieds, you might justifiably wonder whether I actually do mean to rent my own apartment. I think I need to buy another paper."

# twenty-two

With Lily off running errands, I had my first chance to be alone—at least in between nurses poking at me and checking my vital signs. I welcomed the solitude to think about how to find Laurence's murderer.

Homer had to squeeze in time for this investigation between cleaning up after drug dealers, gang members, outraged spouses, armed robbers, and crazed junkies. What's more, he kept getting diverted by fritto misto, potato salad, and Sherele. Progress with Homer was likely to be slow, and I wasn't willing to give up chocolate cherries and cognac for long.

Even more important, I had a certain advantage over detectives who'd had years to dig themselves into a rut. I knew Laurence and his world much better than they did.

I'd read enough mysteries in my life to know that the police would be looking for means, opportunity, and motive. But Homer seemed stuck on the standard motives: money and sex. Puny concerns. To a chef who has been willing to spend sixteen grueling hours a day, from age fourteen, preparing food that is going to disappear in moments but might be remembered forever, even money and sex pale before the driving force: professional pride.

For motive enough to murder, that's where I'd look.

I'd already ruled out burglary and other random crimes. This wasn't a break-in, it was a poisoning. Laurence had obviously known the murderer, had allowed him in the restaurant while he was working or had brought him home after work, changed into a bathrobe, and had a drink with him. Except for the botched attempt to make it seem like a sexual encounter, the scene was a sociable one.

I'd let Homer follow the dollar or whatever motives excited him. To me this was a crime against gastronomy, and its answer was hidden somewhere in the kitchen.

I lay with my eyes closed to discourage conversation from the steady stream of nurses, and I let my mind comb the last few days for clues. Ordinarily I'm a list maker, but at this point I didn't want to take notes. I wanted to free my thoughts.

I returned, in my head, to my first visit with Jeanine, to CityTastes, and on through the week to phone messages and restaurant visits, to my encounter with Borden at Laurence's apartment, to the funeral, and, finally, to last night's wake. By the end, I was dozing, halfway between remembering and dreaming.

Laurence returned to my dreams. He just picked up where he'd left off before, as if my nap hadn't been interrupted. He leaned down to the huddled white figure bound in lipstick-red knots. My heart started pounding. Once again I realized that this person in the white cape was familiar. Laurence pulled back the hood to reveal a face.

I woke up in a panic. Too early. I hadn't seen the face. But my mind flew back to CityTastes. And to an odd moment, though I hadn't thought anything of it at the time. Another incident, from later in the week, floated to the surface, beginning to fill in the blanks. Then the wake last night. Three nearly insignificant events added up.

I knew what was wrong. I knew why Laurence had been murdered. I knew who the figure in white was.

And I knew just the food to trap him.

When Lily returned, I asked her for the stack of messages. I was ready to give the hospital a list of visitors to admit. But first I had to make a call.

"White House."

"The pastry kitchen, please," I asked the operator.

"'Allo." Roland Mesnier, though White House pastry chef since the Reagan administration, always sounds as if he's answering the phone in Paris rather than in Washington.

"Roland, it's Chas."

"Chas, I was so worried about you. And the President, too. You are okay?"

"I am. And I appreciate your concern. Tell the President thanks, too."

"Is there anything I can do for you?"

"I was hoping you'd ask that. I do need something. I know it's a big imposition, but it would mean a great deal to me."

"You know you can ask me for anything. What do you want? Chicken soup? You know, I get these very good chickens from the Amish in Pennsylvania. And even if I am a pastry chef, I can make absolutely superb chicken soup."

"No, Roland, Ari has already brought me some chicken soup."

"Oh, well, my chicken soup could not be so good as Ari's chicken soup." He sounded defensive.

I hurried to reassure him. "I'm sure your chicken soup would be wonderful. But what I need from you is something that nobody else in the world could do so well."

"If you say so." Roland's tone revved up to a swagger.

"I've been thinking about the little pastries you made for the Japanese state dinner. The ones that looked exactly like sushi. They were so exquisite."

"Ahh, Chas. You have such a good memory. I am flattered that you remember them. Would you like me to make you some? For me they are nothing. A little rice. Butter cream. Marzipan colored with licorice."

"I wondered how you got the marzipan so thin that it looked perfectly like seaweed?"

"That is my little secret. In fact, I have worked out an even better way since you tried it. I will show you. I will start making them right now. The President is going out to dinner anyway."

That got my reporter juices flowing. "To dinner? Where?"

Roland gave a little laugh. "Sushi, yes. Gossip, no. I will send a messenger with the sushi as soon as it is ready, but it must sit and rest several hours. Do you wish to have it tonight, or will tomorrow be soon enough?"

"Tomorrow morning would be perfect."

Tomorrow was Saturday. Most restaurants would be closed for lunch. Just the right time to invite a visitor. And to catch a murderer. Tonight I would plan my strategy and rehearse.

True to her promise, Sherele showed up in a nurse's uniform. I laughed until my sides hurt.

"Dying is easy. Comedy is hard," she declared as she unloaded a platter of raw vegetables and dip from the bag she was carrying.

"Who said that?"

"Some actor. Dead, no doubt. How are you feeling, Chas?" She peeled the plastic wrap from the platter. It was definitely not hospital food, with its crisp, bright jicama, golden beets, and sugar snap peas.

"I feel fine, Sherele." I reached for the jicama. I love the way it's juicy and crisp at the same time. "Tired, though. The doctor says I can go home tomorrow afternoon."

"That's excellent. But I'm not going to let you go home to an empty refrigerator. I want to know what time you'll be there so I can bring you some good food to build you back up." Sherele plumped my pillows and cranked up my bed, then arranged the vegetables on my bed tray and the small hand-thrown pottery dish of dip alongside.

"Thanks, Sherele, but I think I've got plenty of food at home already." The dip had sesame paste and soy sauce, maybe a little ginger and garlic. Definitely lemon—or it could be lime. Wonderful.

"Plenty? Oh, yes, I know about your plenty. Vietnamese leftovers from a couple of days ago. A doggie bag from some steak house you went to last week. You've probably got more thousand-year-old eggs than any Chinese restaurant in town, and you cured them yourself." Sherele had settled beside me and pulled a small brush out of her purse. She handed me a lipstick and mirror as she began to gently untangle my hair. I hadn't thought about looking nice for the last eighteen hours.

"You know, Sherele, we hardly ever talk about men." That would divert her from my sloppy food-storage habits. "Don't you find that odd?"

"Why should women always be talking about men? That's what they think we always have on our minds. I, for one, wouldn't give them the satisfaction."

"Bullshit, if you don't mind my saying so. I think we're just afraid to admit that we care."

"I don't notice you caring particularly, Ms. Live-Alone-and-Love-It. Sure, we appreciate a pair of bedroom eyes and a cute ass. But women like us, honey, busy as we are, it just isn't real high on the list."

"Even after last night?"

Sherele reared her head back and peered down her nose at me. A skeptical expression.

I pushed on. "You sure seemed to give Homer Jones a high priority last night."

"Ahhh, Homer. Now there's a man who knows how to wear clothes."

"You mean, 'Just a pretty face,' huh?"

"No, I wouldn't quite say that. I did sense some smarts underneath his designer haircut. It's just that I like to take these things slow."

"You mean safe."

"Maybe that is what I mean. I've learned from experience that the same guy who gets a hard-on from finding out you're a big-city newspaper critic loses it as soon as he realizes that out in the world with you he's not going to always be the center of attention. And before long, he sees you as a ball-buster. I've learned to play it low-key and keep it quiet. See them in your own living room rather than out in public."

That hit home. I hadn't thought of Dave having had his own reasons for keeping our relationship private.

Naahhh, I argued with myself. After all, he's a newspaperman. He's got as many groupies as a restaurant critic. Maybe.

"Hey, Chas. Where'd you go?" Sherele waved her hand in front of my face.

"Oh, sorry. Just thinking." I wished all the more that I'd talked to Sherele about Dave earlier. "It's a funny life, being a critic."

"You can say that again. People think it's all glamour. Spend your life seeing plays. Or eating in fine restaurants." Sherele stretched out the word "fiiiine," then bit into a slice of yellow beet.

"You probably eat more good food than I do," I complained.

"No doubt about it. You've got to go to all those

bad restaurants, while I only have to go to the ones I like. And I get to eat at home when I want."

"On the other hand, I'm not forced to see every bad play that comes along," I said.

"Night work. That's another problem. How do you find time to date when you're out at the theater or eating professionally several nights a week? It's hard enough to find a time to pay your bills," Sherele agreed.

"Or wash your hair."

"Or keep up with *Seinfeld*."

"Aw, c'mon. You don't watch *Seinfeld*." I assumed Sherele was teasing.

"How else am I going to stay apprised of what you honkys are thinking?" Sherele rolled her eyes and waved her hands, minstrel style.

"Maybe I should watch it myself, to find out what we honkys are thinking."

"You know what I find the hardest part of being a critic?" Sherele kicked off her shoes and propped her feet on the bed, reaching over to massage her toes. "I don't really get to enjoy the plays anymore. From the moment the curtain goes up, I have to be thinking about how I'm going to write my review."

"You have it worse than I do on that score," I sympathized. "I have days to think about my reviews, and I get to make several visits to a restaurant first. You've got to start churning out your prose as soon as the curtain goes down."

"It's a challenge, but I like to spin out my ideas fresh from the experience. I never liked take-home exams when I was at Harvard; I liked to get in there and get the test over with. There's another problem, though. I really miss opening the paper in the morning and reading a review of a play I haven't seen yet."

The foot massage looked tempting. I pulled my knees up and pulled aside my blanket, wiggling my toes in the hope that Sherele would notice how neglected they were. She did, and she began to rub her thumbs hard along my instep. That felt like the best thing that had happened to me all day.

"Aahh, that's great. You're right, there's a loss when you turn your pleasure into work. It's kind of like when I was a kid. I loved to read in the summer, when I didn't have to, but those same books were a task when a teacher required me to read them."

"Just what I would have said. But not to anybody besides you. It would sound too much like Donald Trump complaining about how much time it took to count his money."


Somebody else understood the problems that accompany too much of a good thing. The head nurse, Hilda, arrived leading by her rear, having used her hip to push open the door. Her arms were piled with trays of food. Sherele, who had sneaked in against all the rules, slid her chair back and tried to look inconspicuous.

"What are we going to do with these, Ms. Wheatley? More keep arriving every five minutes. Lord, I've never seen so much parsley in all my life." Hilda deposited the trays on the windowsill, stood up straight, and rolled her shoulders. She unstacked the trays and lined them up on every available surface: sink, TV, extra chair.

Hilda went on: "Flowers are so much easier. They don't require refrigeration. And you can send them on to the children's ward or a nursing home when they get to be too much."

"Why don't you send these on to a nursing home? Or call D.C. Central Kitchen. They'll pick up this food and distribute it to soup kitchens."

"Caviar? Smoked salmon?"

"Why not?" I hate the attitude that if you're poor you shouldn't be allowed to taste good things.

"All right. I'll check with our toxicologists and see what they think will be safe, and I'll send it all along. Anything you want to keep?" she asked, eyeing the trays as if they were covered with spiders.

"Not now, thank you. And I'm sorry this is causing you so much trouble. But I would like the cards from the trays so that I can send thank-you's. And there is one food delivery I'll definitely want to keep. It will be arriving tomorrow morning. It's from the White House."

Mention of the White House perked her up. "That sounds safe enough."

She piled up the trays again and hoisted them, averting her head from this probable toxic waste, then turned to leave. She looked at Sherele—who had slipped her shoes back on—as if she'd just materialized out of thin air.

"Who are you?"

"I'm Chas's cousin. Just got off work at Prince George's Hospital. Didn't have time to change my clothes."

Hilda looked from Sherele to me and back again. She didn't dare ask.

Stymied, she swept out of the room.

Sherele and I kept quiet until we were sure that Nurse Hilda was far down the hall. Then we whooped with laughter.

"Say, cuz," I said, once we'd calmed down. "Seriously, what is going on between you and Homer Jones?"

"Nothin' but a hot game of telephone tag," Sherele said, beginning to gather her purse and coat.

"But you are keeping your answering machine on."

"Sure. I'm not that jaded. Nor am I being particularly quick to return his calls. I think that the man has some complications in his life, and I plan to give him plenty of time to simplify it before he complicates my life."

Sherele always had a sixth sense about people. I told her so. "You're right, if my understanding is correct. A few days ago he was talking about proposing to some woman. But I don't know him well enough to guess whether he meant that literally or he was exaggerating just to get me to give my best restaurant recommendation."

"I'm getting the impression that there's something going on, but I'll just wait and see how things play out. Truly, I like the guy. He's worth a little patience. In the meantime, much as I'm enjoying this idle chatter, I've got to go. One more thing: I really would love to see Lily. I keep missing that girl. Please tell her I'll track her down as soon as I get the lifestyles section off my back."

Alone again, I returned to my scheme. I'd yearned

to talk to Sherele about it, and I wished I could get Homer's thoughts. But I couldn't bring myself to put my suspicion into words yet. It was just a hunch. A wild card.

Once I confided in anyone else, I'd be embarrassed if I turned out to be wrong, as I already had been with Bebe, Borden, and Ari. Thinking up a little test was one thing, but the prospect of voicing an accusation out loud, and bringing other people into it, made my evidence sound absurdly flimsy. Better to share my suspicions after I'd conducted my experiment.

The one person I believed I could talk to freely without being ridiculed was Lily. But I couldn't take her into my confidence because she had a role to play. And if she knew what was going on, she might play it awkwardly. It was safer to let her just carry it out naturally.

Lily called to see if there was anything she could bring me tonight. I told her that she shouldn't bother coming back, and asked her to call my mother to reassure her again, since I didn't feel up to it at the moment. And to call Ari and tell him I was too tired for visitors tonight but that I would love to see him and Paul tomorrow. I added that I'd need her to bring some fresh clothes in the morning. And I suggested she bring along the real-estate section because I had an idea for her apartment hunting.

Lily asked me if Dave had called. I mumbled my answer—which was no—and yawned elaborately. I was ready for a long night's sleep, I said. And I wished the same for her.

## twenty-three

The uninterrupted night's sleep was glorious. I didn't remember the nurses removing my tray of vegetables and dip, or taking my temperature, or fussing with any other parts of my body. I didn't remember any dreams. Or any fears. I slept as soundly as my attacker obviously wished me to sleep—though not as long.

Homer wasn't exactly being conscientious when he called first thing Saturday morning. Police business was a thin veneer of an excuse.

"How're you doing, Chas?" It was back to Chas. "I wanted to tell you that we've run those glass fragments through the lab, but this being the weekend, we won't get final results until at least Monday. We do know you were right about that sports drink the chef drank, but it's too early to know about digoxin. And we couldn't retrieve any prints."

"I appreciate your calling me, Homer. Actually, I've got an idea or two I'd like to talk to you about if you've got time." I'd been thinking of a way to get

Homer's assistance without my risking public humiliation.

"All the time in the world." Homer didn't sound
polite, he sounded discouraged. He listened to the
basics of my plan with no protest, not even a comment. Just a few "uh-huh"s and "why not"s.

"Homer, what's wrong?"

"Wrong? What do you mean?"

"This isn't like you. You haven't even told me what
you made for dinner last night."

That got a tinny laugh. "I guess I've got other
things on my mind besides food today."

"Anybody I know?" The subject between us had
changed. All for the better, as far as I was concerned.

"Can't stop being a detective now that you've
started, huh? Of course it's somebody you know. If
you don't mind my asking, did I do something
wrong? I can't get that girl to answer my calls."

"Maybe she doesn't like getting involved with men
who are already involved."

"Involved? What would make her think a thing
like that?"

"Homer, you may be a good detective, but in your
personal life, you leave clues lying about for anybody
to see. Remember asking me for a restaurant recommendation last week?"

"That didn't work out."

"She didn't like the restaurant?"

"She didn't like me. She decided to go on a diet.
She said she was sick of having to talk about food all
the time. The funny thing was, I found that I was
relieved. "

"A message you wouldn't mind my passing on to the right person, I imagine."

"No, Chas. That's not what I intended. I didn't mean to put you in the middle of this. I guess I just needed to tell somebody about it. I've got nobody else to talk to at the moment, and you do seem to have shown up right in the middle of my life all of a sudden. I want to thank you, but I don't want to burden you further. I'll deliver my message myself. If I can get your friend to answer the phone. Otherwise I may have to go and park myself in front of her house."

"I don't know how she'd feel, seeing herself as catching you on the rebound."

"That's not the way it is at all," Homer said, sounding defensive. "Well, I admit that the timing looks that way. But I'd say I was just lucky. I'd have fallen for Sherele even if I'd first caught sight of her walking down the aisle. Or in eighth-grade English class. No, I wouldn't even put it that way. She's the woman I've loved all my life—I just hadn't gotten to meet her yet."

Wow. And I thought Homer was passionate about fried zucchini. A current of envy ran from my fingertips to my toes. Where the hell was Dave, and why wasn't he calling?

I missed Dave—even though I still didn't know whether to believe his denials about playing around with Dawn.


Homer wasn't the only frantic man looking for me to solve his problems this morning. Den Ranger had to be desperate if he was working on a Saturday, and he was. Bull was demanding a Sunday wrap-up on Laurence's death. So Den had left me a message yesterday, but I hadn't even noticed it when I'd flipped through the stack Lily had given me. This time he told the operator it was an emergency.

"Sorry to call you so early, Chas." Den sounded rushed. Surely he wasn't facing a deadline at nine A.M.

"That's all right. They get you up at dawn in the hospital."

No murmur of sympathy. Den was all business. "I just needed to check that there was nothing new on the murder of this chef, you know, for the Sunday wrap-up I'm doing."

"You might talk to Homer Jones about a glass I found in the restaurant. And if you call me back later this afternoon, I might have some new information for you."

"This afternoon? How early?" Den sounded hesitant.

"Not too early. As late as you can. Close to deadline."

"Great. I was afraid you meant earlier. I'm trying to sneak off to the races as soon as I finish a few calls, and I'd hate to have to come back before the trifecta. How's five o'clock? That'll give me plenty of time to write the story before the first run."

"Sounds good to me."

"Thanks, Chas. You're a pal."

The races had gotten me thinking. Hamilton Asterling was known to play the ponies. He'd even hung around the track with Den in the old days, the way I'd heard it.

I mustered up the courage and broached the subject with Den.

"You used to go to the track with Ham from time to time, didn't you?"

"Sure did. I'll never forget the time I talked him out of some dumb-ass, long-shot double he wanted to play, and it won. The guy actually fired me. For a day. What made you bring up Ham?"

"Well, it's the funniest thing." I was trembling, not laughing. "I was having an argument with one of the residents here about myth and reality."

"Myth?"

"You know that old myth, that you can tell the size of a guy's dick from the size of his feet."

"That ain't no myth, sweetheart."

"Well, this resident, knowing I worked for the *Examiner*, said the myth was wrong. And used Ham as the most famous example. Said that everyone knows that, even though our illustrious retired editor's hands and feet are delicate, he's hung like the horses he plays."

Den gave a few coughs and chuckles. "In my day, doctors didn't talk about such things with girls."

"In the old days, doctors weren't girls, you chauvinist codger."

"Maybe I'll have my hemorrhoids looked at after all, if hospitals nowadays are filled with lady doctors talking about the size of cocks."

"Well, am I right?"

"I forgot now who was taking which side of this argument. But I'd put my money on the myth. At least as far as Ham Asterling is concerned. He's a little guy with little feet and a tool to match."

"Are you sure?"

"Listen, Chas, guys always know these things. Locker rooms, showers, steam baths. We just know."

"Thanks, Den. I owe you a drink. By the way, have you met our new investigative reporter?"

"The dame? Yeah."

"So what do you think?"

"Good legs, good hair."

"Aw, lay off it, Den. You know what I mean. What kind of reporter do you take her to be?"

"I'd watch my wallet."

"Huh?"

"Bulldog of a reporter. Would wrestle the Chief Justice to the ground without a qualm. She'll get the story. But I—"

"Why do you say that?"

"Just a feeling."

"But she's a Pulitzer Prize winner."

"So was Janet Cooke."

"Den, you're a peach. I owe you two drinks. Or better yet, a scoop. I'll talk to you this afternoon."

I felt great. If Dawn had lied about Ham, there was no reason to believe her story about Dave.

Back to trapping a murderer, I started working the phones, sidetracked slightly for personal business. Dave wasn't home, and as usual I couldn't tell whether his answering machine was actually working. I left him a message anyway, telling him I had something of great importance to discuss.

Then I spent the next hour calling back people who'd left me messages. Mom wasn't home, and hardly any of the chefs were at their restaurants on a

Saturday morning, which suited me fine. I really just wanted to quickly thank them electronically, and get on with the rest of the calls. The few I needed to talk to in person I tracked down at home. Then I told the nursing staff that I didn't want any calls.

The timing of my scheme was going to be tricky. If Lily wasn't too late, if Roland's delivery wasn't too early, and if Homer would stay cool, I might carry this off. Otherwise, it was going to be an embarrassing mess.

First step: Lily. She arrived with plenty of time to spare, bringing the newspaper and a bag of my favorite lemon-poppyseed scones. She peeled off her cardigan and two pullovers, unwound her six-foot mohair scarf and piled the debris on the window-sill.

"You look much better, Mama," she said, plunking herself on the bed and curling up beside me.

So did she. "And you look as if you've caught up on some sleep," I told her as I wrapped my arms around her. Lily can be so cuddly when she's feeling good.

"I guess we're both in relatively good shape today. But I'm still worried, Mama. As soon as you get out of the hospital, you're going to go right back to your promiscuous eating. And the murderer is still out there."

"I can be more careful, Lily. Besides, I think this is going to be over soon. I've got some ideas."

"Tell me."

"I will. But later. First I've got an idea for your

apartment hunting. I want to look at the real-estate ads with you. The point is, I think you need to start looking today if you're going to get the pick of the rentals coming up in the next month."

Lily wasn't about to protest changing the subject to feature her. She unfolded herself and pulled the classified section from the newspaper, then drew up the chair beside the bed so we could both read the ads at the same time.

We debated various locations, marked the interesting possibilities, then circled three listings that looked promising enough that I wished I could go look at them with her. I was enjoying the process so much that for the moment I forgot what I'd planned for the rest of my day.

As if to remind me, Marcel and Marie Claire bustled in, encased in a cloud of worry. Marie Claire enveloped me in a hug, clucking about how pale I looked. As she turned to wrap her mothering arms around Lily, Marcel awkwardly approached my bed, nibbling on his lower lip and kneading the pair of gloves he held in his hand.

I didn't want to stretch this out any longer than necessary. As soon as we'd gone over my medical updates and begun to broach more general subjects, I turned to Marie Claire and asked her if she would do me a very big favor.

"Of course, my dear. I was going to insist you let me do some shopping for you anyway," Marie Claire responded, as I knew she would.

"It is shopping that I need. In a way. I need you to take Lily to look at three apartments. She's going to move here, and she doesn't know the neighborhoods or the real-estate market the way you do."

Lily looked up in surprise, her jaw set and her eyes flashing in alarm. I knew she wanted to strangle me, but she wouldn't hurt Marie Claire's feelings by voicing her protest. I'd counted on that.

"Lily's moving here? How wonderful. We'll all be so happy to have her back home." Marie Claire flushed with pleasure as she took Lily's hand in both of hers. "Lily, if you don't think I'd be intruding, I would love to look at apartments with you. Your mother knows I've always been interested in decorating."

Lily looked as if she'd just bitten into something blazing hot and was going to have to swallow it.

"And I remember when you dabbled in real estate," I encouraged Marie Claire.

"When would you like to go, my dear?"

Marie Claire addressed her question to Lily, but I answered it.

"Right now, if you could. The good apartments get snatched up so fast in Washington. We've found three really interesting ones that are having open houses, and I think Lily shouldn't wait until tomorrow."

Marie Claire was surprised, but ever gracious. She hesitated only slightly before she agreed, then insisted on her own that she take Lily right away.

Lily was still trying to swallow what I'd fed her. She looked a little nauseated.

"I'll entertain Marcel while you're gone," I promised. "Some other chefs will probably be coming by, and we'll have plenty to talk about. I really appreciate this, Marie Claire." I did. And I tried to throw an apologetic glance toward Lily, but she didn't meet my eyes.

I felt like scum. I kept reminding myself that this was a matter of life and death.

# twenty-four

Our first moments alone were like a blind date you'd wish on an enemy. Marcel isn't a talker under the best of circumstances. Most of the verbal interaction in his life consists of giving orders and chastising underlings. Even with his pals, he tends to communicate in bursts of passionate discourse rather than even exchange. The fact that I was about to write a review of his restaurant was the least of our barriers.

So I made small talk. Babbled. About the weather and Lily moving back home. Anything I could think of except restaurants. I also kept surreptitiously hitting the call button at the side of my bed to summon Hilda. She wasn't listening.

I grew so desperate for conversational topics that I was about to ask Marcel if he'd seen any good movies lately. And I know that chefs never get to the movies. In the nick of time, Hilda came to my rescue.

"Here's the tray you wanted for your lunch, Miss Wheatley. My, isn't it beautiful. I'll just leave it right here, and when the proper lunch trays are sent up, I'll bring along your beverage."

Hilda marched out to the tune of my thanks.

Marcel had perked up at the sight of the tray. Food is more arousing than women and more exciting than soccer to an aging chef. For the first time since his arrival, Marcel stopped biting his lip and twisting his hands.

He stood as close to my bed as possible without touching it. He gazed patiently and lovingly at the tray as I peeled off the foil and revealed a geometric triumph of sushi, rows and rows of sushi, every fishy hue radiant against black seaweed and white rice.

"This is not hospital food, is it?" Marcel wondered, awe in his voice.

"Far from it. One of the chefs sent it. Isn't it gorgeous?" I hoped he wouldn't ask me which chef, but I was prepared to lie if he did.

"Very beautiful. I have always been most impressed by Japanese cooking."

"Why don't you try some? There's way too much for me." To encourage him, I took a piece and bit in, rolling my eyes with the deliciousness of it. A little overplaying my role, but it was truly wonderful.

"You wouldn't mind? Perhaps just a taste."

I held the tray toward Marcel, turning it so that the seaweed-wrapped rice rolls with their tuna-pink centers were closest to him. He took one.

"Very unusual texture," he said as he licked the creamy residue from his lips.

"Creamy. I know. But what do you think about the taste?"

"*Bon*. Good." Marcel's eyes shifted from me, bounced from wall to wall looking for a safe place to settle.

"Have another. Not too much horseradish for you?" I held out the tray again, this time aiming toward him the oval pieces piled with tiny bright-red grains of roe. He took another.

"I like horseradish," he said around a mouthful of red and black. "And I am very fond of this black seaweed."

"Marcel, that's licorice." I said it softly, so softly that the words only gradually seeped into his mind.

"You mean that funny Japanese leaf, the one that tastes like anise crossed with mint?" His hands were twisting again.

"No, not shiso. And not seaweed. Licorice. Real licorice. And the red roe is sugar."

"I don't understand." One hand reached to wipe his mouth, as if he could erase the taste, or the fact of his having eaten.

"The tuna, Marcel, it's butter cream."

"Why butter cream?"

"It's dessert."

Marcel crumpled. He seemed to shrink as he huddled in the chair, looking at me as a dog looks at his master after he's been caught polishing off the rib roast.

Pity wasn't in my emotional vocabulary at the moment. I was enthralled by the pursuit.

"You can't taste, can you?"

Marcel's eyes were rimmed in red. They were pleading with me, but he didn't make a sound.

"I should have realized it when you complained about Patrick O'Connell's tomato and jalapeño sundaes at CityTastes. You thought they were dessert." In my rage I'd thrown off my blanket and sat up, as if I were going to leap out of bed.

Marcel shrank back, still mute.

"That's the reason you didn't notice how rancid the salmon tarts were when you tasted one at the memorial."

He squeezed his eyes closed, as if my words were blinding him.

"And that's why your *soupes en chemises* were so awful at CityTastes."

Tears rolled down Marcel's cheeks. But my last accusation roused him to a faint, miserable protest.

"No, Chas. I can still cook. I know I can still cook."

I ignored his protest. I went straight for the jugular. "That's why you killed Laurence."

I was trembling with anger. Now that I had voiced my accusation, it actually seemed true for the first time. Marcel the friend had been transformed into Marcel the enemy. "And that's why you tried to kill me."

"No, oh no. That's not the way it was. I didn't kill him. And I never, never would have harmed you." Marcel was blubbering, his words thick and runny with tears.

"I don't believe you." My trembling receded. Now I was cold. Cold and hard. I needed to get a confession out of him. "Why should I believe you? Laurence discovered that your taste was gone. He was going to tell the investors in New York. He was going to kill your partnership. Of course you murdered him."

Marcel looked like a puny rag doll after years of a child's mistreatment. His head was in his hands, and I found myself talking to his cowlick, listening to muffled protests.

"I didn't kill him. I could not have killed him. I just went to argue with him and to plead with him. I thought he might change his mind if I explained to him how well I have been running my restaurant even when my sense of taste is gone."

"You went there to kill him. You took digoxin with you. You planned it, and you poisoned him." My voice was raw and icy as the scene began to take shape in my head. The brutality of it, the murdering of a life-long friend in cold blood, enraged me.

"No, I didn't kill him. I swear I didn't kill him. It was an accident."

"An accident? How does a massive dose of digoxin get to be an accident?" I snarled at Marcel, my hands clenching so hard that they ached. They ached for his neck to be between them.

"I didn't! I swear on my mother's soul that I didn't. It was an accident. I could never do such a thing. It was Laurence who plotted and planned, who wanted to hurt me. He was the guilty one."

I began to understand something about confessions. I couldn't just accuse Marcel and expect him to cave in and admit what he'd done. He wasn't ready to proclaim his guilt. But he clearly wanted to talk, to unburden himself. He was ready to defend himself, and if I let him talk himself out, maybe he'd also incriminate himself.

I needed his confession. There might be no other

way to tie him to the murder. I took a deep breath and calmed my voice.

"I hadn't thought of it that way, Marcel. I guess I didn't try to see it from your point of view. It must have been awful for you. How long has your taste been gone?" I asked in a tone I hoped didn't sound as smarmy as it felt.

"It's been six months. Ever since that operation to stop my snoring. The doctor never warned me that this could happen. He said he told me, but he never did. And there's nothing that can be done about it." A sob broke through.

"Nobody knew?" I tried to put sympathy into my voice.

"Only Marie Claire. It wasn't so difficult to keep up the pretense. I can often just look at a dish and tell how it is going to taste. Besides, at my stage of life, I hardly ever do any actual cooking." The words were tumbling out.

"I always had everyone else taste the sauces along with me, so I could follow their lead. Not even my sous-chef knew of my problem." Marcel had revived a small measure of dignity. He was sitting up straighter, though his shoulders were slumped in submission.

"At some point Laurence found out," I prodded.

Marcel's eyes weren't focused on me. They no longer roamed the walls for a place to land. They were focused on some middle distance. In the past, I supposed.

"My friend for so many years. Almost like a son. And yet he showed no sympathy. He treated it like a bad joke. What people call a sick joke."

"You told him?"

"Certainly not. He guessed. He dealt with it the way he dealt with everything else, like a contest. Winning and losing. He trapped me. One day he insisted I taste his quilts. He said he was experimenting with a new way of cooking them and wanted my advice. I told him that I thought the filling did not have quite the right texture, that it was soft, like a paste." Marcel stopped, as if cowed by the humiliation he was recalling.

"Like a paste?" I had to keep him talking.

"A puree, not the solid feel of his usual smoked salmon filling." Marcel's jaw clenched as he stopped, then started again. "He started to laugh. It wasn't smoked salmon. It was eggplant. He had made up a whole batch of his disgusting quilts, filled with eggplant. Just to play a joke on me. Such trouble he went to. Just to be cruel."

"But he had his reasons." I squelched a small bubble of authentic pity. I dared not divert myself from egging Marcel on to say more.

"The man had no honor. He didn't really care whether I could taste or not. He didn't even care about our years together in France, when I taught him and guided him. It didn't matter to him that I could still run a kitchen better than anybody, even without being able to taste the food." I'd never heard Marcel talk so much. Now that he'd started, the words kept flowing.

"I can touch the food and know from the texture whether it is right. I can hear, when the sauce is simmering, whether it is thick enough. I can see what is the right color of brown, how smooth it is. Nobody knows more than I do when it comes to cooking the fish so it is juicy, or keeping all the flavor in the vegetables.

"And most chefs never taste what they are cooking anyway. Laurence knew all that. He just wanted to get rid of me and have it all for himself. I begged, and he refused to listen."

"So you killed him."

"NO!"

I forced myself to relax, to take a deep breath and unclench my fists. Homer had told me that murderers have a drive to confess. Dave had once said that silence is an investigator's best weapon.

So I shut my mouth.

Marcel started again with denials: "I am not a murderer. You know I could not be a violent man."

He went on to excuses: "There are things worse than death. You can kill a man's life without killing his body. A man does not have the right to destroy another man's honor, to take away his livelihood."

Marcel was working up to it. I could hear it in his accelerating emotion. He was steeling himself inch by inch, tightening his stomach, straightening his spine, locking his shoulders. His jaw clenched, his mouth grew firm. He looked like a man facing a firing squad and still refusing to squeal on his comrades.

His eyes fastened on mine. I knew it was time.

Marcel started telling his story. "Chas, I went to see him after I finished cooking for CityTastes. I waited for him to finish. I stood outside in the dark and watched for him. Of course he invited me in for a drink."

A drink? THE drink.

Marcel was in no hurry now. His tale wandered. He described the cold and how he'd kept his coat and gloves on inside Laurence's apartment. I didn't want to interrupt him yet to ask about his being in the restaurant first, so I just let him continue.

He told about Laurence pouring them both a calvados. Marcel had been so nervous he'd felt close to screaming. He'd realized he hadn't the faintest possibility of being tactful. But he'd plunged into his rehearsed speech anyway. He'd tried to persuade Laurence not to tell the investors about his disability. He would do anything Laurence asked in return. He spoke of loyalty. He talked of their decades of friendship. He wound up begging.

"Nothing moved Laurence. In fact, he was so unconcerned that he interrupted me right in the middle and complained that he could still smell fish on his clothes. He said he needed to change his clothes."

Laurence had left Marcel to stew and gone to take a shower. All the while, Marcel paced the living room and practiced what he would say.

When Laurence returned, in his robe, Marcel was so nervous he was about to snap. In fact, he spilled his drink, and Laurence had to go and find him a towel.

"I wanted to kill him."

I'd been waiting to hear those words.

"God must have heard me," he continued.

That wasn't the accomplice I'd had in mind.

Marcel's eyes fastened on mine for the first time. "God struck him dead."

"C'mon, Marcel. You didn't give him a little help?"

"I helped by doing nothing. He handed me my drink and, as if my thoughts were a loaded gun, he collapsed. His heart gave out."

At that point, Marcel's underpinnings gave out, too. Once again his voice broke. "I let him die. I just stood there and did nothing. I didn't help. I didn't call an ambulance. I thanked God, and let him die."

He sobbed the last few words. Then he poured out his wordless grief until his sobs turned into dry heaves.

It could have been ten seconds or ten minutes that I watched him from my rumpled bed, thinking it was a flimsy, ludicrous judgment seat. I couldn't think of a thing to say. Marcel seemed utterly incapable of another word.

Yet there was one more question.

"You haven't talked about when you met him earlier, at the restaurant."

Marcel sprang at me with a low growl. More than ever before, his beaky face looked like a bird's, but this time a vulture's. He knocked the tray of buttery sushi rolls to the floor and whacked me across the face with his hand.

I was slow to react. I'd barely managed to scoot halfway toward the far end of the bed when he came at me for a second blow. This time he had in his hand the small, curved, stainless-steel tray I'd assumed was on my bed table in case I had to throw up. This surely wasn't the way it was supposed to be used. I couldn't raise my arm in time to ward off the blow, but it didn't hurt as much as I'd expected. It only glanced off my temple weakly.

"Drop it!" That line was Homer's.

I was wondering what had taken him so long.

Homer deposited Marcel in the chair from which he'd sprung, pulled his hands behind his back, and handcuffed them. Then he came to examine me.

"You okay?" Homer swept back my hair to peer at the temple Marcel had bashed, then turned my face to see how my cheek had dealt with the first whack.

"No physical harm," I said.

"A small bump," he corrected me.

Then he reached to shut off the tape recorder hidden in my tissue box. He walked over to Marcel, who was curled around the arm of the chair. Homer stood silently over Marcel, who no longer seemed to register his presence.

Homer read him his rights, then asked, "What happened to the glasses you drank from?" His voice was jarring in the quiet room.

To my surprise, Marcel answered conversationally, as if Homer's presence needed no explanation. "I put them in my pocket, then threw them away."

"You planted the lipstick smudges?"

"I was afraid. I wanted it to look as if a woman had been there, and maybe he'd had a heart attack when they . . . you know."

"What else did you do?"

"I found some stockings, and I . . . sort of . . . put them around the room. The kind of thing . . . one under the couch." He broke down again. "And now I miss him. I loved him. He was my family. Oh, Chas," he wailed, "I'm sorry. I didn't mean to hurt you."

Homer gently took hold of Marcel's left arm and unlocked the cuff, helping him to stand upright. "I think we should let Ms. Wheatley get some rest now, while we go and talk someplace else. How about you and me going down to the homicide office and filling in the rest of this story."

"Am I under arrest?"

"Well, not quite yet. At least not as long as you're willing to come along and see how we're going to work this out."

Marcel stooped to pick up the gloves he'd dropped on the floor. He wrapped his coat around his shoulders like a cape, and shuffled to the door as if he'd suddenly become an old man. At the door he turned, belatedly remembering I was there. He held up one hand in a kind of immobile wave and said, "Tell Marie Claire."

"Doesn't she know?" I realized he'd meant for me to tell her that he was at the police station, but he immediately understood that I was asking whether she was aware of his involvement with Laurence's death.

"No, she was still in Mexico. And I didn't have the heart to tell her the next day when she came back. I just wanted to forget that I'd been there. You'll have to tell her."

Now I really felt like Marcel's latest victim.


Once I was alone, I had time to agonize over what I hadn't accomplished. I'd dragged only half a confession out of Marcel. Still worse, if what he'd said was true, I'd implicated him without uncovering the killer. Instead of extricating myself from danger, I'd pulled Marcel in with me.

Was he a killer or a callous bystander? My life was revolving around accusations and denials. I'd closed Dave out by not believing his denials. Was Marcel going to be locked up because he had no support for his?

I wanted to be out of this sterile room full of sickness and death. I craved going home and crawling into my own bed. But I couldn't leave yet. I had to wait for Lily. And that meant I was going to have to face Marie Claire. I certainly didn't want to do that in my pajamas.

The nurse called someone to clean up the mess from the overturned sushi, and I asked her to turn my phone off. I couldn't deal with one more well-wisher. I took a long, hot shower and dressed in the jeans and somber turtleneck Lily had picked out for me to wear home.

Marie Claire and Lily arrived while my back was turned. "You look absolutely elegant," Marie Claire said. I jumped as if I'd been stung.

"Mama, one of those apartments has real possibilities," Lily burst out, too excited to stop for a hello. She'd apparently forgotten she'd been railroaded into this field trip. She started sloughing off her scarf and sweaters.

Marie Claire looked around with a question in her eyes. She walked over to the window and peered out, leaving her purse on the sill as she began to unbutton her coat.

"Where is—" she began, but I interrupted her.

"Look, there's a problem," I plunged in.

Two faces paled before me.

"Are you . . . ?" Lily asked.

"Where is Marcel?" Marie Claire spoke at the same time, her eyes searching the room as if she might spot him in the closet or peeking out from behind the curtains. Moving faster than I'd ever seen her do, she rushed over to the door, then looked up and down the hall.

"He's with Homer Jones, the detective."

"The detective? What is wrong? Why?" Marie Claire's eyes opened wide and her hands flew to cover her mouth.

She must have guessed. She didn't look mystified, she looked horrified.

"It's about Laurence's death," I said stupidly, stating the obvious.

"Marcel had nothing to do with Laurence's death!" Marie Claire's voice hadn't the faintest uncertainty.

"I'm afraid he did. You were away, so you wouldn't have known, but he went to see Laurence that night."

"He did no such thing." It wasn't just an answer, it was a proclamation. Marie Claire's eyes narrowed and hardened into an expression totally alien to the face I'd long known. Her stare felt like poisoned arrows, and her tone warned me that I must purge such thoughts from my mind. Lily backed toward the door, ready to retreat from this threatening scene.

"Marie Claire, I'm sorry. I'm so sorry to have to tell you this. But it's true. Marcel went to Laurence's apartment the night of his death. Marcel confessed to me about arguing with Laurence, and about planting lipstick stains and stockings to make it look as if a woman had been there. He saw Laurence die. He saw him die and did nothing about it." I rushed through the telling, trying to squeeze in the news before Marie Claire could interrupt me.

"Oh, Mother, how could you!" Lily, who never called me Mother except during the moments she hated me, stood uncertainly, her eyes darting from Marie Claire to me. "That's why you sent us out! How could you use me like that, like some kind of child?" She looked as if she were about to pitch a tantrum. Instead, she grabbed the scarf and sweaters she'd just begun shedding, then turned and ran out the door. I didn't know hospital doors could slam.

Marie Claire had murder in her eyes. I began to edge off the bed, on the far side.

"You're lying. He wasn't there." Her voice was choked with anguish. Her pink cheeks grew dark, her soft wrinkles taut with fury.

"Why would I lie about such a thing? He told me himself. He confessed it all. It's even on tape."

She threw her head back and brayed at the ceiling. "I didn't know. Oh, God, I didn't know. How could I have known?" It was a prayer full of fear.

She lowered her head and stared at me. All sound and motion stopped, as if the frame had been frozen and the volume turned low.

"You bitch."

Her voice terrified me. I'd been expecting a shout, but it was a quiet accusation. She was keeping it low. She didn't want any passersby to hear.

She continued in a menacing near whisper, "You always have to stick your nose into everything, don't you? I saw you catch him in his mistake at CityTastes. He'd always been so good, so careful. Until that night, when he was upset and he let down his guard. You're always so smart, always judging everybody. One mistake, and you were ready to destroy him. Nobody knew. Nobody but Laurence. And then you."

I reached for the buzzer on the side of the bed, but Marie Claire had anticipated that. Faster than I could find it, she yanked it from behind the bed so that it dangled out of my reach.

The woman was quick. And strong. As I leapt off the far side of the bed, she shoved it to pin me against the wall. The force knocked the wind out of me. It also smashed the bottle of wine Ari had left on the table. As the red puddle snaked across the floor and the smell of boozy grapes filled the room, Marie Claire picked up the jagged bottle and brandished it. She began to swing it back and forth like a hypnotist mesmerizing me into staying in my corner.

"Look, Marie Claire, I'm sure he'll get out of this," I pleaded. Maybe I should have screamed, but I was afraid that would provoke her to slash me. "He was only a witness, a bystander. The police will catch the real killer, and then they won't care about Marcel not having helped him."

I was blathering, and Marie Claire obviously didn't

believe me. I wasn't sure I did either. But as I watched her watching me, saw her thinking about how to punish me for endangering her husband, I didn't know what to do but keep talking, while hoping that someone would come to take my temperature.

"His sense of taste doesn't really matter so greatly, Marie Claire," I said with as much persuasiveness as I could muster. Not much at all.

The bottle kept waving, as if seeking more red liquid—from my veins. Where was everybody? I looked out the window in the futile hope I could signal to somebody that I was being threatened by a madwoman.

The only weapon I had to fight back with was my blather.

"At his age, the sous-chef does all the cooking, everybody knows that. The chef is really the teacher. And Marcel is a great teacher. Besides, he still has his sense of touch, which is even more important. Marcel himself said that chefs never taste what they are cooking anyway. Even Beethoven could still compose after he went deaf." With that lame ending, I ran out of words.

"Beethoven did not depend on publicists." Marie Claire swung the broken bottle like a scimitar.

"You, of all people, know that a restaurant's success is not about good food." Swish. The movement of the bottle punctuated each sentence.

"It is image. People have to trust that the chef knows what is good." Swish.

"Sheep that they all are, they can't taste for themselves." Swish.

"They can only taste what the chef tells them is good—or what you tell them." Swish.

"If they lose confidence in the chef, no matter how great he is, they will go elsewhere." Marie Claire's voice slashed so fiercely that I was mentally ducking her blows.

Marie Claire had slowly edged forward as she swung the bottle. She was just a few inches from the foot of the bed. She must have thought she was cornering me. I mentally mustered my strength, counted a silent one-two-three, then shoved the bed as hard as I could.

It didn't work. I was weaker than I realized. The bed moved only a few ineffectual inches.

It gave me enough room to escape from my corner, though. I grabbed Marie Claire's purse from the windowsill and threw it at her. I hardly expected it to fell her, but as I hoped, it distracted her momentarily. I scrambled back on the bed, ready to leap free on the other side and strike back. The metal tray Marcel had slugged me with was on my bedside table, and I could use a pillow to protect myself from the jagged bottle.

Once again Marie Claire was faster than I anticipated.

She threw the bottle.

I ducked, but for no good reason. The bottle smashed into the door on the other side of the room. She hadn't been aiming at me after all.

Marie Claire grabbed her purse off the floor. "I'll get you for what you've done to Marcel." She was rooting around in it, and suddenly I was afraid she had a gun.

A makeup kit, then a wad of tissues, flew out of her purse as she rummaged through it. My breathing grew fast and shallow.

I almost didn't hear the knock at the door.

Dr. Bannister edged the door open and peered in tentatively, as if fearing he'd be interrupting me deliciously in the midst of breaking some hospital rule. I would have welcomed even a nurse wielding a rectal thermometer.

"May I come in?" he asked, clearing his throat but not waiting for an answer before he stepped into the room.

Marie Claire, crying into her tissues, one glove and a comb trailing behind, just missed slamming into him as she fled through the door. I started to shout a warning, to yell for the doctor to stop that woman. But before I could get the words out, I thought better of it. Had Marie Claire really been attacking me, or had I overreacted to her unfocused rage? Besides, my goal at the moment was to be released from the hospital, not to risk being considered worthy of further observation or to have to wait for the police to come. I'd call Homer to tell him about Marie Claire's weird behavior as soon as I got home.

I leaned back on my pillow and concentrated on slowing my pulse lest Dr. Bannister decide to take my blood pressure before he signed me out.

"So." He paused, looking me over from head to toe. "How are you feeling?"

"Perfectly fit, Doctor. Ready to go."

"Looks like you've had a little accident here," he

said as he took in the broken bottle and puddles of red wine.

"Oh, I'm sorry I made such a mess. Somehow I knocked over the bottle. And the buzzer fell behind the bed, so I couldn't call the nurse, and I couldn't find my slippers so I was afraid of stepping on glass..." In my nervous relief my mouth was running on automatic.

"Don't worry, we'll get someone in here to clean this up right away. You just stay right there until they come. We wouldn't want you to get cut, not after that quick recovery of yours. No, definitely not. Especially not when you are just ready to leave." He began to back out the door, wrinkling his nose at the mess.

"Dr. Bannister." I stopped him at the door.

"Yes?"

"Thank you for saving my life."

"That's my job. Now you remember to watch that cholesterol."

# twenty-five

I took a taxi home. That's how lost I felt. For once I was too tired and depressed to walk, and I wasn't even sure I could find the way.

The flowers in front of my apartment door—from Helen, dear and thoughtful boss that she was—didn't help. She'd sent them to my home instead of to the hospital so I could enjoy them longer. But I wasn't ready to take joy in anything.

Lily wasn't there. I knew she wouldn't be.

I dropped my infamous red-and-black coat on the floor and my bags beside it, kicked off my shoes, and huddled in my soft velvety platform rocker. My mind was occupied with refereeing an argument inside my head.

How could Lily blame me? Maybe because I blamed myself.

How did I get into this mess? Easy—I walked into it on my own two feet. Then stuck them both right in my mouth.

I could no longer even justify being angry with Marie Claire for going berserk at my expense. She hadn't actually hurt me, and probably wouldn't have. I'd seen her protect Marcel before, and even admired her loyalty. You had to give a woman leeway when you told her you'd just dynamited her whole life.

I watched the shadows creep along the bare wood floor, very slowly nudging the light into a corner.

The phone rang, and I listened to Bull telling my answering machine that he wanted me to give a speech to some dental society his brother belonged to, and he needed to know by Monday so the program could be printed. I guess even the executive editor of a major metropolitan newspaper has to grovel before his family.

What could I do to make Lily forgive me?

Maybe I could start practicing on Dave. I pulled myself up from the chair with such difficulty I might have been sitting there a month. My legs were stiff as I hobbled over to the phone.

Dave's machine answered. I wondered if he, too, was listening to the calls without moving to join the conversation. If so, my message didn't tempt him to take an active role.

I called Den Ranger and briefly filled him in on the events. For once I appreciated that the guy doesn't ask many questions.

I was ready to retreat back to my chair but the ring of the phone caught me off guard. My hand was on automatic: I picked it up.

"Chas, sweetie, are you all right?" It was Paul.

"Not really." My own voice sounded more distant to me than Paul's.

"Maybe I can help. I can't talk long, but I wanted to tell you that Lily is here. She's talking to Ari. When she told us what happened, I realized you must be awfully upset, so I called the hospital. Why didn't you let us take you home, darlin'? You shouldn't be alone. Would you like me to come and get you?"

"Thanks, Paul, but I think being alone is just what I need right now. What's Lily going to do?"

"Ari is teaching her the facts of life. Well, I don't really mean the facts of life. She's known those all too well since she was thirteen. But he's explaining the realities of people. Of Laurence, anyway. God knows it took Ari himself long enough to learn."

"She's so angry with me." I squeezed my eyes tight, trying to stem the flow of tears.

"No, she's just looking for someone to blame for the world being such a hard place. You're the safest bet, because she knows you'll always be there for her no matter how hard she is on you at the moment."

"Tell her she's right. Tell her I love her, and that I didn't mean to hurt anybody. I don't know . . . I can't really think now what's the right thing to tell her. I'm just too tired."

"You must be feeling terrible. We all are, about poor driven Marcel. Did he really do it? No, you don't have to answer that. We'll keep Lily here until she simmers down. And by then she'll be ready to listen to how even Ari was ready to kill Laurence, and how I would have had to turn him in." Paul laughed.

I didn't. If Lily had run out on me at the hospital because I'd set up Marcel, what would she have done if she'd known my suspicions of Ari?

• • •

The shadow had swept away all the light by the time I curled back into my chair, this time with a crocheted blanket I'd bought in Paris's Marais district, where Laurence and I had gone to search for old kitchenware in the waist-deep bins. I waited to hear voices break through the silence, invited by my answering machine. None called. No Lily. No Dave.

Instead, a voice broke through my front door, following a knock. It was Sherele, smelling of chicken soup and apple strudel. Her Jewish mother phase.

"Girlfriend, you look like hell," she said warmly, setting her packages down right where she stood and tucking strands of my straggling hair back into their hairpins.

Sherele, much more efficient than her pearl-gray miniskirt and skimpy tangerine satin top suggested, fixed my place up in a jiffy. She hung up my coat, stashed the contents of my bags, turned the radio to her favorite jazz station, and set the soup and a teakettle on the stove. I followed her around helplessly, unable to do more than deliver a nonstop monologue about everything that had gone wrong today—everything except Dave.

Ten minutes later I was talked out, seated at my dining table with a cup of tea and a slice of still warm strudel in front of me. The napkin was folded into a triangle.

"Soup later. Bad as you feel, I think you need to start with dessert." Sherele sat down across from me, digging her fork into a piece of strudel even bigger than mine. Not for the first time, I wondered whether I should try the all-dessert diet that seemed to keep Sherele so thin.

"You're just beating up on yourself, honey. As the bard said, 'Who can be wise, amazed, temperate and furious, loyal and neutral, in a moment'?"

"Which bard?"

Sherele wrinkled her nose and opened her mouth to utter something cynical, so I amended my question.

"I mean, which play?"

"*Macbeth.*"

"See, a tragedy. Just as I figured."

"A well of wisdom. And as Ms. Macbeth said, 'Things without all remedy should be without regard; what's done is done.'"

"That's for sure. But Shakespeare got to ring down the curtain. I've got to hang around forever cleaning up the mess I've made."

"Don't worry too much about that, honey. We've got Homer to help."

That snapped me out of my whining. "You've talked to him? What's happened with Marcel?"

"That wife of his pulled herself together and hopped on down to homicide with a lawyer in tow. They took Marcel right home. Homer says he had mixed feelings, not so much because he thought the law ought to be holding the guy hostage, but because Marcel himself was feeling so guilty that he wanted to go to jail. The poor slob thinks he deserves to be locked up."

"That's the best argument I've heard for his innocence. Of course that leaves us without a murderer again," I said. Sherele and the strudel had revived me. I was back in investigative mode. I got up to help myself to the second course, a family-size bowl of chicken soup.

I held the pot toward Sherele to offer her some, but she waved it away. "Don't want to lose the taste of the strudel in my mouth quite yet."

A sentiment I should practice.


As if he'd smelled the strudel all the way down at the homicide office, Homer showed up just as I was getting ready to put it away. He was bristling with nervous energy.

Sherele invited him to sit beside her on the sofa, but he couldn't be still. He asked how I was doing, he asked how Sherele was doing, he wondered what smelled so good, he guessed whose jazz trumpet was crooning from the radio. And all the while he strolled nervously around the room, picking up a paperweight to examine, running a dust-seeking finger along a windowsill, uncovering and peering into a handcrafted wooden box, pulling a loose thread from a curtain.

"Homer Jones, you've just got to sit down and stop picking on this entire living room. You're going to have it in shreds before long." Sherele tapped the pillow beside her, as if calling her dog to heel.

Homer heeled. He plopped down on the couch, positioned his hands firmly on his knees, and poured out his frustration.

● ● ●

After Marcel had been sprung—or pushed out into the cold if you saw it from his point of view—Homer got to thinking about what a wimp Marcel was. Not the kind of guy to plan such a bold and simple murder, he thought. Yet his motive rang true to this experienced detective.

"I kept coming back to the motive. It fit so well. The timing fit so neatly with the investors' meeting Laurence was calling in New York. The method fit with someone who knew Laurence intimately and could drop by casually late at night without raising any suspicions. Someone who knew about Laurence's heart condition and that he was already taking digoxin. This motive made the case feel solved." Homer was up again, pacing, absently patting his pockets like an ex-smoker looking for ghost cigarettes.

Sherele tried to interrupt to ask whether he wanted something to eat, but he didn't even seem to hear her. She shrugged and unfolded herself from the couch, briefly stroking his cheek as she passed him on her way to the kitchen. She was about to administer her restorative strudel once again.

I was thinking about the subtext in the room. Homer was immobilized. Sherele had switched into action on his behalf.

Of course.

A jolt of inspiration propelled me off the sofa. "Maybe the motive was right but it was pinned on the wrong person," I said, joining Homer in his pacing.

Sherele's head peered around the kitchen wall. She looked as if she'd just heard Romeo, instead of killing himself, stop and suggest that maybe the family doctor could revive the apparently dead Juliet. "Now that's what I call using your head," she said.

My inspiration hadn't made much impression on Homer. He didn't even slow his stride. "Who's that you're suggesting? Who are you figuring to have the same motive?"

"It's Marcel's motive." I was thinking aloud. "His disablity, his humiliation. His life about to be washed down the drain by Laurence."

"I got that far," Homer said.

"But maybe the deed was done by his surrogate, his protector." I paused, unable to resist drawing out the moment a bit.

"Marie Claire," Sherele and I said in unison, then high-fived each other.

Homer cocked his head and thought a minute, then rolled his shoulders, loosening himself up to refute us. "Ladies, I must confess, that thought did cross my mind. After all, what kind of woman has her lawyer ready on a Saturday afternoon? Without even calling down to the station first to find out what is going on? That woman is cool. She wasn't nervous or apologetic. She didn't ask any questions. Definitely cool. Too cool."

Sherele and I did a little dance of joy as she swept a plate of strudel off the kitchen counter, setting it on the table with a flourish.

"You're forgetting something, though," Homer said. He looked pleased, but I couldn't immediately tell whether that was because of the strudel or the flaw in our argument. "Remember, Marie Claire was in Mexico when Laurence was poisoned." Definitely smug.

Sherele showed her pique by leaving the napkin unfolded.

Homer strode toward the table, paused to admire the strudel, then sat down and dug in his fork. He ignored us both while he rolled his eyes to the ceiling and savored a bite.

"Aah, even better than my grandmother's."

Did Homer have a Jewish grandmother?

Before the question blurted out of my mouth, another thought popped into my head. I left Homer to his strudel and went into my bedroom, which also serves as my study. From an unruly stack of papers on the third shelf of my bookcase I pulled what I wanted: "The Metropolitan Washington Airports Authority Flight Guide."

"Take a tip from a journalist, and never leave home without a flight guide," I said when I returned, waving the booklet. "The only way Marie Claire could have arrived from Mexico City Monday morning was if she took a flight after midnight. She wouldn't have done that."

Homer continued eating. I hadn't even made him pause.

"I had that same thought," he said maddeningly. "And you're right. She didn't leave that late. In fact, she was supposed to arrive in Washington Sunday night, in plenty of time to poison the chef if she was so inclined. But her flight was delayed by mechanical difficulties so that it didn't arrive at Dulles until Monday morning."

I wasn't ready to let go of my idea. I leafed through the airport guide, asking impatiently, "Where was it delayed?"

"Orlando," Homer answered, scraping his fork along his plate to round up the last flakes of strudel. No doubt he was trying to signal Sherele to offer him another piece, but her attention was riveted on me.

"The fact that her flight didn't arrive until Monday morning doesn't necessarily mean that Marie Claire herself didn't arrive until Monday morning," I suggested, my fingers stumbling as they searched for the Orlando page.

"You mean she took another flight?" Sherele was getting up to speed on this.

"Here it is! Arriving at National Airport, nine P.M.," I crowed. Another flight had left Orlando Sunday night in plenty of time for her to adulterate Laurence's last Gatorade.

Homer worked his mouth into a disgusted little frown and got up to offer himself another piece of strudel. "Unlike me, it was full."

"The flight?" I was incredulous. Homer had been way ahead of me on this, and hadn't even let on. He'd just let me think I was Sherlock Holmes to his Watson, whereas all the while he was Holmes and Watson.

"I checked," he explained, digging into the second piece of strudel, which I felt like snatching from him. "Yes, ma'am, the only other flight from Orlando to Washington that she could have taken that night was full. Besides, it would have been noted if her seat was empty when the flight took off the next morning."

"She traded tickets with someone," I insisted,

standing right over Homer so I could grab his strudel if he continued to piss me off.

"It would have been easy," Sherele said, hemming him in from the other side, daring him to contradict us. "She'd already gone through passport control. It would be a cinch to offer a wad of money to make it worth some woman's while to stay overnight in Orlando at the airline's expense and arrive in Washington the next morning."

I could see the scene in front of me. "She dropped by the restaurant to give Laurence a piece of her mind and a dropper full of poison, and then checked into a downtown hotel. Finally, her secret deed done, she could taxi out to Dulles the next morning in time to retrieve her luggage and be welcomed home by her unsuspecting husband." I nodded to Homer, resting my case.

"Presuming it and proving it are two different matters, Chas," Homer said, trying to tone down my imagination.

But it was veering off in a new direction.

"Marcel didn't know. Of course." The implications shook me. "That means he was the one who turned her crime into murder, because he just stood by and let Laurence die."

Sherele gave a low whistle. "Marcel was, without realizing it, sort of confessing to a murder committed by his wife!"

Homer gave his fork one final lick and stood up. "I've got an idea."

For the next hour he played the phones, making calls out on mine and getting incoming calls on his beeper. They had to do with doctors and lists, interviews and flight attendants. Homer demanded and cajoled, shouted and whined. He got busy signals, he talked to answering machines, and he turned on his formal homicide-detective voice to interview the two airline officials he could track down live on a Saturday night. He zeroed in on one final call.

"I have a feeling about this one," he told us as he dialed. "This flight attendant is a woman. Experienced. Friendly. The kind who might have noticed something.

"Hello, Mrs. Stern? This is Detective Homer Jones . . ."

He got it.

Mrs. Stern would never forget that flight, as it had caused her to miss playing tooth fairy for her daughter's first lost tooth.

She also remembered the woman in seat 19C. Rather, the two women in 19C. The reason was, she'd been admiring Marie Claire's rings on the first leg of the Mexico flight, which made her notice that the woman with the fabulous jewelry wasn't on the continuing flight in the morning. Now she recalled something that had struck her as odd: She'd caught sight of the woman with the rings as she passed the baggage claim Monday morning at Dulles. Yet in her hurry to get home, she hadn't really thought twice about it until Homer started questioning her.

"We've got her!" I crowed. Marie Claire's attack on me at the hospital had become real once again. I wanted her punished.

"What about the poison? How could she have gotten hold of that in time?" Sherele asked, always the practical one.

"As it happens," Homer launched this pièce de résistance with enough relish to drown a hot dog, "Marie Claire was returning from helping her sister-in-law put her brother's affairs in order. He died last month, you know."

Homer nodded at me, and I nodded back, getting the drift. Then he went on. "That was the first series of calls I asked our men to make tonight. Coincidentally," he drew out every syllable, "her brother died of heart failure. Even his medicine couldn't help him. Digoxin, of course. But unlike the digoxin that is prescribed here in the U.S. of A., the digoxin in Mexico is often the liquid kind. Far more concentrated, our medical examiner tells me. And far easier to dissolve, say, in a glass of Gatorade."

"Or a chocolate-covered cherry, or a shot of cognac," I reminded him.

"Right. Gotta go." Homer gave both of us a hug at once—he really was in a hurry—and disappeared. Heading for Marie Claire and Marcel in McLean.

Uncharacteristically, Sherele put the dishes in the sink and left them there. I made a move to wash them, but she pulled me away and settled me back in my chair. She lit one of the candles I keep on my mantel and moved it to the low table in front of the sofa. She put on a record, one she'd given me for a birthday, to go with the old-fashioned non-CD record player she'd bought me the year before that. The music was the kind of moody, saxophone-strong jazz that I don't understand and only play as a background to parties. Tonight, though, it began to make sense to me.

We sat silently while the music stroked some pain

that I couldn't reach on my own. Sherele had her head back and her eyes closed, tense lines between her brows showing that she was awake. We sat waiting, hardly saying anything, letting the music try to comfort us.

Sherele had dozed off by the time Homer rang the buzzer, and stumbled sleepily to let him in. Once inside the door, he leaned against it as if reluctant to come too far into the room.

"Ladies, I blew it." His words came slowly. "I was too late."

We didn't ask, "Too late for what?" We just waited.

Homer took a deep breath and said, "He was dead when I got there."

"Marcel? You mean Marcel?" My voice was hoarse and thick. Somehow I was sitting on the floor.

Homer nodded.

"And Marie Claire?"

"She's gone. Disappeared."

Homer perched himself on the edge of my rocking chair while Sherele helped me up off the floor and sat me next to her on the sofa, her arm around my shoulders. Homer's eyes roamed the room, avoiding ours, while he took himself to task. "I should have figured it out sooner. Or acted faster. But I was busy tracking down every little piece of the puzzle before I took responsibility for my hunch."

He restlessly shifted in his seat, leaned back and sat forward again, while Sherele and I silently watched him work up to the rest of the story. I only heard it in fits and blips, as if through a fog. I felt numbed to the core. But the tale seeped in.

Homer had gone out to Marcel and Marie Claire's house in McLean, and found it dark. Nobody answered the door. So he walked around and peered in windows, finally finding a kind of study or office in the basement with high windows at ground level. A figure was inert on the floor.

Since Homer didn't have jurisdiction in Virginia, he'd called the local police, then entered the house with them. Marcel was dead. There was a suicide note wadded up in the wastebasket. Marcel had blamed himself for Laurence's death. And he blamed himself for being the reason Marie Claire had poisoned Laurence. It was all his fault, as he saw it.

The rest of the house was empty. It was empty of people, empty of Marie Claire's clothes and her jewelry. It was a sure bet that tomorrow Homer would find that her bank account was empty, too.

"What's next?" Sherele could still talk; I could not.

"The Fairfax County CID is checking the airports. I figured she might be heading for some French-speaking country. She could have taken the shuttle to New York, so I've alerted the police there. She's probably already on an international flight somewhere.

"She took her car, and if she's flying rather than driving, we might luck on to it and narrow down the search to one airport. But by now she's had plenty of time to get away."

"Do you know any friends who'd have an idea where she'd have gone?" Sherele asked me.

"That's why I'm here," Homer said. "Restaurant

people are pretty hard to talk to on a Saturday night. Their sous-chef and maître d' brushed me off, saying they hadn't been able to find Marcel or Marie Claire themselves, and that they were just trying to get their full house fed."

"Did you tell them?" I paled at the thought of Georges, the unflappable maître d', trying to face the death of his beloved Marcel in the midst of a Saturday service.

"No, I didn't want to raise any alarms until we found Marie Claire. I suggested something vague, a sick relative they might have gone to help, but nobody at the restaurant knew anything more. I tried to call the sister-in-law in Mexico, but she's away. The neighbors didn't have anything to add. So I hoped you might have an idea of where Marie Claire could be headed." I could feel Homer looking at me until my breathing returned to normal and I raised my eyes to meet his.

"France?" he prodded.

"No, she had no relatives left there."

"Yeah, I figured she'd be afraid of extradition there anyway."

His prodding helped. I suggested, "I remember her talking of some cousins in Canada. Quebec."

"We'll look into that. But I'd be surprised if she took off for Canada. It's too cooperative with the U.S. for that to do her much good."

That jogged my memory. "She had an old friend— her best friend, she once called him—in Cuba. In fact, she visited him once when Marcel went back to France for his August vacation without her. I think they'd been fighting."

"Now that's interesting. Do you have any idea how she went to Cuba? By way of Canada?"

"No, I'm sure not. She talked about practicing Spanish before she got to Cuba, in an airport on the way. Let me think. A place where there had been an earthquake, and she was still nervous about it. Nicaragua. That's it."

Homer was off the chair and across the room to the phone in what seemed like one leap. I heard only bits of the conversation. "Miami." "You've got the schedule?" "Dulles or National?" "Call them anyway."

He came back considerably more slowly. "She'd be connecting out of Miami, the flight schedules give her plenty of time. But the flight to Miami left," he checked his watch, "more than two hours ago. A two-hour flight. So, for now, she's lost. We might be able to pick her up in the morning if she takes the next flight to Managua. But she could be going by boat. Or laying low and finding another passport."

Sherele looked sadly at him. "Don't worry. You'll find her."

"Maybe," Homer said, though he didn't look as if he meant it. He was so stricken by his slipups that when he sat down, he didn't even hitch up the knees of his pants to protect the creases.

It didn't matter, because he stood right up again. His pager was beeping.

By now Homer had that trip to my phone down to its barest minimum. "Jones here," he growled after he dialed and waited for an answer. Then he waited some more, but as he did, a grin spread across his face. "You don't say. Sure thing. I'll meet you there."

Homer was strutting when he hung up. He did a little dance on his way over to me and bent down to give me a kiss on the cheek. "I thank you, Ms. Wheatley, from the bottom of my heart." Then he leaned over and did the same to Sherele. Maybe not for the same reasons.

"You've got her?" I asked, some part of me marveling that I'd already turned my dear friend Marie Claire into an anonymous "her" whom I was glad to have arrested.

"Yes, ma'am, we've got her. Remember how this window of opportunity for murder opened up to her because her flight was delayed? Well, opportunity can knock on both sides of the door. Her flight to Miami was delayed at National Airport. Mechanical trouble. It isn't leaving until tomorrow morning. All the passengers are staying at a nearby hotel. She's on her way to being booked."

With that, he picked up his coat and came back for another kiss on Sherele's cheek, not bothering to even things up this time. "I hate to leave so soon, but I've got to go talk to this lady, hopefully before her lawyer friend has time to find his way back into town."

After Homer left, I roused myself for one more task. I was, after all, a journalist. With a little glee over having the chance to wake him up, I called Bull. I had to tell him about Marie Claire's arrest in time to tear up the front page and get the story into the late editions. At the end of the conversation, after thanking me profusely, he made sure to get my commitment to speak at his brother's dental society dinner.

# twenty-six

I don't want to think about the rest of Saturday night. Or Sunday, for that matter. The time felt like a wake, but a wake for live people as well as dead. Lily came back and mourned with me, Sherele shuttled back and forth between her apartment and mine, somehow coming up with a fresh batch of food each time. The bells—both phone and door—rang endlessly.

Jeanine and Borden telephoned from two extensions—at Jeanine's house, I gathered. They sounded more relieved at having the murder resolved than angry with Marie Claire. Jeanine had never had much good to say about Marie Claire in the first place, and now avoided mentioning her arrest altogether, as if her fate were beneath notice. Borden relished every detail. As usual he evaluated everything purely in his own self-interest, talked about reviving the New York project with Jeanine and about taking up the mantle of the sole surviving new-wave French restaurant in town. I half expected him to claim stewardship of La Raison d'Être as well as Chez Laurence.

Brian came by to pick up Lily, who was going back to Philadelphia to pack up her things. He was going to drive her there and stay a couple of days, then bring her back with all of her worldly goods. I would have thought he'd be in the way while she was dismantling her Philadelphia life, but the guy looked so shell-shocked that I could see why she'd invited him along.

"Good-bye, Mama." Her words were muffled in my shoulder as she hugged me. "We'll talk later. I promise. And I love you."

She was gone. For the moment, I was glad. She'd been right that it would be better to talk, really talk, later.

Sherele was unpacking the latest meal—afternoon tea, I supposed—when Bebe rang my bell. And while we really didn't have much to say to each other, I was slightly flattered that she was still seeking my wisdom. She set about helping Sherele set out the tea things, recalling from her last visit precisely where everything was stored. I admired that, particularly since I was so washed out that I'd hardly been able to get up from my rocker-womb all day.

Bebe was even more competent than I remembered. By the end of her visit she had extracted promises of introductions to several theater managers from Sherele. Bebe was on her way to her next career. And Sherele was on her way home, where she had a date to defrost barbecue with Homer.

• • •

Ari and Paul came around dinnertime, carrying a hamper of most aromatic things. My refrigerator had never been so well fed, I told them, though it wasn't much of a compliment since my refrigerator is hardly ever fed anything but doggie bags anyway.

Their bringing food was no surprise. What was unexpected was that they brought along Georges and Stanley, the maître d' and sous-chef of La Raison d'Être and now its only surviving managers.

"You won't be reviewing us, will you, Chas?" Georges asked, seated primly on my sofa as if he were afraid it was going to attack his pinstriped suit.

"Of course not," I answered, wondering why he had even asked such an obvious question.

"I know it isn't proper to ask a favor of you," Stanley chimed in, sitting on the floor with his knees propped up and his chin on them. I was used to seeing him stiff and pompous in his chef's whites. He had a much friendlier look in jeans and well-worn sweatshirt from a Lexington, North Carolina, barbecue place. "But Georges and I are going to try to carry on in the restaurant and eventually buy it out. It will be hard to live down its reputation now, and maybe it won't work. But we have to try."

"For Marcel's sake, too," Georges added.

"I wish you luck," I said lamely, wondering what this had to do with me.

"Ari is going to help me until I feel fully in control of the kitchen," Stanley said.

I looked over at Ari, raising my eyebrows. That would be difficult, especially since he was entering the holiday party season.

"Stanley doesn't need as much help as he thinks he does," Ari said, answering the question my eyebrows were asking.

"I don't understand what you mean about a favor," I told Stanley.

"I was just getting to that. Of course we wouldn't want you to review us during this transition. And I know you wouldn't do that anyway. But what we wanted to ask, if we don't offend you by doing so, is whether you would consider reviewing us as soon as Ari cuts us loose on our own. We will need every bit of help we can get in order to overcome the bad vibes the place has."

"Why, that's not even a favor. It's what I would do anyway," I reassured them.

"I told them that, too, but they were so nervous that I thought that it would help them to hear it from you," Ari said.

And so everyone was repositioning, stitching up wounds and readying them for healing.

That left one major unsolved problem: I had no restaurant to review tomorrow.

And it left one wound that had not yet gotten attention: Dave.

I had blown it. Homer's self-accusation came to mind. Yes, I blew it, too. I had refused to risk taking our relationship public, thus suggesting to Dave that I had no confidence in him. Then I had proved it by accusing him of a humiliating disloyalty, and I had refused to believe his denial.

No wonder he'd dumped me.

Now I was faced with a lesson I should have learned long ago. Hunger is the best seasoning. In relationships as well as in dinner. I'd never before appreciated how very much Dave suited my taste.

By Monday morning I had myself under control, though barely. After I hadn't heard from Dave by Sunday night, I shooed out all my fellow mourners and went to bed. Not to sleep so much as to think.

First I reviewed all those fine times Dave and I'd had together. Kind of like going through a family album. Then I made the case against him: Not only had he left me weak and defenseless in the hospital to go out who-knows-with-whom on Friday night, but he had never shown up as promised on Saturday. He didn't even call the entire weekend to see whether I was alive.

I was ready to get over the guy.

Monday was going to be the first day of the rest of my life. I even vacuumed my apartment before going to work. All the while I worried about my restaurant column, its Friday deadline long past now that it was Monday. First I decided to throw myself on Helen's mercy and ask her if she could just not run a restaurant column this week. It would be the first time I'd missed a deadline in ten years, but certainly these were extenuating circumstances. Then I talked myself out of that. I'd write a tribute to two dead chefs. That's what people were going to be talking about anyway. It wasn't going to be easy.

I not only walked to work, I walked the long way. By way of Georgetown, Key Bridge, and back across Roosevelt Bridge and the Mall. The day was sparkling, and Washington looked like a moving postcard as I passed all the major tourist sites on my route. I'd started so early that I witnessed three distinct waves of commuters creeping in their cars across the bridges and along the choked highways. A few joggers nodded to me along the Virginia bikeways.

The shuttered storefronts of Georgetown, the Key Bridge vista from the university spires to the Watergate and Kennedy Center, the flicker of Kennedy's eternal light at Arlington Cemetery, the riverfront view of the memorials to Lincoln and Washington all put this week's tragedies in perspective. The world stood vast and firm as we few mourners quavered.

The only gathering in front of the *Examiner* this morning was a small clutch of smokers, drawing in their last tar and nicotine before starting their workdays.

The few reporters already at their desks spoke words of support as I passed them. There was no sign of Sherele—which didn't surprise me in the least after what must have been a late barbecue night. No editors had arrived yet, and my particular part of the newsroom was empty. So was Dave's.

The task ahead of me was monumental. Mail was piled in boxes at my feet. My computer message list took several minutes just to scroll through. Voice mail chastised me, saying that my mailbox was full. I cleared a small space on my desk and opened up the *Washington Post*, savoring the pleasure of seeing it try to catch up on our Sunday scoop.

I picked up my phone to start wading through voice mail when the New Message light flashed on my computer. I clicked my message button and read,

"Hi, babe. I'm back at last. That was quite a coup you got for the *Examiner*. Sorry I missed the great moment."

I looked back and saw Dave, his back toward me, hunched over his terminal.

"Back from where?" I wrote, ordering my computer to Send Message.

"From the wilderness rendezvous with that organized crime source. Didn't you get my message?"

"What message?"

"The one I left with the nursing station Saturday when your phone was busy. Didn't they tell you? I called back later, but your phone was turned off. I also left a message on your voice mail to back it up, because I knew you couldn't access your home answering machine from the hospital. You got that one, didn't you?"

I turned to look at Dave again, and this time I noticed his backpack, the one he used instead of luggage, sitting on his desk.

I had to reassess my last days' reassessments.

But I'm not one to make the same mistake twice.

"We need to talk. But I know you're under a lot of

pressure today, and so am I. How about tonight?" I sent the message his way.

"Chas, I really enjoyed our working together last week, and figure we should get to know each other better. How would you like to go out to dinner with me? Or take me out to dinner with you? I'll even buy a sport coat if necessary." That was the message from Dave that next popped up on my screen. Huh? It didn't make a lot of sense.

I heard a wolf whistle, and turned my head to see Den Ranger sitting in front of his computer, grinning at me. A knowing snicker came from another desk, then a catcall from a third. I looked around to see everybody in the newsroom watching me, some people even standing up so they could see better.

I turned back to my computer, embarrassed by the attention and mystified as to its reason. Then it became clear. Dave had hit the wrong button. Instead of sending his message to me privately, he'd accidentally sent it to the entire newsroom. Or maybe not so accidentally.

# TABLE MATTERS

By Chas Wheatley
*Examiner* Staff Writer

Coppi's Chocolate-Hazelnut Calzone and
an All-American Peanut Butter Variation
(Serves 6)

Food writers don't feel comfortable giving recipes with brand-name ingredients: too commercial. They use generic descriptions instead. But sometimes, as with Nutella, only one company makes such a product, and it seems a little silly to send readers out searching for "chocolate-hazelnut spread," which nobody is likely to recognize without the brand name. Thus, this recipe, which originated at Coppi's restaurant on U Street, comes right out and specifies Nutella, the same thick, creamy chocolate-hazelnut spread that Paris street vendors use to fill their crepes. But Nutella isn't always easy to find here, and it is expensive. Therefore, this recipe includes an easy, delicious, homemade, very American peanut butter alternative. The result is still a rich, oozy chocolate filling that is wonderful with yeasty pizza dough.

*For the dough (1 1/2 pounds):*

1/2 cup warm water (110 degrees,
        or slightly warm to touch)
1/2 cup warm milk (whole, 2%, or skim)

1 package ($\frac{1}{4}$ ounce) active dry yeast
$\frac{1}{2}$ teaspoon salt
3 cups flour, more if necessary

*For the filling:*
$\frac{2}{3}$ cup sugar
$\frac{1}{3}$ cup unsweetened cocoa powder
$\frac{2}{3}$ cup milk (whole, 2%, or skim)
1 teaspoon vanilla
$\frac{1}{2}$ cup smooth peanut butter
       or:
$\frac{3}{4}$ cup Nutella chocolate-hazelnut spread
Confectioners' sugar

Make the dough: Put the warm water and warm milk in a large bowl and sprinkle in yeast. Let stand 3 to 4 minutes, then stir to dissolve. Stir in the salt and 2 cups flour. Gradually stir in about 1 more cup of flour, using only enough to form a soft, slightly sticky dough. Knead 5 to 10 minutes. Lightly oil the bottom of a clean bowl and roll the dough in it to coat with oil. Cover with a towel and set in a warm spot—80 to 110 degrees—to rise for 2 hours, or until doubled in bulk. Punch down and knead for 1 minute. After rising, dough can be used immediately or formed into a ball, wrapped tightly in plastic, and refrigerated, then brought to room temperature for baking.

If not using Nutella, make the filling: In a medium saucepan, stir the sugar and cocoa powder until blended. Gradually stir in the milk. Bring to a boil over medium heat, stirring constantly, then lower heat and simmer for 2 minutes. Remove from the heat and let cool for at least 5 minutes. Add the vanilla and peanut butter, stirring until smooth. Let cool thoroughly.

Make the calzone: About 45 minutes before serving, preheat the oven at its highest temperature, up to 500 degrees. If you have a pizza tile, heat it in the oven.

Divide the dough into six pieces. Roll each piece into a circle 6 to 7 inches in diameter, about $\frac{1}{4}$ inch thick. Spoon 2 tablespoons chocolate-peanut-butter filling or Nutella in the center, then fold dough into a half-moon over the filling. Pinch the edges together and fold bottom edge over top, crimping to seal well. Place on an ungreased cookie sheet, leaving 2 inches between each calzone. Bake until well browned, 12 to 20 minutes depending on your oven. Remove from the oven and sprinkle with confectioners' sugar. Serve immediately.